THE WOLF WORE PLAID

TERRY SPEAR

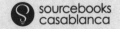
sourcebooks
casablanca

Published by Sourcebooks Casablanca, an imprint of Sourcebooks
P.O. Box 4410, Naperville, Illinois 60567-4410
(630) 961-3900
sourcebooks.com

Printed and bound in Canada.
MBP 10 9 8 7 6 5 4 3 2 1

To Winnie Pang, who has been following my books from the beginning and who jumped right in to suggest writing about Enrick MacQuarrie next. He is all yours, lassie! Though you might find a few lassies wanting you to share him!

CHAPTER 1

"We've got trouble," Lana Cameron, the baker, said to Heather MacNeill, motioning with her head to the big glass windows of Ye Olde Highland Pie Shoppe in the village near the MacNeills' Argent Castle.

Heather glanced out the window and saw Lana was right. Heather had been hoping the rumors about having more problems with the Kilpatrick brothers wouldn't come true. But redheaded Robert and his equally redheaded brother Patrick were climbing out of their truck, looking around to see who was eating at the café tables outside and then speaking to each other before they entered the shop. They both looked like wary gray wolves.

They should be. After Patrick had killed the wolf Heather was going to mate, she'd wanted to end Patrick herself. The only thing stopping her was that the fight had been her mate-to-be's fault.

Lana joined Heather behind the counter. "Did I tell you Enrick MacQuarrie came in when you were gone yesterday afternoon?" Lana raised a brow and gave her a smile.

Heather frowned. "On purpose?"

"Of course he came in on purpose."

Heather let out her breath in annoyance and folded her arms. "He came into the shop when he knew I wasn't going to be here?" As owner, manager, and general hand-on-deck, Heather was nearly always there, though she was training Lana to take over whenever she had to be away.

Lana let out a long-suffering sigh, placing her hands on her chest and looking heavenward. "Aye, if 'twere up to me, I would chase the hunky Highlander all through the heather until I had him pinned down to a mating. But alas, he doesna see me as a pro-spective mate."

Heather continued to frown. "Me then? Why come when I wasn't here? On purpose."

"He is a hardy warrior but with feelings running deep for ye." Lana was keeping in character with her role here at the shop. "'Tis you he wished to see, but he fears you're still in mourning over Timothy and doesn't want to approach you too soon for a courtship."

Heather didn't lose the frown. Lana couldn't be serious. Was she up to a bit of matchmaking where none would be possible? "He has never had time for me...ever. He's a workaholic. He doesn't believe in having fun. He's a...stick-in-the-mud." With her. Not with others. She folded her arms and let her breath out in a huff. "Okay, so then what did he do?"

"He asked me how you were feeling."

"And you said?"

"Good." Lana laughed.

Heather curbed the urge to sock her.

Lana sighed again. "That you were ready to date if he would get on with it and start making an overture. Don't expect too much at first. I'm not sure he took me at my word." Lana smiled, then frowned. "Just think, if he were your mate..." She motioned to the windows where the Kilpatricks looked unsure about coming inside or not. "He would toss them out on their ear if they came inside. Or at least Enrick would make them shake a bit in their boots. They wouldn't be as cocky as they are otherwise."

Protective, oh aye. Enrick and his two brothers were protective of her when Heather chanced to go to the MacQuarrie castle. But the brothers thought she was too wild, too impetuous. And that irritated her. She'd overheard them talking to her brothers about it on different occasions, how difficult it was to keep her in check. She sure didn't need a mate who felt that way about her.

What was wrong with wanting to do things on the spur of the moment? To take a chance at doing something fun and whimsical? That was who she was, and she wasn't changing to fit some male wolf's concept of the perfect she-wolf.

Take her business here. It had been a risk to start something like this, and a few had said she couldn't do it. Well, she proved she could. She'd worked hard to make her dream come true. And it was her dream, no one else's.

"Oh, I've got to tend to the bread." Lana hurried off to check on it while Heather glanced back at the glass door.

She was seriously surprised Enrick had come to talk to her friend and feel her out about Heather's thoughts on dating again. As much as she'd had a crush on the wolf forever, he *wasn't* the one for her. She'd figured that out a long time ago.

Then she thought again about the current situation. Enrick wasn't here to serve and protect, so she was on her own for now.

As far as she knew, the Kilpatricks and their McKinley cousins had been furious they hadn't gotten the film contract to have a new fantasy film shot at the McKinleys' castle in the Highlands. They would be even madder once they learned the MacQuarries had gotten the contract to have it filmed in part at their castle and on their grounds *instead*. Since some of the MacNeill wolves would be participating with the MacQuarries as extras in the film, and the MacNeills were McKinley rivals, there was bound to be trouble at some time or another between them. Had the Kilpatricks already learned where the shoot was going to be held, and that was why they were here? She knew they weren't here to tell her they were sorry for Patrick killing Timothy. Patrick had felt perfectly justified, and truthfully, he had been.

The MacQuarrie pack leaders were keeping quiet about the film location for now, although they'd told Heather's pack leaders because they needed some of their men and women to sign up as extras. Heather knew because she was going to be in charge of the MacNeill female extras during the filming. She hoped the McKinley wolf pack would leave the pie shop out of their quarrels, though the Kilpatricks—members of that *lupus garou* pack—had been passive-aggressive of late with both the MacQuarries and the MacNeills at pubs or wherever they chanced to meet. That attitude was sure to escalate once word reached the world on where the film would actually be shot.

Heather had her cell phone out, just in case she needed to text her pack leaders for some Highland wolf muscle.

The aroma of fresh bread baking, of hearty beef stew bubbling in a cooker, and of sweet pastries filled the air as Lana brought out another loaf of Scottish soda bread from the oven. In full view of the customers, she made buttermilk bread and soda bread in a brick oven, just like in the old days. Originating in Scotland, the bannock bread made of oatmeal dough was cooked in a skillet, so it was made in the shop's kitchen. The ladies working in the shop were all wearing long dresses with narrow sleeves, long tartan overskirts, boots, and wimples. Lana's kilt was the Cameron tartan of red, green, and blue, while Heather's was the blue and green tartan of the MacNeill clan.

Heather's pack leaders—gray wolf cousin Ian MacNeill and his red wolf mate, Julia—had assisted Heather in establishing the shop a year ago to help some of their wolves remain gainfully employed and Heather achieve her dream. Julia had loved the idea of Heather sharing several of the clan's old-time recipes with the world because Julia was American with Scottish roots and had fallen in love with all things Scottish when she joined them a couple of years back. Since the wolves lived such long lives, aging a year for every human thirty, many of them had been around for a very long time. Heather had wanted to own a shop like this since she was always cooking for Ian and his brothers, and she'd wanted to share the old-world charm of the recipes she'd personally prepared. She just hadn't had the means to do it on her own without the pack leaders' assistance.

Heather manned the cash register as a man and his wife paid for two venison and cranberry pies.

The woman said, "We've been wanting to come here since the shop opened. It's so fun, and best of all, the food is great. I love your costumes too."

Heather smiled. "Thanks, I'm so glad you enjoyed the visit." No one could accuse them of wearing costumes that weren't true to the late medieval period. Though about that time, some of the women were casting their wimples aside.

Agreeing with his wife, the man nodded to Heather and carried out the pies as the couple left.

The medieval Highland theme of the shop and the food brought in customers locally and from around the world for a unique dining experience. Who wouldn't want to try something different?

Everything was going fine, busy as usual, when the two men of the enemy wolf clan finally walked into the shop, making Heather feel as if they were turning her sunny day into something dark and dangerous. The brothers glanced around at the customers eating and visiting. Were they checking to see if any of her clansmen were there, ready to stop them from whatever they were up to?

She sure wished a whole bunch of men from her clan were sitting there eating right now. She suspected the brothers might have gone on their way then.

The *lupus garous* attempted to look easygoing, when she knew they were anything but. Their clan had been fighting with her people through the ages. They'd been pirates in the old days and were still trying to cheat or steal from others. Robert epitomized cunning and deviousness. He was a cutthroat who wouldn't hesitate to kill someone who got in his way. His brother went along with everything he did.

Heather wanted to tell them they weren't welcome here, but she didn't want to cause a scene in front of her customers. As long as the

Kilpatricks were behaving themselves and had *only* come to shop, she would just have to deal with them and leave her feelings out of it.

Lupus garous had to take care of their own kind if they were involved in criminal acts. They didn't want a wolf incarcerated long term, even if the rogue wolf could control his shifting during the full-moon phase. So if the Kilpatricks caused any trouble, Heather couldn't call anyone other than her own wolf-pack leaders to handle it.

A chill ran up her spine as she eyed the brothers with a wolf's wariness. Sometimes, men worked in the shop, but not right this minute. Ironically, many of the clansmen who cooked and served there had sworn they would never want to work under medieval conditions again, but they got a kick out of the nostalgia at the shop. They did have modern ovens and stoves and fridges in the back to keep up with the growing business's orders and, of course, fresh running water instead of having to carry the water from a well like they did in the old days.

Three women were in the back cooking, and Lana was still baking bread, while two servers were filling trays with the meals. Another woman was handling takeout orders.

Robert Kilpatrick, the older of the two brothers, gave Heather a small smile. It wasn't warm or friendly or reassuring in the least. More calculating. She didn't trust him or his brother.

Even though Heather knew Patrick wasn't at fault in her fiancé's death, she still didn't like him. She was certain the men's appearance in her shop meant trouble. Anytime she or other pack members had dealings with them, there were problems.

Another couple of customers entered the shop: two men, all smiles, wearing New York City T-shirts from the Big Apple, jeans, and sneakers. Americans? Maybe.

The Kilpatrick brothers glanced at them, but the Americans ignored them and continued to the counter. "We'll take two of the steak pies," one of the men said.

One looked suspiciously like the star of the movie they would be filming at the MacQuarries' castle, Guy McNab. Heather smiled brightly at him. "Aye, sure." She rang up their orders and noticed Lana glance at the two men and her jaw drop.

Don't burn the bread or drop it, Heather wanted to tell her.

She wanted to ask if they were here because of the film, but she couldn't in front of the Kilpatricks. She was dying to know if the one man was Guy, or maybe it was his stunt double.

The Kilpatrick brothers were reading the sign listing all the meat pies. Realizing she was watching them, Robert smiled at her a little again. It still wasn't a friendly smile. Patrick didn't bother. They sauntered over to the glass case filled with sweet desserts on display: clooties (fruit-studded dumplings boiled in a cloth), black buns (Scotland's currant-and-raisin-filled version of a fruitcake), shortbread cookies, empire biscuits (shortbread filled with jam and topped with a bit of icing and a cherry) and millionaire's shortbread (Heather's favorite, a shortbread base topped with layers of caramel and chocolate).

A Canadian customer was taking pictures of the medieval decor: brass lanterns and swords and shields, and a bow and quiver of arrows, and was sharing them with friends and family, which always helped Heather's business. Paintings of Highlanders in ancient kilts—in full color and with a textured look to give them an aged appearance—hung on the stone walls. Wolves and Irish wolfhounds joined them in some of the portraits. Of course, the pairing was kind of an oxymoron since wolfhounds took down wolves in the old days, but the *lupus garous* had raised wolfhounds as pets and hunting dogs from early on. Of course *their* dogs hadn't hunted the wolf kind.

Heather glanced outside and noticed another family taking seats at one of the tables before they came in to order. Eating outside was perfect for nice weather like today—sunny, warm, breezy. No one in the pack had envisioned the shop would be such a success when it first began, though Julia, a well-known romance author, had written about it in some of her stories, encouraging visitors who read her books to check out the pie shop while on vacation to the area. Even the locals loved it.

Heather smiled at a lady from Wales who came up to the counter to get a sweet dumpling to go. She chose a clootie dumpling filled with sultanas and currants, bread crumbs, sugar, spice, milk, and golden syrup. All these ingredients had been mixed into dough, which was boiled in a cloth in water, then dried in the oven. Heather boxed the dumpling for the woman and set it on the counter, then took the money for it and thanked the woman before she left.

The shop had started to get party requests for medieval meals, and it looked like they would need to expand their staff and building to accommodate the orders. Not only that, but Heather's shop was contracted to help cater the main meals during the film shoots. The MacQuarrie staff were contracted to prepare whatever she didn't make for the main meals. She was thrilled and hoped the shop continued to be a success.

"We've heard so much about your shop that we had to come and check it out," Robert said, leaning against her counter.

She didn't believe him for an instant. Her phone was sitting on the ledge below the high counter and out of his sight, so she started to text Ian to see if he could send some backup, other than her three brothers—Oran, Jamie, and Callum, who would just as likely kill the men and ask questions afterward—if she needed the help.

The doorbell jingled again, and she looked up to see who it was, afraid it would be more of the Kilpatricks' kin. Instead, Enrick MacQuarrie pulled the door closed behind him, and a bit of relief washed over her. Now *he* was a welcome sight. Not for his supposed interest in dating her. That was so far-fetched, she couldn't believe Lana would even think it. But Heather knew he would be all protective when it came to her or any other she-wolf of the MacNeill pack.

She didn't send the text message to Ian, figuring Enrick would deal with the Kilpatricks if they gave her any trouble.

Not that she was totally reassured. Anything could go wrong, and she sure didn't want Enrick hurt either.

He looked so much like one of the men wearing a New York T-shirt while they waited for their steak pies that he could have been his double. Ever since Guy McNab had made it big as a film star in America, Enrick had been mistaken for him whenever he ventured out of the area.

Enrick was the middle triplet brother of Grant and Lachlan MacQuarrie, tawny-haired and good-natured—except if he was defending the pack members or his friends, then watch out. He had a warrior's heart, yet Heather had seen a real soft side to him too—playing tug-of-war with the Irish wolfhound pups, chasing the kids around the inner bailey in a game of tag, growling as if he were a wolf in his fur coat and making the kids squeal in delight. She'd seen him playing with his brothers as wolves and he was totally aggressive then, not wanting either of his brothers to win the battle between them. And in a snowball fight, he was the fastest snowball maker and thrower she'd ever seen. If they played on teams, she wanted him on hers.

So he did let his hair down, so to speak, with the kids and with his brothers and others. With her? He clearly thought she was trouble.

At least he was a wolf with a pack friendly to her own, and she smiled brightly at him, glad he was here in case she needed him.

There was no smile for her, his look instead dark and imposing as he glanced from her to the Kilpatrick brothers, still trying to figure out what they wanted to buy. She hoped Enrick wouldn't start a fight. They had so many customers, and she didn't want to see a brawl break out in front of them. It surely wouldn't help business.

Robert pointed to the sign on the wall listing the kind of pies they sold. "We'll take a couple of the steak and kidney pies to go."

Okay, so they weren't causing trouble. Yet. They hadn't noticed Enrick's arrival, and she hoped he wouldn't cause things to get ugly when the other men were behaving...for the moment. Enrick was observing them with a do-anything-I-don't-like-and-you'll-die look.

Robert leaned against the oak countertop. "We hear there's supposed to be a movie filmed at one of the castles nearby."

As her heartbeat quickened, Heather's gaze darted to Enrick's, and he raised his brows at her. Man, she was about to give the secret away in that one little glance at him. She knew he would question her next, once the men left. He could probably hear her heart suddenly beating way too fast.

"We had a movie filmed at our castle a few years back, but that's it." Heather placed their order with RUSH stamped on it. She'd never used the stamp before, but this was certainly one of those times it came in handy.

"Not *that* film. A *new* one. More of a...*fantasy*," Patrick said, "featuring wolves, even."

"At the MacNeills' castle? No," she said, shaking her head. She wasn't lying. Ian MacNeill swore they would never have another film shot at their castle. At the time they'd been in dire straits financially, and the only way to keep the castle solvent was to do the film. Wolf packs had to keep their identity secret. Having tons of nonwolves traipsing through Argent Castle and the grounds could be problematic. Her pack had had to send a couple of newly turned wolves to stay with the MacQuarries, just so the human cast and crew wouldn't have the surprise of seeing the newbies shift during the full moon.

Several female members of her wolf pack would really love a chance to playact in another film though. Heather was waiting on a call from Colleen MacQuarrie, confirming how many would get a chance to be in the new film being shot at the MacQuarries' Farraige Castle. Heather sure was excited to take part too. Maybe she'd even get to see Enrick fighting in good form on the battlefield.

A few minutes later, one of the other MacNeill women brought out two steak and kidney pies in a box. Heather thanked her and began ringing up the sale, wanting to get the brothers out of there quickly without making it appear she was trying to rush them out of the shop. Her alpha leaders had talked with Enrick's pack leaders about having the movie filmed at Farraige Castle because the MacQuarries would need the MacNeills to send reinforcements for the battle scenes and others shot around the keep. But it was all hush-hush so she didn't know if Enrick was aware of that yet. And Robert and Patrick could very well have served as a couple of the extras who got into a fight with her people during the earlier film and were looking to stir up trouble again.

"I think you know," Robert said, glancing over his shoulder at Enrick, finally noticing she had a wolf warrior watching over things, standing off to the side, arms folded across his chest. She just hoped they wouldn't fight!

Stiffening a little, Robert sneered at Enrick who didn't move a muscle, just stared him and his brother down in a wolf-to-wolf confrontation like he was ready for the fight, come and get it. They didn't need whiskey to make them cantankerous. All they needed was their clan pride and, in this case, their wolf-pack pride too. The battle between the clans had been going on forever. Stealing cattle, horses, brides, land; fighting for more power since the beginning. The quest for more land and power was always an ongoing condition.

As soon as she finished up at the shop, Heather was in fact meeting with the MacQuarrie leaders and Grant's two brothers, Enrick and Lachlan, so she wouldn't have to keep the news secret about the film too much longer, and she was glad about that.

Robert paid for the pies. "We know the film is being set in

Scotland at one of the castles. You better not have lied to us," Robert said, while Patrick grabbed the box with a jerk. And then the two stalked out the door.

At least they hadn't fought with Enrick, and they did buy something. Miracles did happen sometimes.

"Hi, Enrick, did you need something?" she asked, relieved beyond words that the men had left without causing any real issues.

"Are you okay?" Enrick asked, looking genuinely concerned.

CHAPTER 2

ENRICK HAD SEEN EVERYTHING THAT HAD GONE ON, SO Heather knew he didn't believe the Kilpatrick brothers had done anything to her. She figured he was more worried about how she felt concerning Timothy, the man she was to mate, and dealing face-to-face with his killer today. Yet Enrick couldn't seem to just come out and say so.

Though she had loved Timothy's wild manner and decisiveness, he couldn't or wouldn't control that darker wolf side of him that was always ready to battle the enemy wolf clans, no matter who else the fight might hurt or if it was even called for. The pack leaders had met after the killing and determined Timothy had been at fault, but that didn't lessen the hurt Heather had felt at losing him. It did make her angry with him for starting the physical fight and getting himself killed though.

She tried to tell herself it was better she hadn't mated a wolf who was so reckless that he might have left her to raise a couple of kids on her own at some point later in their lives. She appreciated Enrick asking how she was feeling. He might be as growly as all the other wolves combined, but he knew when to fight and when to leave it for another day. He never drank too much, so he always had a clear head, unlike Timothy. She'd loved him, sure, but he'd had his faults. Enrick did too. Everyone did. So it wasn't like she would ever end up with Mr. Perfect Wolf, nor did she want that.

No one had shown any interest in courting her after Timothy died. It had happened two years ago, and she felt as though she was being judged for his actions, that selecting him for her mate said the same about her. She'd considered leaving Scotland and going somewhere else, hating to live with the stigma of what he'd done, though everyone said she was not to blame.

But she couldn't leave her friends and family behind. Argent Castle was her home—always had been and always would be. She felt connected to it, to her family, and she would never leave. Without it, she would be less than whole.

Patrick had said something derogatory about what he'd do with Heather if she was his mate, and *that* had set Timothy off. So yes, Patrick had started the fight with words, but he had defended himself with a *sgian dubh* knife because otherwise Timothy would have beaten him to death. Two of the MacQuarrie men had tried to pull Timothy off Patrick, but when Timothy was like that, he was like an old Norse berserker on steroids. After the beating Timothy had given him, Patrick had a crooked nose. Instead of setting it, he left it, thinking it showed his prowess to the lassies. *Jerk.*

Heather wished none of it had ever happened. Words were just words. Ending someone's life, miserable as it was, was something else.

"I'm fine." She shrugged. "They didn't do anything or say anything hurtful."

"I was just...making sure." Enrick frowned. "So, a movie is being filmed at your castle again? I thought Ian would never agree to that." Enrick studied her expression, breathing in her scent. It wasn't that he was trying to catch her in a lie; it was just a natural condition of being a part-time wolf.

Heather was sure she was giving him a ton of mixed messages—concern, anxiousness, relief—and he wouldn't know it wasn't just because of the Kilpatricks having been there. "Uh, I'm sure Ian wouldn't agree to that after the last time. So what did you come in for?"

Enrick looked at the sign featuring the variety of savory meat pies and bridies—Scottish hot pockets smothered in brown sauce—as well as soups, burgers, and baguettes.

"I'll get the Scotch pie. You know how my pack leader is. Colleen has wanted to try it—beans and chips, smothered in brown sauce. She has been talking about the pies ever since she heard about them, and no one has made them at the castle since she has been there. Since I happened to be in the area..."

Right. He just happened to be in the area, checking up on Heather for her brothers since she might suspect someone from her own clan of doing the same thing.

"Good choice. It's fresh out of the oven." She sent the order back with a note it was for Enrick MacQuarrie, and a couple of minutes later, one of the MacNeill ladies brought it out boxed up for him, all smiles. All the ladies were interested in the two unmated MacQuarrie brothers, so Heather wasn't surprised, even though she hadn't put a RUSH stamp on the order.

Enrick smiled at the lady and she smiled back, blushing furiously, then headed back into the kitchen.

"I'm surprised to see you in here," Heather said.

"I was surprised to see the *Kilpatricks* in here."

"So you came in to protect me."

"If I hadn't, Colleen would have had my head."

"Thank you."

Enrick paid for the pie but hesitated to leave. "Are you sure a sequel to the film isn't being made at Argent Castle? After the film came out, the reviewers said the scenery and costuming and battle scenes were better than anything they'd ever seen. I always suspected another movie would be filmed there, maybe not a sequel but another Highland period piece. Or at least they'd try to convince Ian to use his castle for another film."

"They had great reviews for good reason. The 'costumes' were ours and perfectly authentic. Anyway, no, Ian's not allowing another movie to be filmed at the castle. Why? If he did, would you want to fight in it?" The MacQuarrie brothers had been having trouble with another clan during the last filming and hadn't been able to take off to join the MacNeills. The guys were all about fighting. The MacQuarries hadn't had a good battle in a while—even if it was just film-making magic—and she knew the need to fight was in their blood.

Enrick gave her a smirk.

"I thought so. You know that if it's in the works, the ones in charge wouldn't want anyone to leak the details until they're ready to share it with the rest of the pack."

"Then Ian is allowing another one. *Great.*" Enrick smiled, then frowned. "So how come these guys had some idea it was happening when no one else does?"

She sighed. "I didn't say it *was* happening, but if it were, would you sign up to be an extra?"

"If the film is at the MacNeills' castle? Sure. See you around. And thanks for the pie."

See you around? To check on her? Make sure she was behaving herself? He was more interested in being in the next movie. "You're welcome." Except for buying a pie for his pack leader, he was not welcome here just to do what her brothers bid. She sighed as Enrick left the pie shop.

Lana immediately came over and punched her lightly on the shoulder. "You didn't ask him out on a date or tell him anything that would indicate you wanted to go out with him."

"He wasn't here for that."

"Aye, he was here to protect you. And he asked how you were feeling. It helps to have wolf hearing. Coming here has to mean he wants to have something more to do with you. But since he's a man, he's cautious and is afraid of rejection. Oh, and what's this business about a movie being filmed at Argent Castle?"

Heather shook her head. "There isn't going to be a movie shot there. Ian wouldn't hear of it. Trust me."

Enrick wouldn't be happy with her when he learned she had known all along the film was set at *his* castle, not hers, and she hadn't told him. And she even had a role in the film. She glanced at the New York men eating their pies. The star of the film could be sitting here right this minute, but Enrick hadn't even seen him. She was glad he hadn't, or the man could have given it all away.

Enrick had been fuming when he saw the Kilpatricks had parked their red truck at the MacNeills' pie shop. He'd suspected they were up to no good. He hadn't planned to be anywhere near the shop today, yet he'd driven in that direction, not even realizing where he was going until he was there. Subconsciously, he'd wanted to see Heather for himself and learn if she was ready to start dating again. Like her brothers, he was concerned that she would date the wrong wolf. He didn't want to be insensitive about her feelings though.

Her dark hair and eyes had always captivated him. Even now. She'd always caught his attention. But she was not the she-wolf for him, he told himself. He envisioned someone who was a lot less… spontaneous. More predictable. Less out of control.

When he saw the Kilpatricks' vehicle there, the notion of approaching her about a date had flown out the window. Protecting Heather after what Patrick had put her through was all he could think about. Enrick still didn't know what to think of Heather. She had put on a brave face in front of the Kilpatricks, but he'd smelled the tension she'd been feeling too. He wanted to throw the two men out of the shop bodily, but he didn't want to react to them the way Timothy had and get himself in the same predicament.

Since Timothy had been a wolf of the MacQuarrie clan, that had also kept Enrick from approaching her. He didn't want her or anyone else thinking badly of him for not giving her the proper time to grieve, while her brothers were insistent she could just start dating a rogue wolf at any moment.

Enrick had been so busy helping Grant run the estate that he hadn't had time to find a female to court. What with the trouble Grant's mate, Colleen, had from the Kilpatricks and their cousins, and being second-in-command, Enrick had had his hands full. Yet he had seen Heather was making a mistake with Timothy and tried to stop her from courting the wolf. Though from what her brothers had said, if they told her not to do something, she was sure to do it.

Enrick let out his breath. Now she was free and could be hurt all over again, if he and the others didn't watch out for her.

He was much more levelheaded than Timothy and couldn't see mating a woman like Heather. Enrick had been way too much like that until his father had set him straight. Sure, dating her for fun could be enjoyable, but becoming a permanent mate? No. He suspected she liked being with someone who could be more free-spirited, show her a good time, and fight for a cause, no matter if it was uncalled for or not. He was *not* that kind of wolf.

Enrick called his older triplet brother, Grant, on the way back to Farraige Castle.

"Hey, did you hear Ian is having another film shot at his castle? We missed out on fighting in the battle scenes the last time, but if we can manage to get free, maybe the three of us can go over there and fight against the MacNeills." Enrick was always up for a fun-hearted clash with Ian and his brothers. And he hoped during breaks from the shoots he would be able to see Heather and help make sure she didn't run off with some American actors like she'd tried to do the last time.

Once she'd declared she was mating Timothy, Enrick wished he could have stopped the whole dating process at the beginning. Every time he'd seen Timothy with her, Enrick had regretted it. She might be a wild spirit, but Timothy had demons he'd refused to face. Now he was dead, and she'd been left with the collateral damage.

"I was about to call you. We're having a meeting in the conference room as soon as you return," Grant said to Enrick.

"Sure, I'm on my way home now. Be there in twenty minutes." He was going to ask what the meeting was about when Grant spoke again.

"I've got to go. See you in a few minutes."

The line clicked dead. Since Enrick was being called into a meeting in the conference room, he was certain something important was happening.

When he arrived at the castle, he carried the pie into the kitchen and said to a couple of the ladies making lunch, "It's for Colleen. Don't ask." Then he hoofed it to the conference room where portraits of kilted family members past and present hung on the walls, along with the swords and shields of some of their fallen heroes. And portraits of wolves from the early years to today.

A sitting area was situated on one side of the room, and an oak conference table with seating for twelve took up another area.

Since this appeared to be an informal meeting between family members, Grant and Colleen were sitting on a tapestry love seat, and Enrick's younger triplet brother, Lachlan, had taken a seat on one of the leather chairs across from them in the sitting area.

Glass patio doors that looked out on the patio and gardens were open, letting in a warm breeze and sunlight. It was a beautiful day, perfect to be outside, and Enrick would be as soon as he got another chance.

He took a seat next to Lachlan. "What's the trouble now?" Some of the men in their pack had squabbled with McKinley wolf-pack members at a pub this past week. He would have hoped in this day and age they were beyond that. The problem was that wolf shifters all lived such long lives that old battles between clans were hard to forget. And the recent issues their friends the MacNeills had had with the McKinleys hadn't helped. Not to mention that Patrick Kilpatrick had killed one of the MacQuarries' men.

Enrick noticed Colleen was smiling, so he assumed the issue to be discussed wasn't anything troublesome, though the American lass was always coming up with new projects, like making the seawall more secure so kids—and foolhardy adults—couldn't go beyond it, risking being washed out to sea. He figured she had a new plan in mind that impacted all of them.

"We have signed a contract to have a Highland time-travel film made here," Grant said.

Enrick's jaw dropped. He was surprised his brother hadn't told him and Lachlan about it already. He supposed since Grant was mated to Colleen, the pack leaders now made the rules. Or maybe they thought Grant's brothers wouldn't go along with the idea. Enrick was certain it would wreak havoc with their daily schedules, but he knew the MacNeill wolf clan had made a lot of money off having a film staged at their castle, and many of their men and women had fun playing as extras. So he was all for it.

"I ran off two of the Kilpatricks, Robert and Patrick, at the MacNeills' pie shop. They were trying to learn from Heather where a fantasy film was going to be set," Enrick said. "Is this the same one? How did they know about it when we didn't?"

"The location manager of the film checked out the McKinleys' castle, too, but the company chose ours," Colleen said. "We've been in negotiations with them for some time, and we didn't want to say anything to either of you until it was a sure deal. Grant knew you would be on board if we got the contract. I'm sure the McKinleys weren't happy about losing the contract—they were just told today—but they'll be even angrier when they learn the film will be shot at an enemy's clan holdings."

Enrick stifled a groan. Colleen was right. They would be fuming about it. And they would want to get even, despite the MacQuarries having nothing to do with the ultimate selection of the site for the film.

"Wait, the MacNeills had agreed to have the first movie filmed on location at their castle because they were having financial difficulty," Enrick said, worried. "Are we?"

He thought about all the expensive but necessary repairs and improvements Colleen had made to the castle and grounds since she'd arrived and mated his older triplet brother. She had wanted to fortify the stone walls and the towers and the keep, major work and expense, but well worth it in the long run.

Everyone loved her for that and a million other reasons. She'd even trained the Irish wolfhounds to behave and taught pack members how to work with them. Grant and his brothers had been afraid she would get homesick and want to return to America, but she loved the castle and their lands and the pack, and she seemed happy to be here and hadn't said anything about returning there even for a visit. They were glad about that.

"No, we're doing fine," Colleen said. "We've made sure we have a say in who is hired as extras, learning from the MacNeill clan's mistakes. We don't want our enemies showing up to fight us. The Kilpatricks you saw at the shop don't stand a chance of being cast." She frowned. "Did you happen to get me a Scotch pie?"

Enrick smiled. "Of course."

Lachlan laughed. "I was going to get one for Colleen tomorrow afternoon."

Colleen smiled. "Thanks. As soon as we're done here, I'll see if it's as good as Grant says it is."

"It is," Grant said.

"Good. I can't wait to eat it. Okay, back to business," Colleen said. "The extras casting director said they normally would provide authentic-looking period dress, but we've got it already. The director was thrilled that our outfits are really authentic, based on the original weave patterns. Well, the rest of you have authentic costumes. I don't."

"Easily remedied," Grant said, squeezing Colleen's hand.

She smiled at him. "When the MacNeills were dealing with the film production, a weapons trainer was sent to teach the clan how to fight."

The brothers shook their heads.

"We sent them video of our training/fighting sessions and they'll send someone. He'll watch to see if he can give us any tips to improve the fighting on-screen, but otherwise he'll just observe."

Lachlan and Enrick scoffed.

"As if we need any guidance from someone who has never fought a battle in his life. At least not with a claymore," Lachlan said.

Enrick folded his arms across his chest. "Too bad we can't tell him we've been doing this for eons."

Grant agreed. "Since we can't, we'll humor the guy."

"We told them you've had masters teach you the art of sword fighting. The director's staff still don't believe men in our modern age can do it without their guidance and make it look real, but they'll see," Colleen said. "When I first saw all of you in training, no shirts, muscles gleaming, I was totally won over."

Grant laughed, since he'd done the whole fighting scene in the inner bailey to scare Colleen off, not make her a fan.

Enrick knew she'd won the guys over from the beginning because Grant hadn't intimidated her like he thought he would.

Colleen began again. "They want actors in their twenties to forties fighting the battles, though in the real old days they could have been much younger and older. For the women, we'll have a mix of ages. We'll have some children doing chores—young boys sword fighting in the inner bailey with wooden swords or hauling wood in for the fires and young girls helping with washing linens or other chores. Since none of us are in an actors' union, we'll each be paid between $85 and $100 per day.

"They'll be redecorating the castle to an extent and shooting in certain areas that still appear more authentic to the period. They'll also be shooting on the ruins south of the castle, doing a mock setting of before and after. We'll need to keep our people occupied or give them time off while all of that's happening so they'll be out of the way of all the activity. Once the company has the scenes set up the way they want, they'll start shooting."

"No enemy clan will be allowed to be in the film," Grant said, confirming Colleen's earlier comment. "We don't have enough extras for the film, so the MacNeills will send us more men and women."

Immediately, Enrick thought of Heather. Would she have a role in the film? He would have to keep an eye on her if she did. He couldn't shake the need to protect her from any of the male human actors or staff who might want to have a good time with her. Why he was feeling so protective and possessive of her, he didn't know.

At least he would bump into her whenever he could—so it wouldn't look like anything more than a casual encounter—to learn what she was up to as the shooting progressed. Then again, she was so busy with her new shop, he wasn't sure she would have time for anything but that.

"They also want to have trained wolves. They're having difficulty bringing some here, and a local guy can't give them a price they can live with, so Grant said we would beat the other guy's offer and throw in a couple of extra wolves. That's seven in all. We told them we keep them off-site. Their wolf handler wanted to see the wolves, but we told them we have our own wolf handlers," Colleen said. "In the movie, they will be kind of like the *Game of Thrones* wolves, only ours are really shifters."

"Wolves? I hope the script doesn't have them eating people. We need to provide an image that portrays us as the good guys." Enrick hated films where they portrayed evil wolves out to get the good humans as if it were truly the way wolves lived. No wonder wolves had such a bad name.

"They're with the good guys, so they'll only be taking down bad guys," Colleen said.

"I can live with that. So who are the wolves going to be?" Enrick wanted to wield a sword.

"Two will be my cousins. They're big male wolves, a black and a gray. We just need five more volunteers."

"Your cousins are American," Enrick said.

"Exactly, which is why they want to take part as wolves. No Scottish accent required. Though as extras, you won't really have to speak."

"In battle, some Gaelic curses are a necessity," Enrick said.

Colleen smiled. "I'm sure that would lend to the authenticity of the battle scenes then. My cousins still haven't quite gotten the knack of sword fighting, not like you all have mastered the skill. And they'd rather wear jeans than kilts, so their wolf coats will be perfect for an assignment like this. And they are eager to have a role in the movie."

"We'll get their sword-fighting skills up to par before long," Lachlan said. "And somehow we'll convince them that manly men wear kilts."

Colleen chuckled. "I sure think so." She patted Grant's thigh, smiling at him.

"What about you, Colleen?" Enrick asked, assuming she'd have a part in this.

"I'll be watching over many of the activities of the crew setting up the scenes and the women in our clan who will take part. Grant is continuing to oversee the rest of the castle and our people but will lend a hand whenever we need his help."

A knock at the doorjamb had everyone turning to see who it was.

Heather MacNeill. What was she doing here at a private MacQuarrie wolf-pack meeting?

"Hi, sorry I'm late. Ian was giving me last-minute instructions before I left." Heather took a seat near Lachlan. "What did I miss?"

Hell, she already knew about the film deal when she'd said she didn't? Or maybe she hadn't already known about it when she was at the shop. Then he recalled she'd said something about the leaders maybe not wanting to tell anyone about the deal right off.

"Grant and I have told you most of this already." Colleen smiled at her. "Heather is in charge of the MacNeill women who will be extras and the actual scenes they'll be in. We'll need more fighting men for some of the scenes. Heather will coordinate with Enrick, since you will be responsible for all the fighters in the film who are extras."

Enrick's jaw dropped. Again. He could see being in charge of the fighters, but he hadn't expected Heather to be put in charge of the MacNeill extras. Then he straightened. He could still watch out for her, if her brothers or his weren't there to do so.

"Don't tell me I'm a wolf handler." Lachlan's eyes were filled with mirth. He didn't appear to be unhappy about it in the least.

Though Enrick knew Lachlan loved to fight, the idea of being a wolf handler would appeal just as much to his younger brother.

"We have to have someone in charge who they'll mind," Grant said.

"Here are the plans for the scenes they intend to shoot at the castle." Colleen passed copies of the scenes to the brothers and Heather. "They'll have their own people running things, but they can't be responsible for the wolves. They'll tell you what they want the wolves to do, and you'll make it magically happen."

"Our people will get a kick out of that," Enrick said.

Everyone agreed.

"*A Twist in Time*?" Enrick said. "We heard Hollywood was planning the film about two years ago."

"Right, and they planned the film shoots after that. Which means they're about ready to do the shoots here," Grant said.

"Are they're starting the shooting here in the present and then time traveling to the past?" Lachlan asked.

"They're already shooting scenes in New York City. That's

where the story begins in the present. Missy Buchanan, the woman who plays the heroine in the story, inherits a Scottish claymore and is instructed to hand it over to a Scottish lord here at our castle," Colleen said.

"Sounds like the Scottish lord is a usurper," Enrick said, "taking Grant's place."

Everyone laughed.

"And he took over with nary a fight," Lachlan said. "You know in the real old days, he would never have lived that long."

"I don't know," Colleen said. "Guy McNab played a gladiator in another film, and he looks perfectly ripped."

Grant and Lachlan smiled and glanced in Enrick's direction to see how he viewed the news.

"Ah hell." No way did Enrick want to see his clone here at the castle.

"*And* he had to learn how to fight with a sword." Heather showed his picture on her cell phone off to everyone.

"In mock battles," Grant said. "Not in a live-or-die situation."

"Not *him*." Enrick couldn't believe his bad luck. The actor had been the bane of his existence since he'd made it in Hollywood with his last gladiator film and then a hit Viking film.

Enrick looked like his spitting image. The same long, curly blond hair, though Enrick was certain *he* was more ripped than Guy, and he had very similar facial features: square jaw, prominent nose, wide-set eyes, bushy brows, and a mouth meant to kiss the lassies. Sure, Enrick looked similar to his brothers—they were fraternal triplets, after all. But his features made him look even more like the actor than his brothers did.

"He's not a wolf, so that makes a difference," Enrick said. "And he's not Scottish."

"He's American, true, but his ancestors were from Scotland," Colleen said. That was similar to her situation.

Enrick was certain most everyone in his clan would rib him

about it mercilessly, way beyond the short time it took to film the scenes before the film crew was out of there. For years, he suspected.

"Are there any dragons in the story?" Heather asked, changing the subject.

"No, but they do have a wizard," Colleen said. "Just read through the scenes so you have some idea of what our part in all of this will be, and hopefully everything will work out just fine. We have practice sessions scheduled in two days' time, just to prepare our people.

"I need a list of those who want to participate as extras and background actors—women, men, kids, and wolves—by tomorrow afternoon at the latest so I can give the list to Sherry Bright, the extras casting director. Everyone needs to be on time for a shoot. No one leaves a shoot until it's wrapped. In other words, the scene is finished, and the extras are released from shooting that day. The director said it helps to think of this as if you are part of the whole story, playing your important role, just like the main actors are. The same thing for our practice sessions. Whatever job the extras normally have to do during the day will have to be done before or after practice sessions."

"Thinking of ourselves truly playing the role will be easy for all of us to do. We've lived these scenes," Enrick said. "All we have to do is remember what it was like for us back then. But also we know how to fight each other because of all the practice we've had over the years, so unless someone is careless, we shouldn't have any injuries."

"That's what I want to hear," Grant said. "Even though it's a fantasy film and none of this is for real, we don't want anyone to come to harm while playing in the film. The same with the animals. Our wolfhounds are staying with the MacNeills. We're moving our Highland cows to pasture with the MacNeills' for safety reasons, except for three of them they want in a pastoral setting for some shoots. Some of our other livestock also will be moved, though the swans and ducks will remain at the pond. The film director is going to have a scene between the Scottish lord and the time traveler there. Oh, and no one shifts into their wolf, except for those playing wolves, until the shooting is done and we're sure there's no chance of anyone seeing our wolves shift. Those who are playing wolves will be staying at the MacNeill castle and transported here as wolves before the scenes are shot for their role in the story. We don't want to have to turn any humans who happened to see something they shouldn't."

"That would be a disaster. Then we would be stuck with them living here forever," Lachlan said.

"I'd take Guy McNab in and show him our ways any day." Heather placed her hands on her heart.

Enrick scoffed. That was exactly what he was worried about. "You'd be fighting off tons of women interested in getting to know the star better." He knew because he'd been mobbed a couple of times when he was in Edinburgh by fans of Guy who thought Enrick was him and wanted autographs anywhere he wanted to put them. He just hoped Heather wouldn't try to get a date with the star!

Which suddenly conjured an image of her in his arms, with him kissing her and feeling all her curves pressed against his body. Hell. He had to get his mind on track where it belonged.

Heather laughed.

"Besides, that's the role he plays, but in real life, he could be a real ogre," Lachlan said.

Heather smiled at him, but Enrick agreed with his brother.

"Don't *even* think of biting him," Grant warned, just in case Heather needed the warning. Any newly turned wolf could have consequences for all of them. And she was known to be a bit of a wild card.

Grant continued, "They'll have some of their own security

when shoots are going on to keep onlookers out of here, but we'll do most of the security. Since the castle and grounds are quite a way off the road, we shouldn't have much trouble, and it's our property so our responsibility. When the men aren't battling or taking part in other scenes, we'll have them providing security detail. With the McKinley clansmen angry at their missed opportunity, I wouldn't be surprised if we have some issues with them over it.

"I can see them trying to ruin the film and make it seem like the producer picked the wrong castle to use for the production. Enrick, you and Lachlan can be in charge of setting up the security details. I'd do it now, even before the shooting begins, just to make sure the McKinleys don't do anything beforehand to cause trouble. At least Enrick chased the Kilpatricks off at the pie shop. I'm glad he was there to help Heather deal with it."

Heather's kissable lips parted.

Not kissable. Damn it. Intriguing. Enrick tore his gaze away from her mouth.

Okay, so he didn't *exactly* chase the men off, but they *did* leave shortly after they realized he was watching them.

"If you have the lists of extras' names sooner than later, just give them to me and we'll get started with the paperwork on our 'cast,'" Colleen said. "We'll start scheduling dress rehearsals and scene enactments tomorrow. If someone has an important job to do and can't get to it because of the acting requirements, it's up to him or her to make sure their job is covered. As a last resort, if anyone has trouble getting someone to fill their job in the interim, let me know right away and I'll make sure someone covers for them. Okay, if no one has any more questions, you've got your jobs to take care of."

Everyone got up to leave, and Colleen said to Lachlan, "I know you wanted to fight, but you have the most important job. Making sure our wolves show the world just how wonderful they are."

"Aye, I'm fine with it. I've never been a wolf handler before." Lachlan smiled at Heather.

Enrick tried not to frown at him. He hoped his brother wasn't interested in courting Heather. Maybe her saying she'd take in Guy had given his brother the notion she might be interested in courting. Lachlan had never been interested in a she-wolf who could be on the wild side. At least Enrick didn't think so. He frowned at his brother.

CHAPTER 3

HEATHER GLANCED AT ENRICK, AND HE RAISED HIS BROW AT her. Yeah, he would ask her why she didn't tell him what was going on. But she was loyal to a fault to her leaders, and she wasn't supposed to tell anyone about the film deal until they could share with their packs. Not even Grant's brothers. No way would she have abused their trust.

She couldn't believe Enrick had told people he'd chased off the men in her shop! She was going to contradict him, but she figured she would talk to him privately about it after the meeting.

She'd been amused when he sounded as though he didn't like the idea of Guy being the star of the film at the MacQuarries' castle. Around these parts, everyone knew Enrick. But with the real Guy being here? She smiled.

Ever since she was a little girl and her brothers and Enrick and his brothers and the MacNeills had practiced in the heather for real battles to come, she had watched them when she was supposed to be doing chores at the castle. She couldn't help it. She wished she'd been born a warrior, not a lassie. She often played with a wooden sword when she could steal one of her brothers', whacking away at the air where she imagined she was fighting some unseen foe while she saved her people. At least she was a competent archer, since she wasn't supposed to fight with a sword. And the claymores were rather heavy. She thought this whole film business would be fun. She couldn't wait to see how it all worked out, but for now, she needed to return to her castle and begin taking names of all the women who wanted to be in the film.

She had played in the earlier film at the MacNeill castle and found she'd really enjoyed being someone in the background who didn't have any speaking roles. That was easy.

The MacNeill women were just as excited about taking part in the film as she was. She hoped they wouldn't have any troubles while doing it. And she hoped the Kilpatrick brothers wouldn't return to the shop.

Still not believing Heather would know about the film location before he did, Enrick stepped in stride with her as she hurried down the hallway. "You knew all along the film was going to be set here, and you didn't tell me?" She had to know he would give her grief about it. Though he still wondered if she hadn't learned of it until after he'd left the shop.

"Seriously? What would you have done in my shoes? You certainly would have kept the secret if Grant had told you to."

Enrick grunted. He didn't want to admit she had a point. "You led me to believe the film was being shot at *your* castle."

"You believed what you wanted." She smiled at him.

She had such a willful expression when she'd gotten one over on him, though he knew he would have done the same with her if Grant had told him what was going on and nobody else was to know.

"Do you think they'll get you mixed up with Guy during the shoots?" Again, the smile of a vixen.

Enrick wanted to groan out loud. The notion was his worst nightmare. But how would that sound to the she-wolf? He had to keep his warrior persona intact. "My people? No. His people? I doubt it. We won't be wearing the same clothes, and when I speak, I won't sound anything like him. Will you be playing a role in the film?" He knew she had before, so he suspected she would this time too. He was glad she was going to be in charge of the

MacNeill women while they were here, which meant he could see more of her. Watch over her, rather.

"Absolutely. I want to make sure everyone is doing their part, whether preparing meals for a scene in the kitchen, or serving in some other capacity, but I will be overseeing them in 'costume.' What about you? Are you going to be fighting with the men? I thought you might have to be in charge but not actively involved in the fighting," Heather said as he walked her out of the keep and into the inner bailey.

"I'll be fighting with the men. I'll work with them on practicing the scenes and making sure everyone's there when they're supposed to show up, but they'll be taking their cue from the director when the actual shoot begins. That means I get to swing a sword too."

"I figured you wouldn't be able to live with just supervising."

"You figured right."

"Do you think Lachlan is disappointed he's the wolf handler?"

"No. He knows how important showing off our wolves to the rest of the world is. He's proud to do it. Though I'm sure if we don't have the wolves in a battle scene for the day when they're shooting those scenes, he could be one of the fighters."

She tilted her chin down, her brows up, and gave Enrick a scolding look. "*You* chased the Kilpatrick brothers out of my shop? They paid for their pies and left without anyone causing any trouble. Not even you."

Enrick shrugged. "After they saw me, they didn't stay to hassle you about the location of the film further." He cast her a wolfish smile.

———————————

Enrick paused and glanced around the bailey at the men doing their daily chores, and Heather knew his mind was on task, just where her own needed to be.

"Why did you really come into the pie shop? It wasn't just to pick up a pie for Colleen." Heather was sure it wasn't. She swore her brothers had sent him, but maybe he had a hard time showing his feelings and it had nothing to do with her brothers.

Enrick smiled at her, but he wouldn't say.

She sighed. "See you later. Maybe you'll be a real film star after all this is over and done with."

Scoffing, Enrick shook his head. "I would always be known as Guy's clone. Besides, it's just a job like any other."

"As if you really believed that. The chance to get paid something extra for a day's fun of fighting exercises?"

"The fighting will be different, orchestrated to an extent, not like we usually fight in practice. I'm sure the whole keep will be in an uproar while they're shooting scenes, so I'm not sure it will *all* be fun. But I'm certain we'll have a big celebration when it's all over with."

"That would be fun. See you later then." Heather walked to her car and called Ian, while Enrick headed toward some men cleaning out the stables. "We're all set. I'm getting together with the women to find some volunteers, and then after Enrick learns how many extra men they need to fight the battles, he'll get with me and I'll let you know."

"You can handle that too," Ian said. "No need to include me in on it."

"You're not going to get involved in the film this time at all?" To an extent, Heather wasn't surprised.

Ian laughed. "Last time was enough for me. I told Grant what a nightmare it had been and advised him not to do it. But the money is good, I have to admit. It saved us the last time."

She knew the nightmare he was referring to was because of the fight they'd had with their enemy and for no other reason. Sure, Ian hadn't liked other people coming in and telling his people what to do. And the filming had disrupted their business. But Ian had met his mate during the shooting, and that had made everything worthwhile. Heather wondered if Julia would take part in the film this time. Like Grant's mate, Julia was an American with Scottish roots. Ian had trained her with a bow and a sword, but for the film, the director didn't want any women fighting in the battles.

Heather wondered just what they would have the wolves doing. Would they also hire horses for the scenes? Probably. Taking part in the film was going to make her year. She was so glad Ian had asked her to do this job. She was beginning to think everyone worried about her being untrustworthy where strangers were concerned. She had no intention of biting anyone and turning someone into one of their own kind. What if she did that to some guy and she had to mate him to teach him all there was about their kind?

Just because a bunch of the American actors in the last film had asked her to show them some fun places to go. Scottish hospitality being what it was, she had been all for it. Until her pack leader, his brothers, and *her* brothers had intervened. What did they think she was going to do? Have a lovefest? Though she suspected they were worried more about the Americans' intentions than hers.

She finally arrived home and hurried into the castle where Julia had set up a meeting with her for all the eligible women who were interested in playacting in the new film. She wasn't surprised to see nineteen women eager to fill the roles.

"The chance to work with Guy McNab? Oh, yes, choose me," one of the women said.

Heather laughed. "You know Grant said no one is allowed to bite the guy."

"Grant's no fun," the lady said.

"Well, Ian wouldn't go along with it either." Then Heather got to work asking which roles the women would want to play—washerwomen, a mother chasing after her kids, some in the kitchen, some serving meals, some feeding the chickens. By the time she was through with assignments, she thought she had enough volunteers to supplement the MacQuarrie women.

She called Colleen and said, "I've got nineteen volunteers. If you need more, let me know. I'll send the list in a message."

"Thanks," Colleen said. "I knew I could count on you. I'm just going down the list I have, and I think between yours and mine, we'll have it covered. You told the ladies they can't bite Guy McNab, right?"

Heather smiled. "Uh, aye, that's a prerequisite for taking part in this."

"Oh, we need one lady with a baby. The baby has to be at least fifteen days old. I think you have one with a four-week-old, right?"

"Yes."

"And if you have a pregnant mom, we can use her too. But not too far along. We want to make sure we don't have any sudden births during the shoots."

Heather laughed. "That could be a disaster. Can you imagine if it was multiple births, like we often have, and she wants to birth them as a wolf? We have one woman who is eight months along. I'll see what I can do." Then they ended the call and she smiled at the MacNeill women. "You're all in. Colleen will hand over the list of extras to the casting director, and we'll begin shooting soon. I'll get with all of you in the morning as to what you'll need to do, and we'll practice the scenes at the MacQuarrie castle as soon as they're ready for us."

Then Heather's brothers stormed into the room, looking ready to do battle. She figured they'd heard about the Kilpatrick brothers showing up at her shop and speaking to her. She glanced at Lana, who quickly looked away. Heather should have told her not to say anything to anyone about the incident, but she knew word would have spread from the MacQuarries' pack to hers anyway. She sure didn't want her brothers tearing into the Kilpatricks.

CHAPTER 4

AFTER THE INCIDENT AT THE PIE SHOP, ENRICK FOUND HIMSELF heading over there daily to check on Heather and the other women working there until the shooting of the film began. After that, Heather would be working all the time at the MacQuarrie castle, and someone else would be taking charge of her shop. It didn't matter that her MacNeill kinsmen often dropped in, too, and that a couple of the men were actually working there every day on her oldest brother Ian's orders to ensure nothing untoward happened. Enrick still felt it was his duty to see that she and the others were safe because word had gotten out about the location of the film. And the Kilpatrick brothers might want to punish Heather for lying to them.

Oran and Callum, two of Heather's other brothers, were there today, each eating a venison pie. Both of them straightened and inclined their heads in greeting when they saw Enrick drop in for yet another pie for Colleen. Enrick was certain Heather's brothers—and everyone else who worked there—believed there was more to him showing up every day than just to buy his pack leader a different meat or sweet pie. Especially since he'd never done so before.

He usually just left after he made sure everything was fine and paid for Colleen's pie. She'd actually budgeted for it, so he didn't have to pay for them every day. This time, he would order a steak pie for himself so he could visit with Oran and Callum.

Three women were ahead of him in line, and business was brisk again today. Even though Heather was busy with the orders, she'd caught his eye and smiled brightly. She seemed to enjoy his daily visits, and for now, that was all they could afford to see of each other because she practiced scenes with the women after she closed the shop, and he was working on the scenes with the men and getting his other business done. He was afraid she would get suspicious about him being there to watch out for her because her brothers had asked him to, which would make her furious. But that wasn't the only reason he was there.

When he finally reached Heather, he ordered the steak pie for Colleen to go and one for him to eat there and an Irn Bru. "I'll join your brothers and give them some company."

"Good. All of them have been in my hair way too much of late. Your pie will be right up. I guess Colleen is enjoying hers."

"Aye, she is. Colleen said every one of them has whet her appetite for more."

"That's good. I'm glad you're here. I feel safer. If the Kilpatricks are even thinking of dropping by, once they see your car, they'll think twice about it, especially since you ran them off before."

Enrick smiled at her. She would get him back forever for telling his family he had chased the Kilpatricks off.

"I can't wait for the filming to begin." She motioned to the notices posted near the register.

"Subtle."

"It's brought in business. Patrons are eager to hear what it's like to work with the director and work beside the stars."

"I'm sure they're like anybody else. Working to earn a living," Enrick said.

"Except they're famous. The day you chased off the Kilpatricks, a man was eating in here who looked just like you, like Guy."

"I didn't see him."

"You were too busy giving the Kilpatricks your warrior-confrontational look, telling them if they did anything you didn't like, they would die."

Enrick smiled. "We were born with that look down pat. Was the man the star?"

"I think it might have been his double. He just didn't seem star-like, more down-to-earth. Are you getting excited about the film shoots?"

He grunted. "It's a nightmare."

She chuckled. "Ian warned Grant what a mess it could be."

"Aye. We never visited Argent Castle when the filming was going on at your place. We might have thought about this differently. With them staging the scenes, it's a mess. Humans running all over the place. We're not supposed to run as wolves, but everyone is anxious to have things back to the way they were so we can shift when we want to." No one was within hearing distance, so Enrick didn't worry about mentioning wolves.

"Same with us. Ian said you could come out and shift at our castle anytime. No problem at all."

"We appreciate that. I'm sure some of our pack members will be glad to take you up on it."

"I heard some of the cast is coming tomorrow."

"Aye, including Guy McNab." Enrick really wished they would get a new star for the film before they began shooting.

"Has anyone mistaken you for him yet?"

"Hell yeah. I had some woman all excited to see me when he wasn't supposed to be there yet. I was working out with Lachlan, sword fighting, and she was watching us, especially me, and looked eager to speak with me every time I caught her eye. I stopped the fight before Lachlan won because I was so distracted. I told her I wasn't Guy McNab, and I think I ruined her day. She turned three shades of red. Worse, everyone had to needle me about it."

Heather smiled. "*I* wouldn't get the two of you mixed up. I bet she's avoided you since then."

"Aye. She was only interested in the genuine article."

"As a Highland warrior, you *are* the genuine article. I heard the weapons instructor arrived and was giving you tips."

Enrick sighed. "The poor guy is trying to keep up with us."

"I bet."

One of the women working in the shop brought the pie out for Enrick, and then a couple came into the shop to order, which was Enrick's cue to let Heather get back to work. He would sit with Oran and Callum and visit for a bit. Heather handed over Enrick's steak pie on a plate. "I'll have the other ready for you when you are returning to the castle."

"Thanks. Tomorrow's the big day. See you at the castle," Enrick said.

Heather took a deep breath and nodded. "I just hope I don't mess anything up."

"You'll be great." Then Enrick took his pie to the table where Heather's brothers were sitting and joined them.

"Here again." Oran forked up more of his venison pie. "Our brother Jamie said you were in here yesterday to check up on things. We're glad you're watching out for our sister."

"Aye. It doesn't hurt for some of the MacQuarries to show their presence here." Though he was the only MacQuarrie he knew of who was dropping by. Enrick noticed two MacNeill men were servers, wearing kilts and swords, with *sgian dubhs* tucked into their boots.

Patrons had flocked to see the battle-hardened warriors serving meals, along with a pretty lassie or two. It gave the place a real rugged feel. Enrick knew some men swapped off at the shop to work in the past, but now it was a regular occurrence until the film was shot and finalized. Though they might do the same thing when the film was done, just in case they had any backlash from the Kilpatricks and their kinsmen afterward.

"Are you ready to be a warrior?" Enrick asked.

"Aye. I'm ready to fight ye." Oran raised a brow, smiling.

"You will never win that battle." Enrick began to dig into his pie.

Oran laughed. "You will want to fight Cearnach, eh?"

"Aye. He and I have been sparring for practice when I haven't been sparring with Lachlan, but you can gang up on me, too, and I'll still be the winner."

"In your dreams. When you're flat on your back in the mud, you'll take back those words. You are watching out for her while the Americans are at your castle, aye?" Oran motioned with his fork to Heather, who was taking payment for another couple of orders.

"As much as I can. In truth, we're both keeping really busy so we haven't had a lot of free time to do much else. And when she's done with practice, she's off to keep up with her shop."

A lady at a table near them was taking notes and tried to take a surreptitious picture of them with her cell phone. Way too obvious for a wary group of wolves not to notice.

Oran leaned over and said to Enrick, "Methinks the woman believes you are practicing for your role as the lord of MacQuarrie castle."

Enrick sighed. "In other words, she believes..."

"You're the star. Shows what she knows," Oran said under his breath.

Enrick laughed.

Callum agreed.

"Well, keep an eye on our sister, as much as you can. Your brother and Grant are also, of course. We appreciate the help." Oran raised his mug to his lips to take another swig.

"I was remiss in not doing anything to discourage her from seeing Timothy."

"Ha, she's too headstrong. If you had said anything against him, it would have made her that much more eager to see him. We hoped she would see the truth about him before it was too late, and in the end, she did, just not in a good way." Oran paused. "You know why she disobeyed me and my brother to watch us battling in the heather when we were younger? She wanted to see you fighting. She's always wanted to be where you are."

"A young lass's folly." Enrick had known it, but at that time, he was more interested in fighting the guys than being smitten with a lassie.

"Why do you think she jumped at the chance to be in charge of the women in the film?" Callum finished his pie.

"She wanted to take part in it. Just like she took part in the other film at your castle. Who wouldn't want to do that?" Enrick wasn't going to take it for granted that she planned to enjoy this herself.

"You know what a job that will be? Colleen could have done it. Julia even. Any other number of women could have. Or men. Heather's overwhelmed with orders at her shop. She's extremely successful. And she loves it here. It's given her real purpose since Timothy died. Why do you think my pack leaders and yours put Heather in charge?"

Enrick sat back in his chair and glanced at Heather. She was frowning at her brother and then shared the growly expression with Enrick. He smiled.

"If you let the opportunity to really get to know her slide this time, I swear, you will not be seeing her again."

Callum nodded.

Enrick frowned at Oran. "I'm not here to date her or mate her." He figured Oran and his brothers suddenly had some notion this was all supposed to lead up to a mating. It wasn't. He was just doing what they all wanted to do. Protect Heather from herself, particularly with outsiders possibly hitting on her and her taking them up on it.

"And you will make time for her during any breaks you have during the day and at night." Oran raised a brow, challenging Enrick to agree.

Callum again agreed with his brother.

Enrick couldn't believe his pack members and hers were endeavoring to matchmake, if this wasn't just some fantasy her brothers had. Maybe because they were tired of her not having a decent mate to watch over her, day and night, and they thought Enrick would be the right one for her. Especially since she'd had interest in him when they were both young. "Did Heather put you up to this?"

"If she knew what I told you, she would give me a dressing-down, believe you me. All of us feel the same way about you dating her, so don't screw it up." Oran frowned at him.

Enrick wanted to laugh, but he knew from Oran's expression he was dead serious.

"You will tell her you've dated other lassies over the years so she knows what kind of a cad you are. She thinks you have been working too hard or you would have asked her out already. Dinna upset her with the truth, but get it out in the open. It will go easier for the both of you if you're clear on that score," Oran said.

"The truth is I did not think we would suit." As wild as she could be. She was always dating some wolf. And the wolf she'd dated seriously had been as wild and carefree as her.

Enrick wasn't like that. Not any longer. He was down-to-earth, a hard worker, played hard, but not with the she-wolves. She was a free spirit, and he would have wanted to rein her in if they had courted. So it was best if he watched out for her, but beyond that?

Still, once she'd established her shop, that had seemed to channel some of the bubbly energy she always seemed to have. And she loved the shop and her customers and everyone working for her. Truly, this was a new side to her he hadn't expected. He had thought the shop would be something she did on a whim, and within months she'd close the shop down and be off on the next wild adventure.

It wasn't that he didn't like the way she was. He did. And that was the trouble. He was afraid they would butt heads when she wanted to do things he didn't want her to do, for her own safety and well-being. Take Timothy, for instance. Enrick had tried to tell Timothy she *wasn't* the one for him, not wanting him to hurt her with his recklessness, but that hadn't gone over well. Enrick had sported a black eye for four days over it. And Grant had told him to leave the situation alone, that it would sort itself out eventually. Well, it had, but not like any of them had predicted. Enrick had thought she would just dump Timothy before things went too far.

Enrick raised his tankard of Irn Bru to Oran and Callum in friendship. He figured that was the easiest way to set their minds at ease. He was not dating the lass and certainly had no intention of mating her.

CHAPTER 5

THE NEXT MORNING ALL THE *LUPUS GAROU* EXTRAS ARRIVED AT the MacQuarrie castle much earlier than needed. It was a time for the clans to enjoy a visit with each other before the shooting began, and the ladies were eager to get a glimpse of Guy McNab as soon as they could. The guys said they weren't interested in seeing the female star since she wouldn't be a wolf, but most of the women didn't believe them. She was a dark-haired beauty with dark-brown eyes, a goddess on the silver screen. And from what Enrick had read about her, if any of it was true, she was sweet and funny, and liked to cook and hike and read books, a down-to-earth kind of woman.

Guy had tried to ignore Enrick whenever he was nearby. Enrick wasn't sure why the actor didn't care to see him. Guy was fine with the double, Larry Rogers, being there. In fact they seemed to be good friends, which Enrick learned often happened as the stunt double would do the riskier stunts or other scenes as needed. Who would ever have thought Enrick would be reading up on the stars like this?

Maybe Guy liked Larry because he would take the riskier shots for the actor, while Enrick just reminded Guy he could be replaced by a *real* Highlander if the film called for it. Enrick smiled.

The director mistook Enrick for Guy when he first arrived to speak with the star, and Enrick was a little bit amused. "Guy's over there." Enrick motioned to Guy who was watching them, probably wondering what *that* was all about.

"Well, hell, you're a doppelgänger of Guy if I ever saw one."

"I get that sometimes," Enrick said.

The director slapped Enrick on the back. "Stick around. If

something happens to our double, I might just be calling on you to take his place."

Great. And Enrick didn't think that in a good way.

Then they got down to business and began shooting some milling-around scenes in the inner bailey that morning before it rained, while Guy and his entourage rode horses into the courtyard. He and the others dismounted, some of Grant's groomsmen taking the horses to the stable, and then Guy headed inside the castle with the other men who had ridden with him to eat a meal.

Heather had been so busy with meal preparations—and making sure the women all took their places in the kitchen and knew who was to serve the meals in the great hall and how they were to do it—that Enrick hadn't had to worry about her. Her brothers hadn't mentioned him seeing her in a courtship way again, for which he was grateful. He could imagine her getting word of it. She would be furious, and he was afraid he would lose her friendship. Since he wasn't dating her, he didn't think there was any need to mention anything about having dated other women. She had to suspect he had over the years.

Everything went fine while Guy sat at the head table with his wizard adviser and others of importance, including the heroine from another time period. They hadn't filmed the scene where she first met Guy, carrying his claymore sword to him from the present day to his day. They wanted to do it on a sunny day after the battle scenes were shot, if everything worked out as they planned.

Enrick was dying to see how things were going for Heather, but he needed to stay out of her and the other women's way and out of the view of the cameras.

"She's doing just fine," Lachlan told Enrick. They were both in full battle dress, Enrick because they had a battle scene that afternoon and Lachlan as handler of the wolves.

Enrick knew if her scene was a disaster, he would hear about it, because several of their people and the MacNeills were dining in the great hall as background actors for effect.

"Got to go," Lachlan said, going to a room set aside for the wolves. Then he let them out and the wolves raced off to the great hall like they were supposed to and settled at the foot of the head table, tails wagging, sitting tall, eager to catch the scraps of food the lord tossed to them.

Enrick had to see this, and since Lachlan was in charge of the wolves, they both found a spot to watch from.

Guy tossed strips of fish to the wolves, and they caught them in midair.

Enrick smiled. Colleen's cousins had said they wouldn't eat any off the floor, even though real wolves would.

So they'd caught the fish for the shoot, thankfully. He could imagine them turning up their noses at the fish on the floor and not looking wolfish at all.

Then Guy tossed a bone to the wolves and the cousins were to fight over it. Again, they caught it in midair, which was a sight to see.

They were growling as they played tug-of-war, and then one finally wrenched it away from the other and trotted off to leave the great hall and chew on his bone in peace.

When William was out of sight of the cameras, Enrick and Lachlan gave him a thumbs-up.

The other six wolves milled around, pretending to look for scraps of food on the floor.

Two got into a fight over a piece of food, per the script. In the meantime, Guy was talking to his wizard, the wolves just a sideshow. But they were doing an excellent job. Enrick was proud of them.

Who would ever have thought some of their *lupus garous* would be acting as wolves in a film for the world to see, when in truth they never wanted to show that part of themselves to the world?

Then Heather entered the great hall with a tray of food. Enrick swore she was prettier every day he saw her. He suddenly saw trouble ahead. Somebody had tossed a large bone on the floor, and he was afraid she was going to trip over it. It wasn't part of the scene, and he didn't want her to twist her ankle, take a spill, and maybe even injure herself. He didn't think of the cameras or ruining the shoot. All he thought of was rescuing Heather from potential disaster.

He dashed into the great hall, heard a hush go over the "court," and grabbed Heather's arm at the same time he was taking hold of the tray so she wouldn't drop it when he startled her. Her eyes were huge. He quickly kicked the bone out of her path and released her with a slight bow of his head, ensuring she still had a steady grip on the tray, then hurried out of the great hall as if this all had been planned.

She continued on her way, the director never calling cut, so Enrick wasn't certain if they would reshoot the scene or that her part—well, and his—could be cut without causing any trouble. He could just see her spraining an ankle, and though their kind healed in half the time it took humans, he hadn't wanted to ruin the opportunity she had to have this role in the film.

"Nice save." Lachlan slapped Enrick on the back when he was out of the camera's view.

"I hope she doesn't kill me for wrecking her scene."

Lachlan smiled. "She will appreciate that she didn't injure herself. Even if she had managed to move the bone out of her path, she might have wobbled the tray too much and lost the food. You never know. I would say that was hero material, and if you're looking to *finally* court her, you stand a chance."

Enrick was frowning as Heather set the mugs of ale at one of the tables. "I'm not looking to court her. Do you think she saw the bone?" She would *really* kill him if she had planned on pushing it out of her way and Enrick had bolted into the great hall and embarrassed her to pieces over a nonexistent danger.

Heather had been so startled when Enrick rushed into the great hall and grabbed her arm to keep her from tripping over the bone that her heart was still racing to the moon and back. She'd seen the bone and was intending to kick it out of her path when he ran out to rescue her, nearly giving her a heart attack.

She'd expected the director to stop the scene, but—she sighed as she carried the empty tray back to the kitchen—she guessed her part wasn't important in the scheme of things and it would end up on the cutting-room floor.

"Ohmigod," Lana said, giving her a hug, and so did some of the other ladies who were tending to the cooking, ready to serve the food again if they needed to reshoot any of the scenes. "I can't believe Enrick dashed out to grab you so you wouldn't kill yourself on that bone."

"I saw it! I wasn't going to trip on it." Heather set her empty tray down on a table.

Their mouths agape, the ladies all looked at her, their eyes rounded, and then they started to laugh.

"I can't believe the director didn't call 'cut'!" Lana said.

"I'm sure the scene will be tossed." Not that Heather was really upset about that. She loved being in the film and doing all the stuff in preparation for the scenes. It would be something she could remember for the rest of her life. Especially the part about the hero named Enrick who had come to her rescue. If he hadn't done that, it would have been a mundane bit-part scene for her. Sure, she would love to see herself in the final version of the film, but truly, Enrick's impromptu save had made her day.

"Well," Lana said, placing her hands over her heart, "Enrick could rescue me any day."

"He only has eyes for Heather," Colleen said, coming into the kitchen. "Go easy on him, will you, Heather?"

Heather sighed. "I'm way too much of a wild spirit for him. He would want someone…much less wild, if he ever decided to mate. If he hadn't grabbed my tray of drinks and food, I would have dropped it because of his sudden and unexpected appearance. So he's just lucky it all worked out."

"Good. So you're not going to give him a tongue-lashing." Colleen smiled.

The ladies all giggled.

Everyone was saying it. Enrick was courting Heather…in his way.

"I've got to make sure we don't have any more takes." She hurried off to the entrance of the great hall and watched, along with some others who had some roles in the film during this scene. She wondered if Enrick was still watching the great hall with Lachlan at the other entrance. Lachlan would be there to pretend to control the wolves when they weren't needed any longer, but Enrick was probably off getting ready for the battle scene. They would film it for several days. Tents in the field. Two camps, the enemies' and the good guys'.

Heather and some of her kitchen staff would be preparing meals at the hero's camp in the movie. She wondered which side Enrick was on. He would definitely have to be a background actor. He might not even be allowed to be in the film since he looked so much like Guy, unless he wasn't seen in any of the close-up hand-to-hand fighting.

She still had her role in the camp, but during the fighting, everyone could watch the scene unfold. She couldn't believe how much fun it would be, not just watching the magic happen on the screen, but to see parts of it from front-row seats, so to speak, while the scene was actually being filmed.

It was time for the battle to begin. Before everyone took their places in the field, getting ready to go into battle, she heard Enrick say, "Has anyone seen Heather MacNeill?"

Heather wondered what he needed her for.

"She's in Guy's camp, but she's going to the top of the hill where she can watch you fight," Lachlan said.

Then she saw Enrick jogging into camp, looking for her, and she smiled at him. She hoped he wasn't worried he'd upset her with the rescue at the meal.

"Hey," Enrick said, seeing her and taking hold of her hands, "I'm sure sorry I messed up your scene."

"You *saved* me."

His brow was still deeply furrowed. "You didn't see the bone?"

She couldn't lie about it and let him think he had truly saved her because others knew the truth and the word most likely would get back to him. She squeezed his hands. "You did what you had to do."

He let out his breath. "Great. You had seen it."

"What if I'd kicked it out of the way and lost my balance and dropped all the drinks and food? We would have had to cut the scene and couldn't have restarted until someone could clean up the mess. I would have been so rattled, I probably wouldn't have been able to do it again."

He smiled and pulled away. "As long as you're not angry with me. I've got to go off to battle."

"Wait, which side are you on?"

"Your side." He winked and ran off.

For the big battle scene in the light rain, they ended up with three hundred extras from the MacNeill clan and the MacQuarrie clan, some Camerons, some MacDonalds, seventy horses, and all the main characters who would battle it out. Enrick knew shooting the scene would take at least a week, longer if they had a lot of trouble.

Between action and cut, the director was watching a laptop, hoping he got all the shots he needed. It was important that no one was seriously injured, though every day there would be injuries. The director was fortunate they had hired so many *lupus garou* extras who healed quickly. Minor bruises, strained muscles, and cuts went away in a couple of days.

Grant had been there, too, to make sure the director didn't do anything that would put his and Ian's people at too much risk, or the animals either.

In the rain and mud, the shooting was taking place for the third day in a row. Enrick didn't know if they were making headway on the fight scenes or losing ground. The director called cut, began again, and cut. Enrick felt the whole effort was more grueling than when they'd had to fight a battle straight through.

And at night they would be able to wash up and sleep in their beds and prepare for the next day's shoot after a hearty breakfast.

That night, Enrick entered the keep after cleaning his boots outside so he didn't track mud through the castle after doing battle in the mud all day. He'd washed his hands, too, and was ready to take a shower when he saw Heather talking to Lana, nodding. He knew he should just keep going and get his shower. He had to smell bad, and he certainly was covered in enough mud to look bad. If anyone had pointed a camera at him while he was battling with Ian's brothers, no one would have thought he looked like the star of the film.

Heather raised her brows at him and smiled.

He took a detour to speak with her. "So what do you think?" As if she spent the whole time watching him fight in the rain. She was all clean and dry, so she might not have been out there that long. He wouldn't blame her if she hadn't bothered.

Lana said good night and headed to the corridor where she and Heather were sharing a room during the shoot.

"I think you did pretty good against Cearnach and his brother Guthrie. Why in the world did the two of them gang up on you in the first place?" Heather asked.

"I'm surprised you would have noticed. Even though we had a routine we'd practiced, two of Ian's brothers ganging up on me wasn't in the plans. I would have thought you'd be watching Guy."

She tilted her chin down at him as if she thought he was making fun of her. "Nay. I can see him closer in the film than I can from where we observe. I was more interested in my cousins fighting you."

"I spoke too soon when I said that one couldn't give me enough of a workout." Enrick stretched his muddy arm out. "I'll be feeling that tomorrow."

She smiled. "I'll see you in the morning then. I wasn't thinking the battle scene would take that long. At least it's supposed to clear the day after tomorrow. I can't wait for the scene where Guy is supposed to swim out into the sea and then return to see the heroine standing there on the beach with his sword where he first meets her."

"That's after the battle scene is finished, right?"

"Right."

"I imagine his double, Larry, will do that scene."

She chewed on her bottom lip, as if pondering her next words carefully. "Do you need a back rub?"

Enrick smiled. Hell yeah. He should have said no. He didn't know why he hesitated. Then he reasoned she was just being nice. A friend. And she didn't mean anything more by it than that.

"Take a shower, and I'll meet you in your room."

"Are you sure you don't mind?" he asked, frowning, still kicking himself for not saying no.

Heather sighed. "Aye. After you rescued me at the meal, I want to reciprocate. I can't save you on the battlefield, so this will have to suffice."

Okay, so that worked. She was only trying to thank him. No one could see more in it than that. "I'll see you in a few minutes."

Enrick headed up the stairs to his room, removed everything, then carried his clean boxer briefs with him into the bathroom. He would leave his regular clothes all muddied up because that was how the shooting would begin tomorrow again. In the old days when he fought, that was the way it was. With seeing Heather in a few minutes, he grimaced at the notion.

He hurried to scrub off the mud and dirt all over his skin, soaping up like crazy, and rinsed off in a hurry. After drying off, he pulled on his clean boxer briefs and put his dirty ones in a laundry bag.

He thought he'd have to call on Heather to let her know he was done, but when he left the bathroom, she was sitting on his chair, looking at her phone.

She had some lotion on the table next to her, and he suspected she planned to rub that on him. He frowned at the lavender label.

"Are you ready?" she asked.

"Uh, yeah, thanks, Heather."

"You're welcome."

He lay down on his stomach on the bed, and she spread the lavender lotion on his back, then began to knead his back muscles. God, that felt good. If she could do that for him every night, he would reconsider the notion he wasn't going to mate a lassie like her.

———

"Do you remember that time we were having a big snowball fight the first big snow of the season?" Heather felt if they were going to continue to see each other for the next couple of months or more like this—well, not exactly like this, but working and living in the same castle—she had to tell Enrick what had happened all those years ago.

"Aye, we had a great time."

She thought he was remembering a different snowball fight. "When you were nearly knocked out?"

"Aye, you sure could pack a punch."

Her jaw dropped, and she stopped massaging his muscles. She couldn't believe he'd known all this time. Had Lachlan told him the truth? "You knew?"

"Aye."

She couldn't believe Enrick had never said anything to her about it before this. "But your brother claimed he'd done it."

"So I could save face. How would it have looked if a fierce Highland warrior was knocked on his arse by a sweet lassie and the snowball she'd thrown?"

She chuckled and began rubbing his muscles again. "Seriously? You knew and you weren't angry with me? Lachlan told me never to tell you the truth because he wanted to take credit for knocking you down all those years ago."

Smiling, Enrick shook his head. "Everyone who'd seen what had happened—though most were preoccupied with throwing their own snowballs—said you had the hots for me, or you wouldn't have tried to knock me out."

"Ha! I did not have the hots for you. So they thought it was the reversal of the caveman and his woman then?"

"Aye, something like that. I didn't think I would ever hear the end of it."

"People just…get notions, whether there's anything to it or not. You and I weren't dating anyone, so they just assumed there was something more to it. When there wasn't."

"Right. When Grant had to take over the management of the castle and made me second in charge of the castle and our people, I was so busy trying to prove my worth that I didn't have time for anything else."

"Like dating."

"Aye. You stayed clear of me for a long time, too, and that had the rumors starting all over again. Were you afraid I would learn you'd struck me with the snowball?"

"I had the biggest crush on you. It was so silly. You and I would never be right for each other."

He tensed a little at her words.

She moved her hands from his lower back to his shoulders. "I felt so bad when I nearly knocked you out. Did Lachlan get into a lot of trouble for what I did?"

"Nay. Everyone knew it was an accident. It could have happened to anyone. The snowball was a little icier, harder. Anyone could have done that. You didn't come to the next snowball fight we had. I thought maybe you'd lost interest in me. Then I learned you were dating other wolves."

"I told you, I finally realized you weren't right for me. Besides, you were always too busy to date *anyone*. Not that I really noticed all that much. I came to see a couple of friends here a few times, but you were always off managing something. The last time I visited with a friend, Timothy saw me and struck up a conversation and asked me out."

"Don't tell me you went out with him to make me jealous," Enrick said.

"Make you jealous? How could I have done that? You were never around. And I told you, my crush on you was over once I came to my senses and realized we would never suit." So why was she rubbing lavender lotion into his beautiful, toned muscles in his bedroom at night as if she wanted more? She quickly reminded herself she was thanking him for his heroic save in the kitchen.

"But I could have been here. And you knew I would hear about it eventually. Lachlan and Grant both gave me an earful over it. Lachlan said if I'd even bothered to ask you out on a date, Timothy would never have had a chance with you."

"He was a hothead," she admitted. "And you wouldn't have

asked me out on a date. I know what you think of me." She already felt her cheeks flushing with annoying heat. Not the sexy kind. The irritated kind. She didn't like that everyone thought she was too wild for her own good. It wasn't like she got herself into trouble all the time, or she did anything too harebrained. She resented it when her brothers intimated she couldn't be trusted to behave herself. Not once had she offered to show any Americans a good time this time.

"Aye, but I couldn't tell you he was a hothead. You had to learn it for yourself."

"I almost mated him!"

"I figured there was something more about him that you truly cared about. I couldn't interfere. How do you think you would have reacted if I told you what he was really like? You would have figured I thought he wasn't good enough for you, but that I didn't want to ask you out myself."

"Would you have? Asked me out ever?"

"Not while you were dating Timothy. He was part of our wolf pack. We have unwritten rules about that."

"Besides, if you had, you would have had to deal with him."

Enrick smiled. "Aye."

"And now?"

He let out his breath in resignation.

Nope, Enrick wasn't the one for her.

She considered just leaving his room, but that would look like she had hoped something more was going on between them. She made herself stay put and finish what she'd offered to do for him— because he had rescued her, even if she hadn't needed the rescue. She began massaging his right arm.

He groaned.

He'd done a lot of sword swinging with that arm. She was glad she only had kitchen duty and serving the meals, and didn't have to participate in the grueling battle scenes the men were doing.

She worked on his other arm with a slow, gentle massage, loving the feel of his solid muscles and trying to imagine he was some other hot Highlander she was ministering to. But it was of no use. All she could envision was the hot Highlander beneath her. "I bet you wish you were more ambidextrous."

"Aye. I've tried fighting with my left arm in case I was ever wounded, but I always revert back to fighting with my right arm."

"I would be the same way. Roll over and I'll take care of the rest of you." She meant his chest and legs, but when he turned over, his smile was so wicked that she blushed. "We're not dating…ever."

His smile broadened. Then he sighed. "You don't know how good this feels."

"Oh, I imagine it does. You were so tense, and now you're so much more relaxed." At least parts of him were relaxed. His cock was straining his boxer briefs. "I guess I should have asked if the lavender lotion was okay to use. I didn't want to work on you with some of that stuff they use for sore muscles. That lotion smells to high heaven, and it would have stayed with me."

He chuckled. "The lavender will make me think of you."

The one Enrick so adamantly wasn't interested in. As she finally finished massaging his ripped chest muscles, his nipples peaked and she straightened. "What time do you go out tomorrow?"

"Right after breakfast and before first light, though it's going to be raining again all day."

"At least we haven't had any trouble from the McKinleys or Kilpatricks. Fingers crossed. I'll see you in the morning."

Enrick rose from the bed and took her hand, and she swore he wanted to kiss her! *No* way was she going there.

Oh, for heaven's sake, all she was doing was giving him a muscle rub. That was all.

She smiled. "See you tomorrow," she said, and then whipped out of his chamber before she got all wild on him and kissed him like she was dying to do and proved her brothers were right.

CHAPTER 6

HEATHER HAD AWAKENED IN ENRICK THE FIERCE NEED TO BE
with her by stroking him into a lustful state. She no longer was
that little girl in the heather, whacking at the weeds with a wooden
sword, or the young lassie who socked him with a snowball
because she wanted to get his attention. Or the young woman who
was going to mate another wolf.

Hell, he'd wanted to kiss her in the worst way. He knew he
shouldn't, but the way she'd been looking at him like she'd wanted
to eat him all up, and the way she seemed ready to move on with
her life...

Nay. He'd never thought of her in a brotherly way. That wasn't
the issue. Once she'd blossomed into a full-grown woman, she
was a real catch. The problem was she was too...unconventional
for *him*. Yet he couldn't stop thinking of her, knowing she'd had a
crush on him early on. Then her words about visiting friends at
the castle and how she'd hoped to catch a glimpse of him. Hoped
he would ask to date her. Then she finally gave up on him to date
Timothy?

Hell. Enrick ran his hands through his hair.

Lying under his covers, smelling of lavender, his muscles feeling great after the massage she'd given him, he folded his arms
beneath his head and stared up at the canopied bed. He would
have fallen asleep while she was rubbing his muscles because she'd
relaxed him so, but he couldn't stop thinking of the way she was
touching him, the way she'd gotten him all hot and bothered, the
way his cock was eager for action.

Even now, he had to quit thinking about Heather and what
she did to him. He needed to sleep because tomorrow would be

just as rough as today had been and he had another several days of fighting in the battle scenes before the filming was done. But he planned to do something special for Heather tomorrow night. A first real date. If she wanted one. Not in courtship, but just to prove they could be friends and go out on a platonic date.

It was hard to plan for because they couldn't leave until the director said the shooting was a wrap. Enrick needed to see where she would like to go, what she would like to do. Maybe they could go to the MacNeill lands and he could run with her as a wolf afterward, if it wasn't too late.

Enrick was thinking of a special inn that had a seafood restaurant with excellent cuisine on the waterfront. They could watch the sun set, if they finished the shoot before that happened.

He didn't think he would fall asleep, but the next thing he knew, it was time to hurry down to eat breakfast before he had to put on his grungy clothes and head back to the battlefield.

In the great hall, Heather was sitting at a table and surrounded by women, so he couldn't mention having dinner with her tonight just yet. He didn't want to text her because he didn't want her to take the offer of dinner the wrong way. He needed to meet with her face-to-face.

He took a seat next to Lachlan. Grant and Colleen were sitting on the other side of the table, Colleen smiling at Enrick.

Lachlan slapped him on the back. "You are late to breakfast, Brother, which means you missed out." He glanced in the direction of Heather sitting with the other ladies.

"Aye, I'm late when I normally never am." Enrick wasn't going to comment on the missing-out part of Lachlan's comment. "I guess the workout I had really helped me sleep." Enrick would never admit it had really worn him out. He hoped the whole pack didn't know Heather had given him a muscle massage last night.

He glanced in Heather's direction, but she was animatedly talking to Lana and some other lasses and didn't look his way. He hoped she hadn't regretted giving him a massage, thinking she had been a little too intimate with him last night.

"Are you taking Heather someplace special anytime soon?" Colleen asked.

Enrick finished off his blood pudding and began working on his eggs, then glanced up at Colleen, wondering why she'd ask him that.

Colleen shrugged. "I've heard all the rumors about the two of you."

Enrick's ears suddenly felt hot, and he raised his brow in question.

Colleen sighed. "Okay, look, I know you don't think you're right for her, but you'll never know if you don't give it a chance. It's not like you have to make a commitment or anything. I swear everyone in the pack—except for you—seemed to know she was trying to see you when she'd come visit her friends at Farraige Castle. They teased her about it all the time. Don't make the mistake of not giving it a chance and letting her get away with the wrong wolf again."

He opened his mouth to speak, and Colleen amended, "If you happen to be the right wolf for her."

He let his breath out. "If all goes well with the shoot today, I hope to take her to the inn for a seafood dinner on the shore to watch the sunset."

"Oh, good," Colleen said. "That sounds really nice. Sorry, I guess I spoke too soon." She glanced at Grant.

Enrick was certain she wanted his brother to do the same for her.

"Heather's brothers have been asking me to keep an eye on things," Colleen said.

"Between Heather and me?" Och. It was enough they'd threatened him at her place of business that one day. Enrick didn't need the whole pack and Heather's brothers' involvement in his affairs. "They don't have any need to know."

"Today, the wolves will take part in the battle, at least one seg-ment of it," Lachlan said, changing the subject, to Enrick's relief.

"No fighting for you, I take it." At least Lachlan could rest up a bit. Enrick almost wished he could "handle" the wolves instead. He must be getting old.

"No. Well, later, maybe. It depends on if we need to do a bunch of retakes with the wolves. The wolves should be fine in their parts, but you never know when you actually get out in the field and they begin filming." Lachlan ate some of his haddock. "Or if the key actors mess up their lines and the wolves have to do their parts again."

"True. I haven't seen your cousins since the shooting began," Enrick said to Colleen. "Are they doing okay in their roles?"

"They're having a blast. So are the others who are serving as wolves. It's the only time any of our kind can play our other halves for all to see—and get away with it." Colleen smiled. "And some of the men, not my cousins, have been out in the field sword fighting when they don't have to be wolves."

"Good. I'm glad everyone who wanted to participate can. Don't you miss it, Grant?" Enrick couldn't imagine not taking the time to fight in a few takes at least.

Grant chuckled. "No. I saw the way all of you dragged in last night. Everyone looked so ready to fight in the morning, and you guys looked done in after the shoot was wrapped up."

"It's a good thing we had lots of sword practice to get into shape beforehand or we would never have made it." They would have been hurting for a few days after all this fighting if they hadn't been working out.

"Concerning injuries that the men battling in the scenes suf-fered yesterday, all the sprains and bruises and cuts were minor. Sore muscles were the biggest injury we saw," Colleen said.

Enrick was glad she was seeing to that. He'd been too worn out and wanting a shower too badly to look into that. Then he saw

Heather getting up from her table and carrying her plate to the kitchen, and he grabbed his plate. "See you later." He hurried after Heather, even though he hadn't finished his breakfast yet.

When he reached her, she glanced at his plate. "You haven't eaten any of your toast or half of your eggs and sausage. You'll need all your strength to get you through the battles until lunchtime."

He set his plate on the kitchen table and grabbed his buttered toast and coated it with blackberry jam. "I want to take you to the Seaside Inn. We can have supper there and watch the sun set. Tonight. After the shooting is done." He ate a slice of toast.

Heather's eyes widened. Then she smiled. "I would love that. Just let me know when, after you're done."

"I'll have to run up to my room and shower and get dressed, but after that, we're out of here." He finished off his eggs.

"That would be fun."

He ate the last two sausages. "Are you going to watch me fighting the others in the rain today?"

She smiled. "Maybe. I might just enjoy a day off and make sure the shop is running fine without me being there, unless I'm needed for something else during one of the shoots."

He nodded. "I've got to run and get dressed in my muddy clothes."

She wrinkled her nose. "Glad it's you and not me. Though I think I would wash my clothes at night and roll in the mud the next day to get the muddy battle look."

He laughed. "You have to have the sweaty smell to really feel in character." Then he set his plate in one of the sinks, and before he could say anything further to her, her breakfast companions walked into the kitchen with their plates. He smiled at Heather and hurried off.

It wouldn't do for him to be late when he was responsible for all the male extras fighting in the battle scene. At least as far as Grant said. The director was of a different mindset.

But Enrick almost felt lighthearted about having dinner out with Heather tonight, as long as the whole pack didn't put too much stock in it. It was just a nice date between a man and a woman. Nothing beyond that.

———

"Are you going to watch the men battling it out today in the rain?" Lana asked Heather.

"I don't know. I want to. I wish it was drier out today." Heather really wanted to watch Enrick. She couldn't help it. She worried about him and the other men out there. "He asked me to go out with him."

"So are you?" Lana raised a brow.

"I guess so." Heather knew Lana was dying to ask her about the date.

"Okay, well, you can tell me how it went. I don't want to go out there today."

"I'll do that." Now Heather had to.

"I can't believe he finally asked you out on a date," Lana said, taking hold of her hands and squeezing, her face alight with excitement.

Heather had known that was coming. "How many first dates have you been on?"

"Tons." Lana shrugged.

"That's what this is. It doesn't mean anything."

"Except for last night."

Heather let her breath out in exasperation. "I shouldn't have told you about last night."

"You couldn't have hidden what you were doing from me."

That was true. As soon as Heather had left their chamber with the lavender lotion, Lana had been dying to know what she was up to, suspecting just what had happened since Heather had been talking to Enrick beforehand.

"See you at lunch." At least Heather could return to the castle and have lunch and get out of the rain. She didn't have to go back out there this afternoon if she didn't want to. She was trying hard not to be overly excited about having dinner with Enrick tonight. She kept telling herself this wouldn't amount to anything and they would prove to each other, at least to her way of thinking, that he wasn't the right one for her.

She got bundled up in her kilt and a waterproof wool cloak, then headed out into the rain. It wasn't bad, just a light rain, as she hurried to the hill that overlooked the battlegrounds. Some of the cameras were situated on top of the hill, too, so they could get a bird's-eye view of the battle. The view was really impressive with some men on horseback in their leather armor and kilts, others on foot, covered in mud and fighting each other, swords slashing and clanging, men shouting, even calling out some choice Gaelic words.

It looked so real.

Then she saw Enrick, though it was hard to tell individual warriors because of the mud they wore. But that was the position Cearnach had told her he would be in when the fighting started. Enrick was slashing his sword at Cearnach, and she admired how they could swing their swords, thrusting and parrying, slashing and defending themselves as they battled it out, even though they were getting stuck in the mud and slipping on it. No wonder the director had to take so many shots to get it right.

Then another warrior shoved Cearnach down and struck at him with his sword. She was kind of surprised, thinking Enrick would be the one to take Cearnach down. Then to her further astonishment, Enrick began fighting the man who had attacked her cousin. What in the world...?

Enrick should have been on the same side as the other man since he had attacked Cearnach. She narrowed her eyes and looked closer. Ohmigod, it was one of the Kilpatrick brothers. Redheaded Robert, she thought.

In a hurry, she fumbled to pull her cell phone from the pouch at her waist and called Grant right away. "Unless I'm mistaken, Robert Kilpatrick is fighting Enrick. He went after Cearnach first and knocked him down, but Enrick is fighting him now." She hoped she wasn't wrong, but she didn't believe so.

"I'm on my way. Where are you?"

"Widow's Peak."

"I'll be right there."

If Robert was in the mix, his brother surely was. And maybe some of the McKinleys. Heather knew why Robert would go after Cearnach. It all had to do with Cearnach saving the Kilpatricks' cousin from their greedy grasp. Robert would never let go of the anger he felt toward the MacNeills for stealing Elaine away.

Even though this play fighting was supposed to be just that, Heather knew Robert would take it further, then think to slip away. No one would be the wiser that he had injured or killed Cearnach. Everyone was so busy making the battle look good that most wouldn't have noticed. But Enrick knew.

Enrick and Cearnach had been focused on each other until Robert attacked Cearnach, so she imagined everyone else would be doing the same, fighting the same people in the scenes, choreographed to an extent.

Grant and four of his men wearing period dress joined her shortly after that, and she pointed down the hill to where Enrick was still fighting Robert. Cearnach was just getting up when another redheaded man struck at him with his sword—Patrick, she thought—and Cearnach parried in defense.

Grant and his men were armed and wet, but they weren't all muddy. She feared for Grant and the other men's safety, too, because she knew the Kilpatricks were out for blood. Grant headed down to the battlefield, his sword at the ready. The other four men were carrying them too. She was glad about that, though she wouldn't feel any real relief until this situation was resolved to the MacQuarries' satisfaction.

Grant and his men headed down the hill to charge into the fight as if they were latecomers to the party.

The director was watching them and didn't say anything, just continued to observe the newcomers to the fight.

She prayed the Kilpatricks were the only ones to suffer injury for starting the attack in the first place.

———————

Despite the seriousness of Robert and Patrick attacking Enrick and Cearnach, Enrick hadn't wanted to mess up the shoot. Not that he'd had much choice. When Cearnach went down and Robert struck at him again, Cearnach managed to fend off the attack despite being on his back in the mud. Enrick was glad about that because *he* slipped in the mud when he tried to reach Robert. Regaining his footing, Enrick immediately dove in to attack Robert and protect Cearnach, giving him a chance to get to his feet.

It was problematic when the enemy wolves attacked them for real, not in choreographed play, because they couldn't just kill them like Enrick wanted to, not on camera and among humans. They had to handle the situation carefully.

As he struck at Robert again, Enrick worried that more of Kilpatrick's kin were fighting his people and their friends, the MacNeill clansmen. If there were fatalities on the battlefield, Enrick thought the company would shut down the film and the MacQuarries would have a black eye over it, just what the Kilpatricks and McKinleys would want.

Cearnach had managed to get to his feet to help Enrick when Patrick attacked Cearnach out of the muddy sea of men. Enrick wanted to warn Grant about the severity of the problem but couldn't get to his phone while fending off Robert. However, Grant and four of their men suddenly appeared behind Robert.

Grant had a sword in hand, and he hit Robert so hard in the temple that the man fell onto his back in the mud, out cold.

Two of the other men with Grant knocked Patrick unconscious, and then Grant said to Enrick and Cearnach, "Are you both okay?"

"Aye, thanks, Brother," Enrick said.

Cearnach nodded.

"Come with us. We need to find any other of their kin here and knock them out before they seriously injure any of our people," Grant said.

Enrick and the others were fighting through the swarm of muddy bodies. They were constantly being engaged in combat, until some of them saw Grant in the middle of all the fighting.

"Keep fighting, men. The McKinleys may have infiltrated our battle. Knock them out cold, if you find any. Don't kill them." Then Grant and the others resumed searching for any of the McKinleys.

The men continued to fight for the film but were also watching for any sign of the McKinleys.

The director finally called, "Cut!"

Enrick was worried the director had stopped the battle scene because of the mess Grant and the others were making while searching for the villains.

When the fighting was stopped, Enrick and Cearnach pushed through the mob of men, trying to reach the place where the Kilpatricks had been knocked out, ready to take them into custody and, reluctantly, give them first aid.

"I know they were around here somewhere." Enrick couldn't smell the brothers' scents since there were so many scents crowding the area.

"Maybe over that way a wee bit?" Cearnach motioned with his hand as he moved through the men.

"Has anyone seen the Kilpatrick brothers in the mud?" Enrick called out.

"Nay, neither of them are over here," one man said, the words repeated in every direction.

"Hell, they must have scurried off," Cearnach said.

Enrick scoffed. "Like a couple of mud-coated rats. The arses."

"Do you think they messed up the shoot?" Cearnach glanced around at the men there.

"Our part in it, maybe. Though I'm sure the director shoots a lot more film than they actually need to make the movie. So we can probably be cut out of it, if anything looked odd."

Then they saw a path being cleared for Grant and the men that had been with him. He looked ready to kill some McKinleys and a couple of Kilpatricks. Since they weren't dragging any McKinleys with them, Enrick assumed they got away or, best-case scenario, only the Kilpatricks had been here.

"Where are the Kilpatricks?" Grant asked.

"No one's seen them. We should have kept a guard on them," Enrick said, wishing he'd thought of it. But he really had believed the men would still be out cold when they returned for them. "Were any McKinleys here?"

"Aye, at least five of them, but when they saw me coming, they hightailed it out of here," Grant said. "We'll have to meet about this tonight."

There went Enrick's dinner plans with Heather, but this was important too. It was dangerous business.

"Was anyone seriously injured by the men?" Enrick asked.

"No one's reported any injuries. One of our men said one of the McKinleys was holding his temple, blood streaming through his fingers. Hopefully, they weren't able to injure any of *our* men," Grant said. "Serves them right if they were injured."

"You were a welcome sight. I wanted to kill Robert for attacking Cearnach, but I couldn't seem to get the upper hand to keep him from killing me when I took him on," Enrick said. "Not in this mud, and not when I'd been fighting for hours and he appeared fresh."

"You will have to thank Heather for sending us to your rescue." Grant motioned to the hilltop where she was standing in the rain watching them.

Enrick was astounded and proud of Heather for most likely saving his and Cearnach's lives and possibly those of several other men by warning Grant about the trouble they were having.

"I have a dinner date with Heather." *Forget* about the meeting. She was a gem and Enrick wanted to do something special with her.

Grant nodded. "We'll have the meeting after your date."

Some of the men standing around them chuckled, listening in on the conversation.

Cearnach smiled. "She's worth it."

"Aye, I know." Enrick saluted her with his sword.

From the top of the hill, she waved back. His worries about having more trouble on the battlefield in the coming days melted away, just a little. "Are you staying on the battlefield, Brother?" Enrick asked Grant.

"Aye. As long as the director doesn't have any trouble with it." Grant turned and they all saw Lachlan headed for them.

"I've sent the wolves out in search of the men to ensure there aren't any more still on the battlefield," Lachlan said. "The director said they'd done their part in the battle today."

"Good, but I doubt the enemy's clan members would linger here. Too many of our men would know them, now that word is spreading about them infiltrating our ranks. Did you talk to the director about it like I asked?" Grant asked.

"Aye, he said he would take a break until we made sure the interlopers were gone or arrested. He's checking on his laptop to see how the scenes turned out," Lachlan said.

"Okay, excellent."

They were waiting, Cearnach asking Enrick where he was taking Heather to dinner, when the wolves began to return to Lachlan.

One of them woofed at Lachlan, telling him the McKinleys and Kilpatricks were gone. If the men hadn't left, the wolves would have been barking, howling, and pursuing them.

Grant told the director they were good to go, and the director called out to begin the shoot again.

An hour and a half before the sun set, the director wrapped up shooting for the day and Enrick sprinted for the castle. Heather had left the hill later that afternoon, which was probably good because he kept glancing in her direction and nearly got cut when he didn't parry quickly enough.

Now, he was in a rush to clean off his boots and then take a shower and meet up with her…where? He hadn't planned that far ahead.

In his bedchamber, he dumped his clothes in a rubber basket he was using until the battle scenes were done, then grabbed a pair of fresh boxer briefs and hurried to take a shower. He didn't want to miss seeing the sunset with Heather for anything.

CHAPTER 7

HEATHER WAS EAGER TO SEE ENRICK AFTER THE REST OF THE shoot and though she had already spoken to Colleen and Grant about what had happened, she wanted to hear Enrick's version. She'd nearly had a stroke when she saw Robert strike Cearnach and her cousin fall.

But when he got up and Patrick struck him, she was ready to get her bow and arrows and shoot both the Kilpatrick brothers herself. She could just imagine the impression that would make on everyone. She assumed the Kilpatrick brothers hadn't gone into the fight with just the thought of knocking Cearnach or Enrick out either. They wanted blood, enough of an injury to stop the film. Maybe even a death, if they could have gotten away with it and slipped out unnoticed.

She couldn't believe the men would go to those lengths to exact revenge.

Her phone jingled, indicating she had a text, and she saw it was from Enrick. *I'll meet you at the front entrance.*

I'm ready, she replied.

He was soon jogging down the stairs and taking great strides across the common area to reach her. He took her hand, like they were on a real date, and led her outside. Despite telling herself this was just a superficial date, she couldn't help but love his warm, firm grasp on her hand, as if this truly meant more to him.

The rain had stopped, and she was grateful for that. She had stood out in it long enough today to be thankful it was done for tonight at least.

Enrick looked down at her, all smiles, and didn't seem in the least bit angered over the incident on the battlefield. For which she was glad.

Then she saw Lachlan and her brothers following Enrick and her outside. She frowned at them.

"Bodyguard detail. Grant's orders," Enrick said. "It's to keep you safe, so I'm all for it."

She'd thought she and Enrick would have a nice dinner together alone, but she was glad for the protection, just in case, though she wished her brothers weren't the ones coming with them. They wouldn't just be looking out for trouble but cataloging everything that went on with her and Enrick.

Lachlan and her brothers were dressed in clean kilts, had swords swinging at their hips, and were carrying *sgian dubhs* in their boots, as if they were celebrating a special Scottish occasion, but this way their weapons wouldn't look out of place in case they needed them.

"You look good all dressed up, though I still like you all grungy in your plaid," Heather said to Enrick. "A rugged look of a time in the past."

"But for a date?" he asked, opening the car door for her.

"This is really good. You smell nice too."

He smiled at her and got into the driver's seat. The other men were following behind in Lachlan's car.

"This is a date of sorts and I probably shouldn't bring it up, but are you okay? I mean, you don't look like Robert injured you, but that had to have been such a shock to find him trying to fight Cearnach," she said.

"It was. Robert *wasn't* just trying to injure him either. He was trying to kill him. I'm sure he wanted to do the same with me and then get out of there without anyone being the wiser, with so much fighting going on. I suspect Patrick got sidetracked by other fighters thinking he was just one of the enemy, or Patrick and Robert would have pounced on Cearnach and me at the same time. They had to know one of them couldn't have succeeded. Two of them would have to fight us, at the very least."

"I'm sure that was so. Several minutes passed before Patrick showed up to fight Cearnach. I nearly died when I saw Cearnach fall. I worried he'd been fatally wounded."

"Believe me, I was worried about the same thing, but Cearnach was immediately trying to get up out of the mud and he was able to fend off Patrick's subsequent attack. I engaged Robert before he could attack Cearnach again."

"I saw that. Thanks for saving my cousin. What are we going to do about it?" Heather knew they couldn't just leave it. They had to make sure it wouldn't happen again, and that meant Robert and his brother paying for it.

"Grant will tell Robert's pack leader about the trouble we're having with some of their people. Five McKinleys were identified fighting our men, and they weren't holding back either. Our men have had good training and knew who they were, but like me, they couldn't stop what they were doing and call Grant to have him send men to take care of it. Thanks for saving our arses."

Heather smiled. "They're worth saving."

He gave her one of his wicked smiles that turned her insides to mush. "Hopefully, they won't try it again. Maybe their leader will tell them to cool it. At least we hope so."

"I hadn't wanted to bring it up on our first...um...date, but I haven't been able to think of anything else." Every time she said the *date* word, she felt like Enrick would correct her. They weren't on a date, just a get-together or something.

Enrick let out his breath. "I agree. We'll have a lovely evening, but it's good to discuss issues that can affect us. That have affected us. I'm glad the McKinleys and Kilpatricks didn't begin doing this from the first day of shooting the battle scenes. We'll just have to remain vigilant. Everyone will be on the lookout for more trouble with them now."

"Do you think they'll cut some of the film when Grant took his men through the fighting men, looking for the McKinleys?"

Enrick chuckled. "It had to have looked like Grant was in

charge. I'm sure we'll be shooting some of it over, especially the scenes capturing a bird's-eye view of the whole battlefield. We did some retakes this afternoon, so that might suffice."

"Does that bother you?"

"Well, some, only because of the Kilpatricks and McKinleys' sinister actions. But we might have thought the scene was going well before that and the director had a different idea, so we never know why he decides to reshoot something."

She was glad Enrick didn't seem to hold grudges.

Then Enrick parked at the inn and she felt elated and special as he escorted her inside to get a table. She couldn't believe he'd actually made reservations. This was wonderful, and she was excited to just enjoy the meal and put Robert and Patrick and the rest of their kin out of her thoughts.

She hadn't thought Enrick could have had time to make a reservation, what with not knowing when the director would call a wrap, but this made it even more special to her.

The woman smiled broadly as she hurried to seat them at one of the best seaside-view tables, and Heather suddenly had the impression the waitress thought Enrick was Guy McNab.

One of Heather's brothers stayed out with the cars while Lachlan, Callum, and Oran came inside to take a seat near them. Oran winked at her.

She really didn't want him watching her on her first real outing with Enrick.

When the waitress came over so sweet and smiley, Heather wanted to tell her Enrick was *not* the famous actor, but oh so much hotter. And *real*.

———

"So they're filming the movie at Farraige Castle, aren't they?" the waitress asked, looking for confirmation as she offered them menus and glasses of water. She was asking Enrick as if Heather wasn't even there.

Enrick suspected the waitress would shove a pad of paper into his hands for an autograph. "They are, lass."

"Enrick fought bravely all day in the field." Heather smiled brightly, then started looking at her menu.

Enrick smiled at Heather. He still couldn't believe how her diligence, or interest in him, had saved his and Cearnach's arses.

"Oh my, that must have been a lot of grueling work," the waitress said, her gaze fixed on Enrick as if she was truly in love.

Reading her menu, Heather was smiling, amused, which amused Enrick.

"And they battled it out all the while in the rain and mud too." Heather closed her menu. "I'll have the king scallops in garlic butter with crispy bacon on a bed of rice and a salad. And for dessert, I want the homemade sticky toffee pudding with ice cream." She smiled at Enrick when he must have looked a little surprised she was so hungry. "Watching you get that workout with such a *big* sword gave me a real appetite."

Smiling, Enrick shook his head. Heather was a real treasure. "I'll have the sirloin steak served with onion rings, mushrooms, salad, and chips with pepper sauce. I guess if we're having dessert afterward, I'll have the Scottish raspberry cranachan on a meringue topped with homemade almond praline."

"Sounds good, Mister..." Apparently the waitress wasn't convinced Enrick wasn't Guy McNab.

"Enrick MacQuarrie, brother to Lord Grant MacQuarrie of Farraige Castle."

The woman's face brightened. "Oh, aye, Mr. MacQuarrie. Your meals will be right out." Looking a lot flustered, she hurried off to place their orders.

"Okay, so she still thought you were Guy McNab." Heather sipped from her water.

"Until I mentioned who I was in relation to Grant. No one would lie about being his brother."

Heather laughed.

"Thanks for trying to help. I think."

Heather smiled. "I called you Enrick."

"Aye, but the mention of me battling in the mud made her think I was still Guy." Enrick let out his breath. "I hadn't really planned to go anywhere special while he was still here. I imagine I'll get all kinds of fan interest wherever I go."

"Because you don't get out to the businesses in the area much and people don't know you that well."

"To an extent, they know me, but with Guy's presence here, they want to believe it's him. Though I rarely eat here. When I went to Edinburgh after Guy made it big, all kinds of people wanted autographs and were taking pictures of me."

Smiling, Heather cleared her throat. "Did you give them your autograph?"

"A couple."

"Nay. You couldn't have." She smiled again.

Enrick loved how she seemed to be enjoying their easy conversation and chuckled. "Aye, I did. Not as Guy McNab though. I think I confused the women when they saw my name wasn't the same as his. One said to her friend, 'He goes by an alias. I told you he would, or he would get mobbed everywhere he goes.'"

Heather laughed.

"You're not bothered everyone thinks you're with a celebrity, are you?"

"Are you kidding? I saw a celebrity fighting today in perfect form. A real celebrity. Not the made-up kind." Then she glanced out the window as a new arrival caught her eye.

Enrick glanced that way to see who it was. "Ah hell, speak of the devil." Why did Guy have to come here of all nights?

"You've got to admit, you *are* the spitting image of him."

"*He* is the spitting image of me."

"That's true too."

They watched Guy enter the restaurant with Missy, the leading lady, and seven other people who had come with him. Enrick was glad he didn't have to have a bunch of people tag along with him wherever he went. Then he remembered his brother and Heather's were with them as their guard detail.

Lachlan grinned at him from the other table as he, Callum, and Oran ordered their meals.

Guy was about to be seated when he saw Enrick and did a double take. Enrick inclined his head slightly in greeting. Guy had been too busy doing his own scenes or visiting with some of the cast in the film and hadn't seemed to have taken notice of Enrick much lately.

When the waitress asked if Guy wanted to be seated at a table near Enrick, he shook his head and pointed to another table that didn't have half as nice a view of the water. Enrick wasn't sure what the star's problem was. Was Guy worried people would mistake Enrick for him and Enrick would get all the attention? Enrick suspected now that Missy was with Guy, everyone would get it right.

"The sun is setting. Isn't it beautiful?" Heather asked, getting Enrick's mind back to where it needed to be.

"Aye, that it is, lass." He slipped his arm around her shoulders and watched the sun setting, the pinks and oranges coloring the water in a symphony of colors. It was the perfect spot for a date.

Then the waitress started to serve their orders, and when she saw the real Guy McNab, she nearly dropped Enrick's plate. He quickly secured it from her and set it on the table.

"Was he battling with you today?" the waitress asked, breathless, as she continued to keep an eye on Guy.

"Aye, but not real close by." Which was a good thing, considering the trouble they'd had with the enemy clan. If Guy had been near Enrick, they might have caught close-ups on film of what had been going on with the Kilpatrick brothers.

"You've met him then, aye?" the waitress asked, sounding hopeful, as if he would give her an introduction or something.

"He's the star. I'm an extra, so we're not on a first-name basis," Enrick said, trying not to sound annoyed. If the waitress wanted to speak to the actor, she should go do it. He wanted to enjoy his dinner with Heather in private.

"I've met him," Heather said.

Enrick frowned at her.

"He's nice. If you want to get an autograph, I'm sure he would be happy to give you one." Heather smiled at the waitress.

The waitress served Heather's scallop dinner. "Thanks. Is there anything else you need?"

"No. I'm good, thanks."

"I'm fine," Enrick said.

"Okay, good." Then the waitress hurried off to take the real Guy McNab's order.

Heather chuckled. "Well, I know you aren't happy to see him show up here, but at least now all the women can hit on the right guy. Well, for them. He's not the right guy for me."

"So you talked to him?" Enrick didn't know why that bothered him, but it did.

"Sure. I asked what he thought of the surroundings. I asked if he had ever been here before."

"What did he say?" Enrick cut into his steak.

Heather forked up one of her scallops. "He loved the area, but no, he'd never been here before. But he seemed...well, anxious around me."

Enrick frowned again. "Why? Maybe he was afraid your brothers or I would have words with him."

She laughed. "No. I doubt it. Probably something was bothering him, and it had nothing to do with me. He did ask who *you* were."

"His clone?"

She smiled. "He's *your* clone. You're the authentic deal. He also noticed Grant and Lachlan, since the three of you look so similar, and wondered who they were. Learning who the three of you were seemed to make him even more uneasy."

"Maybe he's worried he can be replaced." Enrick took another bite of steak.

"You would be perfect for the part. *Better* than perfect."

Enrick shook his head. "I would never remember all the lines. We all think it's funny when the actors mess up their lines because they make fun of themselves, too, but they would get tired of all my bloopers if I filled in for Guy."

Heather laughed and ate some more of her dinner as the night settled in. "I'm afraid I would be the same way."

"Did you get his autograph?"

"No. Should I have?"

Enrick was glad she hadn't. "I thought that was what all women wanted."

"Ha! Shows what you know about all women."

Enrick smiled. "What do you think about running tonight?" He was thoroughly enjoying having dinner with Heather and didn't want the night to end, but he was tired, too, though he would never admit that to her.

"I'd love to. As long as you don't think the other guys will mind and it's not too late. You must be tired from all that battling you did today."

"I'm fine. We'll make sure the guys don't mind. Lachlan didn't get as much of a workout as the rest of us, so I'm sure he'll be all for it. If we can't get your brothers to go, we'll find someone else to take their place."

"Okay, super. That will be fun."

Guy's stunt double suddenly showed up at the restaurant and staggered a little. Larry smiled at Enrick as if he were Guy, and

Enrick motioned to the other table where Guy and Missy were sitting. Larry dropped the smile and headed for Guy's table.

"Hey," Guy said to Larry. "Looks like you got started on the whiskey already."

Like a little *too* much. Then another couple of the actors, including the wizard—complete with his naturally long white beard, but no cone hat or long velvety robes—joined Guy and his entourage. Enrick hoped one of the others had driven Larry here.

It turned out to be a great night, and once they were done with dinner, Enrick, Heather, Lachlan, Callum, and Oran left the restaurant. Jamie was sitting outside eating takeout.

"We were going for a run at Argent Castle if you're up for it." Enrick opened the car door for Heather, and she climbed in.

"I'm ready," Lachlan said.

"Aye, me too," Oran said.

Jamie nodded in agreement.

Enrick suspected they would agree to anything to ensure he dated their sister and made it a mating. But he also figured they wouldn't want him to show them up if he could do this and they were too worn out.

"Thanks so much for dinner." Heather settled back against her seat. "It was delicious. I loved it. And the sunset on the water? It couldn't have been more beautiful."

"I was trying to think of something nearby we could enjoy. The company was what made it so special to me."

"This has been grand. I thoroughly enjoyed your company too. I feel like I'm with a celebrity. Thank you."

He shook his head. She laughed.

Heather called ahead to let Ian and Julia know they were coming, and she called Grant to let him know where they were going to be after dinner.

When they finally reached Argent Castle, they parked in the

inner bailey. Heather greeted her cousin Ian, who came out to meet with them. "Some more of the MacQuarrie clan are here who want to run with you, and some of our people too," Ian said.

Enrick assumed Grant had told Ian about the trouble they'd had with the Kilpatricks and McKinleys and were concerned about everyone's safety.

"Grant said he talked to Paxton McKinley, leader of their clan now, and he said none of what happened was his doing. He wants to keep peace between his people and ours," Ian said.

"Then he'd better know what his people are up to and tell them to cease their hostilities. He may be just as vengeful as his brothers that you and your brothers were forced to kill last year to protect Colleen. Maybe he isn't being honest with Grant about his knowledge of this," Enrick said.

"I agree," Ian said. "I don't trust the lot of them, though I hope he's being honest and gets his people under control."

"I'll be down in a minute," Heather said, and went inside the castle.

"See you in a few," Enrick said.

"You can use the side room in the hall to leave your clothes in and shift. I'm sending more men to your castle to help reinforce your security tomorrow too," Ian said.

"Thanks. We sure appreciate it."

"No problem. You would do the same for us."

"I'd better get ready before Heather shifts and runs without me."

Ian laughed. "You're good for her. Have a great run."

Enrick headed inside, hoping things worked out between him and Heather and that everyone wasn't making the assumption they would be together forever. They'd only had their first date, though they'd seen each other enough for a long time. But it hadn't been a close relationship all those years. Not with her gruff brothers protecting her from wolves who might take advantage of her. And not when Enrick thought they wouldn't be compatible.

Several MacQuarrie wolves came out to greet Enrick as he was about to reach the room. Then he saw Heather in her gray wolf coat, bright-eyed, bushy-tailed, and ready to run. She woofed at him as if to say he was late.

He smiled and headed inside the room, stripped off his clothes, and shifted, then joined her and the others.

It would have been nice to run with her alone, but as wolves, they loved running as a pack too. For now, it was important to run in groups for protection. Though he suspected the McKinleys and Kilpatricks would concentrate on trying to ruin the film production and not bother any of the MacQuarries or MacNeills on a wolf run near Argent Castle.

The group of wolves ran off, glad to be away from all the mess of the film production and running free as wolves. They ran up the hills over the green grass and down again, into the woods and all the way to the river.

Enrick was glad it had stopped raining so they could see the sunset earlier and now a full moon hanging in the partially cloudy night sky.

Enrick's brother howled, and that set off the rest of the wolves to join in. Heather's howl was hauntingly beautiful. He hadn't heard her siren's wolf call in a while. And it was music to his soul as she lifted her chin and howled again.

The moon glowed through a smattering of clouds, the night air chillier, the breeze whipping the tree branches about and ruffling their fur. It was amazing how much he wanted to run as a wolf and even forgot how tired he had been. He could go days without running as a wolf, but just the idea that he *couldn't* made him long for it more. Running with Heather made it even more special.

Heather drank at the water's edge and so did Enrick, each turning to look at the other and bumping noses. Heather licked Enrick's nose and he nuzzled her face.

Usually when they went on a run at night, they played, too, but everyone was quiet, listening for trouble, maybe tired if they had fought in the battle scenes today like he had.

He was reluctant to play with Heather in case she wanted to get used to him first, especially since she seemed reserved. It could have been because so many other wolves were here.

Then she nipped Enrick's ear, to his surprise, and he instantly retaliated, pinning her down against the lush green grass. She woofed at him in amusement. He hadn't meant to react that quickly, or that wolfishly, but if his brothers had done that to him, that was how he would have responded.

He quickly licked her face and got off her, to let her know he was sorry for startling her, but she nipped at his neck and raced off along the riverbank and the chase was on. This was the Heather he knew! His forelegs were sore from all the sword fighting but playing with Heather as wolves was worth every twinge of pain.

He heard the others running with them, some in the woods near the riverbank, trying to keep up, others behind them, everyone keeping an eye on one another. Except for Enrick, who was mainly focused on Heather, her tail waving at him like a banner saying: *Come, catch me if you can.*

Still, he was having a hard time keeping this at a first-date level, not wanting to dash in and tackle her, telling all the other wolves she was his in a courting way. Or offending Heather. Not when he wasn't sure where this was headed.

They had run maybe a mile when Heather made a dash for the woods, and then she was circling back to Argent Castle. Everyone was heading in the same direction, eager to call it a night after a glorious run in the moonlight. Enrick moved in beside her and nuzzled her face in greeting. She didn't smile at him, didn't nuzzle him back, both of them panting with exertion. He was afraid that because he hadn't tried harder to catch her, maybe he had annoyed her.

Returning through the woods to the castle, they suddenly startled a group of deer, which in turn startled Enrick and Heather. They both faltered, and then the deer dashed off through the trees ahead. The deer soon veered out of the wolves' path and disappeared. Amused at the way they had both reacted to the sudden appearance of the deer, Enrick smiled at her, but she ignored him.

He sighed. He detested the courtship game. Even if he wasn't courting her. With the guys, he could just be himself.

Enrick and Heather and the rest of the wolves finally reached Argent, no troubles at all on the run, and he was glad for that, though he couldn't help but feel the tension between him and Heather return. He had thought this would be the perfect way to end the day with her.

They went inside, and he met her downstairs after they had both shifted and dressed. The other MacQuarrie kinsmen were serving as their bodyguards while Lachlan stayed at Argent with his "wolves" as their handler and Heather's brothers were staying at their home until they returned to the McQuarrie castle in the morning, bright and early for more battle scenes.

"I'll be more careful about nipping your ear in fun," Heather said on the way back to Enrick's home, sounding annoyed.

"Aw, I'm so sorry for pinning you down like I did. I promise you can nip away and I'll try not to attack you." Maybe that was what had bothered her.

She sighed. "I bet that's what you do with your brothers."

"Aye, you know it. But I should have been more careful with you."

She just shook her head, looking like he didn't get it. "Nay. I got the biggest kick out of it, really. I'm sure everyone who saw us did too."

"Och, not that I want our packs to know about it."

She sighed again. "You just keep being you." She sounded like that didn't suit her at all.

He couldn't be who he wasn't. Yet, hell, he wanted to see more of her. They finally reached his castle and he parked his car.

"Did you want to have breakfast with me?" Enrick still wished he hadn't missed out on having breakfast with her this morning, but he wondered if she needed time with her women friends instead. Or she was just saying she didn't want to be with him. He wasn't sure.

"You know what they'll be saying if we keep eating meals together."

"And running together, and you saving my life and Cearnach's earlier today?"

"Well, true," Heather said. "I guess it's too late to keep up appearances, but hey, if you need to sleep in a little like you did this morning, go ahead. I'll just join the ladies again."

Did that mean she did or didn't want to eat with him? There was no figuring the fairer sex. "I'll be there." Even though he didn't normally set his alarm because he was naturally an early riser, he would tonight to ensure he made it down to breakfast early enough. Still, he wanted to know what had set her off about the run.

He escorted her inside the keep.

She sighed again. "I had a lovely evening, Enrick. Thanks for everything. I'll see you in the morning, either at breakfast or… around."

He wanted to kiss her. He knew he shouldn't, not when things were so up in the air between them. He hesitated. She hesitated. And then she gave him an annoyed little smile and turned on her heels and headed for the stairs.

Ah hell. He hurried after her, telling himself he was not going to catch her and kiss her. That he was headed in this direction because his chamber was up the stairs too.

When they reached the landing, he said, "Heather, wait." He had not intended to stop her.

She turned to look at him, her eyes a little misty with tears. *Ah hell.*

"I'm sorry if…"

She turned away, but before she could take a step away from him, he caught her arm and pulled her close. And kissed her.

———————

Heather had fun on her first date with Enrick. He was a rugged wolf, and as she'd learned tonight, he had incredibly fast response times, as evidenced by him pinning her to the grass so quickly at the riverbank. She'd loved that. He was truly fun to be with. And a romantic—the dinner and sunset were stupendous. But she hated how reserved he'd been with her after he'd taken her to the ground as a wolf, as if he'd breached protocol in tackling her so completely. No matter how hard she tried to tell him, in her wolf way, that she'd gotten a kick out of it, he wouldn't bite. He didn't even come close to catching her in wolf play, when she knew he could have easily caught her. She loved the thrill of the chase, but he had to work for it. Instead, he'd just kept up, and she felt it was out of a sense of protectiveness and not out of a need to play with her in more of a courtship way.

She felt she was doing it all wrong with him. She would never be able to do things the way he thought she should. And that had irritated her. Why should she try so hard to get his attention when it just would never work out between them? And then…he'd kissed her. And that had shocked her to the core.

He'd cupped her face with his large, rough hands and looked into her tear-filled eyes, which she hadn't wanted him to see for anything, and kissed her.

He pulled his hands away from her face, and she could see in his expression, his darkened eyes, that he had to know if this was all right with her. Did he make a mistake in kissing her?

She brushed away the tears spilling down her cheeks, gave him a lopsided smile, which was all she could manage with emotions enveloping her like a massive storm, and said good night. She wanted to kiss him back, to ravish him. She wanted to tackle him in his bed, make wild and passionate love to him. But she knew that would be folly. He was still way too unsure of her and she wasn't sure of him either.

"See you in the morning," she said, quickly pulling away and hurrying off to the chamber she was sharing with Lana, resisting the urge to skip all the way. She swore her feet barely touched the floor as she headed down the hallway. She didn't hear Enrick walking away to his chamber, and she turned her head to look over her shoulder to see what he was doing.

He was watching her, and then he gave her a small, wicked smile. Her heart skipped a couple of beats, and she almost took a misstep. Oh, wouldn't that be just perfect? Falling on her face because the wolf of her dreams had briefly, very briefly, kissed her.

Heather cast him a whimsical smile and continued on her way. She finally heard his footfalls as he moved toward his own room.

She told herself the kiss didn't mean anything, though her lips still tingled with the feel of the light press of his agreeable mouth against hers, the warmth they'd shared heating her, the exquisite pressure that had made her nipples react. Her whole body had thrummed with sudden need!

She walked into the chamber feeling practically light-headed, for heaven's sake. And then she sobered, almost, when she saw Lana brushing out her hair, already dressed in a long T-shirt that proclaimed: GIVE A MAN A HOME, AND HE THINKS HE'S THE KING OF THE CASTLE.

"I still can't believe you gave him a thoroughly intimate massage last night," Lana said, climbing into bed. "I'm glad you didn't tonight." She motioned to the lavender lotion sitting on the dresser. "You can't move too quickly with him. You need to slowly work up to more."

"You chided me for it last night, and it wasn't...*intimate*. Just a basic rubdown. If I'd wanted to do intimate, I would have gone to other...*spots* on his body that would have changed the game."

"Ha! Touching him in any manner ups the intimacy between the two of you. I bet he was hard with need when he turned over so you could massage the rest of him."

Man, was he, but Heather wasn't going to spill all the details.

Lana tsked. "Just the way you are blushing tells the whole story."

She had Heather there. She had almost said no to a wolf run, figuring he'd had three times the exercise he needed today and needed to rest, but she had wanted to run with him.

"How was the wolf run?" Lana watched Heather as she combed out her hair.

"It was great. It's always good to get out and stretch my legs as a wolf." She wasn't about to tell Lana about him pinning her down and then being sorry for it.

"I heard you bit at Enrick's ear and he took you down."

Heather climbed into bed, blushing furiously. Again.

Nothing was sacred in a pack.

But she wasn't going to tell Lana about the kiss.

CHAPTER 8

EARLY THE NEXT MORNING, HEATHER HEADED DOWN THE stairs to the great hall to eat breakfast and figured she would sit with whoever was there first, though she desperately wanted to save a seat for Enrick if he showed up late. She was falling down the same rabbit hole when it came to him. She'd always thought the world of him, and she didn't want her feelings of infatuation to spoil things between them.

Lana suddenly shot out of the kitchen to catch up with her. "Don't save a seat for him if he's late. You don't want to look too eager to win his affection. Let him work for it."

Heather was ready to tell her to quit with all the advice.

Then Lana suddenly grabbed Heather's arm, startling her. She thought something was wrong. "Did he kiss you last night?"

Oh, just great. Just when Heather thought Lana wouldn't ask. Instantly, Heather's face heated.

Lana smiled. "I don't have to hear you tell me. I love how you blush. I'm so glad I don't."

Heather wished she could control that part of herself. Colleen greeted the two of them as they were getting ready to enter the great hall.

"Good morning, ladies." Colleen was smiling brightly. "Are you ready for all the craziness again today?"

"I am." Heather was really enjoying all of this when she knew others were ready for some normalcy to return to their lives.

Lana suddenly gasped. Heather turned to see what had startled her. Enrick had set up a small table for two in one corner of the great hall, complete with a vase of a dozen red roses, and was standing there behind the table, smiling.

Heather was blushing all over again. She couldn't help it. It was a good thing she wasn't interested in courting any other wolves at the moment.

"Enjoy breakfast," Colleen said, as if she had known about it all along. Maybe she had.

"I sure will," Heather said.

"Oh, and tell Enrick he'll look sufficiently muddy in his clothes today and to stop worrying about it."

Heather frowned at her, not understanding her meaning.

"When Grant came back from the battlefield, I had his clothes, and everyone else's, washed. Heavens. We might have lived in them day in, day out in the old days, but in this day and age, we clean the body odor off and just coat them in mud for the film."

Heather laughed. "Good. I'm glad someone took charge and did it."

"You bet."

Lana smiled at Heather. "Whatever you're doing, ignore me. It's working. Enjoy your breakfast."

"You too." Heather headed for the table to join Enrick. He sure looked like he was in full courting mode. What else could it be? She liked a man who could decide on something and go for it. Especially when she felt the same way but was a little uncomfortable about showing it.

When she reached him, she said, "I sure hope you aren't planning to court anyone else."

Enrick got her chair for her and she sat down to have breakfast. Then he grunted as he took his seat. "I'm trying to make sure any other eligible wolf out there gets the message."

She laughed. She couldn't believe it when one of the women came to serve them breakfast: eggs over easy, a side of sausage, and two pieces of toast, with a cup of hot tea already made up just for her. He was having steak, eggs, and toast.

"Lana told me what you always have for breakfast," Enrick said.

Now *he* was the kind of wolf that was a keeper. Heather didn't know of any other wolf who would ask her friend what she liked to eat. "She didn't even hint at what you were up to this morning."

"Good. I didn't tell her what I was going to do last night when I texted her, but I told her *not* to tell you I wanted to know what you like to eat. I wanted it to be a surprise."

"Well, this is a great surprise." From Lana's reaction at seeing the table for two, Heather suspected Lana hadn't known exactly what Enrick had been up to. Heather couldn't have been more thrilled. "I hear Colleen had everyone's clothes washed."

Enrick grunted again. "We love her, naturally, but men gotta do what men gotta do. And smelling nice when we're going to get all stinky again is a waste of soap and water."

Heather laughed and buttered her toast. "Well, I'm glad she did. And thank you for such a special breakfast."

"My pleasure. I was thinking over the battle scene yesterday when Robert and his brother showed up."

She was thinking over the kiss and incredible time they'd had yesterday. Men and women were from different planets.

"I was surprised you would have seen Cearnach and me on the battlefield filled with fighting men when Robert attacked him."

She drank some of her tea. "I knew approximately where you would be. Cearnach had told me in case I wanted to watch the two of you fight. He wanted me to see *him* win. *I* wanted to see *you* put all that practice sword fighting to good use. I kept looking until I saw the two of you. At first, when Robert attacked Cearnach, I thought it was part of the battle scene, but then when you tore into Robert, I realized that couldn't be right."

"He would have been on my side if he was fighting Cearnach to begin with. You were the best sentry out there. After your success at spotting the trouble, Grant is setting some more watchers up on the hilltop just in case we have any further incursions. If anyone sees the enemy out there while they're fighting the ones we're supposed to fight, they're to raise the alarm by shouting, and everyone within their close proximity will stop fighting and take down the enemy. Not permanently, of course." Enrick finished off his steak. "We figure the rogue wolves will know we'll be more prepared for them this time and they'll probably try a different tactic."

"But I was observing just *you* fighting Cearnach. Watchers on the hill won't be able to notice anything but a bunch of men fighting while they are looking at the collective group."

"Aye. That's why the men on the field are to call out the alarm, and those on the hill are to watch for it. With our sharp eyesight and outstanding hearing, anyone on the hill should be able to see it and call it in to Grant."

"Okay, good."

"Are you going to observe me again today?" Enrick sounded hopeful.

She was glad he wanted her to be there for him. "If I'm up on the hill with the others who will be watching out for anyone causing trouble, I'll feel I must do that too."

"Nay. You can observe me. The others will concentrate on all the rest of the men on the battlefield."

She laughed. "You need special protection."

He smiled. "Yesterday, it seemed that was so." He finished his eggs. "Today, I need the lady's favor. Something that aids me in winning the battle no matter what so I can return it to her at the end of the day."

"You know, if we don't end up together, you might regret having done all this for me." She drank the rest of her hot tea.

"Not on your life." He waited for her favor.

"You know we don't wear jewelry because if we have to shift quickly, we could lose the jewelry in the interim."

"You have tied back your hair."

"And when I remove the ribbon, my hair will be down again."

He smiled and held out his hand.

She glanced around and saw a few people watching them, Lana most of all. "Oh, all right." She pulled the ribbon from her hair, and the strands cascaded to her shoulders.

"Beautiful."

She was sure he meant her hair, not her ribbon.

Enrick slipped the ribbon inside his waterproof sporran. "I will endeavor to keep it clean."

"Don't worry about it. I'd rather you concentrate on the fight and don't get injured."

"But this has to be something near and dear to your heart."

"It is. I wore it the first time I saw you battling with your brothers in the heather. It always makes me think of that day."

"When I knocked Lachlan on his back?"

She laughed. "You and Lachlan were both ganging up on Grant, as usual. You knew he would lead the clan one day and needed to be stronger than everybody else. He knocked you and Lachlan down, and you both were laughing your heads off." She smiled fondly at the memory. "I haven't worn the ribbon my mother gave me for years. Not until now when I can see you in battle again."

"Hopefully, I won't have to fight Grant. Speaking of which, I need to change and hightail it out to the battlefield and get all muddy first."

She smiled, but she still felt she had to clear the air. "About last night... On the wolf run, I mean..."

"I should have caught you."

She smiled. "Yeah, you should have. I thought maybe your foreleg was hurting from all the work you'd done fighting in the field." Not really, but she figured she would give him an out.

"Nay. I didn't want to overdo tackling you again. Next time I won't hesitate."

She smiled. "Good. You're not catching me either."

He laughed. "You are a challenge."

They both rose from their seats, but this time she wrapped her arms around his back and tilted her head up for a kiss. If he was going to wear her favor in battle, for good luck, she wanted to add a kiss to the magic and to thank him for such a special breakfast. She hoped she didn't embarrass him. "A good-luck kiss that everything will go well today, and no more retakes during the shoot."

He wrapped his arms around her back, looking down at her, his eyes dark with desire, a small smile playing on his lips. He didn't seem to care if anyone was watching them, and she was glad about that. He tilted his head down for a kiss. Their mouths touched, softly at first, and she was afraid that was all he would share with her. He watched her expression as if measuring her interest. She wasn't letting go of him until he gave her more of a kiss this time.

And he obliged, kissing her like he didn't want to give her up ever. She was so ready for this. Their lips pressed harder and she felt light-headed, her whole body warming to inferno level, her heart—and his—pounding hard.

Their lips melded, caressed, pressed harder, and she felt all warm and wet in her nether region. This felt so good, his warm mouth pressing against hers, until her brother Oran called out, "Mud-bath time!"

She groaned and wondered if Oran didn't like Enrick kissing her so eagerly, or if he truly worried Enrick would forget where he was supposed to be soon.

"Your brother is still a big-brother guard wolf," Enrick said.

She smiled. "That's what I figured."

Enrick gave her another brief kiss. "I'll see you later." And then he hurried off before he missed his cue.

Lana soon joined her before Heather could think of anything more than the kiss. Lana took hold of her arm and led her out of the great hall after she left her dishes in the kitchen. "Wow. Amazing. I didn't think he would ever get to it, and when he did? Wow."

Heather smiled. Yeah, that was what she would say about it too. It was utterly amazing.

"Okay, like I said, strike my advice. Keep doing what you are doing to win over the hunky wolf."

Heather began thinking about watching the shoot. At least it wasn't raining, though it was foggy, and she hoped that wouldn't allow the enemy clan to sneak into the battle today.

"Are you going to watch the men? What am I saying? Of course you're going to watch Enrick fighting." Lana smiled. "I can't believe he took your ribbon to wear in the battle today. This is getting serious."

"Maybe."

Lana smiled at her. "You are thinking of something nice to do back. I can tell by the way your brow is furrowed."

"I was thinking about a picnic on the hilltop for lunch."

Lana laughed. "Okay, what do you need me to do to help make it happen?"

Six hours after the initial call was made to start shooting the scene—most of the early part of the day they'd fought in fog and the ground had still been muddy—they had the mandatory lunch break. Enrick had noticed a lot of activity up on top of the hill near the end of the last scene, and he was trying not to get distracted.

When the half-hour break for lunch was called, he saw Heather waving to him to join her on the hilltop. He wondered what was up.

Cearnach slapped him on the back. "I think my cousin has lunch ready for you. I have to say you outdid all of us with the special breakfast you gave her this morning. I could tell she was thrilled."

Enrick was glad he had done it. He'd worried he was pushing

the relationship too fast too soon, until he knew he'd upset Heather for not chasing her down while running as a wolf and then not kissing her like he'd wanted to before they retired to bed last night. "See you in a few."

Thirty minutes wasn't long for a lunch break when he needed to return to the castle to wash up before eating. But Heather lifted a bucket up and motioned for him to join her.

"You have all the luck," one of his kinsmen said.

Enrick did.

He hoofed it up the hill, hoping he looked like he was fresh to start a new battle and not like he was already dragging.

He still wanted to keep downwind of her just in case he didn't smell too fresh. He couldn't believe she'd want to have a picnic lunch with him while he was all grungy. But this was nice. And it was typical of Heather and her spontaneity.

Enrick reached the top of the hill while everyone else went into the inner bailey where Colleen had set up stands for anyone who wanted their full meals there. Catering was being handled by the castle staff and through Heather's shop. Most of the ladies who were doing scenes later were helping out with the meals. A craft service was providing snacks and drinks that were always available during the day and night while the shoot was going on. They also were responsible for cleaning up the trash.

"This is great. I would think you would wait to do this after the battle scenes were done so I wouldn't be quite so muddy." He washed up in the bucket, and she handed him a towel to dry off.

"After you took me out to a beautiful sunset dinner last night and made such a special effort for breakfast? I couldn't wait. And it's sunny now and the weather's perfect. Who knows what it will be like in a few days when the battle scenes are done? Besides, if anyone *hadn't* seen what you did for me for breakfast, I had to make sure they all knew I wasn't dating anyone else for the time being."

"Aye." He smiled and sat down next to the waterproof MacNeill tartan picnic rug she'd set out with a picnic basket and water.

"I would have served wine, but you're still working."

"Tonight, if you don't have any plans, we could have wine together." He took a bite of the pie. "Hmm, the steak pie has to be from your shop. They're so good. And this is my favorite kind of meat pie."

"You're right. The pie is from my shop. Catering the meals has been a real boon to both my business and your pack, since they help with making the meals."

———————

"Colleen knows how to make us happy. This is sure delicious. So what do we do tonight?" Enrick sounded eager to go on another date.

Heather was glad, but she had already made plans. That was one of the reasons she wanted to have lunch with him today, even if he was mostly muddy. She didn't mind. "Colleen wanted us to do something special for Missy, so some of the ladies are going into town to celebrate her film venture here and have a nice Scottish meal."

"Are any men going with you?" Enrick asked, looking serious now, typical Highland wolf who was courting a she-wolf and wanted to make sure she remained safe. Particularly because the McKinleys and Kilpatricks were causing trouble for them.

She could just imagine if the McKinleys or Kilpatricks discovered what they were doing, the difficulties they could make for them at the restaurant. "I think Grant was going to ask you and several others if they would come with us as a security force. I believe Missy has a couple of bodyguards too. So we should be well protected."

"Okay, good. I'm sure Grant's talking to everyone about it at lunch break. And he knew you would mention it to me."

"Of course. So are you coming?" Heather knew she didn't have to ask.

"Are you kidding? We're courting. Aye, I'll be there. After I've cleaned up a wee bit."

It wasn't long before they'd enjoyed their lunch and a visit, and he'd gingerly kissed her, not wanting to get her all muddy before he returned to the battle.

"This was really nice. I wouldn't be surprised if you don't start a trend."

"Or you."

He smiled. "All right. I'll see you tonight." He kissed her again, and then headed down the hill where the men were beginning to gather.

It was back to the trenches for the warriors, and the lookouts joined Heather on the hill. She carried her picnic basket to the keep and cleaned everything up, then was going up the stairs to her room to drop them off when she saw Guy McNab heading into the conference room. She knew Lachlan was out with the wolves to do their part in the battle, and Grant was downstairs talking to Colleen about business, so why was Guy wandering around in parts of the castle where he didn't belong?

Wasn't he supposed to be fighting in the battle? They should be in the middle of swinging their swords by now. Unless the man entering the conference room was Guy's double, but he shouldn't be up here either. She went up after him and soon reached the conference room. Inside, Guy was looking at the pictures of wolves and clan leaders. She was fairly certain it was Guy and not Larry, his stunt double.

"Can I help you with anything?" Even though she didn't live here on a regular basis, she felt it was her duty to safeguard things since none of the MacQuarries probably knew about Guy's transgression.

"No, uh, sorry, I was just… I shouldn't be here."

She could have been a fangirl and told him it was okay, but

she didn't want him or anyone else thinking they could wander around the castle when they weren't allowed to unless Grant and Colleen gave them permission.

"You're right. These rooms are off-limits." She thought it was odd he would do this now. Why not ask the MacQuarries if he could? She was sure they'd give him permission, but he had to ask, and he needed to be escorted around the off-limit areas.

He glanced at the photos again. "Sorry. I just…wondered what the rest of the castle looked like."

Then he hurried out of the room and she followed him down the stairs, making sure he left the castle. She wondered if his double was doing the battle scenes and Guy didn't have to be out there for the moment.

As soon as he walked outside, she went to tell Grant and Colleen what had happened, just to give them a heads-up.

"Thanks for taking care of it," Grant said. "For liability reasons, and because we're wolves, we don't want anyone wandering about the castle unsupervised. Even though nobody's supposed to be in wolf form, you never know when someone might be talking about our wolf halves."

Heather sighed. "I agree. I thought he was supposed to be in the battle fighting. I guess just the peons have to."

Colleen laughed. "I suspect his double is doing some of the more difficult scenes, if Guy has a part in this right now. Though I'm surprised he wouldn't be standing by."

"Right. I'm off to take care of some things for my shop and then I'll get ready for tonight. Oh, and thanks again for suggesting I help cater the food for the shoots. I couldn't be happier."

"You're so welcome. You deserve it. And tonight will totally be fun. Missy is really looking forward to it and was amazed we invited her," Colleen said.

"You never know, but she might mention us in all the tabloids," Heather said.

"True. Oh, that reminds me, Julia is joining us. She said she might include a film star in her next romance novel."

Heather smiled. "Julia would, too. She needs to watch the shooting of the film."

"She will as soon as Missy has more scenes with the hero. I'll see you and all the others down here at six. The shooting should be ended for the meal by then."

"See you then." Heather couldn't wait, but she was glad Enrick would be there too.

CHAPTER 9

THAT NIGHT, ENRICK WAS SEEING HEATHER IN A NEW LIGHT. She was so excited about spending time with the female star of the film. He really hadn't thought she would be so fangirlish, but he loved seeing her having fun. She and the other ladies were happily talking to Missy in the dining room of the inn, while he and six other men were seated at two different tables nearby. He, Lachlan, and Heather's brothers were five of the men. The other two were Missy's bodyguards, and they sat at a different table.

Lachlan said, "Some of the men were taking Guy and a few of the key players to a special pub tonight. I didn't think you would be interested in going."

"No way." Enrick drank some of his beer. Watching out for Heather was the only thing on his agenda.

"We all were asking Heather if we could have joined you to enjoy the picnic on top of the hill," Lachlan said.

Enrick shook his head. "If it weren't for the film, we would have some of our dates in privacy."

"We think this works well," Oran said, his brother agreeing.

Enrick scoffed. "What are you going to do when she has a mate who will protect her?"

"We'll always be there for her protection. Maybe not always with you, but if you need us, you can always count on us to be there for her," Oran said.

"And me too," Lachlan said.

Which went without saying. Enrick's brothers would always treat Heather like their own sister and watch out for her, even if Enrick didn't mate her. She was like part of their extended family.

"I was glad we didn't have any more trouble with the enemy

clan during the battle scenes today," Lachlan said, "and the wolves did really well."

"Aye, they could spread their feet and stay on the top of the mud better than we could." Enrick spoke low so none of the humans in the restaurant would hear them. "I overheard Colleen's cousin William bit one of the men he wasn't supposed to though."

"Uh, yeah. He felt awful about it. He said the man who was supposed to be there had moved position, not that it's that hard to do with all the fighting going on. As soon as he bit into the man's arm, he knew he wasn't padded as heavily as the man he was supposed to have bitten. He let go right away before he did any serious injury. The one he was supposed to bite hurried into position and yelled at him in Gaelic, which of course Colleen's cousin didn't understand. But he was shaking his sword at him, and William recognized him as the one who had the extra padding and attacked him," Lachlan said.

Enrick frowned. "Did they reshoot the scene?"

"No. And the other man was trying to hide the fact he was hurting."

"What about his injury? Was it bad?" Enrick suspected it hadn't been or he would have heard from Grant or Colleen about it.

"William didn't break the skin. The man had some teeth marks, bruising, but nothing serious. We all have padding so we hopefully don't get cut by a sword accidentally." Lachlan drank some more of his beer. "Okay, so we have a new development."

Enrick and Heather's brothers were all ears because they suspected it wasn't a "good" development.

"The director wants to have the wolves bite two of the main villains' arms during a final battle scene." Lachlan started digging into his fish.

"Nay." Enrick couldn't believe Grant would go along with it. He ate some more of his chips.

"Aye." Lachlan shook his head. "I didn't expect that to come up when they began shooting this project. But it's something the director wants now. He was really impressed how well our wolves work with the men in the battle scenes. And he wants to have that added touch for the final scenes with two of the main villains. We've made sure the wolves who will be involved know the man is a human villain, not one of our extras. And to go gently. They'll be two of the stand-ins for the villains, and they're human. We can't have anyone turning a human by accident."

"I didn't realize the wolves were going to have to bite a human stunt double," Enrick said again. "That's awfully risky."

"Aye, you know how the director is always coming up with new stuff to make the story look even better. I had to talk to Grant and Colleen about it. It's a hard deal because we said the wolves could bite the men on the battlefield, no trouble at all as long as everyone was padded enough. So then why can't they bite a couple of their main cast members—well, the doubles—if they are wearing the same amount of padding? Anyway, Grant and Colleen said they would think about it, but they lectured the wolves who actually would bite two of the men, in the event they did it. They have to make it look realistic, like a dog with a chew bone playing tug-of-war for keeps, but not to really sink their teeth in, which could crush the bone."

"What about a couple of our men who could pretend to be the villains? No close-up shots of their faces, but all the action being done would be with our wolves and a couple of our men. If they accidentally are bitten through the padding, no trouble," Enrick said.

"We discussed it, but the director wouldn't go for it. If we do it, we're going to have the men involved wear double the protection, and the wolves will be growling up a storm like they're really tearing into them so it sounds vicious enough. We want the men to be pulled forward without resisting too much, but the director says it won't be realistic enough. The actors really need to fight back."

"Well, hell." Enrick just hoped nothing would go wrong!

Heather glanced Enrick's way and he suspected she had heard some of their conversation, courtesy of their enhanced wolf's hearing. She was frowning. He felt the same way, but he didn't want her worrying about it. She'd been having a good time visiting with the other ladies and the costar of the film.

Then suddenly, a couple of men got up from a nearby table and headed over to the women's table. Enrick wasn't too concerned. They weren't wolves. And Missy's bodyguards were on high alert, too, watching the guys. But the two men only handed her napkins and pens to get Missy's autograph.

Then a couple of ladies from another table approached her, since Missy was so cheerful about signing autographs for the men, and asked her for some too.

Everyone finally finished dinner, and the women got ready to head back to the castle. Enrick wanted to ask Heather to ride with him, but Oran shook his head at him.

"Let her visit with the lasses a bit. You kissed her enough this morning. No telling what you did with her on the hilltop at lunch." Oran smiled.

"I was a muddy mess and didn't want to get her clothes all muddy." But Enrick went along with the plan and they followed the women's car back to the castle.

As soon as they were parked, though, Enrick caught up with Heather before she retired for the night. "About breakfast…"

"Yes, I'll sit with you, but we don't have to have a separate table."

He smiled. "Sure. That was special. We'll eat with the others. But together."

"I'll save you a seat if you get up late."

He chuckled. "I am never—well, almost never—late."

"I'm sure you needed the extra sleep the other night." She smiled, then frowned. "Did I hear right? That the director wants our wolves to attack some of the human actors?"

"Aye. It could be a recipe for disaster."

"I'll say. I sure hope Colleen and Grant can change his mind." Heather wrapped her arms around Enrick's neck. "Good night, Enrick. I'll see you in the morning."

Then they kissed. His hands on her waist, he was enjoying the sweet wine she'd had at dinner, the sensuousness of her lips, the feel of her soft body pressed lightly against his. He kissed her mouth slowly, building up the passion, his body reacting to hers at once.

"Hmm, Enrick," she said, and her words were spoken like a sweet siren's, willing him to carry her off to his chamber.

Man, did he want to.

"We need to run again," he said. "So I can catch you properly."

"If we could do it here, I would. It's too far to travel back to Argent Castle tonight."

He considered asking Grant if he and Heather could take a brief run in the woods, just the two of them, but Grant had made the ruling for good reason. "I agree. Tomorrow night then?"

"Aye."

"We'll have dinner with Ian and Julian and the others."

"Okay, we can do that." It almost made him feel as though he was having dinner with the family, as if seeking their approval to date their kin. "Tomorrow night then." He was going to start kissing her again.

She smiled a little and pulled away, as if she was afraid this was going to go too far. "Night."

"Good night, lass. See you at breakfast." He sighed as he watched her go, but then he got a text from Grant. *If you're not in bed yet, come to the conference room for a meeting.*

Enrick sighed and headed to the conference room. *What now?*

Lachlan was there already, and so were Colleen and Grant.

"Yeah, Grant?" Enrick took a seat on one of the sofas.

"I need three of our men to volunteer to have the wolves

practice on them to ensure they don't bite through the new padded sleeves we're making. Two will do the actual attacking, but we'll have another wolf on standby, just in case," Grant said.

Enrick raised a brow.

"Not you or Lachlan. You have enough on your plate. I'll need Lachlan supervising the practice. I need you, Enrick, to round up three men who wouldn't mind volunteering for the job."

"I can do that." Enrick wasn't opposed to having a wolf attack him for the exercise, but he did have a lot of other work he was responsible for. He didn't want to voice out loud the real concern he had with this.

Grant finally did. "Okay, so we all know the consequences, should one of the men be turned. As much of a concern as this is, we'd even considered getting real wolves for the job."

Enrick shook his head; Lachlan's eyes widened.

Grant waved his hand, dismissing the notion. "It wouldn't work. The wolf owner would have to supervise the wolves, and he might not even be able to use them in such a scenario. We're human, so we can be told what to do in a situation like this. The real wolves could get into the fight so much with the men they were attacking that they turn on each other in a squabble, run off, who knows?"

"True." Enrick ran his hands through his hair. "Okay, worse-case scenario?"

"One of the human stunt men gets bitten? We offer to take care of him. Full medical care, a stay at the castle," Grant said.

Enrick noticed Colleen was sipping from her tea, quiet.

"Live here rent-free for the rest of his life at the castle," Lachlan said.

"Armor," Colleen finally said. "We have the men wear armor on the arm that the wolves attack. The padding will cover it so no one will ever know they have armor on."

"The wolf is supposed to pull away the padding and then you see the blood," Grant said.

"And if it's for real, and not pretend?" Colleen said, annoyed. "They wear armor. It's the only way you will agree to it. They can have a cut in the scene and do whatever they want with blood, removing the armor easily, replacing the torn-up protective padding. We can make sure it works. But they use armor to protect them, or we have our men serve as the doubles."

"Unless they sign a waiver saying if they get bitten by a wolf and turn into one, they don't hold any of us responsible," Lachlan said.

Everyone smiled.

Grant patted Colleen's leg. "They wear armor. You heard the lass."

Enrick prayed that it would work.

Grant called the director, who was waiting to hear from him about how this would go. "You can meet us in the conference room. I'll have Lachlan escort you up."

Lachlan saluted Grant and hurried off.

Within a few minutes, the director and some of his staff were sitting in the conference room, ready to hear the verdict.

"The men wear real armor on their arms the wolves are supposed to attack," Grant said.

The director was frowning.

Grant opened his mouth to speak again, but Colleen jumped right in.

Enrick and Lachlan were always surprised when she did that, and amused that Grant let her have her say.

"They are *real* wolves," Colleen said. "And no matter how much training you give them, they're still partly wild. We can't risk having them tearing into the men that much. What if they forgot their training and their wild wolf half took over? These are not wolves that have been bred down into what you might think of as your pet poodle. They're wolves, through and through. A wolf's normal bite is around 400 pounds of pressure per square inch. If they're fighting something or someone, it can be as much as 1,200 pounds. You wouldn't want any animal biting down that hard on your arm."

The director's eyes widened a bit. "Sure."

"Lachlan has the job of training the wolves to bite through the padding on the volunteers' arms and not dent the armor underneath when the stunt men wear it for their final scene. We're not changing our mind about this. The liability issues are too great, should a wolf accidentally bite through the padding."

"All right, Lady Colleen," the director finally said. He smiled. "I was going to agree already. I never would have likened them to a poodle, but I get your point. And I agree. We wouldn't want to have the liability of a wolf accidentally crushing a man's arm."

Enrick was glad the director had finally agreed because he knew Colleen wouldn't change her mind about it.

Grant had even looked into the backgrounds of the two human stunt men who would get "bitten." Both had wives, kids, parents, and siblings. It would be a veritable disaster if they were turned and had to leave their families behind. No way did Grant want to have to control the catastrophe that would be. Well, any of them, because it would be on the whole pack to keep a newly turned wolf in line.

CHAPTER 10

Heather finally had her important role to play again, as an extra in charge of the kitchen staff as they prepared the actual meal for the next scene. Enrick was busy with security, though she thought he was still wearing his grungy kilt from being in the battle that morning.

Maynard, a grizzled old gray wolf who had been in charge of the kitchens forever, *wasn't* supposed to be in the old kitchen during the film. Heather was running the show, and she knew that rankled the older wolf. She understood he felt he was being pushed out of his "home" so to speak, but Grant and Colleen had agreed to use the kitchen to shoot some of the scenes, and their decision overrode Maynard's need to be in charge of things there.

Grant had given him time off to just have some fun wherever he wanted to go, but Maynard's whole life was wrapped up in food preparation, and it was killing him not to be there while Heather was managing the situation.

"You can't be in here, Maynard," Heather said to the growly wolf. She'd told him several times already in various ways: cajolingly, humorously, determinedly, but now she was just telling him like it was. "You're not cast as an extra. The director only envisioned women being in the kitchen. He said it was all right if you wanted to serve some of the food." She knew that would go over big with the cook and manager of the kitchen staff. *Not.*

"I've been working in this kitchen for—"

Well over three hundred years, but he couldn't say that as some of the film crew were within hearing.

"...a long damn time."

"Aye, and you will have your kitchen back as soon as the shoot is done. You hardly ever use this one." Heather suspected he didn't like that she got to do the majority of the catering for the meals from her shop instead of him from the castle kitchens. His food was excellent, no doubt about it. There wasn't anything wrong with her getting the contract, but Maynard had taken exception to it.

If anyone was to eat at "his" castle, they ate *his* food.

Heather let out her breath in exasperation as the stubborn wolf wouldn't budge and everyone preparing the meal had to make their way around him. No amount of talking to him was going to change his mind. She pulled her cell phone out of her pouch at her waist and called Grant. "Hi, Grant. Maynard is still in the kitchen. He doesn't want to listen to me, but he can't be in the scene."

"Let me talk to him."

"Aye, thanks, Grant." She handed her phone to Maynard. "It's for you."

Maynard took the phone from her. "Aye? Aye. All right." Then he handed the phone back to her, scowled at her, and stomped out of the kitchen.

She asked, "Are you still there, Grant?"

"Aye. I told Maynard he has the day off to go fishing, and I want to eat whatever he catches for dinner tonight."

Heather smiled, then she frowned. "Does he like to fish?"

Grant laughed. "Aye, when I tell him I'll eat the catch."

"Okay, good. We're about ready to do this. Talk to you later."

They had just finished the last battle scene outside, having needed only a couple of hours to retake a couple of scenes, so all of the men involved in that were returning to the castle. Some would be sitting in the great hall eating the meal next.

For the scene she was in charge of, the wizard would show up unannounced and inspect the food for the lord, making sure nobody had tampered with it. The lord of the castle had received so many death threats—in the film's story line—that they were constantly on guard.

Of course, the magic would appear on-screen when the wizard just would "poof," using his wizardly abilities, and appear.

Heather and her female crew were busily preparing the meal in an authentic way in the old kitchen where they'd preserved the history of the castle. The fires were going strong, orange and yellow flames licking the bottoms of the large, black cast-iron pots filled with fish stew. Everyone had practiced making the meal beforehand, since they only did this for historical celebrations of their past, and they had a few more helpers than they were used to from the MacNeill clan. Plus Heather had never done this here, so she'd needed the practice. They also had some of the women and a couple of men working in the lower level of the castle where they baked the bread in ovens of the period. Cameras were set to roll down there after the scene above was shot.

Heather knew it was about time for her "crew" to pause their actions in the old kitchen, while the director called "Cut." Then they were to hold their positions while the wizard hurried into the kitchen from a side entrance to inspect the meal.

But then a woman in traditional Highland dress, who Heather didn't know, suddenly showed up in the kitchen. Heather thought maybe the woman had a speaking role and the director had added her at the last minute.

Heather frowned at the woman as she hurried over to one of the pots and added something to the fish stew, then turned to do the same thing to the other pot. Heather didn't like that she was adding ingredients to the pots that she hadn't approved of beforehand.

Everyone else should have been watching what they were supposed to be busy doing in the rest of the kitchen, while holding their positions. So Heather thought only the director and his film crew and she had noticed. She kept thinking the woman and her actions weren't part of the script. Yet the director and actors had improvised on several occasions and no one had told her or Enrick about the change of plans at the time, so she thought this could be another situation like that.

Still, Heather felt a sense of disquiet. Maybe the woman was pretending to add poison to the meal for the sake of the film. But what if she *did* add something that truly made everyone sick? What if she was one of the Kilpatrick or McKinley family members and she had been paid or coerced to cause trouble for the MacQuarries?

Heather moved closer to her, but the woman ignored her, and that was when Heather smelled her scent. She was a wolf! And she wasn't supposed to be here.

Heather reached into her boot to whip out the *sgian dubh* she always wore when she was in her long kilt and grabbed the woman by the arm. Heather held the knife at the woman's ribs before the woman could hurry out of the kitchen and vanish. If Heather was wrong about the woman, the director wouldn't be happy with her and they would have to reshoot the scene.

If the woman was with an enemy clan and she'd added something bad to the stew, Heather might have saved them from disaster.

"Who are you, and what did you put in the stew?" Heather asked, squeezing the woman's arm as she struggled to get free. Heather couldn't really use the knife on her and the woman knew it, but Heather wasn't losing her grip on her no matter what.

They were supposed to pause all their actions for the magical arrival of the wizard. Instead, everyone who was working for Heather turned to watch them, mouths agape. Lana, who'd been deboning fish, eyed the situation and then ran out of the kitchen, also not part of the story line. In a couple of minutes, Enrick and two other men in full battle dress rushed into the kitchen, still grimy from the recent fight scene. Enrick looked just like Guy, so Enrick couldn't have been a guard in the film, if the director was keeping this impromptu scene in the story. Though Heather couldn't imagine why he would if it messed up their story line. Though the director seemed to like to let things develop organically and often left things in that weren't in the script.

The wizard suddenly walked into the room, like he was supposed to do, but he appeared surprised to see the changes to the scene.

"Who are you?" Enrick asked, taking hold of the woman's arm as Heather released her other arm. His grip was much firmer and made the woman's dark eyes water.

"She put something in the stew," Heather said, slipping her *sgian dubh* back into her boot. She hoped Enrick could put fear in the woman to get her to confess her crime. "I was afraid she put something in it that would make everyone sick."

"Or kill them. Kill you, milord," the wizard said, improvising as if this was part of the story all along, looking stern and growly, just as growly as Enrick looked. Except Enrick's expression was *not* playacting.

Heather knew he wanted to force the truth from the woman because they needed to ensure no one was hurt by whoever had sent her. She kept thinking the director would call "Cut!" And then they would have to sort out what was going on before they could set up for the scene again. But he didn't.

"Take her to the dungeon for questioning," Enrick said to his other two clansmen. Then he told Heather, "Your diligence will be rewarded." Even though he still looked as stern as could be, she saw a glimmer of promise and a smile in his expression. "I must wash before the meal." Then he stalked out of the kitchen with purpose.

Still shocked about the woman's guile and deceit, Heather was wrapped up in thinking about Enrick's promise, and then she was thinking back to the situation at hand, wondering what was going to happen next.

Appearing deep in thought, the wizard stroked his long, white beard. "Mayhap the treacherous woman should eat some of the stew." Then he made a motion to indicate he was vanishing.

Heather thought that was a good idea.

The director called, "Cut!" He rubbed his chin in thought. "I take it that was for real? The woman was trying to sabotage the meal?"

"Aye, she's not one of either the MacQuarrie or MacNeill clans, and if she's not one of your actors, I'd say so. We'll have to empty the pots and clean them out, but we can pretend to serve the food from here and have fresh bowls of stew made in the new kitchen. Since you only show us delivering the food to the tables after this scene, we should be able to make it work," Heather said.

"What about the woman?" the director asked.

"Enrick will call the police." *Not.* The woman was a wolf, so they had to handle it themselves. They would keep her hostage until they learned the truth. If her clansmen knew she'd been caught, maybe they would cease hostilities, but Heather was certain Grant wouldn't let her go until they had finished making the film here. That could be about three months. The wolves lived by their own rules, and they couldn't have one of their kind going to jail. Not if they might shift sometime during their incarceration.

"Good. She was deliberately hiding her face from the camera, and her hair was covered in a veil." The director frowned. "Do you have a woman who looks similar in build who could play the part of this woman? I want a scene where the two men who came to take the woman away watch her being interrogated in your dungeon. She will be stoic, not revealing the truth, stubborn, loyal to her clan, and then the wizard will force her to eat the stew and she'll fall from her chair, dead."

None of the women volunteered for the role. Heather figured that was because they all wanted to continue as background actors and didn't want to lose their fun job by expiring in the dungeon too early on.

"I'll do it," Colleen said, entering the kitchen. Heather guessed she'd been watching things for a while. "I filled out the paperwork to be a background actor in reserve, in case any of the women became indisposed and I was needed."

"You're American," the director said.

"Who is of Scottish descent and who owns the castle with my husband, Grant. And you said the part to be played is a nonspeaking part."

"Lady Colleen, it's a deal. And, Heather, if you can get ahold of Enrick and have him send the two guards to meet me in the dungeon, that would work for me." Then the director switched his attention to the wizard, who had returned to the kitchen to learn what his role would be in all this. "We'll check out the dungeon, set it up for the interrogation, and give you some lines to say. The lady will do her part, and we'll be done with it. In the meantime, if the ladies can prepare a meal for the great hall, we'll start the scene there as soon as we're done with the other and the baking scene. That one is a really short take."

"What about Enrick's voice? Will we have to dub in Guy's over it?" one of the director's staff asked.

"No. I liked the way he was so gruff and feral. I don't think anyone will notice the difference in the end," the director said.

Heather smiled. He was that. Then she frowned. And for good reason.

Colleen said to Heather, "I'll have Maynard take care of preparing the meal in the new kitchen while you help serve the meal when the shoot is ready. That will cheer him up."

"I thought he went fishing for Grant's dinner."

"Maynard hasn't left the castle yet. He was still getting ready to leave. I sent him a text when we learned of the trouble here, and he's eager to help out where he can."

"Okay, good. That will work." Heather was glad Maynard was able to participate in the work he loved doing.

As the director left with Colleen and the wizard—who glanced back at Heather and winked at her—the director was saying to him, "You won't lay a finger on the lady. You are all powerful. But she is proud and determined not to bend to your will. You will be conceited, then fatherly toward her, then finally give up and have one of the men feed her the stew. She will eat it because she knows she has no other choice."

As his voice receded down the hallway, their footfalls growing more distant, Heather hurried to text Enrick.

The director wants you to send the two guards you had with you in the kitchen to the dungeon to play a part there. The woman isn't being interrogated there, is she?

No. We have her in the conference room. I'll send the men to the dungeon and have a couple more guards come up to take their place to watch the woman.

Thanks, Enrick. And Colleen is playing the woman's part in the dungeon.

Does Grant know?

He might not.

All right, I'll let him know. And thanks, Heather. You saved everyone's arse today. I meant it when I said I plan to reward you for it.

She smiled and responded, No reward needed for that. But I'm looking forward to seeing what you have in mind. The director was impressed with your acting skill and voice, by the way. You never know. He might call on you for a future film.

You too. When your friend Lana came running out of the
kitchen to warn someone, she saw me and told me you
had pulled your sgian dubh on the woman so quickly,
no one knew what was happening. Immediately, I was
on my way with the men to rescue you.

Heather hadn't needed protecting! She texted: Or her?

She deserves whatever she gets. Grant's having the stew
tested for poisons or other ingredients that would
make anyone sick.

Okay, good. I've got to get ready for the next scene.

See you when the director calls, "It's a wrap."

As soon as Heather put her cell phone away, a man was removing the contents of each pot of fish stew and placing them in sealed
containers. Then he left. All the women hurried over to give
Heather hugs.

"If you hadn't stopped her, Guy could have been deathly ill or
dead," one of the ladies said as if no one else on the set mattered.

"Or more of the people. Though some just pretend to eat,
close-ups show people sampling the food," another lady said. "And
some like the food so much, they want to-go boxes."

"I was hoping I didn't really screw up the scene. I'd thought
maybe she was pretending to tamper with the stew and was one of
the cast's speaking actors, but then I smelled she was a wolf."

"She's not one of ours," one of the MacQuarrie women said.

"Thanks to Lana for running off to get Enrick and the other
men to assist in taking charge of the woman. I was afraid I was
going to lose my grip on her and have to tackle her to the stone
floor." Heather wouldn't have let the woman go no matter what.

The ladies all smiled.

"I was just glad Enrick and the other men were nearby when I raced out for help," Lana said. "You were the true hero."

Everyone agreed.

"I'm so glad Lady Colleen offered to play the role of the saboteur," one of the women said. "I know one of us would have had to volunteer, but I want to take part in some of the other scenes."

Heather smiled. "I suspected as much. I'm glad she did too."

"I can't believe the other clan would stoop so low," one of the ladies said.

"I can. It's a matter of honor and pride that they didn't win the contract to have the film at their castle. And they've always been vindictive. We'll just have to stay alert."

CHAPTER 11

THAT NIGHT, ENRICK TOOK HEATHER HOME TO HAVE DINNER with her cousins and brothers, and he hoped no one in Heather's family would make a big deal of him dating her. Lachlan came with them to stay with the wolves afterward and would return with Heather's brothers and the wolves in the morning. Since Enrick and Heather planned to run as wolves following the dinner, some of the MacQuarrie clan also had come to run as wolves. They would all watch each other's backs on the return trip home.

Of course the conversation centered on the concern about the food contamination and the continued effort by the McKinleys and Kilpatricks to disrupt the movie.

"They won't stop," Ian said, then took a bite of his chicken.

Julia motioned with her glass of wine. "Heather, you are a true heroine."

Everyone thought Heather was. Enrick figured if they were living in ancient times, and he was lord of the castle and had mated her, she would be managing the castle and fending off the enemy while he was with the troops in battle. He'd never seen her in that role before, as a leader, intent on saving everyone else. Proactive, not waiting for someone else to see the trouble and react.

Heather blushed. Enrick smiled and reached over and squeezed her hand.

"Aye, if it was not for Heather eyeing Enrick with such interest on the battlefield," Oran said, "who knows what might have happened."

She gave her brother a growly look. So did Enrick. He was feeling super protective of her. She was with him this time, not just seated at the table at a gathering of the families in charge of the two wolf packs. She would usually be on the opposite side of the table down at the end, if she was even here, not in the center with him, since he was representing the leadership of the MacQuarrie pack. He enjoyed the shift in dynamics between them.

Oran smiled. "It's true."

"I was watching Cearnach, too, since he is our cousin and bragged how he could beat Enrick on the playing field. I had to see if it was so." She bit into her bun so vigorously that Enrick thought she would have bitten her brother if they'd been in their wolf coats.

Enrick glanced at Cearnach and smiled, amused he'd been bragging to his kinsmen about besting him in the fight. The rivalry between their clans was mostly in fun, though tempers would flare over she-wolves sometimes.

"Och, if Robert hadn't knocked me down, I would have swept you off your feet in an instant," Cearnach said to Enrick.

Everyone laughed. Enrick and Cearnach were so well matched that either of them taking the advantage was solely due to a misstep by the other.

"How did the female saboteur infiltrate the castle?" Julia asked.

Enrick could just imagine Julia adding the plot to one of her romance stories. "Everyone was so busy that the woman, dressed just like one of the ones in the kitchen-scene shoot, slipped by practically unnoticed. Those who caught a glimpse of her thought she was one of the MacNeill women they hadn't seen before and she was in a hurry to reach the old kitchen. They just figured she was about to be late for the shoot. They didn't know shooting had begun. The saboteur was unknown to us. And she hid behind her veil and wimple. Ultimately, it was my fault because I'm in charge of security and—"

"Nay, it wasn't." Heather looked sharply at him, surprising him at her vehemence in contradicting him. "Grant has you taking on way too many jobs as it is. You can't fight battles in the film and then expect to be in charge of the security for the grounds and the castle, for heaven's sake."

He appreciated that she was sticking up for him, but he often had an unfathomable number of bonnets to wear while taking care of business at the castle. No way would he have told Grant he couldn't handle all his jobs. "Aye, but it falls on me to—"

She shook her head and waved her half-eaten bun at him. "You are *not* infallible, and anyone who had half the jobs you are supposed to do would have missed the woman sneaking into the castle too."

He smiled, loving her tenacity as she stuck up for him. But he really didn't believe he was faultless. "But I have many—"

"Too many tasks. Do you want me to talk to Grant about it?" Heather arched her brows and looked like she fully intended to, whether Enrick agreed with her or not.

He had the greatest urge to pull her from her seat and kiss her like there was no tomorrow. If she did talk to Grant about it, which Enrick didn't want her to, he could imagine his brother being totally amused.

A number of people chuckled under their breaths.

Enrick did *not* have too many tasks. Grant did. He oversaw the whole of the castle and everything else pertaining to their wolf pack, with Colleen's help, of course. And Enrick did assign jobs to others, so it wasn't like he was solely responsible for every little detail and was so anal that he couldn't delegate. He was still responsible for his tasks, whether they were accomplished or not. Just like what had happened concerning the woman slipping through their defenses.

Heather's brothers were smiling at Enrick. They knew what he'd gotten into when he'd begun to truly court her. He could handle it.

Enrick cleared his throat. "I've made sure we have guards posted at all the doors to the keep 'round the clock. We do shut the gates to the castle and grounds, but if someone were to sneak in and hide during the day because of all the people there—between ours, the MacNeills, and the film crew—I wanted to make sure he or she didn't get any farther than the front door of the keep."

"That sounds reasonable," Ian agreed.

"I heard they kept the scene like it was and you actually were the hero when you came to take the saboteur into custody," Julia said. "How did seeing Heather holding on to the woman with her *sgian dubh* in hand make you feel?"

Enrick swore Julia was taking mental notes to include all this in a future book. "I was angry, quite frankly. Heather shouldn't have had to do that, but I was proud of her for reacting so quickly and decisively. I was glad she wasn't hurt, and she managed to avoid injuring the woman—mainly because the film crew was shooting the scene. At that point, we didn't know if the woman had poisoned the soup to cause sickness or something as serious as death."

Heather smiled up at him. "You were perfectly growly. Even the director said Enrick had that feral look about him and wanted to keep the 'scene.' The wizard attempted to look just as angry, but he came in a distant second."

"Enrick's shared that look once or twice with me," Lachlan said, making light of it.

Enrick chuckled. "Aye, Brother, you know not to take my sword when I'm off to battle."

Lachlan's eyes sparkled with merriment. "I couldn't find mine."

The rest of the dinner centered around what was coming next for the movie. When Heather said, "The director wants the wolves to bite two of the villains' stunt men," there was an audible gasp among those dining there tonight.

Enrick sighed. "Aye. We've made preparations to have the stunt men wear a piece of armor, not the lightweight stuff they use today for movies but the really heavy-duty armor, just over the arm the wolves will bite."

Everyone looked at Lachlan to see his take on it since he was handling the wolves. "We've been practicing every day, making sure the wolves look like they're really getting into tearing the villain to pieces without injuring anyone. So far during the practice they had today, they haven't bitten through the armor, so it should be fine."

They hoped. Anything could go wrong and it could be a disaster.

As soon as the meal was done, Enrick was eager to play with Heather in the woods as a wolf, and this time? He was going to catch her if she played chase.

Heather was eager to play with Enrick and hoped he wouldn't be afraid to have some fun. They had barely begun the run when he nipped her ear, gently, in a teasing way. She tackled him. Or at least tried. He was a big, muscular wolf, and when she wrapped her forelegs around his thick, furred neck and nipped at his muzzle, he smiled. Okay, so she wasn't going to pin him to the forest floor like he'd taken her down to the grassy riverbank so effortlessly.

He wasn't giving in, either, which she was glad for. She didn't want a wimpy male wolf to play with who would tuck tail and fold just to find favor with her. But she had to admit she was a little frustrated he was looking so smug and immovable.

He licked her face and then bit at her neck in a gentle play bite, and she rigorously bit his neck back. He woofed at her in amusement and then retaliated and pinned her to the ground. She loved it and woofed in pure pleasure. His chest against hers, he licked her face and nibbled on her ear. She licked his face back and she loved this. She couldn't budge him, though, and when she quit trying, he began to move off her and she leapt out of his path and whipped around and nipped at his tail. He woofed at her, enjoying the wolf play as much as she was.

This was what she'd hoped for the first time she'd tried to play with him. She was vaguely aware other wolves were nearby but keeping lookout in the event the McKinleys or Kilpatricks were in the area.

Then she raced off and Enrick was in hot pursuit. Yes! He was going to chase her and…then he was pinning her to the ground again.

Okay, so she might need a little head start. She hadn't expected him to catch up to her *that* quickly with his longer legs and faster stride. She laughed at him in her wolf way and his eyes were filled with amusement, maybe lust, and that was when she smelled how turned on he was.

Hmm, so was she. She licked his muzzle. And he nuzzled her muzzle with his own. Then he moved to let her up and she rubbed against his hot, huggable body, showing him he had done just the right thing. She loved a challenge! She didn't want him to make it easy on her. And she did want him to play with her.

They walked for a while, bumping into each other in playful camaraderie, their heads swinging around to make the connection, licking each other's cheeks, and moving on again, exploring, smelling the scents of rabbits and deer that had passed this way before.

Then she dashed off, hoping he didn't tackle her this time as he took off running, speeding up, catching up to her, but this time running beside her. Yeah, perfect. He seemed to be learning her cues on what she wanted him to do with her as a wolf. She loved it.

Then she saw two Scottish wildcats, their larger skulls and longer limbs differing from domestic house cats. She and Enrick came to an abrupt halt, not wanting to scare the wildcats off. Their fur was covered in stripes with a tabby pattern. Bushy, ringed tails, black at the tips, whipped back and forth. That was all she saw before the wildcats disappeared into the undergrowth.

Seeing them had made her run with Enrick even more special. The wildcats were on the endangered list now, and she rarely saw them on a run in the woods surrounding Argent Castle. They would have refuge on the MacNeill lands, but she was sure they were afraid of the big bad wolves. She wondered if Enrick had seen them around his castle.

Then she heard a couple of wolves bark, both in scolding.

Now what?

Something crashed through the brush wearing part of a fern frond. Chipper, one of the MacNeills' wolfhounds, greeted her as if he'd been let out to play. She knew he hadn't. She woofed at him to go with her. He usually minded her. He needed to be in the kennel with the rest of his mates for the night.

Chipper play-bowed to her, wanting her to play. She nipped at him like a mother dog would, telling him playtime was over.

Then a couple of teen boys in the distance called out, "Chipper! Chipper, come here!"

She howled to let them know Chipper was with her. She loved the wolfhounds and often played with the puppies after dinner before they went to sleep.

She and Enrick corralled the dog back to Argent Castle. She knew he wouldn't run off now, not when all the wolves on the run with them began to return too. Chipper felt like he was just one of the pack.

"Coming!" one of the teens shouted. That would be Matthew. He was supposed to be putting the dogs up for the night. She hoped Chipper was the only one that had gotten away from him. Lewis, Matthew's friend, would be the other with him. They'd both been prone to getting into trouble until Ian had put them in charge of the wolfhounds. With some responsibility, they were turning out to be fine young men.

But Chipper could be sneaky, so she knew to keep an eye on him when the kennel was locked for the night.

Suddenly, Matthew was in front of them, panting, trying to catch his breath. "He made a mad dash for it when Lewis arrived at the kennel."

Lewis looked just as flushed, trying to get his wind.

She woofed at them, telling them it wasn't a problem. All was well.

Matthew secured a leash to Chipper's collar. "Sorry for interrupting your wolf run. We wanted to go, too, but we had to put up the dogs first. Then we ended up running anyway, but not as wolves."

She smiled at him. Life had a way of working out like that. At least she'd seen the wildcats and had enjoyed playing with Enrick. When they finally reached the castle, Ian was waiting for them. He gave Matthew and Lewis a stern look.

It was mostly for show, but they took it for real.

"Sorry," both of them said, waiting for him to release them.

"Put 'em up. Just let that be a lesson to you not to be in such a hurry." Ian raised his brows at the boys.

"Aye," they both said, and hurried off to put Chipper with the rest of his packmates.

Ian smiled at Heather and Enrick as the other wolves went inside to shift and change. "Hope the boys didn't cut into your run too much."

She shook her head. They had to return to the MacQuarries' castle and get some sleep.

Then she and Enrick ran inside the keep, and she went to her room and he went to the area where the other wolves were getting dressed.

She shouldn't even be considering it, but she'd love to join Enrick in his room tonight.

CHAPTER 12

ENRICK FIGURED HE'D DONE EVERYTHING RIGHT AS FAR AS running and playing as a wolf with Heather. He wasn't used to tackling a she-wolf like that. He had never played with one in courtship. Well, actually, at any time really. He always played with the bigger, rougher males.

He felt he was too big, and he didn't want her to feel overwhelmed. He certainly didn't want to accidentally injure her. But she seemed to love his maneuvers anyway.

He was grateful for that. He was also glad they'd seen the wildcats. He could tell that had made her night.

It didn't take long for her to come down the stairs to join him, and then everyone who was going back to his castle got in their vehicles and took off.

"I did it right this time, correct?" Even though Enrick was fairly certain he had, he still wanted to make sure as he drove her back to Farraige Castle.

She laughed. "I never thought you would tackle me so fast the second time. The first time, aye."

He smiled. He'd been amused she thought she could outdistance him for long. "Seriously, though, you were all right with it, weren't you?"

She smiled, her eyes alight with joy. "You bet. I've played with male wolves before who were so eager to please and so beta-like. I didn't want that. I wanted to really play with you the way you play with your brothers and mine and my cousins. I just wanted to be one of the guys."

He laughed. "I am so glad you are not just one of the guys. That wouldn't be fun at all."

"Okay, well, yeah, not in that way. I just didn't want you to treat me like a wilting flower."

"I was afraid I'd overdone it the second time I pinned you down."

"If I'd thought so, I would have bitten you to tell you to back off. You would have known." She patted him on the thigh.

He chuckled. "Okay, I guess you would have." So that made him feel better. He wanted her to let him know if something between them wasn't working for her.

He didn't know how to approach her about having dated other women before and not asking her to date him, too, though he suspected she might know already, as gossipy as pack members were. Yet Oran's words kept coming back to haunt him. Tell her, before they got too much farther in their relationship.

Maybe if he mentioned his shortcomings, it would help. "I've always been…focused on work and…" Hell, that was feeding right into what Oran said she already believed about him. "I can be really conventional. Boring even."

She nodded.

He hadn't expected her to agree. He smiled. "Staid, I guess you might say."

She glanced at him, waiting for him to get to the point.

How in the world was he supposed to mention that he had dated other women but never asked her out on a date, when he would have loved to, without telling her Oran had told him to speak to her about it? Not that he meant to protect her brother, but Enrick didn't want her to think they'd been talking about her behind her back.

"I've dated women who are like me."

She nodded. "Boring."

He chuckled. "Uh, yeah." So far she didn't seem to think anything ill of him for it.

"I know all about them. One date and you wouldn't date for a long time after that."

He frowned at her. How had she known about it? She and he lived at different castles. And he'd never seen her at his when he had dated other women. Her brothers had been sure she didn't know anything about it.

"Right." Those women didn't suit him either.

"They weren't right for you. Lachlan told me."

Lachlan. Hell.

"You didn't ask me out because I was too fun-loving."

Enrick smiled. That was one way of putting it.

She sighed. "If you had, you would have had the time of your life. We both would have."

"I think you might be right."

"I am. I thought of chasing after you, but I was afraid that would just scare you more." She smiled at him.

He laughed. "I don't scare easily."

"Oh, I don't know about that. Anyway, I was surprised to see you in the shop to chase away the Kilpatricks. I thought maybe you had changed your mind about me. Lana told me you were concerned how I was feeling."

"Aye." Despite not believing they were suited, he realized he'd begun to think differently about her. He was seeing her in a whole new light. Maybe if he'd given them a chance earlier, he would have seen her that way back then. Maybe they both just needed to change before that could happen.

"If you want to know the truth, I'm not as reckless as you probably think I am." Heather folded her arms.

He smiled at her.

She frowned at him. "I'm not. I only act that way when you're around so I can get your attention."

"I'm not really all that dull all the time."

"Oh, nay, you're about the most fascinating man I know. The women you dated wouldn't have seen that in you." She smiled.

"Fascinating."

"Aye. Truth be told, if we have snowball fights in the future, I want to be on your team."

"I want that too. You're deadly in a snowball fight."

She laughed. "Sorry. I really hadn't meant to hurt you."

"I wanted to see you after that and let you know I'd been amused, not angry with you over it. Then time passed, and I figured you wouldn't even remember about it, so no sense in bringing it up."

"You wanted to see me?"

"Aye, but you made yourself scarce."

They finally arrived at Farraige Castle and headed for the stairs to their chambers. He was going to escort her to her room this time, but instead, she took hold of his hand and led him to his.

Her impulsiveness was rubbing off on him and he let her into his room, not sure what she had in mind.

"I'm staying the night. Don't bother to try and talk me out of it." She began to remove her hair clip and he laughed.

"I won't." He removed his T-shirt and laid it on a chair. "What will Lana think? She'll be worried when you don't return to your chamber and will tell Grant to call out the guard."

"I told her I was staying with you if all worked out tonight at dinner at my castle, so don't worry about me." Heather sighed and pulled out her phone and began texting. "I'm sending her a text to tell her that's what I'm doing for sure. I can see her worrying and knocking on your door just to make sure I am here."

Enrick was glad Heather was texting. He could just imagine the uproar Lana would cause if Heather didn't.

She glanced at his dresser and saw her hair ribbon lying there, nice and pristine. She smiled.

Yeah, he hadn't given it back. He would have if she asked for it, but he'd kept it on his dresser as a keepsake of his time on the battlefield with her favor in his sporran.

Then he slid her cardigan off her shoulders and let it drop to the floor. He put his hands on her shoulders and caressed. Her warm hands were on his waist and the heat of her fingers seared him all the way through. He couldn't believe it had finally come to this. Not a mating, but maybe in the future…

He leaned down to kiss her and she eagerly kissed him back. He loved the feel of her hot lips against his mouth, the way she speared him with her tongue, and pressed her body against his.

His cock would have been standing at attention if he'd been undressed. Instead, it was straining for release, feeling her pressed against it, making him even harder. He groaned as he wrapped his arms around her and held her tight, wanting to keep her like this forever.

He nuzzled her face and she nipped at his ear as if she were a wolf in play, only in a sexy way this time. When they'd played as wolves and he'd pinned her down, he'd been turned on and had thought about the afterward—here, like this with her. He had planned on playing it by ear, but he was glad she had taken charge and made it clear this was just what she had wanted, too, as she wrapped her arms tighter around him and pressed harder against his body.

He groaned and ran his hands through her long, silky hair. "Beautiful."

"Hmm." She kissed his bare chest and licked a rigid nipple, sending an electric shock straight through to his groin.

His cock jumped and she rubbed her lithe body against him. She wasn't making it easy for him to slowly seduce her the way he wanted to. He was ready to rip off her clothes and take her right then and there.

He pulled off her wool shirt and tossed it aside, then leaned down to kiss her throat, his tongue laving a path to a breast, taking hold of the edge of the lacy cup of her bra and pulling it down with his teeth.

She moaned and arched her back, the connection between her pelvis and his cock making him stifle another groan.

He laved her dusky nipple with his tongue and then pulled at the taut peak with his lips. She grasped his shoulders and held on as if she were going to collapse at any second. He smiled and let go of her nipple, then reached back to unfasten her bra. He pulled the straps down her arms, and once the bra slid to the floor, he cupped her creamy breasts in his hands and gently kneaded them.

Her skin was soft and kissable. He caressed her skin with his lips, loving the feel of it against his mouth.

Back to kissing her enticing mouth, he felt the heat building in his blood, their hearts pumping hard.

She smelled of the piney woods and the fresh breeze from their wolf run, of lavender, woman, and sexy wolf. Her musky scent was an aphrodisiac and their pheromones were spinning out of control. This had never happened with him with any other woman he'd dated. Heather made him want to go further than he'd ever gone before with a she-wolf.

She ran her hands over his biceps, feeling them, squeezing, rubbing her body against his arousal again, telling him she was interested in every bit of him. Not just the kissing.

She reached down and began to unfasten his belt, and then his jeans. He did the same with hers, unfastening and then pulling the button from the buttonhole. He realized both of them were wearing their hiking shoes. That wouldn't do.

He took hold of her shoulders and sat her on his bed. Man, he'd never thought he would be sleeping with her tonight. He leaned down and untied one of her shoes and pulled it off, and then the other. He slipped off her wool socks next and massaged her left foot and she leaned back against the bed, hands in her hair, and purred.

He was thinking of the night she gave him a massage. Now he got to reciprocate. Except he didn't have her lavender lotion to use. He switched to the other foot and gave it the same gentle massage before sliding his hands up her jeans and pulling down the zipper, then slipping them off her hips and pulling them the rest of the way clear.

He quickly dispensed with his boots, socks, and jeans, then slid his boxer briefs off.

Looking appreciatively at him, she smiled, waiting for him to get on with business. He was certainly ready to oblige but he hesitated, wanting to make sure.

She reached her hands up to him. That was all the encouragement he needed.

He pulled off her panties and tossed them to the floor and joined her in the bed.

He began kissing her mouth, his naked body pressing against hers. She was hot and moving against him, her touching him making him starved for her. Their lips caressed and pressed, her hands running over his bare back and settling on his arse. He groaned with the need to take this all the way.

Then he moved her with her back to him so he could ply her feminine core with his strokes. Hooking her heel over his leg, he began running his fingers over her slick clit, her body thrumming with desire, her wetness telling him she was ready for his penetration, if they were going for a mating.

She was pressing her buttocks against his rigid cock, making him desperate to bring her to climax.

He leaned down to kiss her naked neck, and she angled her body so she could capture his mouth in another sizzling kiss. Tongues teased each other and then she sucked on his tongue, making his cock jerk against her buttocks. Vixen.

Dipping his finger into her wet sheath, he stroked her clit faster, his mouth still fused with hers, and this time he managed to suck on *her* tongue. She cast him a wicked smile, her eyes heavy-lidded, filled with lust.

He kissed her again, enjoying the feel of her soft, moist lips pressing against his, and then she arched her back against his body.

He knew she was ready to come, and he kept stroking, harder now, coaxing the climax out of her.

He was enthralled with her and already thinking of where this could lead. A mating, if everything worked out, and the she-wolf who had always captured his imagination would be his very own wolf for all time.

But he also kissed her deeply as she let out a muffled cry. He didn't want everyone in the castle to hear her cry of exultation, though the stone walls were thick so they helped to soundproof the rooms, and the solid oak doors did too. But with their wolf hearing...he didn't want her to feel embarrassed.

She relaxed in his arms for a minute, her smile telling him she was well pleased with the way she was feeling. And he was glad about that. Then she rolled over and began to stroke his full-blown cock, while kissing his chest. She switched her attention to licking his nipples, and red-hot need shot straight to his cock. He kissed the top of her head, and she moved up to kiss his mouth again, her hand firm on his arousal, giving him just the right amount of pressure and speed, and he groaned with the action.

If he'd had any doubts about them going this far, they had flown out the castle window.

She moved her sweet mouth to one of his nipples again, and that time she suckled, and he came in a volcanic explosion. He'd known he was near the end, but man, that pushed him right over.

She continued to milk him to the end, his hand stroking her back, feeling hotly satiated. He hoped she wouldn't want to leave him tonight, though he would understand if she wanted to keep up appearances, should anyone know what they were up to. But he wanted to hold her close all night long.

"Be right back," he said, leaving the bed to take a shower. He kissed her real quick, then headed into the bathroom. But she needed to clean up, too, he figured, and she soon joined him.

Hell, this was one damn great way to shower, he thought, as he soaped her all up and she reciprocated.

———————

Ohmigod, Enrick was such a keeper! Heather wasn't sure if this was a one-shot deal, staying with him like this for now in his chamber, or if he wanted to do this for longer on a sort of trial basis. But she was sure ready to do it every night, as long as things worked out between them. She hoped not too many in their packs would learn about it and that any who did wouldn't share with the rest of his pack and hers. She knew Lana wouldn't say a word, not wanting to divulge Heather's secret.

Heather could imagine her brothers giving Enrick fits for not just mating her first. She knew they really liked him as a friend and were eager to have him join the family if Enrick mated her. But she and he had to be sure about this.

Right now, she was in heaven, still feeling the heat wafting through her, the tingle of climax still making her feel special and wanted and beautiful. She had imagined how this would be between them, but never like this. Never this real, or hot, or exquisite. And the shower? That extended the pleasure all over again.

He turned off the shower and then they were out of it, drying their hair, her concentration on him drying the rest of his beautifully toned body. He smiled to see her interest. She kissed his chest and hurried back to the bed and climbed under the quilts, ready to dream about one sexy Highland wolf. Minus his kilt.

"I'm glad you're still here." Enrick set his towel aside and climbed under the covers with her.

He pulled her against his body, and she was glad, though she didn't expect to be wrapped up in his arms all night long. This was a nice way to end the lovely time she'd had with Enrick today.

He was stroking her arm when she said, "I'll need to leave early in the morning."

He glanced down at her, a smile playing on his lips.

"Not to hide what we're doing, for heaven's sake, or I would leave now."

He tightened his hold on her almost imperceptibly, but she loved how he was showing he didn't want her to go.

"I didn't think to bring a change of clothes."

"Ah," he said, and kissed the top of her head. "We will wake early, then, and you can change in your bedroom. Then what? Do you want to meet me in the great hall for breakfast, or I can pick you up at your chamber?"

She wanted to tell him to pick her up from her chamber—they were courting, after all. But she didn't want him to feel like he had to be with her every second of the day when they were free.

"I'll meet you downstairs so you don't have to wait for me."

He smiled again.

"Not to let on that we had been together."

His smile broadened. The rogue.

She closed her eyes. "It would just take you out of your way, and you might as well save a seat for me in the great hall."

"Aye, I will do that."

CHAPTER 13

EVEN IF HEATHER DIDN'T WANT TO SOUND LIKE SHE WAS trying to cover up that they had been together in his chamber all night, Enrick was sure she was feeling a little self-conscious. It was understandable because they didn't have the privacy they might have if they weren't living in a castle with a pack of wolves.

Everyone was interested in learning if a wolf couple would end up mating. It kept the circle of life going for the *lupus garous*.

He would have liked to escort her to the great hall, to prove to everyone they were "together." But he understood her reasoning and that was fine with him too.

What he hadn't expected was to wake this morning, still cuddling Heather and find the light was streaming in through a separation of the curtains hanging over the window. Och, they were late!

He didn't want to alarm Heather, but he needed to make sure security was in place and they hadn't had any more breaches into their domain. He didn't think Heather had anything to do for the film shoot this morning, at least that he could recall. But they were so late, they'd even missed breakfast!

They would have to rush down and try to grab something to eat.

"Hey, sleepyhead," he said, kissing her forehead.

She slowly opened her eyes and smiled up at him. That was enough of a reward to get him through whatever missions he had to do for the day.

Then she frowned and looked in the direction of the window. Her hand shoved at his chest as she tried to scramble out of bed. He stifled the urge to laugh because he was in as much of a rush to get out of bed and dress as she was, once she was out of his arms and began throwing on her clothes.

"You should have woken me." She frowned at him as she jerked her wool shirt over her head, dispensing with her bra, and shoved her legs into her jeans, not putting on her panties.

"I just woke up myself, lass." He was pulling on his long shirt, trying to get dressed as fast as she was.

"Sorry, I just planned to have a lot more time than this." She grabbed the hair clip she'd had in her hair last night and hurried to pull her hair back.

"I'll get us some breakfast while you're changing in your—"

She raced out of his chamber, barefooted and with socks, bra, and panties shoved in her boots as she made a beeline for her chamber down the hallway.

He smiled and shut the door, then finished dressing. He thought of texting Maynard and seeing if he could whip them up a breakfast, but he knew the kitchen manager never fed anyone between meals. Unless it was Colleen. Not even Ian could change the crusty old Highlander's mind at times. When the kitchen was closed, it was closed. If someone had to eat, they could make a meal for themselves, but they had to clean up after themselves too. Maynard had his reasons. Clansmen and women would traipse through there all day, if they had their way.

Enrick headed out of his room and strode down the stairs, intent on reaching the kitchen and making a meal, despite figuring he could have a fight on his hands with Maynard if he was still there.

To his surprise, Maynard was busy making breakfast. Maybe for himself? Maynard frowned at Enrick. "I probably shouldn't say anything, but…"

"Then don't," Enrick said, heading for one of the fridges.

"Don't bother. I'm making breakfast for the two of you. Next time, get up a wee bit earlier."

Enrick smiled at the old cuss. "I owe you."

"Aye, that you do."

Enrick knew Maynard had been frustrated with Heather and her pie shop and then taking over the kitchens for the film, so he was surprised the old wolf would do something so nice for her.

"How did you—"

"Know? Heather texted me saying if you didn't get breakfast you would faint during a battle scene, if you had to fight one today."

Enrick knew that had to amuse the wolf. He smiled. "She said that, did she?"

"And I knew she would wilt if she didn't have a good hearty breakfast to carry her through lunch. What were you thinking?" Maynard scrambled the eggs.

"We had a long run last night as wolves and—"

"Och, you were together last night." Maynard waved his spatula at Enrick. "Don't you go upsetting the lass after all she's been through over Timothy."

Enrick hadn't intended to, but if they decided they weren't meant to be together, he knew he would end up hurting her no matter how much he didn't want to.

"Her brothers were in here asking about her. And about you. Wondering why they didn't see the two of you at breakfast. They were afraid the two of you had a spat."

"Well, we didn't." Enrick poured some coffee for himself.

"I know that. They shoulda figured where this was headed."

"It's not—"

"Aye, I know that, or the lass would have mentioned it to me."

Now *that* surprised Enrick. He hadn't thought she and Maynard were getting along that well. Maybe things had changed between them when Maynard had been able to make the food for the scene in the new kitchen after the woman had sabotaged the food in the old one.

"She knows her stuff," Maynard said, motioning to the kitchen. "And, out of the goodness of her heart, she shared a couple of her recipes that she uses to make her own meat pies, because they're so popular at her shop. I'm not undercutting her business, mind you. But I'm making them for myself and Colleen, for Ian also if he wants."

"And me?" Enrick asked, hearing footfalls hurrying in the direction of the kitchen. Heather's light footsteps, he imagined.

"Not you. You buy them at her shop. Keep her in business." Maynard served up the eggs, haddock, toast, and bowls of oatmeal. He smiled like a chipper young wolf when Heather walked into the kitchen looking flustered. "Morning, lass. Sit yourself down and enjoy your breakfast." Then he set the food out on the kitchen table the staff used, or family used if they could sneak into the kitchen and grab a bite when Maynard wasn't around.

"Oh, thank you." Heather gave him a hug and a kiss on the cheek. "You are my hero."

Maynard chuckled and raised a brow at Enrick.

He wanted to shake his head at Maynard, but instead he kissed Heather briefly because she didn't appear to be in the mood for anything more. She was in too much of a hurry.

"Later," Maynard said, and discreetly left the kitchen.

"Wasn't it lovely of Maynard to do this for us?" Heather asked.

"It sure was." Enrick wasn't about to mention how shocked he was at this turn of events.

"We can't do this anymore," she said, waving her buttered toast at him, and then hurried to coat it with strawberry jam.

"I'll set an alarm clock." Enrick wanted her in his bed with him at night. They'd finally come this far, and he didn't want to take a step back.

"Nay. We can't let this happen again. Maynard was being kindhearted to make us a special breakfast just because we couldn't drag ourselves out of bed this morning."

"We can set our phone alarms too." Enrick would do anything to keep up the status quo, for now.

She finished her tea. "It would have been bad enough if we'd been on time and our clansmen would be speculating what had gone on. But this? It's a catastrophe."

Enrick fought smiling because he knew she was upset about it, but to him, this was a natural order of things to come. It was inevitable after all they'd done yesterday and then last night that they would be so exhausted this morning that they accidentally slept in.

"You were supposed to be in charge of security." She finished off her eggs.

"Aye, and I have people in place to take care of things. As soon as we're done, I'll check on it."

"You are always so…" She paused, searching for a word.

"Anal?"

"Punctual. I am too, for the most part, but there are times when I'm not. You are *always* punctual, except for the other morning when you came down for breakfast later than usual, and I feel I've led you astray."

He reached out to take her hand and squeezed it with reassurance. "Everything will get done that has to be done. I think you're right in saying Grant has put too much on my shoulders of late."

That earned him a little smile.

"Did you talk to Grant about it?" Enrick really hadn't thought she would.

"Aye, I did. He agreed with me."

Enrick laughed. "Good. I'm glad he didn't think I put you up to it."

"He knew you would never do that. You have too much pride."

Enrick chuckled again. "I want you in my bed tonight. I swear I'll borrow a dozen alarm clocks and have them set so we won't be able to shut them all off before we're wide awake and we'll be on time for breakfast in the morning."

She took the last bite of her haddock. "All right. If I see a dozen alarm clocks sitting in your room tonight, in addition to our two cell phones, I'll take you up on it."

He let out his breath in relief.

She smiled. Then she frowned. "But they have to be set for an hour before we're to arrive down here. Oh, and this time, I'll pack a bag and I won't have to run through the castle to my chamber in my bare feet."

He smiled. "You have a deal."

Lachlan came into the kitchen with "his" wolves and smiled to see Enrick and Heather finishing up breakfast. "Grant told me I needed to check on security, but if you have a minute after you eat, you can do it. I need to get the wolves ready for the beach scene."

The wolves drank from a big water dish usually reserved for the wolfhounds.

"Aye, I'm on it." Enrick rose from his chair and carried his empty plate and bowl to the kitchen sink. Before he left, he took Heather in his arms and kissed her. "Lunch together?"

"I'm going to the shop with two of my brothers to make sure everything is going okay at lunchtime. Now go make sure the bad guys don't cause any trouble." Heather got a text. "It's from my pack leader. Got to run."

"See you in a few hours then." Enrick was so glad she was staying with him. He needed to ask who had alarm clocks though. As soon as Heather hurried off, the wolves left the kitchen and Enrick asked his brother, "Do you have an alarm clock you can spare?"

"So the two of you don't come down late for breakfast again?" Lachlan sounded amused. "Sure."

"Okay, good. I just need another ten."

Lachlan laughed.

"Hey, this is serious. She won't stay with me tonight if I don't have a dozen clocks in the room."

Lachlan laughed again and slapped him on the back. "Go take

care of business. I'll see if I can round up some more clocks, but of course I won't give a reason for the need."

"Good. Thanks, Lachlan." Then Enrick was out of there, praying nothing had gone wrong with the security because of him not being there earlier to check it all out.

CHAPTER 14

THAT MORNING, THE BEACH SCENE WAS ALL SET UP AND Spencer Emerson, an actor playing one of the main villains in the movie, was supposed to have his role in this scene. He had taken an interest in Heather, and she'd tried to pretend she hadn't noticed.

She hadn't meant to speak with him or have anything to do with him, but she'd forgotten he would be in this scene, and like usual, he had to approach her. She admired him as an actor, but that was it.

At first, she hadn't really paid any attention to him as they were standing on the beach, waiting for the scene to be set up. She figured Spencer was a flatterer, and she'd seen him smiling at other clanswomen. A womanizer. Only it wouldn't work with the women here. That had to be a real shock to him.

He might have a rakish, wolfish personality, but the real wolves weren't taken in.

Thankfully, her brothers and Enrick and his brothers hadn't been around to see the way Spencer had been all smiles with her anytime he'd caught her eye. He'd struck up a conversation with her a few times, but she was always in a hurry to get something else done somewhere else and was on her way someplace. Though she couldn't help but be a little flattered by his interest in her, she reminded herself he did that with all the women. She could just imagine what his model girlfriend, the one he left behind in Los Angeles, thought of his behavior.

Maybe that was why he was more intrigued with Heather than the other women in the two clans. She didn't give him the time of day. Some men liked a woman who wasn't an easy catch. She had news for him. She wasn't interested in being his catch now or ever. Though she did love his character in the movies. He was a strikingly handsome villain. He was great in the roles she'd seen him play in. He was so vile that she was ready to terminate him herself whenever she watched him in a movie. And she knew if he was in it, it would be a riveting film.

For this film, he had a jagged red scar across his cheek, courtesy of a fight at some point or another between him and the hero. In the story, Spencer was after the enchanted sword and the woman connected to it.

Now, he moved in next to Heather on the beach where the heroine would first meet the hero in the film. The villain would also step in to make his presence known, but they were still waiting for the arrival of Guy's double, the director swearing he was going to dock his pay for being late to the set. And fire his ass if he didn't show up promptly.

"Would you like to show me some of your Scottish hospitality?" Spencer asked Heather.

She hadn't meant for her jaw to drop in reaction to his question, but she was appalled. Julia and Lana were standing near her and both heard his question, their eyes rounded.

"Sorry, no."

Spencer folded his arms, frowning, looking perfectly ominous as if he could change her mind with his lethal look.

She smiled up at him. "I love your character in the movies, no matter what part you play. You're the perfect villain."

He smiled at her.

"In real life, you are way too much of a flatterer."

He frowned again. "Too much, do you think?" He shrugged. "It's part of my character."

"It's part of your personality," she corrected. Then she glanced back at the director, who was on his cell phone looking ready to have a meltdown.

Missy was standing nearby, and she looked tired and ready to do anything but this right now.

"I meant I would take you out someplace nice. I think you have real acting talent. I even have some pull if you ever wanted to get into the business. I saw the scene where you pulled your knife out of your boot and held that woman hostage. It was so natural, it looked like you had done so on countless occasions."

"I have. It comes in handy on dates." Not really, but she had used it on countless other occasions in the past for defense.

Julia chuckled. Lana smiled at her. So did Spencer, but Heather was sure he didn't believe her.

"So no date?" he asked, looking really surprised she would turn him down.

Heather shook her head. Seriously? She supposed women were all after him because he was a popular American movie star. She would love to know how many women he had already asked out from the castle.

She was only down here on the beach today because Julia wanted some company, and she was Heather's pack leader, and so Heather had dragged—ha!—a very excited Lana with them because she was dying to watch the scene. Yeah, seeing the stunt double pretending to be Guy swimming naked in the sea was what had Lana super interested in being down on the beach. Julia had her notebook and was taking notes already about the setting as they all waited for Larry to turn up. At least Heather hadn't been late to the party.

The good news was it turned out to be a beautiful day, sunny morning, blue skies with a smattering of fluffy white clouds, a sea breeze, just perfect.

If the double ever showed up for the shoot!

———————

Enrick was making sure they had plenty of security up on the cliffs overlooking the beach scene that would be taking place next. They

had everything in hand, so he was returning to the castle. He wondered where Heather was. He knew she didn't have a scene to take
part in right now, and he was glad they'd resolved the issue of her
sleeping with him again tonight.

He was nearly to the keep when he got a call from the director himself. Which surprised the hell out of Enrick. They were
finally done with the major battle scenes. He was hoping he hadn't
screwed things up by missing a reshoot or another scene. "Yes, sir?"

"Guy's double is sick, and we've got a scene to shoot now. You
look just like Guy, so we'll increase your pay for any scenes where
you serve as the double if you're interested. I'll ask your brother
Lachlan if you don't want to do it, but you look even more like
Guy, so if you're agreeable, let's do this. I don't believe Grant
would want to do it, and he said he'd put a couple of men in charge
of security so you're free to handle it."

Enrick was both honored with the prospect of being the hero
in the story, but annoyed Guy would get the credit while Enrick
did whatever Guy didn't want to do. "Aye, sure, what did you need
me for?"

"The beach scene. We need you in the costume Larry was
going to wear and, well, you'll come down to the beach like Larry
was supposed to do. We're all set up. Time is money. Grab Larry's
clothes from wardrobe at the keep. We'll film you coming down
the stairs. Walk down with a good steady speed. When you get
down to the beach, you'll strip and take a little swim in the sea.
Your brother, Grant, said you were good for it."

Enrick would kill his brother. Hell, here Enrick thought the
reason he was needed was so the actor wouldn't have to walk up
and down all those stairs. Not that getting naked before shifting
into his wolf was any big deal when it came to his pack, but being
filmed getting naked for the whole world to see was a whole other
story. Then again, no one would ever know that Enrick, instead of
the film star, had done it.

"Aye. I'll be right down." At least as fast as he could travel the two-thousand-and-six-hundred-feet worth of stairs from the castle to the beach after returning to the castle, stripping, and putting on the new clothes. He would prefer his own, but he'd have to wear a duplicate of the clothing Guy would be wearing.

Enrick didn't see a sword and scabbard with the clothes in wardrobe. If he were a warrior and going to the beach alone for a swim in years past, he would have armed himself with a sword at the very least. He dashed up the stairs to his room and retrieved his sword and *sgian dubh*. After he was "properly" attired, he headed out of the keep and finally reached the stairs.

The director called, "Action!"

Two cameramen began shooting Enrick from different angles. It was very different going from fighting in a sea of warriors during a battle where he might never have been seen on the silver screen to being the center of attention, spotlighted by the cameras. He tried not to feel self-conscious, but he couldn't help it. Most *lupus garous* didn't like to be in the spotlight like this.

He made his usual fast walk down the stairs, not slowly as if he were doing this for the camera, but in a manner that said he was in great physical shape and had purpose in his warrior's stride.

He glanced over at the gathering of people out of the cameras' view nearer the bottom of the cliffs on the sandy beach and saw the female star of the film waiting for her part in the story, looking bored, yawning, and fussing with strands of hair whipping across her face from the sea breeze. She was frowning as she waited to get her part over with. He didn't know what her role was, or what he was supposed to do exactly. He'd only briefly scanned the scene to make sure they had proper security.

Then he saw Heather, Lana, and Julia, with a couple of other lasses from their clan standing nearby. Julia was taking copious notes, and he figured she was going to use the idea in one of her books. Heather smiled broadly at him. So did the other women.

Ah hell. He had envisioned no one from either clan seeing him like this, not until the film came out, and then they might think he was Guy all along. He would never hear the end of this.

The director called, "Cut!" when Enrick reached the beach.

"You're going to use the same purposeful stride to that point on the shore and strip out of your clothes right there with your back to the camera," the director said, pointing to the spot. "Then walk into the sea, swim out a good distance to the halfway point where that first boat is, pause, look out to sea, up at your castle, and then turn and swim back. You won't see anyone on the shore until you reach it, and suddenly the heroine will appear as if by magic, her hand on your sword."

Heather chuckled.

Enrick couldn't help but smile at her.

Several others chortled.

The director frowned. "You're wearing a sword already."

"Aye. In the distant past, any warrior worth his salt would be armed wherever he went."

"Okay, that sounds good. Missy will have brought your old sword from her present world. Your sword"—the director glanced at the *sgian dubh* handle sticking out of Enrick's boot—"and your *sgian dubh* will be left on the beach, along with your clothes. When you return from your swim, you'll walk out of the water and grab your kilt to put it on, but then you see the heroine standing there with a sword in her hand and you hold your kilt in front of your crotch and stare at her for a moment, surprised, shocked, furious to see her. She could be from the enemy clan. You have no idea who she is, and she'll be wearing clothes foreign to you, her hair pulled back in a ponytail, unlike the women of your period in time."

"I will be holding onto my shirt first," Enrick said. "Not my kilt. The shirt is worn under the kilt."

"Uh, yeah, you'll grab up your shirt, hold it in front of your crotch, bunched up like a hardened warrior would do, and then I'll call 'Cut!' and have Guy and the other actors take over from there. You'll be done, but stick around in case we need to retake any of the scenes."

Like walking down the stairs? Or swimming again? Enrick sure as hell hoped not.

He noticed some of his men in boats out in the water waiting to rescue him if he had trouble. All three of Heather's brothers were in one of them. Even though Enrick had never had any difficulty doing this and loved to have a vigorous swim on a hot summer's day, he was glad the boats were there, just in case he got a cramp.

"Action!" the director called, and Enrick moved through the sand to the spot where he would strip with his back to the cameras.

It was a warm and sunny day in the Highlands, though the water would be cold. Enrick stripped off his borrowed clothes at the same rate of speed he normally did, not in a rush and not super slowly like he was doing a striptease for the camera. He paused, looking out to sea.

The director didn't say anything, so Enrick hoped he was doing everything right. He stalked toward the water with purpose, trying to ignore the fact that several eyes were upon him, and attempting to soak up the sounds and smells surrounding him instead. At least with the battle scenes, they knew they were supposed to be the good guys fighting with Guy or the bad guys fighting him and his men, and it felt more like it had a beginning and an end. Here, the scene felt out of context for Enrick.

He better get paid a lot more money for this, or Grant was making it up to him. Enrick didn't mind swimming in the sea— when it was *his* idea!

Enrick started walking into the water, and everything was quiet except for seagulls screeching high above and the waves crashing on the shore. He tried to pretend this was any other day that he might take a swim in the cold water, and not that his every move was being filmed for all time. Or that he had an audience of people watching him from the shore.

The smell of fish and briny water filled his senses as he waded out, and when he was finally deep enough, he dove into the water. He wasn't sure that was what the director wanted since he hadn't said so. Enrick rose to the surface of the choppy water, expecting the director to call "Cut" and have him do it again, just swimming out when it was deep enough, but maybe the director thought that if Enrick usually did it this way, it would look more natural.

At least it was for him. It took him a few minutes to adjust to the cold water pressing against his skin, but as he swam out as far as they'd wanted him to, his muscles warmed with the effort. He was hoping he wouldn't get a cramp while he was swimming. That would sure ruin the take. And then he would have to do it all over again. Or Lachlan would have to take his place. No way did Enrick want his brother to show him up! Especially not in front of Heather.

When he thought he had swum out far enough, he took his glances at the castle, the men in the boat smiling at him, thumbs up, one raising his sword in salute. Hell, Enrick truly would never live this down.

He turned and started the swim back. Though swimming in the sea wasn't on his list of things to do today, it felt good taking a dip in the cold water on the hot day. He still wanted an increase in pay for doing it. All he could think about was getting back to shore and hopefully doing what he needed to without having to redo any of this. He hated having to do things over anyway.

Once he returned to the shore, he tried to look as imposing as any Highland warrior would, which was easy to do if he thought about facing down Robert Kilpatrick, minus his clothes and dripping wet, his skin covered in goose bumps. He finally reached his clothes on the shore, or his double's, technically. He lifted the long shirt off the sand and held it up and, without thinking, shook off the sand, like he would have done, and belatedly realized the director hadn't called for that in the scene.

He was trying to figure out how to bunch the shirt up in his hand to cover his crotch to make it look natural, but it wouldn't work. He would have held it up and pulled it over his head, if he was doing this for real and not staged, so instead, he held the shirt in one hand, letting the remainder fall to the shore, one muscled leg exposed and let his gaze settle on the heroine, so the top of his shirt was crumpled in his fist, and the rest hanging loose and touching the sand.

The heroine was standing a long distance from him. She was wearing black jeans and black, low-heeled boots and a black tank top—her period clothes while she was in New York City before she was whisked away to a much earlier century to the beach below his castle.

Her hands were gripping the hilt of a claymore, the point of the sword embedded in the sand—which was something a warrior would never do. Then again, she was a woman from the future, so what did she know?

Her eyes were huge and round, her mouth gaping—part of the scene, of course.

He suspected they'd situated the sword with her there for the scene and she hadn't been carrying the heavy weapon around.

Then the director called, "Cut!"

To Enrick's profound relief, that was his cue to move out of the scene. The hero quickly took Enrick's place, all freshly wetted down, his hair dripping wet, his clothes dry and not sporting even a speck of sand. Enrick suspected the water they doused Guy with wasn't half as cold as the water Enrick had swum in. They might have just sprinkled some water on his skin in truth.

As soon as Enrick moved out of the way so they could begin the close-ups of the high-paid actors, three of their Hollywood warriors with speaking parts ran to protect the hero from the woman with the claymore, who couldn't have wielded it unless she'd had magical powers. All seven wolves raced to join them.

Enrick wondered if they would add a magical glow or something to the claymore to make it appear enchanted. Why hadn't Guy grabbed up his sword and defended himself, instead of waiting for his own men to protect him? In the movie version, at least.

If it had been for real, Enrick would have, sans the clothes. Nothing mattered but dealing with the perceived threat. It would have appeared more real, and much more intimate, if he'd tackled the heroine to the sandy beach with his naked body. Sounded more plausible and a hell of a lot more fun. Though the only one he was interested in tackling was Heather and plying her with kisses.

In the meantime, though, Enrick headed toward the stairs, wearing the shirt and kilt. The hero was doing the same on the beach for the film while his men seized the heroine. The wolves stood next to Guy as if they were protecting their lord.

Enrick thought about having a nice hot shower.

He realized, damn it, he couldn't take one yet. He had to wait near the beach to see if the director needed to reshoot any part of the scenes Enrick had been in.

Enrick wasn't expecting Heather to run after him with a supersize towel. When she reached him, she began to push up his long shirtsleeves and dry his arms. He smiled down at her and whispered, "Do you get paid to do this?" Not that anyone would hear them, as far away as they were now from the filming of the actors.

"Oh, aye. It's a privilege to wipe down the lord's cold, wet body," she whispered back.

"I'm a warrior and impervious to cold." He cast her a smirk.

Heather smiled as she made him lean down and towel-dried his hair. "You may be, but they were worried *Guy* would take a chill and they had him dripping with warmed water. With you, the water had to be ice cold. You might have noticed Guy didn't have any goose bumps on his skin."

"I really didn't look. As soon as I was dismissed, it was time to get out of there and all I could think of was taking a nice hot shower." With Heather, it would be even better.

"But it's not a wrap yet."

"Aye. I realized that, belatedly."

Heather reached down with the towel to wipe his legs dry.

He smiled at her. "You know you could do this more often for me."

She shook her head. "I don't want you to take a chill. You're now Guy's double for any of the scenes he can't or won't do. Everyone—their people and ours—is counting on it."

"What?"

"Aye. There's a lot more money in it for you, and the director said he's been watching you and you're perfect to fill in for Guy when he can't do the scenes."

"What happened to his regular double?" Enrick had thought this really was just a one-shot deal.

"He was drunk, got into a brawl at a pub last night, got sick and couldn't work today, so the director fired him."

Enrick shook his head.

"Guess who picked the fight?"

Enrick let out his breath in disgust. "Don't tell me. The Kilpatrick brothers."

"Aye. Robert and Patrick were giving him grief about being an American pretending to be a Highland lord. It was partly Larry's fault. He's got a drinking problem and a temper, but still, if Robert and Patrick hadn't been egging him on, everything might have been fine."

"Did they know he wasn't Guy?"

"I don't think so. One of our men who stuck up for Larry said Robert called Larry by Guy's name, but Larry didn't correct him. Our man knew it wasn't Guy because he could smell the difference."

"So the Kilpatrick brothers thought they could take out the main actor. Bastards."

"Right. Now you're the new double since you look even more like Guy than Larry does, and you're already warrior material so you can take over all those scenes."

"Like making love to the heroine?" No way did Enrick want to do any of those scenes. With Heather in private? Hell yeah. He wondered why Heather had the towel in the first place. Had she been planning to wipe Guy down instead?

Heather paused and frowned at him. "I think Guy believes those are safe enough for him to do. Grant said he would take over the duty of making sure our people are ready for the battles they have to do later if you have to stand in for Guy instead." She sighed. "I don't know how they're going to cover up the discrepancy between the two of you though."

"What discrepancy?" Enrick didn't care one whit about it. They could just do some postprocessing fixes, he figured. As long as he didn't have to do a bunch of retakes on any of the scenes. And he was only teasing Heather about making love with the heroine on-screen. He wasn't interested in her in any way, and he figured it would show if he tried to act like he was.

"You're bigger than he is."

Enrick flexed his muscles. "I'm sure I spend a lot more time working out with a sword than he does, despite that he was in a Viking and gladiator film recently."

"I don't mean your muscles."

Frowning, Enrick glanced down at Heather. "What then?"

She smiled impishly, her face reddening a little bit.

He was about to laugh out loud, thinking she meant his cock, but stopped himself, not wanting to get into trouble for messing up the shoot, if anyone should catch his laughter on the wind. "I'm not sure they can do anything with that in postprocessing." At least he thought that was what she meant.

"Don't let it go to your head. All the girls will think he's got the biggest one around, and that it grew some since the last film where he was showing it off."

Enrick chuckled. "So you were taking measurements?"

Heather turned even redder.

"You had a towel ready to wipe down the double's wet body?" Enrick didn't like the idea that she might have been drying Larry's skin, either, or Guy's. Someone from the film staff should have done it.

"Nay, for you. As soon as Colleen learned you were going to do this, she had one of the other ladies bring the towel down to me. Lana and I were keeping Julia company because she's taking notes, just in case you wondered. Anyway, Colleen told me you were going to swim in the sea and that you could use a towel to dry off."

"What if Lachlan had done the scene instead?" Enrick raised a brow.

"No way would you have let Lachlan take your place, but if you had, I would have generously handed him the towel."

That was what Enrick wanted to hear.

They sat down on the bottom of the steps and watched the scene play out, when Enrick hadn't planned on watching any of this. She brushed the sand off Enrick's feet, and he pulled on his socks and boots.

The main villain suddenly entered the scene and fought the hero and the two guards on the beach, attempted to grab the sword but couldn't manage it, and then vanished. Or at least on film he would. The wolves had taken off down the beach before that had happened, no help at all.

"If this had been for real, you wouldn't have waited for your trusty guards to come and protect you," Heather said.

"I was thinking the same thing." Enrick smiled at Heather, glad she was here for him. "And I would have tackled the woman, but I was thinking of you being in her place."

"Were you really?"

"Aye. She doesn't hold a candle to you."

"Thank you." Heather snuggled next to Enrick. "I think the whole production is fascinating. I can't wait to see it all come together in the film. It's intriguing seeing it in bits and pieces, and then seeing it as one continuous film, though we won't know which parts could end up being cut. Hopefully not your scenes. Still, knowing the production was done here in your castle makes it all the more fun, and seeing friends and family in the roles, even as background actors, is really exciting too, don't you think?"

"Aye." It's definitely something they would talk about for years to come.

"Oh, and by the way, I want to talk to the woman who tried to poison us, once the director calls it a wrap."

"I'll go with you." Enrick was surprised she wanted to talk to the woman again.

"She still hasn't told anyone who made her do it?"

"Nay. But we did learn she'd added salmonella to the stew."

"People could have died! Maybe she'll open up to a woman."

"The one who caught her in the act and held a *sgian dubh* on her?" Enrick raised a brow at Heather.

Heather smiled. "Someone had to do it."

CHAPTER 15

WHEN ENRICK AND HEATHER REACHED THE SMALL, WINDOW-less room equipped with a twin-size bed covered in a blue and white quilt, a blue chintz chair, and a small, round table, they found the woman who'd contaminated the meal. She was sitting on the chair, looking superior and not in the least bit contrite for what she had done. Her chin was tilted up, her arms folded defensively across her waist, her whole posture telling them they weren't going to get a thing out of her.

"I'm Heather, and you are...?" Heather was irritated with the woman, who appeared to feel no remorse for what she'd done.

The woman pursed her lips. She was pretty and petite, with a small face and beautiful long, dark hair under her veil. Her blue eyes narrowed in contempt. "I know who you are. Patrick killed your intended. You act like we're the only ones who start things—"

"Patrick had."

The woman frowned. "Timothy was a hothead. Did he tell you he had dated Robert and Patrick's sister?"

If the woman thought she was going to upset Heather with news she didn't already know, she was wrong. "Aye. She hid the fact she was a Kilpatrick from him. He told me all about it. When he learned she was their sister, he stopped seeing her."

This was not supposed to be about Heather, damn it.

"Is that what he told you? That he didn't know who she was? Of course he did," the woman said.

"Aye, but it doesn't really matter now, does it? He's dead, at the hand of one of her brothers who started the confrontation. You being here has nothing to do with any of this. Unless you did it out of some misplaced sense of revenge on behalf of the Kilpatricks' sister."

The woman didn't say anything, and Heather suspected it wasn't the case.

"Did you know what you were doing when you added bacteria to the cauldrons?" Heather figured the woman had to have. Why would she have worn the same kind of costume they were wearing, sneaked into the castle, and in front of all the other people who were busy in the kitchen while the filming was going on, added something to the fish stew and not have had a clue as to what she was doing?

Looking anywhere but at Heather's gaze, the woman didn't say anything.

"Who told you to add it to the stew?" Heather hoped they could at least get that information out of the woman.

Enrick was looking so growly that Heather thought he might be inhibiting the woman from speaking.

"Enrick, can you leave us alone for a few minutes?" Heather didn't want to dismiss him, but she thought she might get somewhere with the woman if he was not hovering over them.

He cast the woman a hard look, then nodded to Heather and left the room. She was glad Enrick didn't appear to be annoyed with her for wanting to question the woman alone.

Heather shut the door and sat on the bed. "Okay, so who told you to do this?"

At first the woman was mute.

"We'll learn the truth soon enough. You're not protecting anyone, and they don't care that you're here and can't return home. They'll let you take all the blame, and no one has even asked about you, concerned for your welfare." Heather had asked Colleen and that was what she'd told her.

The woman let out her breath in a huff. "Robert Kilpatrick."

Heather was surprised she'd finally told the truth, but wasn't surprised to learn it was him. She tried not to hold the ongoing conflict between the clans against them, but it sure ticked her off that Robert would do something this dastardly.

THE WOLF WORE PLAID

"Why?" Heather was certain she knew why, but she wanted to hear the truth from the woman.

"He's still furious your cousin Cearnach MacNeill took Elaine in when Robert had use of her and her properties. Then the MacQuarries got the contract to have the movie filmed here and he was doubly angry. You're getting paid for the use of your wolves, the horses, the castle and lands, all of you working as extras, the fame and glory. He couldn't be any angrier than he is that you got the contract. If it had been a clan we were in league with, we could have at least taken part in the film, if nothing else. Though I'm not sure that would have satisfied him."

"All right, I totally get that. What I don't get is why *you* would stick your neck out for him."

The woman looked down at her hands clenched in her lap.

"Ohmigod, you love him!" Not that Heather could believe anyone could love that bastard, but then again, some women loved guys who were up to no good, so maybe that was the deal with her.

"I didn't say I loved him," the woman quickly snapped.

But the color in her cheeks said otherwise.

"And he loves you back? Which is why he hasn't said one damn thing about you being taken prisoner?" Heather hated seeing one-sided love affairs. She suspected if Robert had wooed the woman, it was to coax her into doing something dastardly for him.

The woman looked down at her lap again.

"He knows about it. It's not like you just vanished and he's been trying to figure out what happened to you. Your pack leader has been called on this one. He's furious Robert would stoop so low as to do this. To have you do this. Yet what does Robert do? What does Paxton do? Nothing. They don't care if you rot here. They aren't asking for your release. Bargaining for it. Nothing. You'll be lucky if we release you and you're only banished from your pack."

The woman's gaze shot up to meet Heather's.

"Aye, that's what happens when you commit a criminal act for a wolf who doesn't have the pack leader's permission to do something that can negatively affect the whole pack." Heather couldn't believe the woman would be so naive as to not realize that.

"Robert said he got permission from Paxton."

"Okay, well, then either Robert lied, or Paxton lied. And guess what? They're saying you're the one who took it upon yourself to do it. No one asked you to."

"Nay. That's a lie."

"Who do you think they're going to believe? Robert, Paxton, or you?" Heather hoped the woman would realize she was sitting between a rock and a hard place right now.

The woman slumped on the chair. Aye, they wouldn't believe the woman for sure.

"Do you have proof Robert ordered you to do this?" Heather suspected she didn't.

The woman shook her head. "Robert said Paxton wanted this done and he knew I was the best one for the job. He didn't put it in writing."

"To cover himself. So it wouldn't fall back on him."

The woman ground her teeth.

"Does he have the same feelings for you?"

The woman didn't answer her.

Heather suspected not, or the bastard would be making some attempt to get her released. Not to mention he wouldn't have sent her on this dangerous errand in the first place. "Tell me your full name, and we can let Paxton know who you are, at least. Apparently, Robert is denying he even knows who you are."

The woman's eyes widened, but she didn't say anything.

"Despite your attempt to sabotage the fish stew and make everyone deathly ill, the director's keeping the scene, but someone else played your part at the end when she dies for her deceitfulness."

The woman swallowed hard. "It would have just caused people who ate it to have stomach cramps and diarrhea. Nothing that severe."

"Salmonella? What if someone had died from it? How do you know it wasn't something that could be deadly? Robert's a liar, a thief, and not honorable in the least. And here you would be the one to take the blame for it."

The woman bit her lower lip, and Heather was hoping she was considering the possibility she was telling the truth. "He said it was just laxatives."

"It was salmonella. You did it willingly?" Heather asked.

"I'm a McKinley."

"So you're saying you did it willingly and your clan backed Robert's actions, even though both of them are denying it. That it wasn't just Robert's idea."

The woman didn't say anything more right away. "I...I thought it was laxatives."

"Did you know about your people attacking ours on the battle-field before it happened?"

The woman smiled. Heather wanted to wipe the smile off her face. She had been beginning to feel sorry for the duped woman. Not now.

"Do you know of any other plans they have to try and sabotage the film?"

The woman shook her head. "Even if I knew, I wouldn't tell you."

"Fine. You can stay here until they're done filming the movie." Not that Heather made the rules. That was Grant and Colleen's job. But she figured it didn't hurt to say it, and if they said something else to the woman, it wouldn't matter.

"How long will that be?" That was the first real sense of alarm the woman had displayed.

"Three months. Maybe longer." Heather didn't think it was for that much longer, but she didn't want to tell the woman that.

Heather opened the door to the room and said to Enrick, "Can we torture her?"

He chuckled and led Heather out of the room and locked the door. "Did things not go as planned?"

"No. And you *weren't* supposed to laugh when I mentioned the torture business. You were supposed to take it very seriously."

He chuckled again.

"She admitted to poisoning the food, though she said she thought it was laxatives. She was glad to have done it and knew about the men attacking ours beforehand. Other than that, she claims if she knew of any more plans to attack our people, she wouldn't tell us about them. She says Robert had Paxton's sanction for doing this, and of course there's no proof either man told her to do it." Heather was so annoyed. "Can we at least lock her in the dungeon? She could always shift into her wolf, but it just doesn't seem right that she has a nice little room to stay in after what she pulled."

"Let's take a walk in the gardens." Enrick smiled at Heather and took her hand. "That's where she's going. The dungeon. Now that she has admitted she did it and has no regrets."

"Robert Kilpatrick *was* behind the poisoning. And from what I gather, she loves the bastard."

"See, lass? You did get more out of her than any of the rest of us had. If he loves her back, I'm surprised he's not making demands to have her released." He pulled out his phone and began texting Grant.

"I think it might be a one-sided love affair, wishful thinking on her part. I wish we knew what else they were planning to do to sabotage the film."

After putting his phone back in his pocket, Enrick rubbed her back. "Even if she did know, they might change their plans, worried she would tell us what they were."

"True. Do you think they'll try to pull anything else?" She hated them for trying to ruin things for the clans, she thought as she and Enrick made their way out of the castle and into the gardens.

"Aye, I wouldn't put it past them to continue doing stuff to cause us trouble. There's not a whole lot we can do about it other than deal with them as problems arise." He drew her into his arms. "Concerning a more important matter, I want you to know if I'd been less of a workaholic and did something about how I was feeling about you, I would have asked to court you a long time ago."

She smiled up at him. "Oh, really? You were afraid of me. I was much too...wild for you. I'm sure you thought I was irresponsible."

Smiling, he shook his head. "It was that wild part of you that got my attention. The first time you socked me in the head with a snowball, you got my notice. Well, before that, when Lachlan stole a kiss from you and you clobbered him."

She laughed and walked with Enrick through the rose gardens, breathing in the heady floral scent of the pink, red, and white roses.

"I always wondered: If I'd stolen a kiss from you, would you have done the same to me?" Enrick glanced down at her.

"You will never know. Lachlan did it on a dare. If you had too? Maybe. Maybe not." She really didn't know what she would have done. Probably socked him too. The time with the snowball? She was just trying to get his attention, and she hadn't meant to hurt him.

She led him to the gazebo, and they took a seat on one of the benches overlooking the sea. The rest of the gazebo was surrounded by a privacy hedge, and pink climbing roses cascaded over the top of the frame. Even from the castle they were screened in privacy.

Enrick put his arm around her shoulders and pulled her close. "We saw you watching us while we were in sword practice. Your brothers said you were a troublesome lass."

"Ha! They were the ones always getting into trouble. Oran, Callum, and Jamie did so many crazy things that I'm surprised they're still around today."

Enrick smiled, then grew serious again. "They always said you were a wild little wolf."

"I was."

He sighed. "Yeah, I think that's why you always intrigued me. I didn't want to upset you if I had assumed you wanted to date, and you weren't interested or were still feeling bad about your fiancé. Sometimes our kind never seek another mate."

"Nay. It's been two years since he died. I'm still angry with him for fighting Patrick and getting himself killed. But it made me change my mind about him too. If he had lived after what he'd pulled with Patrick, I would have called off the mating, no matter how anyone would have felt about it."

"I would have been glad."

She smiled at Enrick, then frowned. "I didn't respect him for what he'd done, how hotheaded he had become. At one time, I think his wildness appealed to me."

"You dated him longer than I'd thought possible."

"Aye. I…kept delaying the inevitable. I didn't even realize I was doing it, and truthfully, he didn't seem to care all that much. But if we'd been mated wolves, then had children, he would have had to be a good father and not start brawls or teach our kids to behave that way.

"I'm sure, after what I'd witnessed, he wouldn't have settled down and raised them like a levelheaded father should. I'm still angry with Patrick too. I felt he could have cut Timothy and not fatally, but maybe not. Timothy was much bigger than Patrick and could have easily killed him with his bare hands. I do blame Patrick for instigating the trouble. But if Timothy had ignored him, that would have been the end of it," she said.

"I agree on all accounts. I still can't understand why Patrick would have used you to provoke Timothy though," Enrick said.

"Because I was there, and Patrick knew he could do it."

"Aye, but—"

"Timothy told me he'd courted a wolf named Bernice Hanover and he learned after a couple of weeks why she didn't want anyone to know they were dating. She was the Kilpatricks' sister. She'd been married and lost her mate while he was fishing at sea during a storm. She really liked Timothy and he really enjoyed her company, but once he realized who she was related to, he knew they would have nothing but trouble from her brothers and the McKinley clan. He ended the relationship. Naturally, she was upset.

"When her brothers learned she'd been dating Timothy and he'd broken up with her, they felt he'd always known who she was related to and that he'd hurt her to get back at the clan."

"Hell, he never told any of us about that. So when the Kilpatricks saw you with Timothy, they felt you were to blame somehow?"

"Maybe they thought he'd been seeing me all along and he'd only pretended to be interested in her. I don't know. All I know is they wouldn't have allowed him to date their sister, once they learned of it. So they should have been glad he'd ended the relationship."

"But they felt he'd used their sister."

"Right. I just didn't want to tell anyone about what Timothy had done. Because she didn't want him to tell anyone he was dating her, it was all very secretive. Since he was planning to mate me, he knew he needed to tell me about it. He felt guilty about having so much fun with Bernice, and then awful about how mad he'd gotten when he learned the truth. She knew just who he was, and she should have known that she couldn't get away with hiding the truth for long."

"Not unless he'd wanted to break free of the family and move somewhere else with her," Enrick said.

"Exactly. He realized what a mess it would be for their two clans and figured neither side would accept it. Enough about that." Heather pulled Enrick's face down to kiss him. She loved his warm lips and willing caress, pressuring lightly, then more as they got into the kiss. She finally pulled her mouth away from his, feeling a little breathless. She really didn't want to get caught out here kissing him that willingly. Tonight? Sure. In his chamber.

She took a breath of the sweet fragrance of flowers. "I sure hope you got the dozen alarm clocks for tonight."

He smiled.

She was serious though. Well, maybe not about the actual number of alarm clocks they needed, but she thought they could use their phones and two backup clocks, just in case.

"I will have, rest assured. I need to get cleaned up after my swim in the sea. I still feel salty and sandy and smell a little fishy. Did you want to come with me?"

She shook her head. "I need to check on my shop. Besides, if I went with you, I could see me missing a date with my brothers to check out my shop at lunchtime. And you know they would come after you then."

CHAPTER 16

WHEN ENRICK ARRIVED AT HIS ROOM TO SHOWER, HE FOUND three times as many clocks as he'd asked Lachlan for. He laughed out loud. There must have been close to three dozen alarm clocks—from digital to the regular old brass ones—sitting on his dresser, bedside tables, and bachelor chest. Not only that, but after looking over several, he found they were all set to five in the morning.

He chuckled as he stripped out of the double's clothing and headed in to shower and found six more clocks sitting on the bathroom counter. Smiling, he shook his head. He was delighted because he figured that would convince Heather to stay with him again tonight. Not that they would use them all. What a nightmare that would be if they all went off at the same time!

He'd never slept that well at night, usually waking around three and then finally falling back to sleep. By five, he was up. But last night, man, he could really get used to sleeping all night with Heather.

When he got out of the shower, it was lunchtime, but when he called Heather, she reminded him she'd ridden over to her shop with two of her brothers and she would see him later.

Wanting to give her some space, he got dressed. But then Lachlan called him. Enrick figured it was about the clocks.

"I need your help tomorrow with a scene, if you can assist me," Lachlan said.

"Yeah, after you came through on the clocks, sure, as long as I don't have to fill in for Guy. So far, I don't think I will have to, though I'll be there ready for it, just in case."

"Aye, that's what I figured. So while you're not doing anything for him, why don't we meet in the great hall to have lunch and we'll talk. I saw Heather was headed out with her brothers to her shop, so I figured you might want to have lunch with us again."

Yeah, Enrick had kind of turned his attention from his brothers and sister-in-law to being there with Heather instead. "Be right there. And thanks for the clocks. Oh, you didn't tell anyone why you were asking for them, did you?"

Lachlan laughed. "Are you kidding? Everyone witnessed you and Heather missing breakfast and they heard that Maynard fixed you a special one, when he never does that. They certainly wouldn't think I would need an alarm clock. There are a few more than you asked for, but once the word got out, everyone was texting me and dropping them off at my chamber. I didn't have the heart to tell them I had enough about two dozen earlier."

Smiling, Enrick shook his head. "I'll meet you in the great hall."

When he arrived, he joined Lachlan and Grant and Colleen at one of the tables. Five alarm clocks were sitting on the table. He stifled a chuckle.

"We have everything covered, if you need to sleep in," Grant said with a smirk.

"Then if they need me to be Guy's double, you'll take his place?" Enrick asked.

"Hell no."

Colleen laughed.

"That's why I made sure you had enough alarm clocks," Lachlan said. "I don't want to have to take his place either."

"I hope this doesn't embarrass Heather too much," Enrick said.

"Heather? No. She'll get a big kick out of it," Colleen said.

Enrick sure hoped Colleen was right.

Maynard had made grilled turkey, bacon, and swiss cheese sandwiches and cabbage slaw for everyone while Enrick looked over the hunt scenes for tomorrow with Lachlan, concerning the wolves and their part in it.

"It appears the way they want this handled is to have the wolves separate. Four will go one way and the three remaining wolves will run off in the opposite direction in the woods while Guy and his entourage are 'hunting,'" Enrick said.

"Right. If you're not playing the hero in this scene as his double, do you think you could help watch one of the groups of wolves? I was going to ask one of Heather's brothers, but it would be great if you could do it."

"Aye, I can do it. I'm not supposed to be needed until the day after tomorrow to play another role for Guy. I'll take the group of wolves that run off to the east." Enrick was glad he could help his brother in this.

"All right. We'll ride behind the group of men he has with him, and when the wolves take off to check things out, I'll go west, and you'll monitor the other group. We'll be in full dress the whole time. Just make sure you don't get in the way of any of the cameras when you ride off to monitor the wolves."

"Right."

Grant said, "If you need any help, just let me know. I'm always on standby."

"Of course," Lachlan said.

"My short-lived role is over," Colleen said, fanning herself dramatically. "One bite of poisoned fish stew and it was at an end. Julia loved it. She wished she could have played the part."

The guys all smiled.

"We still have that scene where the final battle is fought between the hero and the antagonist, where the wolves attack two of the main villains, but they want to do that scene last, just in case anyone suffers an injury," Lachlan said.

Enrick shook his head. "That would be more of a disaster than they can ever know."

"Aye, that it would," Lachlan agreed.

"Let's pray none of the wolves bite through the armor," Colleen said.

"Aye," Grant said, rubbing her back.

After eating lunch, Enrick got a text to see Heather in the study. "I've got to run."

Lachlan smiled. "An important date, no doubt. It's about time the two of you got together."

"I couldn't agree with you more, Brother." Then Enrick left them and met with Heather in the study, glad neither of them had anything to do this afternoon, though he needed to check with security after this. That was ongoing, no matter what else was taking place.

"I wondered why your brothers never took you to task for dating Timothy," he said, joining Heather on one of the leather sofas. He wondered what her version of the story was, since he'd heard Oran's.

Heather smiled. "Really? You should know me better by now. They didn't know about it until it was too late."

Enrick frowned.

She chuckled. "Since then, they've kept a more watchful eye out." She shrugged. "Of course, I wasn't making the same mistake twice. All I cared about was starting up my business and having fun with it. Dating wasn't a priority for me for the last couple of years."

"Until I kicked the Kilpatricks out of your shop."

She smiled. "You are too funny. I must admit I *was* waiting for you to ask me out. You know, it was hard for me to show any interest in you after I was over Timothy. You were a member of his pack, a friend even. I was afraid you wouldn't see me in a good light for wanting to date you."

"Hell, I was dying to ask you out, but I was afraid you would see me the same way." Even though he had a hard time admitting that even to himself, still figuring they wouldn't suit. He realized just how much his dad's counseling him had changed him and his ways, so much so that he'd been afraid Heather might influence him to return to his reckless manner. But she had changed too.

"I'm glad we didn't wait any longer. Since you need to check on security, do you mind if I go with you? I don't have anything else to do today."

"Aye, sure. Get a rain jacket. It's drippy out there."

"Pick me up at my room."

"Okay, I'll do that." That was the first time she'd wanted him to come to her room. He hoped that was a sign of her feeling comfortable with everyone knowing they were together, if anyone was still clueless.

When Enrick arrived to pick Heather up at her room, he was wearing cargo pants, a long T-shirt, a rain jacket and boots, and carrying a hunting rifle. No sense in carrying a sword or *sgian dubh* when he could protect them better with a rifle.

Each of the men on guard duty beyond the castle was dressed for the weather, wearing whatever was more comfortable for them and not making them an easy target. They were also armed with either hunting rifles or shotguns.

So far, they hadn't had trouble with the McKinleys or Kilpatricks except for during the film shoots. That was bad enough, but Enrick was glad it wasn't an ongoing battle through the day and night. He suspected the reason for that was not everyone from the McKinley pack was involved in the shenanigans.

When Enrick and Heather headed out into the light rain to check on security and see if guards were posted where they were supposed to be, she was eager to identify weak spots in their defense. Enrick loved how she wanted to help and offered valuable ideas. That it wasn't just a lark with her, a walk in the park while he had a job to do.

She joked with the guys on guard duty at each of the posts they came to. Of course, the men hadn't been expecting Enrick to bring Heather along on the trek, and they were amused and eager to take a little respite and enjoy the visit, unlike when only he showed up and it was more businesslike. "Any trouble?" "No, all's quiet."

"Good. Let me know if you have trouble." "Aye, I will." And that was usually the gist of the night security checks. Not with Heather. They were fun.

"What knave would take his ladylove on a walk in the night in the misty rain?" one of the men asked, giving Enrick a hard time.

He took it in good humor.

"A braw Highland warrior who is agreeable and wishes to please his ladylove by taking her with him as she has asked. Would you not have done the same if a lady had asked it of you?" Heather asked, her chin tilted up, her arms folded at her waist.

"Nay. She would prove too much of a distraction as I sit at my post. But now if I had Enrick's job of checking on all the guard posts and everything in between, aye, I would. Especially if she was as fair and fun as you."

She laughed, and then she and Enrick continued on to the next guard post. Everyone loved seeing her, and he was grateful for that.

"Now, ye are a bright spot in the night. Here I thought I would only be seeing ol' Enrick on his nightly rounds," another of their men said. "'Tis better than a flask of mead."

Enrick smiled. She was the bright spot in his life. And he realized how much she was in everyone else's lives too.

"I bet you say that to all the lasses who come to visit you while you're on duty," she said.

The man chuckled. "Enrick would have my head if I had a lass visiting me while I was supposed to be guarding."

"That is the right answer," Enrick said and smiled down at Heather.

She sighed. "We will let you get back to work." And then she took Enrick's hand and moved him along again.

"You do realize you are making the men on guard duty wish they had the pleasure of your company tonight, don't you?" Enrick asked her as they moved through the dark woods to the next guard post.

She smiled up at him. "Aye." She was such a vixen.

He was glad their relationship had changed from just being friends to so much more. He paused to think about that for a moment. He was in love. With her. With all her cheeriness and wildness. She might have settled down, done well with her shop, but he realized it was her wildness that really accounted for his fascination with her. Her spontaneity made her a pleasure to be with.

They finally finished the rounds, and she had been a trouper the whole way, despite the wetness and cool air. He hadn't even noticed how long they'd been out because she made the task pleasurable. He didn't plan to drag her out every night. But he wouldn't mind the company anytime she wanted to do this with him. At least until they no longer had to post guards around the clock.

As they headed back to the castle, he asked, "How does Chinese takeout dinner in my chamber sound?"

"Excellent. I haven't had any in eons. I would love jasmine rice and sweet and sour pork and an egg roll."

"Okay, that sounds good. I'll order it when we return to the keep. I'm sure you'll want to get into some dry things before you come to my chamber."

"That will be perfect. I need to pack a bag too."

Now that was what he loved to hear. Until she did it, he kept thinking she would change her mind.

Enrick gave her a kiss in the hallway before she headed for her chamber, and then he went to his and was calling in an order of Chinese takeout for their dinner on the way there. When he walked into the room, he saw the alarm clocks sitting everywhere in his chamber, having forgotten about them completely. Every time he saw them, he smiled.

He set up several candles on the dresser, table, and bedside tables for a romantic evening and lit them.

He'd just changed out of his wet clothes and into jeans and a long-sleeved T-shirt, but nothing else. No boxer briefs or socks or boots.

Then he got a text from Lachlan: I just happened to be in the inner bailey when an order of Chinese food was delivered. Believe me, if I hadn't been armed with my sword, I'm sure some of the other men would have claimed your food.

Enrick laughed, then texted: Thanks for protecting our dinner order with your life.

Lachlan was at his door a few minutes later with a sack of the food, two plates and silverware, wineglasses, and a bottle of wine in a picnic basket, making this a first-class dinner instead of Heather and Enrick just eating the meals from the takeout boxes with plastic forks or chopsticks. "Here you go, enjoy. I think a bunch of us are going to place an even bigger order and have Chinese tonight. Maynard said he was all for it too." Lachlan glanced at all the clocks and the candles and smiled. "I'm taking notes for when I'm in your position. But I won't need the alarm clocks."

"Just you wait, Brother, when you have a lassie in your arms at night."

Lachlan laughed. "I'm getting out of here before she arrives."

"Thanks for bringing the plates and wine too."

"Aye, you have to do it right if you're going to have a candlelight dinner. Colleen told me to bring up the plates and wineglasses. I thought of the wine." Lachlan opened the door and there was Heather, bag in hand, blushing beautifully. Lachlan smiled. "I delivered the food. Getting out of your hair now." Then he hurried off.

Enrick took her bag from her, and as soon as she saw the alarm clocks, she burst out laughing. He laughed too. "I didn't expect them all to show up like that. They're all set to go off at five," he said, serving the Chinese food on the china plates.

She took in a deep breath of the broccoli and pepper beef, jasmine rice, and sweet and sour pork. "No way. One alarm clock and our two phones should be enough of a wake-up call for us in the morning." She started turning off all the alarm clocks but his digital one and then sat down to dinner. "I love the candles and wine. You sure can be a romantic."

"Thanks. I had to scrounge them up from Colleen."

Heather smiled. "I bet she wishes Grant would do something like this for her. When did you find the time to gather up all those clocks?"

"Lachlan did it for me."

She frowned. "He didn't tell everyone why he needed them, did he?"

"He said everyone already knew why I needed them."

She laughed, but she was blushing again.

"What did Lana say about you coming to stay with me?" Enrick figured she would have had something to say.

"It was inevitable. Nothing she could say would talk me out of it."

"Why would she want to talk you out of it?" He hoped Lana wasn't against their relationship because he knew Heather valued their friendship.

"Don't you know she has also had a crush on you forever?"

"No, only that you did. And that's all that mattered to me. She's out of luck. I've…" He hesitated. Was this the right time to confess his love to her? Maybe he should date her longer and give her the chance to feel the same way about him as he did about her. A crush was not the same as being in love with that person. He hated to admit he was afraid of a rejection.

She glanced up from taking a bite of pork. "Aye?" Her eyes were soft, and her lips parted, looking perfectly kissable.

"I don't know if it's too early to say anything about it—"

"You want me to live with you for an eternity." She sounded like she was joking.

He hoped it wouldn't be a shock to her when he asked if she would be his mate.

"Or not." She smiled as if dismissing the notion and sipped some of her water.

"I do."

Her lips parted in surprise.

"Aye, I've given it a lot of thought and I don't want it any other way. If you told me you were running off with Spencer, the villain in the movie, I would have hunted him down and convinced you he wasn't the one for you. That I was the only one for you."

She laughed. "*Who* told you about him asking me on a date? Julia?"

"Lana. She said if I didn't make my claim to you soon, some villain was going to take you away and we'd never see you again."

"Lana did? She is such a contradiction. She'd been telling me to take it slow with you or I would scare you off."

"No way in hell. Really?"

Heather laughed and he loved her laughter. He swore it bounced off all the brass clocks in the chamber in a melodious way, making it even prettier.

"She is working behind the scenes to make this happen, it appears." Enrick couldn't help but be amused.

"Aye. I think if we decided we weren't right for each other, she would make her play for you. There are several lasses who are interested, you know, and she doesn't want to lose out to them, if I said no to a mating. Though she knows she doesn't stand a chance if I'm still in the running." Heather sighed and reached over and took Enrick's hand and squeezed. "I've dated all kinds of guys, trying to get you out of my system."

"Ah, Heather, me too. I mean, lasses."

She chuckled. "I know. One date and they were history. All the women I know said if you ever went out on a date with a woman more than once, she'd be the one you had chosen for your own. I'm all for giving up the dating game. I want to keep doing things like this because it's important to show we care about each other no matter what else is going on in our lives, but I love you, Enrick MacQuarrie, and always have."

"You have made me the happiest wolf alive." He was afraid he was being too impulsive this time, like he'd been in the past. Reckless, foolhardy, which was why his father had taken him aside to tell him someday he would be second-in-command of the pack and he needed to be Grant's righthand man, not a liability. Enrick *hadn't* taken those words to heart until his dad had been murdered, and Grant took over. From that day forth, Enrick had often pushed away that frivolous part of him that could be way too carefree.

"I know why you changed, Enrick. Lachlan told me the talk your father had with you, and when your father died, you truly had to adjust and become the subleader everyone expected you to be. But you're also fun to be with and lighthearted and caring, and you still do things that really are you. That part of your character will always be with you. That's why I love you. I wouldn't give you up for anything." She finished off the rest of her sweet and sour pork and licked her fingers, like he was eager to do.

"That's good to hear because I love you too. And if you're agreeable, you're not returning to the guest chamber to stay with Lana."

"She will be *so* disappointed."

Enrick raised a brow in question, concerned Lana didn't like sleeping by herself in the castle. He would endeavor to find someone else to share the chamber with her if she didn't want to be alone. He wasn't giving up Heather for anything.

"She will have lost out. She's happy to have the chamber to herself."

He laughed. "Good, because I had hoped you would be agreeable to a mating and you would stay here with me through the end of the filming. After that? We'll have to decide, my castle or yours, or something in between."

"That's to discuss at another time." She drank the rest of her glass of burgundy and rose from her chair.

Enrick hastily got up from his and pulled her into his arms. "You are sure? Because when we start, I won't want to stop."

"If you stop, I will never forgive you."

He laughed. He loved her. "Then I have no intention of stopping."

CHAPTER 17

ENRICK'S WARM BREATH CARESSED HEATHER'S CHEEK AS HE nuzzled her face, and she was drawn to his wolf magnetism like she always was. Her feelings ran deep for the Highland wolf, every fiber of her being attuned to his touch. And wanting more.

She ran her hands over his arms, licked her lips, and lifted her head for a kiss. He leaned down and brushed his lips against her mouth in a tender way, and she felt her heart hitch. She wanted to ravish her sexy wolf senseless.

He ran his hands down her back, and they felt hot and large and so good as he caressed her. Their mouths connected again, this time lingering.

"Hmm, sweet and sour, just like I like you." He licked the seam of her mouth.

She nipped at his lower lip. "I am not sour. Sweet? Aye."

He smiled and wrapped his arms tightly around her, giving her a bear hug and nuzzling her hair with his face. "The rain and wind cling to you as if we've just run as wolves in the woods."

She wished they could run again like that, here, and without having to take an army of bodyguards with them wherever they went. "So do you." And like musky male who was getting totally turned on.

Kissing him again, she ran her hands up his T-shirt, stroking his abs. She slid her fingers over his flat nipples that instantly rose to her touch. She gently tweaked them, and he groaned.

Inserting her leg between his, she rubbed his stiffening cock with her thigh. There was something hot and sexy about a man wearing well-worn jeans when his erection was swelling with need.

He slid his hands down to her buttocks and lifted them,

pressing her mons against his thigh. Ohmigod, she felt she could come right then and there. His mouth was on her neck, just below her ear, and he was kissing and licking, his thigh doing a number on her mons. She was way too absorbed in the feel of him working her up.

She pressed her breasts against his chest and slid her hands down to his hips, holding on as their pheromones began to sing to each other. She couldn't help wondering: If she had pushed the issue of dating him sooner, would they have come to this point earlier in their relationship? It didn't really matter, though, in the scheme of things. Because of their longevity, they could make up for it for many, many years to come.

He nipped her ear and she was reminded of the time when she'd done that to him as a wolf and he'd tackled her to the ground. She tackled him to the bed before she gave it any serious thought. She was between his legs, resting against his bulging cock, and he was smiling up at her, running his hands through her hair.

Then she slid his shirt up his chest and kissed his bare skin. He wedged his leg between hers and began to rub again. She wanted to groan out loud. She slid the palms of her hands over his peaked nipples. He moaned and ran his hands under her T-shirt this time, sliding his hands up her back until he found her bra and unfastened it.

She felt sexy and free in that instant. He pulled her shirt over her head and tossed it aside, then pulled her bra straps down her arms. She lifted a bit, pressing against his groin, making him groan again. Never in a million years would she think she would ever be here with Enrick like this.

He pulled off her bra the rest of the way. He sat up on the bed and pulled his long-sleeved T-shirt off and threw it on the floor.

Bare chest to bare chest, she kissed his mouth again, running her hands through his hair and he stroked hers. She loved feeling their bare skin touching like this and was gladder still that they were finally going to go all the way to mate. His fingers felt dreamy in her hair as he slid them through the silky strands. To her surprise, he pulled her legs apart and sat up on the edge of the bed with her facing him.

He began working on her jeans that were a little damp from their walk to the guard posts. At least Enrick had the sense to change before she arrived. She'd been so eager to have dinner with him that she had hurried to pack and then see him. She'd left her wet raincoat in her chamber, so she would have to retrieve it later if she needed it again.

But now she realized she still had her shoes and socks on and he was barefooted and ready for her to pull off his jeans. She unfastened his belt and he undid her button and zipper. She was going to get off his lap to remove her shoes, but he held her in place and slid his hand between her legs and rubbed her jeans-covered mons.

Och, he was doing things to her that were making her dripping wet with need. Forget about damp jeans. Her panties were even wetter.

He was rubbing her clit through her clothes the whole time, and she was way past wanting to be naked with him. Moaning with the overwhelming pleasure of his touch propelling her to the heavens, she unfastened his jeans and pulled down his zipper. His cock sprang free and she was so surprised he wasn't wearing boxer briefs that she looked up at him, her mouth gaping.

Smiling, he moved her aside so he could pull off his jeans. Then he removed her shoes and pulled off her jeans. His fingers got a grip on her panties and he slid them down her legs. He slipped one of her socks off, and then the other.

Man, was he wolfishly sexy. Next time, she wanted to do this when he was wearing his kilt. Then she wondered, had he been going commando the whole time he'd worn his? She wished she'd thought of it before and asked him.

He sat back down on the bed and pulled her onto his lap

again, and she wasn't sure what he had in mind. He lifted her legs so her feet were resting on the bed and then pinned them under his arms. She felt exposed and sexy. At first, he was kissing her mouth, his hands on her breasts, caressing and massaging, then his thumb rubbed the sensitive nipple and she arched her back and moaned. He ran his other hand down her waist until he reached between her legs and began to stroke again. She loved this position so she could touch him too, running her hands up his hard abs, caressing his nipples, kissing his mouth with exuberance.

Every stroke of her clit brought her closer to climax. And she could barely breathe as he continued to touch her so intimately. Then he slid a finger into her and moved it in and out and she practically came. But then he was stroking her again, kissing her mouth, tonguing her, his free hand sliding down to cup her buttock and squeeze.

She loved the way he made love to her, slowly, sensually, not with just the purpose of having sex, but making a deeper connection, showing her he truly loved her, a joining that would make them feel as one—complete.

As soon as he slid two fingers between her feminine folds, she shattered and cried out his name, saying she loved him, and sank against him, luxuriating in the feel of the orgasm as it rushed through her.

"*Tha gaol agam ort.* I love you," he said, kissing her mouth again. Then he slid his hands under her buttocks and lifted her, pulling her closer and pressing his rigid cock between her legs. Every inch of his thickness filled her to the max. The climax still rippled through her, and now she was embracing his cock deep inside of her. Then he began to rock into her, and she thought she would come again before long with the hot, sexy friction he created between them.

Enrick was glad Heather hadn't minded trying something different while he made love to her. Body and soul, they were connected, and he couldn't have loved her more. He rocked into her, thrusting slowly at first, his hands on her hips, speeding up the action and slowing it down, wanting to keep the momentum going, but wanting to last too. With her, everything she did to him, from kissing to touching, made him hard with want. Smelling her sweet scent—lavender and woman and heather from their time out-of-doors, the forest and the rain—turned him on even more. Not to mention their pheromones were driving him crazy. Even her soft moans, breathless moments, and her cry of passion pushed him toward the precipice. He should have done this long ago, claimed her for his own. Made her his mate. Whatever it took.

But at least now it was done. They were together like they should have always been. Through her, he was complete.

She rubbed her breasts against his chest and kissed his throat and neck, his jaw, moving upward until she could reach his mouth and pressed her tongue between his parted lips. She slid her hands around his arse and squeezed. Hell, he thought he had all the control. Between the friction of her nipples rubbing against his chest, her tongue in his mouth, and her hands on his arse, he couldn't hold on any longer.

He exploded inside her and said he loved her in Gaelic, and she smiled and kissed his mouth again.

"I love you too." And then she pushed him back against the bed as he continued to thrust upward into her until he was done.

He wrapped his arms around her and smiled at her smiling face. "You are the most beautiful she-wolf in the world, you know?"

"You are the hottest wolf I know."

Heather only wanted to luxuriate in Enrick's arms until they fell asleep. They were truly mated and this felt so right, but she kept thinking that if they didn't make sure all the alarms were turned off, she could imagine them scrambling out of bed in the morning to shut all of them off.

Thankfully, Enrick was of the same mind. He made the move first, and she left the bed after that. They made sure only one alarm was set and both cell phone alarms, then put them on the dresser so they would have to get up to turn them off. Then it was time for more snuggling, and she suspected they would be making love all over again after they had both rested for a while.

CHAPTER 18

EARLY THE NEXT MORNING, THE JANGLING OF THE ONE ALARM on the dresser, and the five they missed on the bathroom counter, and the music from their phones, had Enrick and Heather groaning, laughing, and jumping out of bed to turn them all off in a hurry.

Enrick shook his head. So much for remembering to check the ones in the bathroom last night. They would have slept, too, if it hadn't been for the alarms going off, as tired as they'd both been.

"We'll have to find time to take a nap," Enrick said.

"Ha! As if we would sleep." She hurried to dress and he did the same.

They both were wearing their kilts, Enrick because he had to watch the wolves this morning in the hunt scene, and Heather in case she was needed at the last minute for some part.

They rushed down to the great hall for breakfast. Heather got a text from Lana. "Lana asked if we're mated yet."

Enrick smiled at Heather. She sighed. "I texted her back to say we were but she's the first one who knows it. We need to let our pack leaders—" She stopped speaking abruptly as she saw Ian visiting with his mate, Julia, and Colleen, Grant, and Lachlan. Even her brothers, who usually ate breakfast before they left Argent Castle, were at the table enjoying the meal.

"It looks like there's no better time than the present, unless you want to wait a bit to tell everyone." Enrick hoped she didn't, but he was willing to do whatever she wanted.

"Oh, we're doing this. I don't want any other lass thinking you're still available." Heather took hold of his hand and headed for the high table.

He smiled down at her. "That was my thought concerning you and the male wolves out there."

"No problem with me. I've got my wolf."

He laughed.

When they joined the others at the high table, Heather brightly said, "It's done. No need to guess about it."

Everyone hooted and hollered at the head table, making everyone else eating breakfast in the great hall turn and clap.

"Yeah, no more even thinking about ogling Heather," Enrick said to the bachelor male wolves in the great hall as he pulled out Heather's chair for her.

"Same goes for you ladies where Enrick is concerned." Heather gave them a bright smile, looking pleased and on top of the world like Enrick was feeling.

"A wedding in the plans?" Julia asked.

"Aye, we just have to figure out where to have it." Heather bit into her egg sandwich.

"At Argent," Ian said as if he was in charge of planning Heather's wedding.

Julia gave her mate a look.

"She's my cousin, and she's in my pack. The MacQuarries will have to come to Argent Castle to celebrate the wedding." Ian sounded adamant, but Enrick knew he would agree to whatever Heather wanted.

She looked up at Enrick. "It's totally up to you. I don't care where we do it as long as you're happy."

"All right. We'll do it at Argent Castle."

"I'm giving you away, as your eldest brother," Oran said.

She laughed. "Can I have any say in my wedding plans?"

"Yes," Julia said.

"Only if it matches what we say," Oran said.

Enrick stifled a laugh. He knew Heather would do whatever she wanted, when she put her mind to it. He would help when she needed him, but otherwise, he was letting her decide.

"When?" Julia asked.

"After the filming is done," Enrick said. Okay, so he did have something to say about it. He was Guy's stand-in after all, and if he was needed, he had to be at Farraige Castle. So did Heather.

"Right. He's the hero of the movie." Heather smiled at Enrick and patted his thigh.

Enrick shook his head. "Stand-in. And Heather has her roles to play, so after the filming is done."

"That goes without saying," Ian said. "Both of you have important jobs to do."

"We can help you figure it out. Colleen, me, and the others at Argent Castle," Julia said.

"Aye, as soon as we are finished with all of this," Heather agreed.

Enrick was glad she had a lot of women who would help her with all the coordinating and such.

Lachlan hurried to finish his breakfast. "Congratulations to the both of you. If you need any advice, Heather, just call on me."

Enrick smiled at his brother. Knowing Lachlan, his advice would be hilarious. Enrick quickly leaned over and kissed Heather on the cheek. "I'll see you at lunch down on the field?"

"Aye, I'll bring the picnic basket."

Everyone was smiling. No one else was getting that kind of special treatment.

"Okay, good. We need to get going if we're going to make this shoot." Enrick kissed her again, and then he and Lachlan hurried off, stopping by one of the rooms where the "wolves" were penned up to let them out.

When Enrick and Lachlan and the wolves reached the ancient forest, a thick fog was rising from the floor filled with ferns, mosses, and liverworts. It was perfect for the scene, making it appear primordial, though he hoped they wouldn't have trouble with security because of how dense the fog was. It couldn't have been more mystical, everything verdant and the leaves and grass shimmering with water droplets. The wolves were running alongside the horses ridden by Guy and some of his warriors, all who were main characters. The wizard was with him, too, wearing long robes and a coned hat.

Several MacQuarries were riding behind the main party as part of Guy's guard/hunting force for the film and Lachlan was also, watching the wolves. The wolves knew their role in the film: run alongside the main party, then stop and listen to something only they could hear and smell, lifting their noses, taking deep breaths of the water-laden air, their ears twitching back and forth, hearing the sounds only wolves could hear. Guy and the wizard would be watching the wolves for their reactions, hoping the animals would help them on the hunt.

Enrick confirmed he wasn't needed to be Guy's double, so he was helping Lachlan with the wolves and just watching the woods for trouble.

The seven wolves ran off into the woods and the party of mounted Highlanders halted their horses, all part of the script.

"There must be trouble ahead, milord," one of Guy's men said, his voice darkly concerned. "The wolves would have alerted us had they found prey."

In reality, if the wolves had been on a real hunt, they wouldn't have made any noise. For the film, they wanted it this way. Silence for the bad guys, barking like darn dogs for prey. Even though Grant had told them it wouldn't be that way.

"Aye, keep a look out, men," Guy said in his rich baritone voice.

In the meantime, the wolves were supposed to be searching the area for the enemy and cameras were filming their movements. Lachlan had taken off after the wolves he was supposed to be watching but was staying out of the cameras' views so he could make sure everything went as planned. On horseback too, Enrick was monitoring the second group of wolves that had split off from the others.

He didn't think anything would go wrong. The wolves knew

just what they were supposed to do. The director had been impressed they could do so many things as if they'd rehearsed the scenes, which they had, but as *lupus garous* that made all the difference in the world.

Suddenly, out of the primordial mist, Enrick saw three wolves racing to meet his wolves head-on. All three were from the Kilpatrick-McKinley clan. He'd seen them with their pack before, though he didn't know them in their human form.

Heart pounding, Enrick yanked his cell phone out of his fur-covered sporran and texted Grant: Three of the Kilpatrick-McKinley clan's wolves are in the process of attacking ours. I'm shifting and fighting them.

Unable to waste precious time waiting for a response—though in a situation like this, it might have been prudent to give Grant the chance to say yay or nay—Enrick dismounted and stripped out of his kilt, shirt, socks, and boots, leaving behind his sword and *sgian dubh*. He shifted into the wolf, hoping nobody caught him at it, though he'd been listening, smelling the scents in the area, and watching for any signs of humans, but he hadn't seen any. He raced to fight the attacking wolves, protecting his own men, furious that the clan would resort to even further measures to disrupt the shooting of the film and give the MacQuarries, and all wolves in general, a bad name. Somebody was going to get seriously injured one of these times. Maybe even killed. Their wolves had brought it on themselves, but his wolves? That would be unconscionable.

Enrick knew that when the wolves fought, the cameras would catch the action, and who knew what everyone would think. He hoped they didn't keep the cameras rolling as he ran into the middle of the fighting wolves and bit one in the neck, holding on until the offending wolf got the message. He would either back off and run away with his tail tucked between his legs or Enrick was going to injure him. The wolf yipped and Enrick released him, hoping the aggressor wolf wasn't pretending to want to break off the attack. The rogue wolf got the message and took off as fast as he could, tail tucked between his legs, the jackass. He was a McKinley, and so were the other two attacking wolves. Enrick didn't know them by their given names though.

He immediately targeted the next wolf fighting Edward Playfair, one of Colleen's cousins. Enrick bit the attacking wolf's leg, letting him know in no uncertain terms he would break it if the other wolf didn't turn tail and run. The wolf yipped in fright and ran off with a limp. The other was fighting with Edward's brother, William, and when the rogue wolf realized his partners in crime had left without him, he whipped around and raced off before Enrick could take him on next.

Enrick's wolf's instinct was to chase them down and kill all of them, without the cameras there to capture the scene because a dead *lupus garou* would shift into his human form. But he needed to make sure his own wolves were okay.

Enrick greeted his wolves. They were panting, chests heaving, the smell of anger and adrenaline rolling off them in waves. Just as much as his scent was giving off the same irritated smell. At least they were not badly wounded, and their healing genetics would help to heal the wounds quickly. A little blood was dribbling on Edward's ear and William was sporting bloody fur on his shoulder. Enrick had been so focused, so angry when he tore into the wolves that he realized his wolves hadn't even retaliated against the rogue wolves. The rogues must have been shocked an alpha was suddenly attacking them.

He knew it meant they would have to reshoot the scene, and he hated that. Not to mention, the director would wonder if they'd made a mistake in trusting the MacQuarries' tame wolves. He was sure they wouldn't believe another group of wolves had attacked them.

Once Enrick was assured his kinsmen were fine, Grant and Lachlan galloped up on horseback, Lachlan in his Scottish garb, Grant in jeans, boots, and a shirt, both their faces red with rage.

"What the hell happened?" Grant asked Enrick, as if he'd for-gotten Enrick couldn't just shift right there in front of them and the film crew who were in the area and speak. Enrick woofed at him, telling him he would return, then raced off to where he'd tied his horse and removed his clothes. Once he arrived there, he made sure no one was around, shifted into his human form, and hurried to dress.

Then he mounted his horse and headed back to the group of wolves to tell Grant, and everyone else within hearing range, what had happened.

"They were from the Kilpatricks' wolf pack," Enrick said, since no one would know that he meant *lupus garous*. Instead, the film crew would think the Kilpatricks had raised a wolf pack of their own. Enrick was glad the director had used the MacQuarries' wolf pack and not a real group of trained wolves. He could imagine what a disaster that would have been. The wolves wouldn't have under-stood the others were not fully wolves. The Kilpatricks would have had to deal with real wolves, not Grant's men who would hold back and not kill their men at that point. At least not in front of the cameras. The real wolves might have killed the Kilpatricks for attacking them, if that had been the case.

"Were the wolves from the pack I wouldn't use because the man had too many conditions and wanted too much money?" the director asked, sounding shocked as he finally made it to the scene of the wolf fight.

"No, but I know whose wolves they are," Grant said vaguely. "We'll take care of it."

Wolf to wolf if they had to. Enrick believed neither of the clans would want an all-out war with another pack, but it would lead to that if they didn't rein their men in. It wasn't like in the old days where the clans—and in their case, wolf packs—would battle to the death and none of it would be reported. The clans would take care of their own dead and dying, and no one would think anything of it. It was just business as usual. Just like it was with the human clans in centuries past.

They had to be a little more careful about how they handled the situation now, particularly when they had a human film crew and others watching what was going on. If Enrick and his wolves could have gotten the McKinley wolves off to an isolated area, they wouldn't have hesitated to kill them. They had to have peace among them, or war. There seemed to be no in-between.

Wolves had to show they wouldn't back down or they would lose the battle.

"Your wolves are injured though," the director said. "We can't have any animals injured in the making of the film."

"They will be as good as new in a couple of days. I'll take full responsibility for them," Grant said.

Enrick suspected the director wasn't comfortable with what had happened. If any animal rights' activist learned of it, they could share that with the world on social media and then what would happen? The wolf packs in Scotland certainly didn't need the bad publicity, but the Kilpatricks and their cousins were too bent on revenge to see that what they were doing could affect the bigger picture for all their kind.

Enrick suspected the problem was with a few of their clansmen, not all of them. Enrick and his kin had to remember that when dealing with the bastards.

Colleen's cousins were two of the worst injured. Enrick wondered if they'd held back because of the cameras rolling, being unsure how far they were allowed to go to defend themselves. The two wolves had never been in a wolf fight since they'd lived here. They'd been in wolf fights between *lupus garou* packs in America, but they were part of a new pack, with new rules and ways of doing things.

Enrick hadn't given a damn about the cameras, only about protecting his new kinsmen and chasing off the aggressor wolves. Plus the brothers were both beta wolves, which probably had something to do with them just trying to defend themselves instead of attacking the other wolves back. He was certain Colleen would be mortified that the other pack's wolves had attacked them.

"Can we go on with the shoot?" The director sounded a bit concerned.

"Aye, sure. One of the wolves is injured in the scene. That can be that wolf, if he's up to it," Grant said, motioning to Colleen's cousin William. "Your men are in a fight. Our wolves will do their part and fight my men who are playing your enemy," Grant said. "The wolves are fine. We have others we can bring in if you're worried about the two that were bitten."

"If you're sure they're okay, we'll go with them. But I am also concerned about further wolf attacks," the director said.

Guy agreed with the director. "Yeah, what if they attacked *us* next?"

That was another thing that differed between Enrick and his clone. Enrick didn't have any trouble taking the real enemy to task. Though he understood how Guy felt. He didn't have big teeth like a wolf did to deal with the other wolves.

"Some of our men are chasing the wolves down. They'll tranquilize them and return them to their owner," Grant said. "They'll be taken care of. I'll show you pictures of them to let you know it's been dealt with. And that no harm will come to the wolves."

Enrick wished he'd been on the detail to take down the wolves that had fought their own. He just hoped his packmates would catch them before they got away. He knew Grant wouldn't be turning them over to the "owner" of the wolves. They would hang on to the aggressors, just like they were holding the woman who had tried to make everyone sick.

At this rate, they could have a bunch of the Kilpatrick/ McKinley clan locked up. But the MacQuarries needed to deal with the ones responsible for ordering the attacks. The problem was that others could still take up the cause and fill their shoes. That was what had happened in the past, and the clans couldn't seem to move forward without taking several steps back.

Colleen's cousins' ears perked up to hear they would still be able to act in the film. They both wagged their tails, trying to show their enthusiasm.

Enrick smiled at them. "They're eager to please."

William even gave a little woof, and his brother followed suit, as if he thought it was a good idea to play it up for all it was worth.

The director nodded. "Okay, let's get on with it."

Everyone took their places again, and Guy and his men were soon fighting the MacQuarrie men, the ones who were supposed to be the enemy, led by a couple of the main villainous characters. The wolves were helping Guy's guards fight the onslaught. William fell onto his side, pretending to be injured, though since he had been wounded in the earlier wolf fight, Enrick hoped he was really all right. After filming was done, Enrick would give William an earful if he had been pretending not to be too badly injured to continue in the film.

In the meantime, the fight went on while Enrick and others watched for any signs of the real enemy coming to cause more trouble. They'd tripled the number of men out there to act as security. Grant had even called Ian to see if he could scrounge up some more of his men to do battle with the enemy clan if they showed their wolf faces there again.

Enrick knew Ian would be all too eager to help.

They continued to redo scenes until the director was satisfied.

As soon as the battle scene was finally over, everyone took a lunch break. The MacNeills served a variety of meat pies from their pie shop, and the MacQuarries provided other meals for some of the staff. Everyone was enjoying having their lunch in the field, just like the Highlanders would have had in the past, minus the modern meals. In olden times, meals might have consisted of something they caught on the hunt and bannock bread cooked over a fire.

Heather was there with a number of women who would participate in the next scene where the campfire was set up. But everyone needed a hearty meal and their half-hour break before they nibbled on some food in the campfire scene.

In the meantime, Grant informed the director that all three aggressor wolves had been caught and were caged in a wolf run until his clan could deal with the consequences. But Grant was handling it. He showed the director a picture.

Enrick knew that in truth the wolves were caged at the MacNeills' castle. Grant would explain more to Enrick and the others in charge at a meeting after the last scenes were shot today.

Enrick realized how different things were for him now. Instead of wanting just to get on with business, as much as this was so important, he was doubly angered at the rogue wolves for interrupting his time with Heather. Tonight, he'd wanted to spend all the rest of his time with her, not dealing with this other issue.

Heather joined him, bringing him a steak pie, knowing it was his favorite of all the meat pies she made. She brought her little picnic basket, water for them because she knew he needed to stay hydrated, and a wash bucket so he could clean up. They had stations set up for everyone else who needed to wash their hands before they ate, but she made him feel like a star by providing his very own bucket of water, like the stars had.

Even the stars ate in the field, knowing if they didn't, the time allotted for their lunch hour would be depleted just coming and going from there.

Enrick and Heather chose a spot away from the others so they could have some privacy. Not only because they were newly mated, but because he knew she would want to know what had happened to everyone on the hunt and he couldn't say in front of the humans.

"They're all talking about it." Heather sounded upset about the wolf attack as she sat down on the picnic cloth.

Enrick sat next to it, though he wasn't muddy like before, and leaned over and kissed her cheek.

She wrapped her arms around him and gave him a real kiss. "Grant said there would be a meeting this evening about it."

Enrick kissed her deeply and then she handed him a bottle of water. He took off the cap and drank a swig. "Aye. At least we caught the wolves."

"They're not going to stop, are they?" Heather glanced back at the rest of the men and women eating their meals.

"I doubt it." Enrick ate some of his steak pie, loving how much steak she put in the pies, making them good and hearty. "This is great."

"Thanks. I'm glad you love it. It's one of the reasons I mated you." She took a deep breath and let it out. "Are the wolves who were bitten okay?"

"Aye, as long as they're not faking it."

"Did Grant mention to Paxton McKinley that the woman who contaminated the fish stew is a McKinley?"

"He did, but since she won't give us her first name, I guess they're trying to figure out who it is. We sent a photo of her, but Paxton said he didn't know who she was," Enrick said. "He wanted her turned over to them so they can question and deal with her, but we don't trust them to do anything but praise her for her actions."

"I agree with that. Still, it doesn't seem like holding her hostage is giving us any bargaining chips. They're still pulling stuff." Heather pointed her slice of bread at Enrick. "What if she's somebody important and that's why she won't give us her name and why they won't admit who she is?" Heather took a bite of her bread.

"Then if her pack leader got hold of her, he would give her hell for this because he hadn't sanctioned the poisoning. He might even kick her out of the pack. You never know."

"That's what I told her. She seemed surprised at the notion. Hmm, I want to question her again. After the meeting we have with Grant following the wrap-up of today's shoot. Maybe she will tell me her name and we can get further with her pack leader over this. You would think they would say something about wanting her back."

"You'd think so. Their wolf pack is darn stubborn. Then again, so are we. But, sure, we can do that after the meeting." Though he wanted to have a quick bite to eat and take Heather to bed! He had to remind himself he had a whole lifetime to enjoy her in mated bliss. But that didn't lessen his need to have her writhing under his touch again tonight.

"Why is your kilt rising?" she asked, smiling at him.

"Och, lass, you know why. Thinking of you in bed with me in the throes of passion after all these blasted meetings is the reason."

CHAPTER 19

After the lunch break, the director had part of the hunting party scenes reshot, this time with Enrick serving as Guy's double to check on the wolves who had been injured. He wasn't supposed to speak, but Enrick did anyway, saying in Gaelic, "Rest well, my friend." Then he ran his hand over William's furry head. William licked his hand and Enrick smiled.

He hadn't had a chance to talk to William or Edward or the other wolf who'd been caught up in the fray, so he guessed William was showing he was thankful for Enrick intervening on their behalf.

Then Enrick left the wolf to speak with one of his advisers and the director called, "Cut!"

Guy quickly took Enrick's place and began speaking while Enrick stood off to the side, watching the woods, the actors, wary in case the Kilpatricks or McKinleys pulled anything more. He really didn't think any more of their wolves would turn up after he'd torn into the three who were now in a cell at Argent Castle.

Heather joined Enrick while four other women were standing by to serve food in the next scene. She snuggled next to him and he smiled down at her, raising his brows.

They had to be quiet, nobody saying a word while the main actors were speaking in the woods to each other.

After seven reshoots of the scene with Guy and his adviser—with one or the other stumbling over their lines, which had everyone laughing and relieved some of the tension everyone was feeling after the wolf attack—they finally got it right.

"Cut!" the director shouted.

The campfire scene was next in a small patch of cleared land surrounded by woods to give the feel of Guy and the others still being on the hunt while eating some of their wild boar catch.

Lachlan had made sure the area was safe with no booby traps anywhere and nothing else that could be a problem. Men were wearing kilts and carrying tranquilizer guns beyond that, watching for any trouble to occur. At night, the wolves' vision was good, so they really could see what was coming if anyone intended to give them further grief.

Enrick had planned to join the security detail until Heather and the ladies came down from the castle to play their part. He wanted to protect them at all costs.

Lachlan glanced in his direction and smirked.

Enrick smiled back and folded his arms, his duty just as important as Lachlan's.

Men set up a nice campfire, tents, and a couple of logs for the main characters to sit on as a boar was roasting over the fire, the one Colleen had ensured was already fully cooked before they set it over the campfire to warm up.

The hunting party took their seats before the campfire, some of the men serving guard duty while the "lord" and his key men were getting ready to eat.

The women were serving "mead," though Guy was drinking water and his adviser was having a soda.

Guy was supposed to pet one of the injured wolves and was trying not to look nervous about it. Though the director said Enrick could stand in for him, Guy wanted to do it this time, since Enrick had made it look so easy and safe.

Enrick got the biggest kick out of Edward licking Guy's hand in an attempt to reassure him that he was friendly, not vicious. Guy's eyes widened, but he didn't pull away, thankfully.

Then the actor returned to his seat by the fire and began to talk to his men about the hunt and how he had to track down the villains and end their miserable lives. They bit into loaves of brown bread freshly baked for them and sliced off pieces of the wild boar with their *sgian dubhs* and ate the food for the scene.

The wizard stood nearby, listening in on the conversation but also glancing in the direction of the woods as if hearing sounds the men weren't privy to.

"What do you hear, Malachi?" Guy asked the wizard.

"There is an ill wind blowing our way."

That was for sure, if the Kilpatricks and the others continued to threaten the making of the film.

When they were finally finished with the campfire scene, the party was filmed returning to the castle for one last scene of the day, torches in hand. Two of the MacQuarries were carrying the injured wolf on a medieval stretcher to show how much the wolves meant to Guy and his men. The other six wolves were walking beside the horses, escorting their lord back to the castle, protecting him and his men. That was another reason the director decided to use the MacQuarries' horses. The horses knew the wolves and were comfortable with them, having been raised with them.

Back at the castle, the director was telling Guy he needed to pet the wolf again one last time today, to make it look realistic, and then get on with his scene.

But William had been groaning from his injured shoulder. Enrick hoped he wasn't truly in a lot of pain. Some of their women had tended to his wound during lunch, Colleen at the forefront, but then everyone involved in the film went back to shooting again.

"No way am I petting the wounded wolf again," Guy said as Enrick, Heather, and others looked on. The actors were seated by the fire in the great hall and the wolves were lying nearby on the stone floor. Two of them were pretending to sleep, and two were watching their fallen wolf on the stretcher. Two were sitting up, ears perked, acting like guard dogs as they watched the people coming in to sit by their "lord." Heather brought him another cup of "mead," and two of his men came to speak to him about the situation with the time-traveling wench.

Enrick knew Colleen hadn't wanted her cousin to do any more scenes for the day and wanted him to rest from the ordeal. He hadn't been in a wolf fight for eons, but he wanted to play the scenes out and then take it easy tomorrow, as they were doing some inside scenes with the hero and heroine.

"Enrick?" the director asked. "Would you pet the wolf?"

"Aye, sure. I'll do it. Just tell me what you want me to do."

"No speaking part in this scene, just comfort the wolf as if the animal were one of your kinsmen like you did earlier, as long as you do it safely. Stand right there, and when you finish comforting the wolf, get up and take a seat on the chair over there and Guy will take it from there."

"I can do that." Enrick's clansmen and friends were all smiling, since the wolf was truly his kinsman.

Enrick was already wearing the double's costume, and he stood where he was supposed to before the camera started rolling. Once the director called "Action," Enrick crouched down and lifted William's head off the stretcher and looked him in the eye. "You did good, lad. Real good. I owe you my life." In Gaelic, he added, "You are a true Highland warrior." He knew William wouldn't know what he said, but he wanted to tell him in a way that meant he truly was one of them and he was proud of him.

William lifted his tail and wagged it lightly as if showing he loved his master but didn't have the strength to give him much more of a wag than that.

"Sleep, my friend." Then Enrick laid William's head gently down on the stretcher, rose to his feet, looking down at the wolf with admiration while the wolf closed his eyes.

Then Enrick turned and walked over to the chair and sat down, trying to look like a warrior, but with compassion as he glanced down at the wolf.

"Cut!"

Enrick knew it wasn't supposed to be a speaking part, but how was he supposed to totally convey his feelings of gratitude to the wolf without *saying* something? The wolf would understand how much he loved him when he spoke to him. And if this had all been for real, he would have done it just like that.

He quickly moved out of the chair so Guy could take his place. The actor was scowling at him, not looking happy in the least. It appeared the director was going to leave the scene as it was— seemed to like how Enrick handled the part.

Not that Enrick would be able to manage long speaking roles he would have to memorize beforehand. He could imagine making a real muddle of it. He'd watched as they'd done take after take when one of the actors had messed up his lines. Or like in the one scene where the enemy was sword fighting with Guy in close combat and hit Guy's sword really hard. Guy's weapon went flying through the air. Which wasn't supposed to happen. Everyone in the vicinity of the flying sword had scattered and then everyone had laughed. Guy too. At least when mistakes were made, he was a good sport about it.

But doing what came naturally for Enrick when it came to filling in for Guy? That worked well for Enrick.

Heather was all smiles as he stood beside her, watching the scene continue with Guy now playing his part to the hilt. He was good, Enrick would give him that, but when it came to certain parts, like being comfortable around the injured wolves, sword fighting, or swimming in the cold Irish Sea, Enrick had him beat.

When the director said it was a wrap, and everyone left to run into the village to shop and eat dinner before retiring for the night, Heather said to Enrick, "You were superb in the role. Don't let it go to your head, but you and William played the part perfectly. I so love your brogue."

"It comes naturally."

She laughed. "Guy was not happy you could show warmth and affection to a wounded wolf and the wolf would show how much he loved you back."

"I had to keep a straight face when the director told me I needed to see him as one of my kinsmen. If only he knew how close to the truth he was."

"I was surprised the director kept the scene after you spoke when you weren't supposed to. Again."

"How could I not speak a couple of words to reassure the wolf he had done well? I could smile at him, rub his bony head, but speaking a few words worked the best."

"And throwing in some Gaelic?"

"That's what we spoke back then. It just suited the occasion."

"William will be sure to learn what you said to him. You showed Guy up for not being willing to comfort the wolf. I'm sure the director wasn't happy with the way Guy reacted when he offered to pet William and looked so terrified in the scene. He didn't pull it off well at all."

"I don't blame him, really. We have a secret understanding. To Guy, a wounded dog could lash out if in pain. A wolf? Even scarier and more dangerous. It made sense that he couldn't do that part. Besides, he's worth a lot more money than I am."

Heather laughed. "You are worth a lot more than some guy that playacts about all this. You're the real deal."

"I would sure hope so. I need to check on William. He was moaning like he was in real pain."

"I'll come with you. I imagine Colleen will be seeing to him, too, so you'd better not get all growly with him if he is really hurting."

Enrick grunted.

Heather smiled up at him. "Colleen will give him enough grief, believe me."

They finally reached the room where William was staying, and sure enough, Colleen was there with another woman who was bandaging his shoulder. Between shoots, they'd moved William to the castle and cleaned the injury, hiding him in his room, but when he had to do his part again, they'd had to remove the bandages and let him shift.

"You'd better not be here to tell me William has to play the injured wolf anymore today," Colleen said, her brow furrowed.

"Nay. I just wanted to check on how severe his bite wounds really are." Enrick frowned to see William's shoulder all bandaged and he couldn't tell how bad it was.

"He'll live, as long as it doesn't get infected. Which it could if he keeps having to remove his bandage to shift," Colleen said crossly.

Enrick understood Colleen's concern. He was just as worried about William. "He doesn't have a scene tomorrow or the next day. We can fill in with another wolf for any days after that."

"No," William said. "I can do this."

"Not if you don't allow the wound to heal," Enrick said. No way did they want him to get sick over playing a part in a film.

CHAPTER 20

THAT NIGHT AT THE PRIVATE MEETING IN THE CONFERENCE room, Grant met with Enrick, Lachlan, and Heather, since they had major roles in the film shoots.

"Colleen is seeing to her cousins at the moment and will join us shortly. All of you know we caught the wolves who attacked ours, and they're currently incarcerated at Argent Castle. We found their vehicle and impounded it. I also called Paxton McKinley and told him if he wants us to start killing his wolves, we'll do so. They are bound to get all of our kind in real trouble," Grant said. "Robert said the wolves acted on their own, and he didn't have control over all the wolves. They were McKinley wolves. Paxton says he knows nothing about it."

"That may be, but I suspect Robert had something to do with stirring things up," Enrick said. "Has Ian questioned the men yet?"

"He and his men tried to question them, telling them they only wanted the men issuing the order for the attacks, but the rogue wolves won't shift," Grant said. "By the way, you handled the situation perfectly, Enrick."

"I wanted to kill them."

"I would have felt the same way you did," Grant said. "I'm glad you used restraint in front of the film crew. Especially since we know the wolves would have turned into their human forms if they had died."

"I so agree." Enrick figured the aggressor wolves hadn't intended to kill their wolves, either, just injure them badly, disrupt the film, and maybe scare the film cast into stopping the filming in the woods, anything to cause trouble.

"So what do we do now?" Lachlan asked.

"Remain diligent. Keep a large security force surrounding the area of the shoots. Make sure the areas where they're shooting are checked over to ensure there are no traps or other issues that could injure anyone in the vicinity. Be armed with tranquilizer guns if we have any further issues with their wolves attacking ours in the scenes. Shoot them if they're not wearing their wolf coats too. Nip it in the bud, as Colleen says."

Colleen stormed into the meeting room, her face three shades redder than Enrick had ever seen it. "I hope you plan to kill the wolves."

She was all about life and living and forgiving. Enrick didn't think he'd ever seen her this riled over the fighting going on between her pack and the instigators, except when Grant was trying to protect her from the McKinley clan and she had been in danger.

"You aren't going to let them get away with this, are you?" she asked Grant, her voice furious.

"Nay, love. Not in this century or any other. But your cousins were not badly injured, and they wanted to continue to play their roles. The men who are ordering these crimes are the ones we're seeking," Grant said, rising from his chair and taking Colleen into his arms. He kissed her cheek. "Your cousins are fine."

"Thanks to Enrick who single-handedly took on the three rogue wolves," Colleen said, frowning at Grant.

"Aye, and he didn't kill the wolves because you know what would have happened next." Grant kissed her forehead.

She took a deep, settling breath. "Right." She sat down on the chair next to where Grant had been sitting, and he retook his seat. "So exactly what are we doing?"

After Grant explained what was going on, Heather said, "I want to question the woman further."

Everyone watched her but didn't say anything.

"Maybe I won't get anything more out of her, but I want to

learn what her given name is. They might deny she's one of them, but if we learn the truth from her, we'll know for certain." Heather sounded determined to learn it anyway.

"I agree with Heather. Maybe her family, once we know who she is, will put pressure on Paxton to cease and desist," Enrick said.

"By all means, question her. I've tried three times without success," Colleen said. "But you had the most luck with her already, so hopefully you will get somewhere with her again."

"It's certainly worth a try," Grant said, everyone else agreeing. "If you have any success with her, maybe you can work on the three wolves who attacked ours."

Heather smiled. "If you need me to try, I will. But I think I might have more luck with the woman."

"Okay, Enrick, you stick with Heather until she's done questioning the woman, then help Lachlan make sure we have plenty of security for tomorrow's scenes."

"Will do." Tomorrow was going to be a good day. Other than a day filming some scenes with the hero and heroine of the story— one at the pond, one in a bedchamber that Enrick didn't have to take part in—he planned to visit with Heather.

But for now, he was off to watch over her while she questioned the woman in custody.

———

Heather had wished she could just enjoy the night with Enrick, but he had to check out the details with the people providing security, and she really hoped she could make some progress questioning the woman.

When Heather and Enrick arrived at the cell in the dungeon, the woman was sitting on a cot and writing in a journal. She'd had a shower and was wearing clean clothes, so she wasn't being mistreated. Only confined. Heather didn't think the woman should have anything she could use to entertain herself while she was incarcerated.

"Your pack leader wants to know your name." Heather stood outside the cell.

Enrick leaned against the wall at the end of the cell block, listening but not intruding.

"Okay, look, if you did this for Robert, not once has he asked how you are or cared to have you freed or anything. I take it this is a one-sided love affair. You're hoping he'll care about you because you did what he wanted you to do. In truth, he really doesn't care whether it was you or any other woman he could get to do it as long as he could convince one of you to go along with the plan. Do you wonder if he asked any others to deliver the contaminants who might have turned him down?"

The woman flinched. So she knew he had asked others and she'd been delighted he finally asked her.

"Were you the only woman gullible enough to do it?"

The woman frowned at her.

"Do you have sisters or brothers who care about your welfare? Parents? Cousins? Does anyone care you are incarcerated? Does anyone even know except for Paxton and Robert?"

The woman remained mute.

"Okay, let's say you're banished from the pack. Where are you going to go? Anyone allied with us won't take you in. Not after what you pulled. Anyone allied with the McKinley wolf pack won't take you in either. Robert? You think he would have anything to do with you if you were banished?"

"My brother wouldn't banish me from the pack."

Heather's jaw dropped. "Paxton's sister? You're Paxton's sister, Catherine?" As far as Heather knew, Catherine was really quiet and did what her brothers told her to do. Heather didn't believe she would get herself into trouble by doing Robert's bidding. But a woman hooked on a heel could be convinced to do things she never would have done without the rogue's influence.

"We sent a picture of you to your brother and he said he didn't know you," Heather said.

The woman frowned at her.

Heather knew Enrick would text Grant as soon as she finished speaking with Catherine and then Grant would call Paxton and tell him they had his sister, of all people, even though he had denied that she belonged to his pack, and see where that led. As far as Heather knew, the brothers had always been protective of their only sister. Robert would be in a world of hurt if Paxton hadn't truly ordered her to contaminate the food.

She suspected now Paxton wouldn't have. Certainly, he wouldn't have sent his own sister to do the deed, unless he thought Grant wouldn't do anything to her because Catherine *was* his sister. But why lie about who she was? Ashamed of her?

Catherine didn't confirm that was who she was, but Heather thought it was her, after she had the name to the face. The packs didn't mingle, so it wasn't like they would see each other at events or anywhere else all the time.

"So when your brother learns we know who you are, then what? He'll ask for your release, or leave you here for doing such a stupid thing? And what of Robert? Will he reward him? Banish him? Kill him?" Heather was hoping for the latter solution so he wouldn't be any more trouble for either of their clans.

Catherine just scowled at her.

Heather smiled. "Always nice talking to you. Next time, you ought to put your faith in a wolf who's not a rogue." Then she left to join Enrick and he escorted her up the stone stairs.

"Man, I can't believe you got that much out of her. I seriously think you should speak with the men we're holding at your cousin's castle," Enrick said and texted Grant to let him know what they learned.

Grant texted him back.

"What does Grant say about it?"

"Conference call now. I suspect he's going to call Paxton with the news, but he'll want us there to verify that's who the woman is and to see what he has to say. I can't believe we sent him a photo of her and he denied she was part of the pack."

"He's going to be angry we know the truth now, I betcha," Heather said.

"He will be, I'm sure. I know if I had a sister that pulled that and threatened to harm the pack in doing so, I would be mad."

"But would you banish her from the pack?"

"Nay." Enrick escorted Heather up the stairs. "I'd probably put a ton of restrictions on her. I would definitely ban Robert, Patrick, and the others who caused trouble and could have gotten us involved in a pack war though."

"I would banish her," Heather said.

Enrick smiled down at her. "What if she was *your* sister? Or one of your brothers?"

Heather didn't hesitate to say, "Aye, I would if she were one of my brothers instead."

Enrick laughed.

"A sister?" Heather shrugged. "I guess I could forgive her if she straightened out. But she would have to do something to earn forgiveness from the pack she wronged."

When they reached the conference room, Colleen and Grant were already there.

"You are amazing, Heather," Grant said.

"I agree," Colleen said. "You need to go and speak with the men locked up at your castle. We've sent pictures of them as wolves to the McKinley pack, but they deny they've ever seen them. No surprise since they denied who the woman was also. See if you can get the men to confess to who they are."

"I don't think it will work as well as me talking to Catherine.

She might have made a slip in calling Paxton her brother," Heather said. "She might have wanted to see if her brother cares, since Robert obviously doesn't."

"Okay, I'm going to call Paxton and see what he has to say about it." Grant got ahold of Paxton and said, "I've got some news for you. I'm putting the call on speakerphone so my brothers, Colleen, and Heather MacNeill, who learned who the woman is who sabotaged our food, can confirm it."

"Who? Everyone is accounted for. Are you sure it's not someone else from another wolf pack? Someone else who has a grudge against you? I told you we've never seen the woman in the picture you sent to us," Paxton said.

"It's Catherine McKinley." Grant didn't say anything more, and there was a long moment of silence.

"Nay. She's gone to see our aunt in London."

"Unless a woman of your clan lied about who she is, and someone intercepted the photo we sent to you and switched it with another, then Catherine has lied to you about where she intended to go. Like I said before, Catherine said Robert gave her the go-ahead to tamper with the food, and he said it was under your orders."

Again, a significant pause. "Hold on."

There was a clunk that sounded like Paxton had put his phone down on a table, then a door opened and closed.

A few minutes later, the door opened and closed, and a breathless Paxton said, "Let me speak with her."

Paxton must have learned Catherine wasn't at her aunt's place after all.

"It'll take a few minutes," Grant said. "I'll call you back."

"I'll get her." Lachlan headed out of the conference room.

Heather felt like she was sitting on a cushion of pins, wondering what Paxton would do about his sister. She couldn't help feeling like the woman had been used by the man she thought she loved. Heather wondered if Robert could feel anything for anyone.

Lachlan finally returned to the conference room with Catherine. She looked glum, and Heather wondered if Lachlan had told her that her brother wanted to speak with her.

"Have a seat, Catherine," Grant said, and she sat on one of the love seats as Lachlan took a seat beside her. "Your brother wants to talk to you."

Her back stiff, she gave a curt nod.

Grant got her brother on the phone. "Here she is." He offered his phone to her, and she got up from the love seat and took the phone, her hand shaking.

She listened for a few minutes, still standing as if that would be easier than sitting while she talked to her brother. Though he was doing all the talking.

"No, he did not coerce me. No, Paxton, you know our aunt and I don't get along." Catherine let out her breath in exasperation. "He said you sanctioned it! No, of course I didn't think to ask you. I believed him." She began to pace across the floor. "You're banishing me to our aunt's place? No." She glanced at Heather. "I can work for the MacQuarries to pay off my debt."

"In my shop," Heather said, feeling the woman needed someone on her side. Maybe it would change Catherine's view of the MacNeills and the MacQuarries. They had to start somewhere.

The woman smiled at her.

"No contaminating the food or you're terminated." Heather smiled sweetly at her, but she meant it. She didn't need someone ruining her reputation. And Heather didn't mean that Catherine would be fired from the job either.

Catherine smiled back at her and the look was one of appreciation, though Heather didn't trust her entirely around the food. Catherine would have to earn that trust. Cleaning tables and the restrooms would come first.

"Aye, that's what I want to do. I'm not staying with our aunt. She hates me because she thinks I'm a useless beta wolf. And if she learns Robert convinced me to do this, she'll be assured I'm just a problem wolf," Catherine said to her brother. "What are you going to do about Robert and his brother? They're the ones that pushed everyone to cause trouble for the MacQuarries." Her eyes widened. "Banishment? At least a dozen wolves are loyal to them. You'll have a fight on your hands." She bit her lip. "Aye, of course, I'll go along with banishing them. Nay. I know he doesn't…" She took a deep breath and let it out. "He doesn't love me. He just used me. Aye, they're treating me well." She glanced at Heather again.

Which made Heather feel a little guilty that she'd said Catherine should be staying in the dungeon and had made the comment about torture. Just a little guilty. After all, Catherine had been glad she'd done what she had, but Heather suspected it was because Catherine had truly believed her brother had called for it.

"They said I would have to stay at Farraige Castle until the film shoot is done."

Grant cleared his throat.

Catherine glanced at him.

"If you're going to repay your debt to us by working at Heather's shop and not cause any trouble, you can return home. That is, if Robert and Patrick and any others who sided with them are banished from the pack and the territory," Grant said.

"Aye." Catherine repeated Grant's words to her brother. "I won't cause any further trouble, Paxton. I thought you were behind all this. All right. All right. Next time I'll ask. Okay? Nay, I understand he just used me. You said that already. I get it, okay?" She let out her breath. "I don't know who the wolves are who were taken prisoner. Aye, I will. The MacQuarries took a photo of me and sent it to you. What happened with that?" She paused, then said, "Robert must have intercepted it then." She said to Grant, "My brother wants me to give the names of the wolves you've incarcerated. I need to see them, and I'll know who they are. He said they won't shift to tell you their names.

And since sending their photos hadn't worked, I'll make a positive identification.

"If they're strictly beta, they would have been influenced by Robert. He's persuasive when he wants to be. It doesn't mean they'll cause any further trouble. Paxton will look further into the others who were involved in the fight against your men and how Robert is intercepting your messages. The men you're holding might have also been three of the five McKinleys who fought with your men during the battle scene. Paxton said he would discuss with you what he will do about their punishment. For sure, he intends to banish the Kilpatrick brothers."

"Aye, I agree to that," Grant said.

"Will you release the other men?" Catherine asked.

"Once we know who they are, and Paxton gives me his word they'll either be banished from the pack or punished," Grant said.

"Aye. Did you hear that, Paxton?" Catherine asked Grant, "Can we go now to see the men? My brother wants to know who they are and resolve this now."

"Aye. My brother Lachlan is returning there tonight, as well as Heather's three brothers. They'll take you, and you can stay at Argent Castle tonight. Your brother can pick you up in the morning."

"What about working off my debt to you at Heather's shop?"

"You can start tomorrow. You'll be cleaning tables and such to begin with. Once we know you're trustworthy, you can help in the kitchen or with the customers," Heather said.

"For how long?" Grant asked Heather.

"A month?" Heather thought that was time enough since Catherine had been jailed already and she seemed to realize she'd been a pawn and lied to. If Robert hadn't conned her, Heather figured Catherine would never have done it.

Catherine frowned. "Sure. You don't think I should do it for longer?"

Heather smiled. "Listen, if you work out fine at the shop, I'll hire you."

Catherine's smile couldn't have grown any bigger, and Heather felt good about the way things were turning out with the woman. She just hoped Patrick and Robert didn't stir up more trouble when they learned they were banished.

She wanted to go with Catherine to hear who the men were. But when she looked at Enrick, his expression said he was thinking he wanted her to be with him, after he did his security checks. He won out.

CHAPTER 21

THE NEXT DAY, HEATHER HAD TO PARTICIPATE IN A SCENE IN the inner bailey and Enrick stood nearby watching her, wearing Guy's double's costume as usual, just in case he was needed for anything. He was helping to provide security for the women since he didn't have another job to do right now. The scene was about a woman near term and getting ready to have the baby. They could have had a woman wearing a Moonbump, a fake pregnant belly, but the director had opted for an extra who was the real thing. He was especially delighted she had an identical twin sister who would substitute for her after the "delivery" of the newborn. And the twin's four-week-old baby would be used as the newly delivered baby for that scene.

Missy, the star of the show, was now wearing the clothes of the period and had been since the scene where she had magically appeared from her time in New York City to the past on the beach below the castle.

This scene called for her to speak with the woman, Lisa MacNeill, who was close to giving birth, and kiss the four-week-old baby the other woman was holding swaddled in a tartan in her arms. No one would know that the same baby wasn't used for both scenes. The point of the scene was to show how Missy now felt like she was part of the clan and was no longer desperate to return to her own time and place. She still spoke with a modern-day New York accent and the clansmen and women had a difficult time understanding her—for the movie. Missy, in the story, was a midwife back home, aiding natural-birth deliveries, and so this was something she felt she could do when the time was right. She felt she could actually make a difference in the mortality rate of infant births, besides the fact she was falling for the stubborn, behind-the-times Highland lord.

Enrick was amused. Had Missy truly lived back in these times, she wouldn't have managed half as well, and she would still have been desperate to leave behind the medieval times and return to all her modern-day conveniences. As many times as he'd seen her on her phone between shoots, he was certain she wouldn't give that up for a Highlander of old.

The pregnant MacNeill woman suddenly held her belly and groaned.

"It is time. Come, we must take her inside the keep to her chamber," Missy said.

Heather and Lana helped the pregnant woman to stand and then headed inside the keep. Heather glanced back at Enrick, frowning. But she didn't say anything, not wanting to mess up the shoot, he thought. Was Lisa MacNeill actually having her baby?

"I can help deliver her child," Missy was saying for the camera. "That's what I do…uh, did back home."

"You're a midwife?" one of the actresses who was supposed to be a lady-in-waiting asked Missy.

"Yes. We even deliver babies in a bathtub filled with warm water," Missy said.

Heather and the other women looked at Missy like the devil had possessed her—for the role in the film.

"Never mind. As long as there are no complications, I can help. But everyone must sterilize—uh, wash their hands with soap and water before they touch the baby or the mother during the delivery. We need hot water and soap."

One of the women took off to fetch the items.

"Cut!" the director called out.

The next scene was shot on the stairs and Enrick was nearby, thinking the pregnant woman was having more trouble getting up the stairs than she should. Unless it was all just acting on her part.

He wanted to rush forth and carry her up the stairs. When Heather glanced back at him, her brow still furrowed, he worried the woman was really in labor. He hurried into the scene, like he wasn't supposed to do, and Heather nodded at him, as if he had done the right thing. Whether or not the director was happy about it.

Enrick swept the woman up in his arms and carried her the rest of the way to the chamber where she was to give birth. Her brow was peppered with sweat, and she was panting through what he assumed were labor pains. It was her first child, so he knew it could take many hours, even days for the process. She probably wanted to shift into her wolf, and she could, once the "delivery" in the film took place and she swapped places with her twin sister, who was standing nearby, waiting to switch with her.

Cameras were in the room where he laid the woman down on the bed. He hesitated to leave. The pregnant woman squeezed his hand in grateful thanks.

"Uh, my lord, I can take care of this now," Missy said to Enrick.

He inclined his head to her, then stalked out of the room. He immediately texted Grant: *I think Lisa MacNeill is having real contractions.*

Grant promptly texted back: I'll send for the doctor.

The doctor was a wolf named Rupert Carraway. He wasn't a member of any of the wolf packs, but he was there to aid any of them who were injured, sick, or giving birth.

Enrick texted him: *I might be mistaken. Or it might take hours before she has the baby.*

Grant responded with, Aye. We will have him see to her, just in case.

Enrick peeked into the room and saw Lisa's face was flushed with pain. Hell. They needed to cut the action.

They were "prepping" her for delivery, and Heather was holding her hand when her irate mate showed up at the chamber door.

Enrick stopped him and shook his head. They would move her

as soon as she said she was ready, unless the doctor arrived and said she was ready for the delivery.

At least that was what Enrick figured.

A wolf wandered into the room, part of the script. It was William, and Missy told him, "Shoo! Your master might be all right with you roaming the halls, but you can't be in here. Go. Now."

When he wouldn't mind her, Heather motioned for him to leave and he turned around and left the room.

"Thank you," Missy said. "I can't understand how his lordship can have those wild beasts around him all the time."

"They are like family...to him," Heather said, and Enrick knew she was supposed to just listen, not comment.

He smiled.

"I suppose you are right," Missy said. "Like owning a pet dog."

No way were the wolves like the dogs. Sure, they were canines, but they mated for life.

Heather wisely didn't say anything in response, but he knew she, and all the other *lupus garous*, felt the way he did.

"The baby's coming," Lisa said in Gaelic in a strained voice, and only Enrick and Heather knew for sure then that the baby was on its way.

The doctor arrived just in the nick of time.

The director, seeing the new man wearing a white shirt and black trousers heading for the room, quickly called, "Cut!"

The doctor cleared everyone out of the room, giving the camera crew the evil eye.

"We need to finish the shoot. We can have Lisa's sister take over the part now, and you can move Lisa to the hospital," the director said.

The doctor turned on him with a scowl. "She is giving birth now. Kindly leave the room."

Heather and Lana stayed. Missy hurried out of the room. The camera crew packed up as quickly as they could.

Two more women, one of them Lisa's twin sister, arrived to

help Lisa remove her clothes so she could shift. Lisa's mate joined them.

Shutting the door, Enrick guarded it so no one intruded who shouldn't. Lachlan soon joined him, smiling. "Hell, who would have ever thought birthing a baby in the film would turn into a real delivery scene?"

"At least the Kilpatricks didn't have any part in stopping the film this time."

"Aye. I saw her mate downstairs before he came up here, and he'd looked like he was getting ready to kill anyone who stood in his way," Lachlan said.

"Do you blame him?"

Lachlan shook his head and folded his arms. "Nay."

Colleen soon joined them. "Since Julia's her pack leader, I've called her to let her know the situation. She was on her way before this but got held up. How are things going?"

They heard a wolf pup give a little cry, then another. Then the wolf pup's cries turned into baby cries.

"Two babies?" Enrick and the others chuckled. "Sounds to me like things are going well."

Colleen knocked on the door and Heather answered it. She pulled her into the room and smiled at Enrick. "Twins. Two boys. They came earlier than expected, but they're doing fine. The second one wasn't expected either." Then she closed the door.

"Just think, that could be you and Heather in the not-too-distant future." Lachlan leaned against the wall.

Enrick hadn't really given the baby business a whole lot of thought. He smiled, thinking Heather would make a great momma wolf.

They heard noise in the room that sounded suspiciously like a secret panel being opened into the next chamber. "Hey, stay here and guard the door. I'm checking out the spare chamber down the hallway."

"Aye."

Enrick stalked down the hall and opened the door to the other chamber and Heather squeaked, her hand to her chest. He smiled. "Sorry. Are you moving Lisa in here?"

"Aye. We're going to clean up the room she'd been in and the director can begin again with Lisa's twin this time."

"Do you need my help?"

"Just to guard the door. Thanks, Enrick." She gave him a quick peck on the cheek and then closed the door.

A few minutes later, a woman came out with bloody sheets. She was smiling though. "Beautiful twins."

He smiled back. "I'm glad."

The doctor finally came out of the room and shook his head. "This takes the cake for a delivery. In the middle of the shooting of a film, no less."

"As long as everyone's all right," Enrick said.

"Aye. The mother is trying to nurse her babies. Don't let anyone into the room."

"Aye, Doc." Enrick took that to mean the mother was in her wolf form, easier to deal with newborn wolf puppies suckling on her teats.

"Congratulations are in order for you mating Heather. That could be you and your mate in a few months." The doctor smiled, slapped him on the shoulder, and headed out.

At least when Heather had their baby or babies, they wouldn't have this circus to deal with.

It seemed like it took forever, women coming in and out of one of the rooms or the other. Heather and Lisa's sister remained in the room with Lisa.

And then Heather finally came out of the guest room and said to Enrick, "We're ready to begin the shoot again in the other room. Lisa and her twins are asleep. Lana, Missy, Lisa's sister, and I will get set up to begin again, since the mother has delivered her baby—as far as the film is concerned. The other two ladies and Lisa's mate are staying with her while the shooting is going on."

"All right."

Colleen came out of the room just then. "Julia just arrived at the castle. I'm going to greet her downstairs. We're all set otherwise."

"Aye, I'll let the director know." Enrick called the director who was taking a break downstairs, while the film crew sat in the hall waiting to set up in the room again, per the director's orders. "We're ready to go."

"How is Lisa?" the director asked.

Enrick was glad he didn't think only of making his film.

"She had two little boys."

"Twins. I'll be. That will be good luck then. I'll be right up. Can the cameramen set up again?"

"Aye."

"Thanks!" The director must have called the lead cameraman because he was suddenly on his phone and said, "Yes, sir."

Then he was off his phone and directing everyone to return to the room. Enrick opened the door for them and was surprised how everything looked as normal as before. Only this time, Lisa's twin was climbing into bed.

Missy took hold of the sleeping four-week-old baby and cradled her in her arms, her eyes filling with tears at the miracle of birth. And then she returned the baby to her "mother's" arms and glanced at Guy, who had come in to see that the woman was all right, along with the woman's film "husband," who went over to the bed and smiled to see he had a healthy boy. Even though the baby was really a little girl.

"Cut!" the director said.

What had been a simple scene had turned out to be a lot more complicated than anyone had predicted. Enrick was glad when they broke for lunch and he and Heather, his brothers, Colleen, and Julia could eat in the great hall together.

"Thank you, Enrick, for rescuing Lisa in the middle of the scene," Heather said, and gave him a big hug and kiss. She wanted to take her hunky hero to bed, but she wasn't sure what he had to do next for the movie shoot.

Enrick kissed her back and squeezed the breath out of her in a way that said he loved her with all his heart. "I was sure you were trying to tell me Lisa was really in labor without messing up the scene. When she was struggling up the stairs, I figured either she was having contractions or she was one hell of an actress. I wasn't waiting to find out."

"I'm so glad you didn't. I could just see her having the babies on the stairs before we even got her to the room. Thanks for calling the doctor. Missy might be a midwife in her story, but she looked a little green when she finally realized the baby was really coming. She probably would have expired on the spot if she'd known Lisa was having two."

Enrick chuckled. "I probably looked that way too."

"No way. You would have handled it like a brave Highlander." She took his hand and they walked down the stairs together. "I'm really glad everything went well for Lisa and the babies, and the director said he wasn't reshooting the scene with you carrying her to the chamber. They had to get Guy in a hurry to come in and check on Lisa's twin afterward to fit with the new scene."

Enrick laughed. "That wasn't part of the script, I take it."

"No. He wasn't supposed to go near the chamber. But when you so gallantly carried the woman up the stairs, he had to finish the scene with an appearance."

Grant, Lachlan, and Colleen were smiling at Enrick and Heather as they joined them at the table to have one of Colleen's favorite Scottish deep-fried mushroom pizzas, with a fresh, thick parbaked base and toppings already applied, then fried until crisp.

"I can't believe I missed all the excitement," Julia said, taking a slice of pizza. "But I was glad to see Lisa and her babies are doing great."

"I thought her mate was going to punch me out when he wanted to get in to see her." Enrick took a bite of his pizza.

"She told me how gallant you were when you carried her up the stairs. Her mate was grateful too. He couldn't believe she wanted to go through with the scene as long as she did. Until she knew the babies were coming and she couldn't hold off any longer," Julia said.

"Had she shifted?" Enrick asked.

"Aye, she did to give birth. Easier as wolves. And then she shifted back for a few minutes to check over her babies. That's when they began crying as babies," Heather said.

Julia took a bite of her pizza, then after she finished it, she said, "If you hadn't heard, Catherine identified the three men who had attacked Colleen's cousins and the MacQuarrie. They're all alphas. Once we reported who they were to Paxton, he banished them and Robert and Patrick Kilpatrick from the pack and the territory. It turned out the three McKinleys had also invaded the one battle scene being filmed. Two others had taken part in the battle, but no one would say who they were."

"I suspect Robert and Patrick and the other three men know exactly who they are. Maybe even others. Maybe even Paxton. But since they weren't caught in the act, no one wants to give them up. That could be a dangerous business as the two men still in the McKinley pack could cause dissent. Hopefully, just for them and not any more for the MacQuarries or MacNeills," Enrick said.

"Agreed." Grant lifted another slice of pizza off the platter.

"Catherine went home," Julia said, "but she'll definitely have a place in my new novel."

"Is she redeemed?" Heather asked.

Enrick rubbed Heather's back. "You know you'll want to read

the book, and you don't want to know all about the story before that."

Heather sighed.

Julia chuckled. "I'm not sure. I'll have to write the book, and if it works out, then yes, but who knows where the story characters will take it."

Heather drank some of her tea. "Well, from what some of our people said, Catherine arrived at the shop early this morning, eager to work, doing anything they deemed necessary."

"Oh?" Enrick said.

"Aye. They had her cleaning the windows first thing, then the tables outside. The ones inside were clean, but the wind blows dust around and the tables outside have to be washed down each morning before the shop opens." Heather picked up another slice of pizza.

"I'm glad to hear she's working out," Enrick said, the others at the table agreeing.

"Me too. We're still watching her. She understands she has to earn our trust."

"Good," Enrick said.

"The men who were banished after Catherine confirmed who they were at Argent Castle were furious she was the one who told Paxton. But she said she is loyal to her pack and to the pack leader. What they did was akin to a mutiny. She wanted no further part in it," Lachlan said.

"That's good. I hope they don't try to take it out on her," Heather said.

"Hopefully, Paxton will realize this and ensure she's well protected." As much as Enrick was angry that she'd pulled what she had in the name of love, at least she'd turned around. He didn't want her paying the price for revealing the identity of the coconspirators.

After the lunch break, Enrick led Heather out of the great hall and into the gardens, glad he could take a break from constantly sitting around, waiting for something to happen.

"Are you sure Catherine's going to work out all right in your shop and not cause trouble?" Enrick was concerned for Heather and her shop's reputation.

"Aye. I suspect if she did something like contaminate the food in my shop, her brother might just banish her too. And I really don't think she wants that. I still can't believe I was the one who pulled a *sgian dubh* on her and I'm the one who she finally opened up to."

"You also were the only one who offered to work with her so she could do a good deed to repair the damage she'd done."

"You know, deep down she might have wanted to get caught. She pretended not to see that I was watching her in the kitchen. She might have been hoping I would stop her and end the whole business." Heather frowned at Enrick. "Are you sure you're not supposed to be down at the pond, just in case they need you?"

"No battles, nothing Guy needs a double for. It's just a scene with talking and then kissing between Guy and Missy. Then some more scenes in the castle and bedchamber, but nothing I need to be part of. We have a ton of security all around the area, watching out for trouble."

Then they heard a woman scream and a man shout out.

Enrick and Heather raced to the garden gate and saw Gutzie, the gander, chasing Guy and Missy away from the pond. The goose, Buttercup, was watching and Enrick swore if she could, she would be laughing.

Enrick probably shouldn't have, but he laughed out loud. Not that the film crew or the terrified actors could hear him. He couldn't help himself. A Highland lord should not be chased off by a gander.

Enrick loped down the hill toward the pond and Heather ran after him. "What are you going to do?" she asked.

He had no intention of kissing Missy in the scene, like Guy was supposed to do. But he could get Gutzie to come to him, hopefully, and he could lock him up for the time being. "Can you get some oats for them, Heather?"

"Aye, sure." Heather ran back to the castle.

Behind him, he heard one of the women say, "Here are the oats, Heather. Gutzie's in rare form today."

"Aye, I'll say. And thanks!"

Then he heard footfalls behind him and saw Heather running to catch up to him with a bag of oats.

"Thanks, Heather." Enrick ran the rest of the way to the pond with the bag of oats clutched in his hand. When he reached the gander returning to the pond, he spoke to him in greeting. "Hey, Gutzie, Buttercup, here are some oats for you."

Both the goose and gander headed toward him for the meal, along with a number of ducks.

As long as Gutzie wasn't making a beeline toward Enrick with his neck stretched forward, head down, and hissing at him, Enrick was in good shape. He hoped.

If he wasn't and the gander tried to bite him, he was sure Heather would laugh this time. Geese had a sharp tip on the end of their upper bills and when they pinched, twisted their head, and pulled back, they could leave some nasty bruises. Not to mention that the bony edge of their wings could beat on a person with some force. He was glad Guy and Missy had gotten away unscathed. With the issues the film had already suffered from Kilpatrick's clan, they didn't need animal trouble from their own.

"You don't ever want to run," Enrick told Guy and Missy as they watched from a distance. Though his advice was shared with anyone out there who might encounter trouble with the geese in the future. "You have to stand up to them and wave your arms around to make yourself look bigger. They'll think you're meaner than them then. You can extend your arm, making it appear you have a long neck and point your finger like it's a beak and tell him, 'No! Don't bite.'"

Enrick didn't think Guy and the woman were going for it, from the way they'd folded their arms and shaken their heads at him in unison. If he had to, he would demonstrate, but he was glad he hadn't had to.

He encouraged the geese to follow him to a shed with a promise of more to eat. Once they were inside eating happily, he shut the door so that the film could go on without the actors, or anyone else, having to contend with the menacing geese. Though he thought it would make for a funny addition to the scene if the gander had chased Guy off and the film star had showed he was only human.

Enrick called out to the director, "The geese are locked up."

"Thanks!" the director said.

Enrick should have realized Gutzie could get cantankerous if Guy and Missy were at the pond and not feeding them anything. It didn't always happen, but with so many people milling about, he was certain the gander was aggravated. His pond, his space.

Enrick was glad he'd been close by to help, even though he hadn't thought they would need him for anything. The security detail had strict orders to watch for Kilpatricks and McKinley men and weren't to budge from where they were positioned, except to do their duty. Chasing after the geese didn't qualify.

"You sure try to show Guy up," Heather said, a sparkle in her eye as they moved out of the area.

Very seriously, Enrick said, "I don't try."

She laughed. "I know the geese have chased you before. Weren't you worried they would do it this time?"

"Not when I had the bag of oats. Besides, I learned my lesson when I was a kid tending to the geese. Particularly when they were mating."

She chuckled. "Aye, my da always warned me not to go near them, or to be really careful when I had to feed them."

They watched Guy and Missy kissing, and Enrick was ready to

take Heather back to bed. She reached over and took his hand and squeezed, smiling up at Enrick. She looked like she had the same thing in mind.

Watching Guy and Missy making love near the pond really wasn't Enrick's thing. He would much rather be making love to his mate.

CHAPTER 22

THE NEXT MORNING, ENRICK WOKE TO HEATHER CUDDLING against his bare chest.

She kissed his chest and smiled up at him. "We were supposed to get some sleep."

"Hmm, tonight," he said, kissing the top of her head and sweeping his hand down her back in a loving caress. He sighed. "We need to get going." As much as he wanted to just stay in bed the rest of the day with Heather, they had jobs to do. "I'll be glad when the shooting is done."

"You know you love it."

The phone alarms and the one alarm clock went off, Enrick having returned all the rest of the clocks to Lachlan yesterday so he could find their owners.

Heather and Enrick scrambled out of bed to turn off the alarms. "Okay, so maybe you're right," Heather conceded after they turned off the alarms. She grabbed Enrick's hand and hauled him toward the bathroom. "Shower first."

"Together."

"Aye. What better way to start our day?"

He scooped his naked mate up in his arms and carried her into the shower. "I couldn't agree with you more."

Enrick and Heather ate a hurried breakfast in the great hall where most everyone had already eaten and left, and Maynard was giving Enrick the evil eye for being late—again. After that, Enrick was busy watching things with Heather and being part of the security force while Guy was supposed to cross moss-covered rocks over a creek to reach the heroine. Missy was waiting for Guy to follow her after having crossed the stones off-screen, and the trick was for him to run across them in his exuberance to reach her.

The film crew had cleaned the stepping-stones the best they could to ensure Guy could make it across without slipping and falling into the creek, which, to Enrick's way of thinking, had diminished the sport of it. Not to mention it looked odd when everything else was covered in moss.

Enrick was standing by in case he was needed to fill in for Guy. In fact, he assumed Guy would want Enrick to cross the rocks because they were wobbly, and Guy wouldn't want to fall and injure himself. But the actor did like doing his own scenes as much as possible, Enrick had learned, and Guy was determined to reach the heroine himself. How hard could it be?

"And action!" the director called out.

Guy headed for the stepping-stones like a man with a mission while Missy, wearing his clan's tartan now, was standing on the other side, waiting for him to join her.

Guy made it across the first four stones, wobbling a little on the last one, but when he took a step on the next one, he must not have balanced himself quite right. He tottered, tilted, and tumbled into the creek. And swore.

For a second, no one said anything, and then he got to his feet in the waist-deep water and smiled at the director, who immediately called, "Cut!"

Missy was laughing then, and so were many of the crew and other onlookers.

Enrick smiled.

Heather laughed. "You probably would have done the exact same thing."

"No way. I have the balance of a cat."

"Hmm, and other moves like a wolf."

He smiled down at her.

In the meantime, Guy was quickly changing into dry clothes. They had several sets for him to wear, in the event he ended up in the creek, and Enrick suspected the director, or his film crew, hadn't had a lot of faith in Guy making it the first time across. Or even several times across.

"The stones are wobbly," Guy said.

"Aye, and they would have been in ancient times," Enrick said, not meaning to say anything to Guy about it.

Everyone looked to see how Guy would react.

Heather punched Enrick in the ribs, undoubtedly annoyed with him for making the comment.

"Any Highland lord worth his salt can make that." Enrick didn't mean to badger him, but to say he could do it.

Heather looked up at Enrick, her expression one of disbelief.

He smiled at her. It was true and she knew it.

Guy's growly look faded, and he glanced back at the stones where some of the film crew were trying to make the rocks more stable.

"Do you want me to do it?" Enrick wanted to tell the men to quit messing with the stones. They'd already done enough to them to make the scene look fake. The stones had been set there centuries ago by people living in the area. Through the ages, lads and lassies had crossed them with never a mishap. Adults too, and no problem at all. He couldn't see that the American star could be that…unbalanced. Then again, Enrick and his kin had traversed many a water crossing in such a manner, not wishing to get wet, and so they were used to judging the slipperiness and instability of the rocks, even if it was a new path they hadn't taken before.

"No, I can do this." Guy had finished changing into dry clothes.

"Aye, you can. Feel the movement in the soles of your boots, adjust before you take the next step. Have confidence and you'll make it." Enrick folded his arms across his chest.

Guy nodded to the director. He was ready to chance crossing the creek again. He must have thought he could manage the first four rocks, and so he hurried across them in a way that said he could do this. Enrick looked on with approval.

But then Guy hesitated at the fifth rock. The one that had given him trouble before. If Guy didn't overcome his fear of that rock, he would never make it across.

He took a step, and another, and that rock became his new albatross as he lost his balance, waved his arms frantically about like a bird trying to catch the wind under its wings and take flight, and fell.

Everyone laughed before they could even see how Guy was feeling about the situation. Enrick included. Not in a mean way. It was just...funny.

Heather sighed.

Enrick glanced down at her. She gave him a stern look telling him nonverbally not to say anything more to poor Guy. But the man needed encouragement if he was going to overcome his shortcomings.

This time when Guy waded out of the water, he was much glummer.

"I'll be right back," Enrick told Heather.

"Enrick," she said in a warning tone.

He leaned down and kissed her cheek. "He needs some more encouragement."

"Aye, but not the way you would offer it, I'm sure."

"Like any of us would when we're trying to overcome what seems an insurmountable obstacle."

"He is an American, raised in a city, not like you and our kin."

"Aye, but he's a McNab. Somewhere in his genetic makeup, he's a Scottish warrior at heart." Enrick was certain of it. He stalked off toward McNab, and Guy frowned at him as he dressed yet again in another set of dry garments.

"You do not need to tell me how to do this," Guy said to Enrick, sounding vexed.

"Aye, I do."

Guy frowned even harder at him.

"Listen, we've been doing this since we were able to walk. I understand this. I'm sure you've had other obstacles to traverse that you had to work at. You'll do this. I have every faith in you. Just don't think of everyone else watching you. Concentrate on your footing. You can do this."

The breeze shifted and suddenly, Enrick got a whiff of a wolf, of Guy standing before him, wet, and irritated, and wolfish. He had to have been wearing hunter's concealment.

Enrick's eyes widened. "Hell, man," he said under his breath. "You're one of *us*."

———

When Guy's jaw dropped and his eyes widened, Heather wondered just what Enrick was saying to him. She really couldn't imagine him belittling Guy, but the Highlanders could be brusque about saying things in a way Guy might not understand and would instead cause him to take offense.

For several minutes, Enrick spoke to Guy and then he finally slapped him on the back as if they were great friends, though Guy didn't look like he reciprocated the feeling. Enrick headed back to Heather out of the view of the camera. Guy was just staring after Enrick, looking dumbfounded.

What in the world had Enrick said to him?

Enrick smiled at her as if she had nothing to worry about, but then his expression changed to a bit of a frown as he turned to watch Guy try to cross the creek again. "He'll do it. He's one of us."

Heather said, "Aye, he's got a Celtic name, so I agree. He will. What did you say to him?"

"Nay…I mean, aye, he's got a Celtic name, but he's one of *us*."

Heather stared at Enrick, not knowing what he was saying. "Kin?" she whispered. "A wolf?" She barely spoke the word. No way. Guy couldn't be. Then she smiled. "Oh, if he *is* one, the single women in both of our clans will go crazy over wanting to get to know him better."

The director called, "And action."

Guy looked so much more confident this time that whether he made it or not, Heather felt Enrick's talk with him *had* helped.

Then Guy began to walk across the rocks, this time taking it easy all the way across, with enough confidence that he could do it, but not so rushed. In fact, he looked like he was really concentrating on his footing, feeling every step for movement. And then he was across. He hurried to see Missy and began talking to her.

Cameras on that side were filming the close-up of the two of them while they said their lines.

Heather swore everyone had wanted to cheer Guy when he made it across the creek perfectly dry this time.

Missy had looked the most relieved of all. Though everyone breathed in a bit of relief, glad to see the shoot was continuing so they could break for lunch next.

Enrick wrapped his arm around Heather's shoulders and leaned down and kissed her. Whatever Enrick had said to Guy must have helped, and she was feeling a lot better about the talk they'd had.

Though she was dying to know more about it.

When they finally broke for lunch, Heather said, "He's really a wolf?"

"Aye, he is. He has been wearing that damn hunter's concealment."

"Why? Did he know we were wolves before he got here?"

"Aye, but we couldn't talk about any of it here." Enrick got on his phone and texted Grant. He paused, texted some more. "Okay, Grant said we'll have to have him come and have a private dinner with us, and we'll discuss all this."

"Wow. He's really a wolf."

Enrick looked down at her.

She laughed. "You're still the real deal to me. He might be one of us, but you've lived here as one of us all our lives. I wouldn't give you up for anything. You did have me worried though. I wondered what you had said to him."

"Only good, hearty words of encouragement."

"Coming from one of you, that's what I worried about."

He laughed.

She smiled and kissed his lips.

They both had Scottish salmon sandwiches for lunch before the next scene played out. She couldn't wait to go to the dinner meeting where they spoke with Guy and learned the whole truth about where his family had come from in Scotland. She knew the single female wolves would all be a-twitter once they knew about him. But like Enrick, she really couldn't wait to return to their chamber to enjoy their mated couple status.

Maybe when Enrick wasn't working, after the film shoot was done, he could drop by and help her out at her shop, if he wanted to. She even wanted to ask Maynard if he had any old recipes he wouldn't mind sharing with her.

"Since you're the second-in-command for Grant and Colleen, I assume we'll stay at Farraige Castle."

"Nay. I don't want you to have that commute day in, day out. We'll either live at Argent Castle like you do now, or we'll find a place of our own."

"Somewhere between. Aye, we can do that."

"But closer to your shop."

That was another reason why she loved Enrick. She wrapped her arms around his neck. "I love you."

"Ah, lassie, I think I have loved you from the time I saw you fall into the creek and had to save you when you were a wee thing."

"You *teased* me about that!"

"Aye, with my brothers looking on and telling me I was going to mate you, what else could I do?"

She laughed. "Well, they were right."

"Aye, they were."

CHAPTER 23

"Okay, let's go meet some more of the family," Enrick told Guy once the afternoon shoot was a wrap, glad Guy had finally come clean about who he was and how he was kin to the clan. They actually had a fair number of women in the clan who were not directly related to the MacQuarries, but their families had joined their clan to ensure they were protected from other wolf packs and clans, while owing their allegiance to their protectors. He suspected they would be ecstatic to learn Guy was a wolf and still unmated.

It didn't take long for Enrick's brothers to arrive at the conference room, and Colleen and her cousins were there too to meet with Enrick and Guy.

He looked a little uncomfortable as everyone waited to hear his story, Colleen offering for everyone to take their seats.

Heather soon joined them and took a seat next to Enrick.

"Okay, so you're a wolf," Grant said, but before he could say anything more, there were a couple of astonished gasps.

Enrick noticed Heather and Colleen exchanging glances, and he swore the women were already making plans. Matchmaking? If one of their kind ended up falling for the actor, they would have to travel all over, not be able to shift when they wanted, wouldn't have a pack to fall back on, and would be leaving their beloved Scotland behind.

Then again, to be with an actor who was seen as one of Hollywood's hottest stars? One of the women might be able to live with it. Being in the tabloids, in the news all the time, might be harder to take.

They could always return here to be with family and get away from all the fame and tabloids for a time.

"You are welcome to come stay with us, even live with us, should you ever tire of being a hero of the big screen," Grant said.

"Eventually, I'll have to quit because everyone will wonder how I manage to look so young over the years and try to learn who my plastic surgeon is," Guy said.

They all laughed.

"That is the problem with stardom," Guy said. "Though I never figured my career would go this far."

"I can't believe you were wearing hunter's concealment," Enrick said, still finding it hard to believe any of this.

"Your grandfather sent my grandfather and grandmother away with my mother and uncle and they ended up in America." Guy shrugged, as if what had happened so long ago didn't matter.

But it did matter, and Enrick suspected that was why Guy had been sort of hostile toward him in the beginning.

"Hell, your family actually lived here? At Farraige Castle?" Grant asked.

"Yeah. They did."

"Why did our grandfather send your family away?" Lachlan asked.

"My grandfather didn't see eye to eye with yours. He fought his rule at every turn. Your grandfather hated to kick the family off the land, but he really didn't have any choice. He couldn't have that kind of constant dissent and still run the pack, my grandmother said." Guy let out his breath and ran his hands through his hair. "You have to know I objected to where the film was being set in the beginning. You can't imagine how much I didn't want to come here, to see the people who were in charge now. But the director loved this castle and he felt everything was right for the film. You were giving the director everything he needed—the castle, grounds, background actors with full dress, horses, wolves even. Hell, you don't know how much I didn't want to see the wolves in the film because I knew just who and what they were."

"Hell, I'm sorry, Guy," Enrick said.

Guy shook his head. "It's not *your* fault. And thanks, by the way, for the pep talk to get me to cross that creek. By telling me I was one of you, that made all the difference in the world. I didn't think it would, but it did."

"Good. I'm glad." Enrick glanced at Heather. She smiled at him and patted his leg, confirming he'd done all right after all. Then Enrick frowned. "You're…you're a distant *cousin* then."

Guy smiled. "Yeah. That must be why we look so much alike. Your brothers, too, but you are the spitting image of me."

"Well, I'll be. This is a cause for celebration." Enrick slapped him on the back. "Despite my grandfather having differences with yours, my brothers and I and the rest of our clan won't let that stand between us. You're welcome to return anytime to join us. You will always have a home with us."

Grant and Lachlan agreed with Enrick.

"And with us too," Ian said.

"Yes, we've been friends forever. And if you're looking for a girlfriend…we have several eligible she-wolves who would love to date you," Heather finished.

Guy smiled. "She's not in the tabloids, thankfully, but I'm dating a wolf right now."

"Oh, the ladies will be so disappointed," Heather said.

Enrick knew the men wouldn't be. They didn't need to lose one of their single lasses to a star in America.

"Thanks for the offer to visit though. I would like that. I guess I can't convince you to join me in America where you could continue to be my double, Enrick. You're perfect. You could teach me more of your sword-fighting skills and some of that Gaelic you were speaking that charmed the ladies and impressed the director, and help me perfect my Scottish brogue."

Enrick chuckled. "My home is here, but truly, you're welcome to come and stay with us at any time and we can assist you with your brogue, weapons training, and Gaelic." He was puzzled though. "Why were you afraid to get near William when he had been injured as a wolf? You knew he was one of us and he wouldn't have harmed you."

"I was staying in character. How would it have looked if I had been all macho and unafraid of an injured wolf? I was pretending to be afraid of the wolf. William."

Enrick would hate to have to playact at all times in front of the camera, and off. He could imagine being mobbed everywhere he went if anyone thought he was Guy. "And swimming out to sea?"

"Are you kidding? I would never have been able to swim in that cold water and for as far out as you'd swum. I mean, I know how to swim, but I stick to my heated swimming pool. By the way, you're a great double. If you had my voice down, you could replace me."

Enrick laughed. "No way. I could never speak all your lines and get them right."

"I don't either all the time."

Enrick shook his head. "This is the life for me."

Guy glanced at Grant and Lachlan. "Not me either," Grant said.

"You're in charge here. Totally understandable." Guy looked at Lachlan.

"Nay, like my brothers, this is home for me, but you'll always have a home with us."

"I have to ask if it's all right if I say we're related," Guy said.

"Aye," Grant said. "It is our honor to be related to a popular wolf like you."

"I will be sure to mention why we look so similar if anyone asks if we're related. I just hope no one realizes Enrick is playing some of my parts and that he's better at them than I am," Guy said, smiling. Then he grew serious. "The other wolves that fought yours... They're from a *lupus garou* pack, aren't they?"

"Aye. We've had trouble through the ages with them," Grant said.

"Then they are my enemy too. Is there any way I can help?"

Enrick appreciated Guy's offer, particularly after what their grandfather had done to Guy's. "No. We don't want you embroiled in this."

"I am. Not only because of them trying to sabotage the movie, but I'm one of you, even if our kin had trouble with each other in the past. I certainly don't hold it against you. I just didn't know how you would react if you knew who I was," Guy said.

"Like you're a long-lost cousin! Hell, you're a wolf like us. That makes all the difference in the world. Do you want to go for a run with some of us tonight?" Grant asked.

"Yeah, sure. I would love to. My grandmother taught me never to resent what had happened between her mate and your grandfather. That they'd both been stubborn asses. She gave him grief for it for many a year because she had wanted to stay in Scotland, but it wouldn't have worked out for them to try and move somewhere else, not without a wolf pack to back them. And she was committed to her wolf, no matter how outspoken or contentious he could be.

"When she was grown, my mother met Douglas McNab in Nebraska. He was a Highland wolf whose family left Scotland to find their fortune in America. We ended up in Montana as a family, no pack. We finally moved to Los Angeles where I've been in theater since I was young, an extra in every film I could get into. To begin with, those that had anything to do with sword fighting. I'd been practicing for years, but not as long as you have, and certainly not in any real battles."

"And wolf fights?" Enrick asked.

"The occasional fight. I saw a cute she-wolf near Bigfork, Montana, when I returned to the state to see other family, and was ready to ask her out when a male wolf came to chase me off. Man, was he growly, and a Navy SEAL to boot. I quickly learned he was courting the woman."

Enrick smiled. "That would do it."

"You're lucky to have Heather. She has real spunk. When I learned she'd pulled a knife on the woman who'd contaminated the food for that one meal, I was amazed and wanted to applaud her. Wait, don't tell me that woman is with the wolf pack that sent the wolves to attack your kin."

"Aye, she is," Enrick said.

"You didn't turn her over to the police, did you?" Guy sounded concerned.

"Nay. We couldn't," Heather said. "Not when she's a wolf. But we've resolved that issue. She's working for me at my shop."

Guy's eyes widened a bit. "And the wolves who attacked your people?"

"They're McKinleys, under Kilpatrick orders. They've been banished from the region and the pack," Grant said.

"They were trying to put the film behind schedule and discredit you and your wolves." Guy rubbed his chin in thought.

"Aye. They were angry we got the contract to have the film made here instead of at their castle," Enrick said.

"Man, I'm glad the film didn't take place at their castle then. I imagine they would have even been angrier with me if they had known who I was related to."

"I agree," Grant said. "It worked out best for all concerned."

Enrick knew how just the touch of fame Guy had was impacting him and his brothers when they went to Edinburgh and fans of Guy thought any of them were him. Now for them to admit they were related to him? Enrick could just imagine everyone wanting to talk to them in an attempt to be friends with Guy through them.

Enrick wondered how Guy handled his fame back in the States. "So how in the world did you find a she-wolf you were interested in courting while you're off making films all over the place and have human women at your beck and call?"

Guy smiled. "You know how we are. The notion of settling

down with one of our kind is the only way to go. Just finding one who wasn't already taken is the problem. Rest assured, I had no intention of ever turning a woman into a wolf. In the business I'm in, I hadn't found any wolves who are actors. Not that I want to mate an actress. I would probably be too overly protective with her if she was off with some leading man somewhere else, while I was in a film at a different location."

"And she would feel the same way about you and some leading lady," Enrick said.

Guy laughed. "Yeah, true. It didn't matter. The social circles I was in, I never seem to meet up with any of our kind. A lot of people believe I'm from the big city, but I'm really from a rural way of life. I finally finished the Viking movie and I had a break. I went back home to Montana, and there she was. Alice Hawthorn, a writer, had joined our small wolf pack, and when I saw her, we just connected. There have been ups and downs, of course. She hasn't wanted to get into the limelight with me, walking down the red carpet at premiere showings, all that bit. I want her to be with me, if we're going to make this work. She can take her work with her wherever we end up."

Julia tilted her chin down and gave him a look that said it wasn't that easy.

Guy smiled at her. "Well, right, that's what she says to me. That traveling around to different locations isn't always conducive to writing. I want her in my life, so I'm hoping we can find a way to make this work." He drank some of his water. "Being around a whole pack here in Scotland that are truly family is a real eye-opener."

"Aye, just wait until they learn you're a wolf like the rest of us. I'm sure you'd have all kinds of interest. Too much interest," Grant said, "so you'd better let everyone know you're courting a wolf already."

"I hate to admit I worry about that. Do you think it would be a good idea if I let your pack members in on the secret? This can't get out."

"You know it. And, aye, they need to know you're one of us. We're like all wolves. We don't let it be known that's what we are, so you won't have any problem with us, and everyone will treat you like the family that you are," Grant said.

"All right. I'm game if you are."

"Aye." Grant smiled.

CHAPTER 24

MAYNARD HAD PREPARED A SPECIAL HADDOCK-AND-CHIPS dinner to honor Guy, and they all went downstairs to the great hall to celebrate their kin's return home to the pack. Grant and his brothers, Colleen and her cousins, Heather and her brothers, Ian and Julia all attended the dinner to learn more about the actor. They enjoyed visiting with him and making him feel like he was a full-fledged member of the pack.

After that, several went with him to run as wolves by Argent Castle, and that became a regular nightly routine for the weeks that followed.

Now the filming was finally coming to an end.

That night, Heather was snuggling against Enrick and he was caressing her arm, neither of them able to drop off to sleep right away.

"Are you thinking about Edward and William biting the villains tomorrow?" she asked.

"Aye," Enrick said. "The other five wolves will be fighting the other villain's men, who are our own MacQuarrie extras, so no problem. But the two who bite the doubles for the villainous actors? Everyone will be on edge about that. Lachlan has tested and retested the arm that will be wearing the armor and extra padding. William and Edward have perfected the chomping down on our men's arms, growling and looking super vicious without biting down too hard. But any mistakes that could lead to turning one or both men could prove disastrous."

"I would not want to be one of Colleen's cousins tomorrow." Heather was proud of them, though, for volunteering to do the job.

"I would do it, but they need two of the original wolves who have been seen in the film up until the end. It seems fitting that two of the wolves that were injured by the McKinley wolves would take down the villains in the film."

"Since they were supposed to be one and the same in the film," Heather agreed.

"Aye." Then Enrick kissed her head. "Let's get some sleep. Tomorrow in the thick of the mist, everything will be decided."

Very early the next morning, Enrick and Heather and the rest of those living at Farraige Castle had a quick breakfast and then cleaned everything up in the great hall for the filming of a breakfast scene. Heather was in charge of that while Enrick watched in the wings.

Everything went according to plan, and then Guy went with his men and the wolves on a hunt.

With his loyal adviser and guards and his beloved wolves, Guy led the hunt for wild boar or deer.

"I believe we should have brought a larger guard force with us," Guy's adviser said.

The wizard agreed.

"We beat him in the earlier battle," Guy said. "By all accounts the villain died of his wounds in that encounter."

Enrick and many of his people and those from the MacNeill clan were watching from behind the scene, anxious to see the final fight between Guy, his men, and the main villains and their men, which were a mix of MacQuarrie and MacNeill clansmen. Enrick wouldn't be fighting this time but waiting to hear if he was needed to be Guy's stunt double. As far as he knew, he wasn't needed.

Then shouts rang out in the woods as the men found themselves surrounded on all sides by the villains and their men. The battle between good and evil was on.

Heather soon joined Enrick and held his hand, looking just as anxious as he felt about the wolves biting the humans. Never in a million years had he ever thought they would have two of their wolves bite humans on purpose!

Spencer, playing the lead villain, fought against Guy, both of them gaining ground and falling back until Guy stumbled over an exposed tree root behind him. He fell and landed on his back. Spencer looked a little surprised. Guy didn't spring to his feet, which had Enrick a wee bit worried.

Heather squeezed Enrick's hand. He shook his head at her, indicating it wasn't part of the scene as far as he knew.

Guy tried to get up, but he looked like he was struggling.

"Cut!" the director called out.

Guy looked crestfallen that he couldn't finish the scene, or at least that was what Enrick suspected. Enrick didn't jump in to check though. He let Guy talk to the director about it. But the film's set doctor hurried in to check on him.

"I pulled a back muscle." Guy appeared exasperated now. "I'm okay otherwise."

"Do you want to try to do this in a few hours?" The director surprised Enrick because time was money, the director was always saying. "We could shoot the indoor scenes now instead."

Now that sounded like the director, though it would still take time to move the equipment to the castle after everything was set up out here for the fight scene.

"It could be a few days before he's able to handle a sword fight. Doing light activities will probably be fine. But fighting with a sword?" The doctor shook his head. "He would aggravate the condition."

Guy grimaced as the doctor and Spencer helped him to stand and moved him away from the battle in the woods. "Call Enrick. He can take my place." Then he saw Enrick headed that way. Smiling in a pained way, Guy shook his head at Enrick.

Aye, Enrick had a wolf's hearing, just like Guy did.

The director got on his phone and called Enrick.

"I'm almost to your location, sir." Enrick had really believed he wouldn't be doing any more stand-ins for Guy, so he was surprised, but he wished Guy hadn't injured himself in the scene. At least Guy would heal faster than a human would.

As soon as Enrick took Guy's place in the woods, the director told Enrick that he would continue to fight Spencer until one of Spencer's men ganged up on Enrick and he was injured. Then there would be a break and then two of the wolves that had been fighting the extras would attack the doubles who would take Spencer and the other main villain's place.

Enrick would then attack Spencer, and Guy's adviser would attack the other, and the two main villains would be dead.

"You will stand over the fallen villains, heaving with exertion, and raise your sword in victory. Two of the extras will be fighting still, and then silence and everyone on your side will shout with exuberance. Any questions?"

Enrick had watched Guy practicing this scene yesterday, so he hoped he would get it right. He nodded, assuming he would figure it out as the scene played through. If the director didn't like it, Enrick knew he would stop them and give Enrick more guidance. He was ready to get this over with.

"All right. Action!"

Enrick fought Spencer as if his life and the lives of his men counted on it, just like he would have done in the old days. He thought Spencer looked a little surprised at the zeal Enrick used in the fight. But that was how he fought, whether in practice or in a battle. It made it real, it looked real, and on the screen, it would be just right.

Then he remembered Spencer had asked Heather to show him some Scottish hospitality. Maybe Spencer thought Enrick was trying to get him back for it. But he wasn't. He realized he was wearing Spencer out, the man swinging not half as rigorously. Enrick wanted to smile, but bit back on the inclination. Instead, Enrick was supposed to fall back, look ready to be beaten, be attacked by the other man, and fall, and then two of his wolves would attack those men.

They were growling and fighting other men for now.

That was when the other main villain attacked Enrick—he'd forgotten about him. Now with fighting two men, Enrick was working up a real sweat. Spencer was driven to beat him, and Enrick knew Heather would be watching. Hell, at least half their people not involved in the battle would be.

Redoubling his effort, Spencer knocked Enrick down as he took another swing at the other man.

The director called, "Cut! Fred, take Spencer's place, and Allan, you take Martin's." The doubles for the main villain actors took their places before the wolves attacked.

"Action!" the director called.

As if in retaliation for seeing their master knocked down, the two wolves tore into Spencer's double and the other man, mindful, hopefully, not to bite through the armor.

In the meantime, Enrick realized Spencer had cut through the padded armor and he was bleeding, damn it. Hopefully not too badly, and the padding seemed to help to stem the blood flow. He finally managed to get to his feet and, with a real effort, readied his sword to kill off Spencer's double—for the film. Oran came in to take care of the other stunt double so the two wolves would release the men's arms.

Enrick fought for some time, every swing harder to make, the adrenaline flooding his system for the fight, keeping him from feeling the pain in his arm. But he was feeling weaker. He finally managed the final blow, pretending to stab Spencer's double in the heart.

The director called, "Cut!"

And the doubles were replaced by the main villainous characters again for their death scenes.

Spencer clutched his bloodied chest as he looked up at Enrick, mortally wounded. "This isn't the end between us. Only the beginning." And then he gave Enrick an evil glower.

Enrick wondered if the guy was supposed to vanish on the screen or something and then come back for a sequel to the movie.

As soon as the scene was done, the director called, "Cut!"

Immediately, Enrick asked the stunt doubles if either of them had been bitten.

"Yeah, man, those wolves can sure bite," the one man said.

The other agreed. "Your men look like they're unafraid of the wolves. I was shitting bricks."

"Let me see your arms."

The men pulled off the padding and then the armor, but neither had a scratch on them.

Enrick breathed in a sigh of relief.

Most everyone was moving to the great hall for a celebratory feast—part of the story—but the director stayed back to see what Enrick was concerned about and patted him on the shoulder. "I told you they would be fine. Your wolves haven't hurt anyone so far."

"Right. Good thing too."

Heather had already left to help take care of the feast in the great hall, so Enrick texted her: The scene was a success. No problem with the wolves biting through the armor.

Heather texted back: Thank God for that. How are you doing?

Enrick texted: I'm good. Headed in now.

Then he slipped his phone into his sporran. He favored his injured arm, the burning pain just now beginning to kick in. He didn't want to worry her, not when it was something minor and she had an important job to do. He didn't want to distract her, but he had wanted to let her know right away that neither of the humans had been bitten.

He and the rest of the people were headed inside when Lachlan caught up with him and slapped him on the shoulder. Enrick groaned.

Lachlan immediately glanced down at Enrick's arm and swore. "You've been wounded."

"Aye, but don't make a big deal of it. I don't want Heather to know until after she's done with her scene."

"She will be furious with us if you don't let her know."

"Know what?" Grant asked, he and Colleen catching up to them. "Fine job on the wolves' part, and Enrick, you were superb while taking Guy's part."

Lachlan was frowning.

Grant asked, "What's wrong?"

"Our brother is injured."

Grant pulled Enrick to a halt and looked over his arm. "Hell, Brother."

"Oh no, Enrick." Colleen immediately took the wool scarf she was wearing around her neck and began wrapping it around Enrick's arm, delaying him from reaching the castle.

Enrick wanted to watch Heather's role in her last scene! And he sure didn't want her to catch a glimpse of him wearing Colleen's scarf as a temporary bandage.

"How's Guy doing?" Enrick asked, changing the subject.

"He's good. He said he could make it through the celebratory dinner as long as he doesn't have to stand up and dance a jig," Grant said.

Enrick laughed. "Poor guy. I was thinking we could put him up here for a while until he needs to go back to the United States for another film production. We could get to know him better."

"Aye, I already asked him. Colleen begged him to stay. Guy said that decided it for him." Grant smiled and hugged Colleen as they walked back to the keep.

"Good. Then he can get the rest he needs and—"

"You too," Colleen said, frowning at Enrick. "I texted the doctor and he's on his way."

"It's just a scratch."

She glanced down at his arm and he did too. A small amount of blood had stained her scarf red.

"I'm so sorry about your scarf," Enrick said.

"Are you kidding? You bleeding to death is more of an issue."

Enrick laughed.

Neither of his brothers did. They both gave him scowls that said he should not take this business so lightly.

"You do realize the last scene they're shooting is of Guy in bed with Missy," Lachlan said, his scowl turning to a smile. "His back might not be good enough to handle it."

"Well, Brother, I am incapacitated." Enrick elevated his injured arm a little to make his point.

"Not that it would stop you when it comes to Heather. I bet for the film you could work around it. And if you're all bandaged up, it would even look more realistic."

"I'm sure Guy can work around it." Though Enrick thought Lachlan might be right. Trying to pretend to make love to a woman in the throes of passion with a bad back could be more of an issue. "How about you? You could play the role, and it wouldn't be any trouble for you."

"Nay. You've got this, if Guy doesn't." Lachlan smiled at Enrick, enjoying the idea a little too much.

"I wonder if they caught you bleeding in the film," Lachlan asked. "You might want to tell the director so he can check it out and make sure Guy is wearing the same wound. Or a pretend version of it."

"Aye, I guess you're right." Enrick texted the director: *I managed to get a little cut while battling it out with Spencer. You might want to see if it shows up in the film.*

The director texted back: Will do. Where were you injured?

My right arm, Enrick replied.

There was a significant delay and then the director texted: Yeah, it shows up on the film, thanks. How are you doing?

Enrick texted: *I'm fine, thanks. Colleen called our doctor to look at the wound.*

Let me know if you need anything.

Enrick texted: *Will do.*

When they reached the castle, Enrick was surprised to see Guy walking toward the entryway with a definite limp to meet up with him. "Hell, we're a pair. How bad is the cut?" Guy frowned at seeing the blood on Colleen's scarf.

"It's not bad. How's your back?"

"A damn nuisance."

"You're staying with us until you're well, and I'll teach you not to fall and break your back during a sword fight," Enrick said.

Guy laughed. "I'll have to show you how to parry better when you're being attacked by a second threat."

Enrick smiled. He was glad they were on the same side.

"I thought you were giving Spencer a bit of grief during the battle. I heard he wanted to take Heather out," Guy said.

Enrick chuckled. "I was just being my usual focused self, until the other villain attacked."

"Hey, I've got to get on set, but let me know what the doctor says about your arm. I have a new scene we're doing before we have the dinner. Missy's got to bandage up my wound that you got in the woods."

Enrick smiled. "You know, on the beach scene, you should have tackled Missy instead of having your guards take her hostage."

"Hell, that's a great idea. Only now my back is injured. You would have to play the role."

Enrick showed him his arm.

"Talk to you in a little while." Guy hurried off as fast as he could with his back hurting him.

Enrick felt for him, but he figured Guy's injury would heal quickly. Enrick wanted to watch Heather next, but since the director was doing the new scene with Missy and Guy and his "new wound," Heather's scene would follow that.

Enrick would have some time to get checked out, since Colleen and Enrick's brothers were ensuring the doctor arrived and looked at his wound. When the doctor removed Colleen's scarf and Enrick had to strip down to his waist, he saw the cut was deeper than he'd thought it would be. The doctor sewed him up, gave him antibiotics, and told Colleen to call him if Enrick started running a fever or the wound looked infected.

"No more fighting for you," the doctor said. "Not for about three weeks."

At least Enrick's fighting days were over, as far as the film went. The battles were all done. The villains dead. The lord victorious.

Suddenly, Heather rushed into the room looking worried and annoyed. "Guy was doing a new scene where he had been injured. He said *you* had been injured and he was stuck having to pretend he had been. And you didn't tell me about it!"

"Aye, I didn't want to upset you, lass."

"I'm upset, all right? Because you didn't tell me. When I was texting with you on the phone, all you said was that the humans hadn't been bitten." She folded her arms and scowled at him.

"Which was true. I wanted to let you know right away."

"And not about you? Were you trying to be all macho, or what?"

"Nay, lass. I was afraid you would be upset and couldn't concentrate on the scene you had to be part of. I didn't know Guy was going to do another scene before that."

"And? You couldn't have told me after that? Fine." She stormed out of the room.

Colleen raised her brows as she considered Enrick. "You should have told her." Then she left the room.

The doctor shook his head. "Let me know if you begin to feel poorly. Otherwise, you should be fine." Then he left.

Lachlan and Grant smiled at Enrick.

"Hell," Enrick said. "I didn't want to worry her."

"That worked out well," Lachlan said. "Did you need me for anything?"

"Nay, thanks, Lachlan."

"Okay. I need to take care of the wolves. They will be at the celebration meal." Lachlan hurried off.

Grant cleared his throat and folded his arms. "You will have to make it up to the lass. But first, if I were you, I would get changed. If you need to be Guy's double again because of his back this time, you'll be ready."

"You won't stand in for me?"

"Me? Nay, you have nothing but a scratch." Grant left the room.

Enrick frowned. He wondered how Missy was dealing with Guy's injured arm. A lot better than Heather had treated Enrick, he'd bet.

CHAPTER 25

FOR THE FILM, HEATHER WAS BUSY WITH HER SCENE IN THE kitchen and serving food in the great hall, the wolves enjoying the feast while she tried to avoid being knocked over by them. She saw Enrick watching her from the other entryway, and she gave him a peeved look. He should have been lying down, not watching her in the scene. She wanted to make love to him, to show him how much she cared about him, if he could handle it after being injured. So he *had* to rest.

She swore they'd always been that way with each other, even if he'd tried to believe they wouldn't suit in years past—seeing her, catching her eye, wanting something he thought he couldn't have, just like she'd felt about him. But now?

He wanted her, just like she wanted him, to scratch the itch she always felt when she saw him. Wanting to be with him, to touch his hand, to press a lingering kiss upon his wickedly pliable mouth. To rub her body against his and feel his cock growing for her. Och! She was already wet with need. After this scene and when he was free, she was taking him to bed.

When she returned to the kitchen, Lana said, "You know the director is wondering if Guy can handle the love scene with Missy in the chamber after this scene is done. What if he asks Enrick to do it instead?"

Several of the women doing kitchen duty for the film paused to hear what Heather had to say. All the filming was going on in the great hall, so they could talk freely in the kitchen for now.

"Enrick is saving his strength for me." Heather loaded up another tray filled with dishes and mugs. "His younger brother, Lachlan, can fill the role. I know Grant wouldn't do it. And Colleen sure wouldn't go along with it."

"And you?" Lana asked, smiling.

Heather sighed. "He will do what he feels he needs to do. But he is wounded, you know."

Lana shook her head. "I truly don't think Guy wants to give up that part of his role either. He has a reputation to uphold on the silver screen. I hope if he does do it, he isn't feeling too much pain. Did you hear how Enrick fought against Spencer?"

"Hold that thought. I need to deliver these to the lord's table." Heather hurried off while two other women carried trays of food and drinks to other tables.

Heather was dying to hear what Lana had to say, but the show had to go on. When she returned to the kitchen, she said, "Okay, what?" She wished she could have been there to watch the battle where Enrick had been injured, but she'd had to return to the castle to take charge of the food preparations for this scene.

"Enrick was a little overzealous in fighting with Spencer and the other villain. Some said because Spencer had asked you out, and Enrick was fighting him for your honor."

Heather laughed. "Okay, so I'm not surprised." Then she frowned. "But I didn't want him injured over it. Do you know he is standing in the other entryway, watching me work? He needs to lie down."

"You do realize he loves you, don't you? I know you were angry with him for not telling you he'd been injured, but he was only trying to keep you from thinking about him when you had a job to do."

"So I'm not thinking about him now?"

"Which is just the point. You learned he was injured, and you're worried about it."

"Aye, I am. But he should have told me." Heather let out her breath. "Okay, this scene is nearly done. And I'm glad I don't have to do anything with the love scene."

Lana laughed. "Nay, their professional actresses serving as Missy's maids will take care of that."

"How do you feel about returning to the shop and baking bread after being an extra in a movie?" Heather asked.

"Oh, I will love to get back to the routine, in truth. It's been fun and I wouldn't have given this up for anything, but I'm ready to return home and sleep in my own bed." Lana frowned. "What are you and Enrick going to do? With him being so important to the pack and leadership, he might feel he needs to stay here."

"I know. I've been thinking about it. I would love to have our own place, a home somewhere in between the shop and his castle. But I don't mind the commute if he needs to be closer to home to do his job."

"Get a home of your own. You'll work it out. Grant wouldn't deny his brother a place of your own."

"We'll see. It's one thing to manage a pie shop—"

"An incredibly *successful* shop."

"Aye, but another thing to manage a wolf pack and a castle."

"All that should matter is being with you."

Heather smiled. But Enrick's position was really important, so she wouldn't make light of his job. He had to be there for the pack.

At the entrance to the great hall, Enrick watched as Lachlan called the wolves to come with him while Guy and Missy left the great hall to do their love scene in the lord's chamber. Enrick thought the wolves weren't needed for any further scenes so they would be free to stay at the castle and shift into their human forms. But he was wrong.

"The director wants the wolves to run into the lord's chamber when he goes to make love to his wife. Guy has to shoo them out of the chamber, the first time ever that she takes priority over his wolves," Lachlan told Enrick.

"I'll go with you then."

Heather was done with all her scenes for the day. Enrick was glad about that. He was ready to spend all his spare time with her and get back to his real job after the wedding scene tomorrow. Unless Enrick needed to be a double, he didn't have a role to play. Heather would be among the background actors at the chapel.

They finally reached the chamber where the love scene was going to be filmed. "You need to be Guy's double if he needs one for this scene," Enrick said before Lachlan motioned for the wolves to enter the room where Missy and Guy were still fully dressed and ready for the director to call "Action."

Lachlan shook his head.

Then the director called, "Action!" and Missy and Guy started to kiss.

Lachlan motioned for the wolves to race into the room, and Guy turned, which was a mistake on his part. He groaned, his back still hurting him.

Enrick felt for him.

"Cut!" The director asked, "Why don't you turn so you're facing the door and then you can chase the wolves off?"

"Why don't I do that part and then Guy can take over from there?" Enrick said, thinking after he said it that he'd lost his mind. He only thought to deal with the wolves, *not* make love to the heroine afterward.

As if he'd read Enrick's mind, Guy smiled at him. The director waited for Guy to say what he wanted to do. "We're good. I'll face the door when the wolves enter."

Lachlan called the wolves out of the chamber to repeat the scene.

Once Guy and Missy were ready, the director called, "Action!" and Lachlan motioned to the wolves to run into the chamber.

Guy frowned and waved his hand at the wolves. "Out, now, all of you!" He winced as he motioned with his hand.

The wolves acted reluctant at first, like they were supposed to, confused that their master would send them packing when they always slept with him in his chamber at night. Then Guy said again, "Go, out, now!"

The wolves reluctantly obeyed, tails tucked between their legs, ears flattened, heads down as they loped out of the room. *Perfect*, Enrick thought.

The director called, "Cut!" Then he called for action again, and the kissing began between the movie stars. Suddenly, Heather was at Enrick's side, slipping her hand in his, squeezing it, smiling up at him, and he leaned down to kiss her, glad *his* back wasn't hurting him and their lovemaking would be for real.

Forget about being a stunt double. Enrick was finished. The job was done. The last shoot in progress for the night. Lachlan was still there if the director needed someone to fill in for Guy. Enrick couldn't quit thinking of being with Heather in the throes of passion, seeking fulfillment in her arms as only mated wolves could, loving her in every way possible.

Sure, she'd looked peeved at him for watching her while she was doing her duty in the great hall, but he couldn't help it. He wanted to be there if she needed him for a rescue. What if she had encountered another bone in her path? Despite appearing annoyed with him, she had glanced in his direction to see if he was there, watching her. Or maybe she had an uncanny sixth sense that he had been looking out for her again.

Not caring anything about his injury, Enrick was taking his mate to bed.

Heather was surprised that when she and Enrick were kissing, he suddenly led her away from the chamber where the scene was being filmed and headed down the hall to his chamber. She thought he might be needed if Guy's back was acting up. She glanced over her shoulder at Lachlan, who folded his arms and shook his head at them. But then he gave her a little smile.

She smiled and mouthed, "Thank you."

Lachlan would take Guy's place if he needed to. She loved Lachlan for giving Enrick the out, and Enrick for wanting to make love to her more than doing his duty as Guy's stand-in.

Sure, she hadn't wanted Enrick to make pretend love to Missy, but she would have backed him on anything he needed to do.

He hurried her down the hallway as if he was afraid the director would catch up to him and say he needed to do the rest of the scene for Guy because Lachlan had decided he didn't want to do it.

"You're eager to make love to me, I see," she said to Enrick.

He smiled down at her. "Aye, lass, always." He swept her up in his arms and carried her the last few feet to his room and opened the door, then walked inside and closed it with his hip. "And nothing is stopping us."

"That's one of the things I love about you."

"You really didn't think I was going to fill in for Guy, did you?" Enrick unfastened her kilt pin and pulled her kilt off her shoulder, letting the fabric fall to her belt in back.

"Aye, when you have a job to do, you don't give up on it."

He smiled. "It was Lachlan's turn."

She laughed. "I don't think he was too unhappy about the prospect." She unfastened the Celtic wolf knot pin holding Enrick's kilt over his shoulder and placed it on the dresser. She pulled the kilt draped over his shoulder and slipped it off, and like hers, it fell to the back of his belt.

Then they began kissing, her hands caressing the back of his head, her mouth pressing against his and then licking, and then kissing again. She cupped his pleated-kilt-covered buttocks and squeezed. She loved the feel of his firm buttocks. She knew he wasn't wearing any boxer briefs under his great kilt, not unless he'd done something differently this time. The idea he was naked beneath that tartan fabric made him all the sexier and more tantalizing.

But then she was naked under hers too. She rubbed her body against his and felt his steel-hard cock pressing against her kilt. "Hmm, you feel so good." She pulled his body even harder against hers.

His hands swept down her back and he nuzzled her neck, his five-o'clock shadow brushing against her sensitive skin. "So do you, lass." He licked her neck, sizzling heat following in his tongue's wake.

Their heartbeats were already ramping up, their pheromones kicking into high gear, her blood heating. She loved the way he stroked her arms, thrust his tongue into her mouth, and pulled her close to feel her breasts against his chest. Her nipples were already sharp points, sensitive to his touch.

He ran his hand down her waist until he caught hold of her long overskirt and long shirt underneath and pulled them up to her waist, then tucked the hems into her belt, exposing her mons to him. She felt naked and sexy, the cool air in the room making her feel even more exposed.

He slid his hot finger between her wet folds and began to stroke her sensitive bud. She clung to him, feeling as though she would collapse on the floor if she didn't hold on tight to his hips.

He stopped for a moment and she said, "Don't stop."

"Too many clothes, lass."

Fine. She agreed, but she wanted him stroking her nub again. She grabbed hold of the belt holding his sporran and sword and unfastened it. As soon as she did, his kilt fell to the floor in a puddle of plaid. But he was still wearing boots and a long shirt. She placed his belt on the nearby chair. She was mindful that she couldn't just toss his belt with his sword to the floor as if his weapon was insignificant. Not as many times as it had saved his life and his kin's lives in a fight to the death.

Then he removed her belt and her kilt fell in volumes of plaid to the floor. She was wearing a long shirt under that and her boots too. He ran his hands over her breasts through the soft fabric, his eyes dark with lust. Then he pulled up her long shirt and tossed it aside. She was quick to lift his shirt next, exposing his beautiful muscular body, and pull it over his head. She noticed his bandaged arm and touched the skin lightly around it. No blood on the bandage, for which she was glad. He lifted her onto the bed as if he didn't want her to worry about his injured arm and crouched down to pull off her boots and socks. She planned to remove his, but he quickly yanked his own off and then moved in beside her as she scooted over on the mattress so he could join her.

Thankfully, he began kissing her breasts and stroking her nub again. And the fevered need to reach a climax shot through her all over again. She was so wet and ready for him. Ready to feel his erection thrusting into her, their bodies undulating in rhythm. Their hearts beating in sync. Their breaths frantic and shallow. And the smell of their sex enveloping them, pushing them into a mating frenzy.

Her body burned for him, waves of desire coursing through her as he licked and suckled a nipple. She arched against his questing finger, wanting his cock to penetrate her slick sheath now.

Then he trailed kisses up her chest, her throat, her jaw, his finger still stroking her with the most imperative mission: to bring her to climax, to make her feel as light as air.

And then his mouth was on hers, branding her with a searing kiss, tongue exploring her mouth, hers taking a turn next. Her hands were cupped around his head, not wanting to give his mouth up, yet absorbing the feel of his finger stroking her nub, drawing her to new heights.

His kisses were insistent, demanding, almost as much as hers were. She clung fiercely to his shoulders, tremors of pleasure stealing her thoughts, driving her to the edge. Maybe because of the way she was digging her fingers into his shoulders, he knew she was getting ready to come.

He dipped his finger inside her core, swirled it around, and the tremors multiplied. He inserted another finger and penetrated her as deeply as he could, simulating his cock, and she arched against him, writhing in anticipation, knowing the climax was nearly there.

He began stroking her nub again, and she cried out, her whole body filled with sweet joy, and she rode the high when he spread her legs and pressed his advantage.

He pulled her legs around his lean hips and began to thrust deep inside her. Then he was kissing her again, his mouth possessing hers, and she licked and kissed and nibbled his lips in return. His eyes were darkened with need, the seduction mutual, loving, and fulfilling.

Every time they made love, it was like discovering a new world, learning more about each other, identifying the nuances that would turn him on and that would turn her on. She moved her legs up higher, taking him in deeper, and he thrust harder.

They were kissing each other, tasting and teasing and deepening the kiss. Still feeling euphoric and now with his body connected to hers, she felt the tide rising, swelling, carrying her upward again. She couldn't believe he could make her come again so soon after the first time, but his wolfish powers of seduction were beyond compare. She was trying to hold off until he came too so they would be in sync.

As if he knew she was struggling to hold on to the feelings rising in her, he slid his hand between them and began to stroke her while he continued to thrust. Ohmigod. It didn't take much for her to shoot straight toward the heavens on the crest of a wave.

She cried out again, and he came this time, exploding deep inside her, bathing her in his hot wetness, continuing to thrust until he was totally spent, groaning with release.

"You are something special," he said, his warm breath whispering against her temple.

"You are my dream wolf come true."

He pulled her into his arms and held her tight, kissing the top of her head as she finally settled against him the way she'd come to love, one leg propped against his in a way that said "Mine." Her arm stretched over his body, keeping him close. Her head rested against his chest, and his hand stroked her back with a gentle sweep of his fingers. At least, that was how they always started out. Sometimes they ended up with him spooning her in the middle of the night, sometimes with him partially pinning her down in a possessive way, but they were always touching, as if they needed that connection that showed they loved each other to the depths of their souls.

Of course, sometimes he ended up between her legs, and they would be making love all over again.

Tomorrow was the last scene of the movie, but all she cared about was tonight and being wrapped up in her wolf. Though she realized she should have asked how his arm was feeling before they'd made love.

"Enrick," she whispered, not wanting to disturb the quiet moment between them, "is your arm okay?"

He chuckled and kissed her forehead. "Now you ask."

She sighed. "Well, if it's hurting, we should just sleep the rest of the night."

"Uh-huh." He continued to stroke her back and she suspected his injury wouldn't keep him from making love to her again.

And it didn't. She loved her strong Highland wolf.

CHAPTER 26

THE NEXT AFTERNOON AFTER THE FILMING OF THE WEDDING scene that morning, the film crew was taking down sets and packing up and departing. The director and the actors were leaving for their next assignments—all but Guy, who was staying for a couple of weeks to get to know his kin and run with them as wolves to his heart's content when his back felt better. He was glad to be part of the family, a wolf pack, a clan. And this would give him time for his injured back to heal.

For two weeks, Heather had been staying at Farraige Castle with Enrick, but they were actively looking for a home closer to her work. He knew she really wanted that, and he wanted her to be happy, most of all.

That night, it was time for Guy to leave Scotland. Since Enrick and Guy had become friends, they would pick up Heather after her shop closed and have dinner together before they took him to the airport.

They'd packed Enrick's car with Guy's bags and were on their way to Heather's shop when Heather called Enrick. He thought she was calling because he was late picking her up, not calculating how long it would take for Guy to get his stuff together to leave and say goodbyes to his new wolf pack.

"The McKinleys and Kilpatricks who were banished are here, trying to break the windows and the glass door. Get help. Hurry!" Heather said, her words rife with urgency and concern.

The heavy thuds of someone hitting the glass sounded on the car's speakers, and Enrick's heart practically stopped beating.

As soon as Heather saw the two Kilpatrick brothers and five other men show up at the shop with baseball bats in hand and swords swinging at their hips, Catherine McKinley grabbed her phone. "Those two men must be the other two who were involved in the battle when they tried to injure your men. I didn't know who they were."

"Good, then we can get rid of all of them at the same time." Instantly, Catherine and Heather were both on their phones, calling for help, Catherine saying, "I know, Paxton. They're coming here to kill us, not to talk. Hurry! Yes, Heather's talked to her mate, he's calling for backup."

Heart racing, Heather dashed around the counter and grabbed a bow and quiver of arrows hanging on the wall and tossed them over the counter. "We have two fire extinguishers and some cleaning sprays we can use on them. Let's get some of the tables and chairs and barricade the countertop." The glass display cabinets were tall, six feet in height, so they would provide a barrier of sorts. "We just need to delay these men long enough to allow help to arrive."

Catherine grabbed a sword off the wall and set it on a table, then removed a shield. "I can't manage a sword and a shield at the same time. They're both too heavy. Maybe we can use one or the other."

"I'll use the bow and arrows, unless you're a better shot than me. I've won first place in a few competitions." Heather wedged some more chairs on top of the countertop, while Catherine carried the shield and sword behind the counter.

"I can shoot, but I haven't done so in a long time." Catherine rushed around the counter and added more chairs on top of the ones Heather had already stacked on the countertop.

Once they'd done all they could with that, Heather and Catherine hurried around the counter, and Heather locked the door to the counter area and kitchen. She began grabbing bottles of cleaning products from under one of the kitchen cabinets that Catherine could use to spray in the men's eyes while she held them off with her bow and arrows.

Catherine grabbed one of the fire extinguishers and set it on the floor next to the selection of cleaners behind the counter. The men were still battering at the glass, and Heather was glad she'd paid more for the bulletproof kind. She had thought with the trouble they had with the McKinleys, it might come in handy if they tried to vandalize her shop. She'd made the right decision that time.

"They look angry they can't break through the glass easily." Catherine set the second fire extinguisher on the floor next to the rest of her arsenal, the sword and shield next to that.

"Yeah, I'm glad I got the more expensive glass." Heather had her bow and arrows ready to start shooting. She wanted to hit the men before they got too far into the shop. She didn't want the men to get close enough that Catherine would have to resort to using the cleaning sprays and the fire extinguishers, worried the men could strike her and Catherine with their swords.

Heather had another thought. "Uh, boil some water."

Her eyes wide, her lips parted, Catherine stared at her.

"This is our castle, and right now, it's under siege. We're outnumbered and the men are a lot stronger than us. We have to do everything we can to keep them from killing us before help arrives. Just, well, start it in case we have time to use some." Heather hoped her call to arms would convince Catherine to get with the program. Though she had to remind herself these men were Catherine's kin. Out to kill her, sure, but they were not faceless intruders intent on murder—they were her own relations.

"Aye."

Of course if they'd been defending a castle, the boiling water would have been poured down on the men who had broken through the portcullis or were climbing the castle walls. At least in a situation like that, the men fighting from the wall walk were some distance from their attackers, unlike with Catherine and her.

Still, if Catherine threw a pot of boiling water at the men, they would have to jump back or get scalded. Heather wished she had another bow and quiver of arrows for Catherine to use. Or at least Heather could use the other arrows. She had ten arrows in all. They wouldn't be enough.

She was just glad she'd added that to her collection of weapons on the walls. She would never have managed to fight the men with one of the swords she had on display. She couldn't see Catherine successfully fighting them with one either.

Then the men broke through the glass door and climbed through the wooden frame. Catherine grabbed one of the fire extinguishers, readying it to use it as soon as any of the men were in range. Heather nocked her arrow to her bow and let the first arrow fly, striking the first man through the door in the chest. She let loose the second one, and that went through his throat. He clutched his chest and throat and collapsed on his face. The other men stared at him for a moment, looking shocked that one of them was down. They looked up and saw Heather nocking the next arrow, and the men scattered outside the broken glass door.

God, if only she could keep them from coming in. It took them a few minutes and a lot of hushed talking before two of them rushed through the door, followed by the rest of them, but Heather was only targeting one of the men as he ran to knock down their barrier on the countertop with a baseball bat.

One arrow released, then two, both hitting the target in the chest. He collapsed and one of the men stumbled over him. Robert and Patrick dove into the shop and slipped next to the door to the counter area while the other three McKinleys took their chances and slammed their bats at the barricade on top of the counter.

Heather was trying to take aim as the chairs and tables went flying, but she didn't want to waste her arrows, and she had to dodge the flying chairs and tables too. *Damn it!* As soon as they cleared her counter where she could get a good shot, she would shoot. Catherine wasn't waiting and blasted one of the men she had a clearer shot at with the fire extinguisher.

The foam spray hit him full force in the face, and he screamed out in pain. He was coughing, the strong irritation most likely causing respiratory distress, his hands on his eyes, trying to wipe the chemical from them. He tripped over one of the men Heather had shot and fell to the floor, appearing to be in agony, coughing and choking.

Catherine switched her attention to the other men, but they'd ducked down behind the display counter, avoiding the spray. Some of the chairs were still on top of the counter, but most were on the floor on Heather and Catherine's side of the counter.

Heather wanted to start stacking them back up to provide a barrier again, but she didn't want to set down her bow. Catherine, likewise, was ready with the second fire extinguisher, both of them tense, their hearts beating wildly. At least they had managed to take down three of the men. But with four more armed men, they were way outnumbered.

The Kilpatrick brothers began beating on the door to the area behind the counter. They would break it in and then the men would come at them from two fronts, to their right and from the front. She and Catherine's efforts to defend themselves would be divided.

Heather didn't want to be faced with that. Divide and conquer—that was what would happen.

That was when she heard Enrick's car racing down the road and finally screeching to a halt in the parking lot. She felt a bit of relief. Enrick was letting Heather know he was coming to her aid, warning the men who had broken in that they had real Highland warriors to fight now, instead of just a couple of Highland lasses.

Heather's brother Oran drove up in his car after that, and

Enrick shouted as he raced into the store. "Heather!" He grabbed a sword off the wall.

"Catherine and I are safe," Heather called out from behind the counter.

Guy was right behind Enrick and also grabbed a sword displayed on her wall. Heather's brothers all ran in after them, each of them already armed.

The Kilpatrick brothers stopped banging on the door, and she saw Enrick fighting Robert, her brothers Oran, Callum, and Jamie fighting the McKinleys, while poor Guy, the newest member of their pack, was fighting Patrick. Heather suspected he'd never believed he would be fighting in a real battle to the death with Highland warriors. Worse, Guy looked like he was in pain. His back? Great.

Heather wanted to push some of the chairs off the counter so she could shoot one of the rogue wolves full of arrows, but the men were moving around so much, she didn't want to wound the wrong person. Suddenly, more cars and trucks were pulling into the parking lot—Ian and his brothers and more of the MacNeill kin, Grant and Lachlan and more of the MacQuarrie men, and even Paxton, the McKinley leader, and some of his men arrived to help out.

━━━━━━━━

Enrick had been so angry the men had come to kill his mate and Catherine that he hadn't planned to give the rogues any quarter. Robert had never seen him fight like that. When they'd fought during the shoot in the rain and mud, Enrick had been fighting for some time, while Robert had been fresh for the kill. But this time, Robert had gone after the wrong person.

Guy was struggling, and Enrick was certain he'd injured his back again. Then the rest of the troops arrived, and Enrick stabbed

Robert in the shoulder. He wanted to take him down. He wanted to eliminate the rogue wolf, but with Paxton now arriving, and Cearnach killing Patrick for Guy, Enrick let Paxton have Robert and the other men who were still among the living. All of them had been wounded though.

"We will take them off your hands," Paxton said, and Ian and Grant looked like they weren't sure that was a good idea. "They tried to murder my sister and your kin. The men who haven't died will cease to exist. You have my word."

"Aye, see to it then," Grant said. "If we ever see any of their faces again, they're dead men."

"Aye," Ian agreed.

"You have my word," Paxton repeated and shook Ian and Grant's hands. Then he told his men to move the prisoners and the dead men to his van and return them to his castle.

Enrick was already headed for the door to the counter and Heather hurried to open it. She threw herself into his arms and hugged him tight, her heart still beating wildly, tears streaking down her cheeks. "You were late," she scolded.

He kissed her passionately on the mouth, not wanting to ever let her go. "I didn't think Guy would ever get out of the castle. He had made so many friends and was having a hard time saying goodbye to everyone."

"I will take full responsibility for our being late," Guy said, his hand on his back. "I'm so sorry."

Enrick could have lost his wild Highland lass if it hadn't been for her quick thinking and tactical planning on the makeshift battlefield. He loved her with all his heart. He hugged her to his breast, unable to release her because he was so relieved she was alive and well.

"They had to have been waiting, biding their time when you were late this one time and I had released the rest of my staff," Heather said.

"I was late sending one of my men to pick up Catherine as well," Paxton said, sounding deeply regretful. "I assumed Enrick would be there and wouldn't leave until someone picked up Catherine."

"It is done," Catherine said, hurrying to turn off the water boiling in a pot and then washing the foam residue off her hands.

Heather gave her a hug. "You were a great warrior."

Catherine hugged her back. "You were a great leader. I would never have thought to use what you had in the shop to our advantage in fighting our enemy."

Everyone was helping to clean up the glass and set up the tables and chairs back in place. Even Paxton and his men—who weren't guarding the van and their prisoners—were helping to clean up the mess. Though Paxton had given Catherine a hug, too, and looked well relieved that she was still alive.

Paxton told Heather, "My pack will pay for all the damages."

"Thank you." Heather finally turned her attention to Guy, who was still holding his back. "You've reinjured your back."

"Think nothing of it. In the heat of battle, it is nothing." Guy gave her a pained smile.

"You'll have to stay with us longer. You can't fly all those hours in your condition. It will kill you," Heather said.

Enrick agreed. He couldn't imagine how being forced to sit so long would affect an injured back.

"I agree," Guy said.

"Dinner at the castle then," Enrick said, figuring they would need a change of plans.

Guy frowned. "No, I was taking you both out." He sounded adamant, especially after what had happened to Heather and Catherine, due to him delaying Enrick's arrival.

Enrick wasn't sure Heather was in the mood to go out for dinner after what had happened. Or that Guy was in any shape to do so.

Grant said, "Go, have dinner like you planned. We'll take care of everything here. Don't worry about it. Then, Guy, you are to go straight to your chamber following the dinner, and we'll have someone set you up with a heating pad and anything else you need to make you more comfortable. Enrick, you and Heather are on your own after that."

Enrick smiled. It hadn't taken long for Grant to take charge of his new pack member and lay down the law. Guy smiled, looking grateful he was truly one of the pack. And Enrick was definitely planning to take care of his bonny lass the rest of the night in his chamber, but when they woke, he was taking her to see a house he thought she would love close to her place. It shortened his distance to Farraige Castle some too.

He gave her another hug before he led her out to the car. She looked reluctant to leave just yet. "Come on, lass. They'll do their best to take care of it. After dinner, we can see their progress, if you would like."

"Aye, I would like that."

Then he would make sure they had a long, extended dinner to give the men time to put her place back in order.

When they returned that evening, men were still putting the finishing touches on the place. Someone had replaced the one spent fire extinguisher, and Heather's sword, shield, and bow and quiver of arrows were again on the wall, minus four of the arrows. So were Enrick and Guy's borrowed swords.

The glass door had been patched, and so had the door to the counter and kitchen that the Kilpatricks had been bashing.

"Thanks to everyone who came to our rescue," Heather said. "I'm so sorry I didn't mention it earlier."

"After what you went through," Ian said, "think nothing of it."

"Aye," Grant said. "All that matters is that you and Catherine came out of it unscathed."

Enrick knew they would have a feast to celebrate the end of hostilities between their pack and Paxton's, though they weren't including their pack in the celebration. If Paxton had eliminated the men who had caused the trouble instead of banishing them, none of this would have happened.

Guy went home with Grant and Lachlan, while Enrick drove Heather back to the castle. "I'm sorry, Heather. I know it was a strain for you to have dinner out with Guy tonight."

She sighed. "I hope I wasn't too much of a wet blanket. Guy needed to do it. He would have felt terrible if he hadn't. Though I know his back had to have been bothering him."

"You were so quiet."

"Guy filled in all the pauses." She chuckled. "Aye, I was worried about the shape the shop would be in. I feel much better after seeing it nearly back to the way it had been."

He figured there was more to her being so quiet at dinner. "Killing the two men—"

"It had to be done. I don't regret it."

"I should have been there." He felt terrible about it. He could have lost her.

She reached over and ran her hand over his lap. "You came in the nick of time. If you hadn't, we wouldn't be having this conversation. That's all that matters. And what comes next."

He raised a brow.

"Don't tell me you don't know what comes next."

He laughed. "You are a warrior at heart, lass. My wild Highland she-wolf is a force to be reckoned with. I love you."

She smiled at him, looking pleased he would say so. She ran her hand over his arm. "I hope your arm is okay after the fight."

"Ah, lass, nothing would stop me from showing you how much I love you when we return home. And that's a promise."

She leaned her head against his shoulder. "That is the reason why I love you."

EPILOGUE

WHEN THE MACQUARRIES FINALLY RECEIVED A COPY OF THE film, some who had participated and the MacNeill pack leaders, Ian and Julia, and Heather's brothers came to watch it in the great hall of Farraige Castle. Maynard made kettles of buttered popcorn for everyone to snack on, courtesy of Colleen who said everyone had to have buttered popcorn at the cinema. Though she also had the sweet, caramel-covered kind for those who ate that variety.

Another showing of the film would occur later for those who couldn't attend this special first showing. Others wanted to see it at a regular cinema.

"Oh-oh, they left the fighting scene in there where you and Cearnach were battling it out with Robert and Patrick," Heather said, cuddling with Enrick.

"I sure didn't think the director would keep any of that."

"You even look like Guy despite the slashes of mud on your cheeks," Lachlan said.

"It looks like the director thought you appeared so ferocious that it was perfect for a close-up," Colleen said.

"Hell, I should have been paid a higher amount for being his double for that scene then."

Everyone laughed.

"They didn't show me in the film," Grant said, though no one had thought the director would keep any of those shots, not when Grant was barreling through the fighters with the other men, searching for any McKinleys who had infiltrated their ranks.

"You looked like you were too much in charge, the real leader of the men," Colleen said.

Several said, "Aye."

When they came to the part where Enrick was walking down all those stairs from the castle to the beach, they would cut some of it, even though he'd walked down them with a good steady pace. It was just too much filler otherwise.

Oran grunted. "Guy couldn't have managed all those steps."

"Nay, he's a wolf like us. He could have. He just didn't want to," Enrick said, sticking up for him.

"He didn't want to swim in the cold water either," Heather said, loving this scene the best.

"I just hoped Enrick wouldn't start to drown, because Callum and Jamie and I would have had to dive into that icy water and save his naked arse," Oran said.

If Oran had been closer to where Heather was sitting, she would have socked her brother.

Everyone laughed though.

When Enrick was wading out into the sea in the film, Colleen involuntarily shivered. "This scene gave me chills just thinking about swimming in the water."

Colleen had been washed out into the sea when she was trying to rescue a young boy, so she had firsthand knowledge of how cold that water could be.

"Me too," Heather said.

"It's not so bad after the initial shock." Enrick scarfed down some more popcorn. "I love this buttered popcorn, Colleen."

"Yeah, it's real butter, not like what they serve in the theater, uh, cinema back home," Colleen said.

Everyone was quiet when Enrick came out of the sea dripping wet. Then he lifted the shirt off the sand and shook it out and held it in front of his crotch, one sexy leg exposed. Heather squeezed his hand. He was so hot.

He leaned down and kissed her.

"Well done," Lachlan said. "I'm glad it was you and not me. Grant told me if Enrick didn't want to do it, I was next on the

Guy look-alike roster to pull the duty. And Grant told me I was doing it."

Everyone laughed.

"You didn't want to go for a swim, Grant?" Enrick asked.

"Hell, I didn't want to be on camera going for a swim." Grant finished his beer.

When they had the scene with the wolves on the hunt, everyone tensed a little. Now when they watched the film, they weren't just seeing the magic of the film production, but also being reminded of all the trouble they'd had with the McKinleys and Kilpatricks.

The filmmakers didn't show any scenes where the wolves were fighting their wolves because it wasn't part of the script, and Heather was sure they didn't want to have the animal rights activists up in arms.

"Good, no wolves fighting in the film," Grant said.

Everyone agreed.

Then they reached the scene where William bit the wrong extra who didn't have all the additional arm padding. William quickly let go and turned his wrath on another man, the one he was supposed to attack in the first place, while the other man was quickly engaged in a fight.

"I'm glad they didn't reshoot that scene and that I didn't injure the other man," William said.

"With all that was going on in that scene, it was an easy mistake to make," Enrick said, everyone agreeing. "These sure aren't all in the order we saw them shot."

"Yeah, I kept thinking they cut out a whole bunch of scenes we were in, but then a few minutes later, there's the scene we were in," Oran said.

The wolves at the meal in the great hall was a fun scene where Colleen's cousins were fighting over a bone.

"Was William supposed to win the bone?" Enrick asked.

William smiled. "We agreed whoever truly tugged hard enough

and got the bone in the end kept it. Though after I left the great hall with my reward, I dumped it."

"I let him have it," his brother Edward said. "It was already slimy enough."

Everyone laughed.

When they came to the scene where Enrick rescued Heather from the bone tossed on the floor, Enrick wrapped his arm around her shoulders protectively.

"Nice save," Colleen said.

"If she'd needed saving," Callum said, laughing.

Enrick smiled and kissed Heather's cheek.

"I love how you spoke to William when he was wounded. I was sure they were going to reshoot the scene since you weren't supposed to talk," Heather said.

"He has a mind of his own," Grant said. "I totally got where the director was coming from when Enrick did his own thing."

Lachlan laughed.

"You too," Grant said.

In the scene where Catherine McKinley contaminated the food with bacteria, everyone booed her. They clapped and cheered when Heather pulled her *sgian dubh* on her and Lana ran out of the kitchen to get help. They cheered when Enrick and his "guards" came to take the villain away. And cheered again when they saw the wizard questioning Colleen in the dungeon. She looked so stubborn and proud sitting on a wooden stool while the wizard tried to get her to confess and tell him who had put her up to it. Then she ate from the fish stew and, within minutes, fell from the stool, dead.

Everyone gave her a standing ovation.

Colleen stood and gave a curtsy.

Then they settled down to watch more of the film.

Everyone laughed out loud when Gutzie the goose ran after the stars of the film.

"I didn't think they would keep that part of the scene. That goose has given more of us trouble than I can remember," Lachlan said. "I've mentioned it before, and I'll say it again: he would make for a nice dinner."

"You would miss him the next time you took a date to the pond," Colleen teased him.

"That's exactly what Guy's and Missy's scene reminded me of. I've told Gutzie a number of times where he's going to end up if he doesn't behave," Lachlan said.

Several scenes later, they had the one where Guy was trying to cross the stones to reach Missy on the other side of the creek.

"They cleaned the stones too much," Jamie said. "Those were ancient mossy stones. They made it look like they're practically new. Enrick should have done the scene."

"If I hadn't talked to him after he had fallen in the creek for the third time, we might never have learned he was one of us. Not just a wolf, but one of the families who had been part of our clan in the old days," Enrick said.

"You still should have done the scene," Jamie said. "It was painful watching Guy slip into the creek two more times. Of course, we were all laughing our heads off, him included, but still, it took forever."

"It could have been me," Enrick said. "Those stones were unstable too. Though they tried to prop them up so they wouldn't be. It didn't work."

"It was just a good thing that Missy didn't have to cross the stones herself," Heather said. "She's a city girl. She said she was glad she didn't have to, or she would have been in the creek more times than Guy was."

The final battle scene was the hardest for Heather to watch, though she noticed several others were also tensing during the scene. Between their wolves biting the two human actors, Guy falling and injuring his back, and Enrick getting cut, it was something she cringed to see.

"I had nightmares the eve before they filmed this scene," Grant admitted.

"You and me both," Colleen said.

William said, "We practiced and practiced with our own people, trying to get the feel of biting and tugging, but not crushing bones. It was probably the most difficult thing I've ever had to do."

"I agree," Edward said.

"That makes you perfectly skilled wolf actors," Enrick said.

Everyone laughed.

The battle scene was over and the villains dead, the celebratory feast over, and the last love scene done. Enrick squeezed Heather's shoulders in a sweet embrace as Guy married Missy on the screen, a woman from the future with ancestors from the past who had been part of his world, in the ancient chapel several hundred feet from the main castle. And they lived happily ever after at Farraige Castle.

The movie ended and it was a feel-good one, Heather thought.

Grant clapped his hands first and everyone followed suit. "Well done, everyone. I'm sure I speak for all of you when I say you did an outstanding job. Colleen and I haven't had time to mention it, but we've already had requests to use our wolves in a couple of other period pieces and one modern-day film. We'll talk about it later. And Guy asked me to convince you, Enrick, to be his double for a new movie. He said you told him no, but he's got a role for Heather to play too."

Enrick shook his head.

"We should do it," Heather said. "It's in Scotland, all about a shipwrecked Highlander who was hired to kill the heroine and her young brother because they know the king murdered his own brother for the crown."

"I can just see me being the one tossed about at sea, half-drowned in the surf, clinging to the rocks, and then finally reaching the shore."

Heather smiled. "Aye, because you are the invincible braw Highlander, and nothing will stop you from completing your mission."

"Except falling in love with the heroine."

"Nay, that part falls to Guy to do. You get all the good scenes."

Enrick laughed. "You just want me to play in another movie so you can advertise it and make lots more sales in your shop."

"Our shop, and aye, though I will advertise it anyway because Guy is our kin."

"I never realized it before seeing the film play out like this, but this is like Guy returning to his ancestors' home and becoming part of it again," Enrick said.

"Aye," Grant said. "He will always be welcome at our castle, among our people and part of our wolf pack, no matter where his travels take him."

"A friend of mine sent me this interview he'd done about his look-alike double," Julia said. "He said Enrick and his brothers are his long-lost kin and that the film had an even deeper meaning for him when he met all of you."

Heather was glad Guy had connected with his family, and she was glad they'd made friends with Missy, who'd vowed to stop in anytime she was in Scotland.

Now, it was time for the final scene as Heather took hold of Enrick's hand and they said their good-nights and hurried off to bed. Tomorrow, they would be moving into their new home between Farraige Castle and her shop. "I keep thinking of you coming out of the water, dripping wet and gloriously naked after you swam in the cold sea."

Enrick swept her up in his arms and carried her to his chamber. "I'm ready to make your fantasies come true."

"And I yours."

Don't miss book one in the Highland Wolf series from Terry Spear

HEART
OF THE HIGHLAND
WOLF

Available now from Sourcebooks Casablanca

CHAPTER 1

THE GHOSTLY FOG MADE JULIA FEEL AS THOUGH SHE HAD slipped into the primordial past. She couldn't believe she'd made it to the Highlands of Scotland where a castle beckoned, filled with secrets, intrigue, and hunky Scots—*with any luck*. Hopefully, none of them would learn why she was really here and put a stop to it.

Nothing would dampen her enthusiasm as she and her friend Maria Baquero headed for Baird Cottage, within hiking distance of Argent Castle—and the *end* of her writer's block.

At least, that was the plan.

After flight delays and missed luggage, they'd had trouble getting their rental car at Inverness Airport—following a mix-up when a Scotsman declared their car was his. Another man had creeped Julia out when she realized he was watching them, and she'd felt apprehensive at the way his thin lips hadn't hinted at a bit of friendliness. But then she dismissed him as she and Maria finally set off in late afternoon with Maria driving the rented Fiat into the deepening fog.

The laird of Argent Castle, Ian MacNeill, had been a royal pain to deal with concerning filming the movie at his castle. Luckily, as assistant director, only Maria had to do business with him. Pretending to be Maria's assistant, Julia was to watch from the sidelines and take notes. But not for the film production. For her breakout novel. Julia Wildthorn was one of the United States' most successful werewolf romance novelists and the only one, she was sure, who had ever suffered a writer's block like this one.

Dense fog obscured the curving road as it ran through rocky land on either side. Pine trees in the distance faded into the thickening soup, which offered glimpses of quaint dry-stone dykes that must have stood for centuries, snaking across the land and dividing someone's property from another's.

Despite Julia's enhanced wolf vision, she couldn't see any better than a human in the soup.

Eyes widening, she caught sight of something running in the woods. Something gray. Something that looked a *lot* like a wolf and then melted into the fog like a phantom.

Heartbeat ratchetting up several notches, she tried to catch another glimpse, her hand tightening on the door's armrest as she peered out the window, her nose almost touching the glass. "Did you see anything?" she asked Maria, her voice tight.

Maria gave her a disgruntled snort. "In this fog? I can barely see the road. What did you think you saw?"

"A…wolf." Julia strained to get another glimpse of what she'd seen. "But it couldn't have been. Wolves here were killed off centuries ago."

Off to Julia's left, the mist parted, revealing older aspen, the bark covered with dark lichen stretching upward, while tall, straight Scots pines and stands of willowy birch clustered close together in the distance. But no more signs of a wolf. Julia blinked her eyes. Maybe because she was so tired from the trip, her eyes were playing tricks on her.

Julia straightened and faced Maria. "Maybe it was a *lupus garou*, if I wasn't imagining it." She smiled at the thought. "A hunky Highland werewolf in a kilt."

She'd never considered she might run across a *lupus garou* in Scotland. Not as elusive as their kind were, hiding their secret from the rest of the world. Unless she bumped into one and could smell his or her scent, she wouldn't know a *lupus garou* from a strictly human type.

"Hmm, a Highland werewolf," Maria said thoughtfully, sliding her hands over the steering wheel, "although getting hold of a Spanish conquistador would be just as intriguing."

An Iberian werewolf whose ancestors had been turned by a wolfish conquistador, Maria was a beauty with dark brown hair and thick, long eyelashes.

Being a redhead with fair skin, Julia turned heads on her own, but the two of them together often stole the show.

Maria was still stewing about the laird who was in charge of Argent Castle. "Laird Ian MacNeill is being a real hard ass about the filming particulars—restricting our use of the castle and grounds, the times, the locations, and who knows what else when we arrive."

"Maybe he won't be so bad once the filming begins." Although Julia didn't believe that—and the sour look on Maria's face said she didn't, either. Julia pulled the laird's photo from her purse. Maria's boss had paid a private investigator good money to obtain the picture. "Exactly how did the guy get a picture of the laird like this if it's so difficult to catch a glimpse of him?"

"The P.I. followed him to a Celtic festival. The laird was surrounded by his men and a couple of women, so the detective snapped one shot right before the laird took part in a sword-fighting demonstration."

"Who won?"

"The laird and his men. According to the P.I., the MacNeills had a real workout against the Sutherlands. Bad blood has existed between them for centuries. The fighting looked so real, he thought organizers of the show might step in and stop the demonstration."

In one word, Julia summed up Laird Ian MacNeill's appearance: *dangerous*.

It wasn't his handsome features—his short, very dark coffee-colored hair, the rich color of his eyes, the rigid planes of his face, and his aristocratic nose—that made him appear that way. Not his broad shoulders or firm stance or unsmiling mouth, either. It was his unerring gaze that seemed so piercingly astute, like he could see into a person's very soul.

That worried her.

In the photo, the man was prime hunk, wearing a predominantly green and blue kilt, an ermine sporran belted in front, and a sword sheathed behind him. From the looks of the hilt partially peeking over his shoulder, the sword served as a warning that he was armed and deadly, much more so than just his looks. He wore a shirt belted, hanging open to the waist, and revealing sexy abs a woman would love to caress. At least this woman would. Just as rugged, his castle sat in the background, formidable, commanding, and resilient.

She could just imagine him wielding that lethal sword against his enemy.

Maria shook her head. "He's arrogant, hard-nosed, too far above us, and on top of that, we're Americans and working—or at least he'll think you're working—with the film crew he so despises. So just remember that in case you're getting romantic notions from that picture of him. He's too wickedly sexy for his own good... or maybe I should say, for *your* own good."

Maria was probably right. Julia wanted to see the laird up close and personal for the sake of writing her manuscript, but she didn't want to hear the disparaging things he might say to her. That would ruin her image of him as the hero type. And if he looked at her the way he did in the picture, she feared he would see right through her.

Just then, they topped the hill and faced a sea of white, curly fur blocking their way. Maria gasped and slammed on the brakes. Julia's heart rapped a triple beat, and she grabbed the dashboard. Like a pastoral scene from an old-time painting, the mob of sheep was making its way to the other side of the rocky glen. Several sheared sheep—ewes, a curly horned ram, and lots of lambs—crossed the road, along with a sheepherder with a gnarled walking stick in hand and his collie.

Instantly, Julia thought about the wolf.

Once the sheep had passed, Maria started driving slower than before and cleared her throat.

"As soon as we drop off our carry-on luggage, I have to drive over to the estate for a meeting."

Harold Washburn, the producer of the film, and most of the staff were staying at a local mansion. Maria had insisted on leasing Baird Cottage, citing its closeness to the castle. In truth, it was to hide that she and Julia were *lupus garous* and that Julia wasn't truly working for Maria.

"At this rate, I'm not going to make it in time. I haven't seen a sign in a while, and… I thought we would have been there by now," Maria continued.

Julia strained to see into the distance, searching for another road sign, but the fog that had parted in places for her to glimpse the trees was again too thick to see a thing.

A shadow of gray bolted across the road. *The wolf.* A gray wolf.

Maria gasped and slammed on her brakes. Julia's mouth dropped open, but the squeal died in her throat as headlights reflected off her side mirror. The headlights barreled on top of them. It was too late.

Rubber and brakes squealed behind them. Heart pounding, Julia braced for the crash, the wolf forgotten.

Bang! The rental car flew off the road like an airborne mini-plane. Then it landed hard, tearing down the incline. Bouncing. Jolting. Teeth jarring. A white cloud filled Julia's vision and she gasped.

A shotgun blast! A horrible jolt. Another bang!

Before Julia could process what had happened, the white air bag deflated, and a snaking wall of rocks loomed before them only a couple of feet away in the fog.

"Hit the brakes!" Julia screamed.

As soon as he heard the explosions ahead, Ian MacNeill slowed his car and watched the road and the shoulders, looking for signs of a collision. Some poor fool must have been driving too slowly in the fog, while another had been driving too fast, hence the horrendous noise in the distance.

His youngest brother, Duncan—which being quadruplets meant only by minutes—peered out the passenger window.

"It had to be a car wreck," Duncan said, his tone concerned.

"Aye." Ian watched for lights that might indicate vehicles ahead. Their wolf hearing was so enhanced that the sounds made could have been some kilometers distant.

"I don't see anything, Ian. Not a thing. No tire skids, no broken glass. But the explosive sounds were loud enough that the vehicles had to have damage."

Unease scraping down his spine, Ian agreed.

Duncan leaned against the passenger door and then motioned toward the incline. "Taillights in the fog, down there."

"And scraps of red metal from a vehicle up here," Ian said as his headlights glinted off pieces of metal and part of a taillight reflector.

He pulled off onto the soft shoulder, turned off the ignition, and exited the vehicle. With Duncan at his side, he hurried down the incline toward the cherry-colored fog.

"Hello, anybody hurt?" Ian called out, his dark voice traveling over the glen. He took a breath and swore he smelled a hint of the acrid odor of gunfire.

No one answered his call, and another trace of unease wormed its way into his blood. Then he heard a moan. A woman's moan.

"Hell, probably a woman driving way too slow and got hit," Duncan growled, quickening his run.

Duncan should know since he'd smashed into the rear bumper of a woman's car just the month before for the same reason. Ian hoped to hell no one had life-threatening injuries.

The odor of burning tires, scraped raw metal, and refrigerant gas leaking from the car's air-conditioning system drifted to them. Then smoke.

"Smoke," Duncan said, racing to the car.

"Hello!" Ian called out again as they scrambled to reach the vehicle smashed into the dry dyke, the front bumper looking like an accordion, the red metal crumpled against the windshield. Glass everywhere sparkled like diamond shards on the ground. The windshield was shattered, and the driver's side window, a spider web of cracks. White sheets of material covered the shattered dash—deflated air bags.

The two rear tires had blown out, and the rear bumper was smashed and the metal torn from its moorings, one end now touching the ground. But Ian didn't see telltale signs of another vehicle's paint on this one. Yet after considering the rear bumper, he assumed someone *had* to have hit the car *hard*.

Ian reached the driver's door first, but the frame was so badly bent that the door wouldn't budge. He peered in through the window as Duncan reached him. No one inside the vehicle. He glanced around, raised his nose, and smelled... petrol, hot and burning.

"Duncan!" Ian grabbed his brother's arm and yanked him away from the car.

Boom! The forceful explosion threw them several meters away, heat singeing their eyebrows and zapping the moisture out of the cool, wet air. His ears ringing, hearing deadened, eyes and nostrils filled with smoke, Ian lay still in the grass, dazed. Then he jerked to a sitting position and looked for his brother.

Duncan was sitting nearby, shaking his head as if clearing the fog from it. "Hell. The driver had better sense than we did." His black clothes were now covered in gray soot and splotches of brown mud.

Ian agreed. "The car had a couple of small suitcases—someone on holiday."

"A lass from the looks of it," Duncan added.

"Aye, one of the suitcases was pink, and I glimpsed a handbag sitting on the center console."

They both watched as orange flames consumed the car. No worry of anything else catching fire, as damp as it was. The rains that morning had turned everything to mud, which Ian's light khaki-colored trousers were now soaking up. Ian stood and wiped the mud off his hands and onto his trousers. "You okay?"

"Aye. Can't hear anything worth a damn. Your voice sounds a million kilometers away. And my head is splitting."

"Same here. Come on. Let's find the woman. She's probably in better shape than we are." Ian cast Duncan a dark smile. "You look like hell, brother."

Duncan snorted. "You don't look much better."

Ian slapped him on the back, and the two made a wide circle around the car, looking for any indication of where the driver would have gone. Heel marks. Not one, but two sets of prints. "Two," Ian said, pointing to the tracks. "Lassies, both of them."

"Do you smell something?" Duncan asked.

"If you mean burning rubber, petrol, smoke, hot metal, and mud, aye. Was there something else you smelled then? A woman's perfume, maybe?"

Duncan tilted his head up, took another deep breath, and then coughed. "Let's move away from the fire. I can't smell anything but smoke. But I thought…" He shook his head.

"What?"

"Nothing."

Ian moved away from the burning car, but something in Duncan's voice made him take another long look at his brother. Duncan was frowning, concentrating, and sampling the air, trying to locate the women.

"Blood?" Ian asked, thinking maybe Duncan had smelled an injury and was concerned about it. The smoke and burning petrol were wreaking havoc with his own sense of smell now.

"Aye, well, that and…" Duncan looked at him with an odd expression. "…the faint scent of wolf."

CHAPTER 2

"I STILL THINK WE SHOULD HAVE STAYED WITH THE CAR," JULIA grumbled under her breath, limping in her heels, her ankle throbbing. She held onto Maria for support as they hurried away from the wreck as fast as possible.

The sound of an explosion at their backs made Julia jump. But they were far from there now. And they heard no more shouts, which worried Julia as her heart thundered spastically. What if the man who had come after them had been injured?

The sweet, earthy smell of rain preceded the start of a shower. Then the raindrops poured down on them in earnest, the plants and earth offering up a cleansing scent.

They would be drenched before they got much of anywhere, even though they weren't letting up on the pace, despite their minor injuries. Julia wished she hadn't taken off her pantsuit jacket to keep it from getting wrinkled by her seat belt. The jacket, being in the backseat, hadn't been on her mind, not when they'd discovered Maria's door was jammed tight and Julia had to help her over the console. Now, the shell of aqua silk Julia wore was plastered to her chest, revealing everything, she was sure. Her linen slacks were in the same shape, molding to her legs, feeling cold and wet like an alien second skin.

"We should have stayed near the car at least," Julia griped, wiping away the steady trickle of water droplets dribbling down her cheeks. "That's what you're supposed to do when you need assistance." She tightened her grip on Maria's arm. "With the car on fire, someone is sure to spot it eventually."

Maria hushed her again.

Julia pulled her to a stop. "All right," Julia whispered. "Why do you think whoever hit us did it on purpose?"

"We were better off getting away from the car before it exploded." Maria took a deep breath and let it out slowly. "But that's not the only reason. I got a death threat before we left L.A."

Uncomprehending, Julia stared at her. "*What?*"

Maria started walking again, pulling Julia along, their shoes squishing and squelching in the mud. "A man with a distinctive Scottish brogue called me on my home phone, angry about us using Ian MacNeill's castle for the film. He said I'd live to regret it. I didn't believe it, *much*… then this happens. But it was more than that."

When Maria didn't say anything further, Julia prompted, "More than that?"

Maria gave her a hard look. "He said you didn't know what you were getting yourself into."

"Me?"

"He knew you had learned of the castle and passed the information on to me. But it was almost like he knew you. *Personally.* And he didn't want you to have anything to do with Laird MacNeill. He sounded like an ex-lover."

"I've never had a boyfriend with a Scottish accent. I don't know anyone like that."

"He said he knew your family. That if you hadn't dumped the investment advisor, he would have had to do something about it. See what I mean? It's like it's personal with him."

Julia wracked her brain, trying to come up with anyone like that, but she couldn't think of a soul. The part about him knowing about Trevor did concern her. Not that her relationship with him was secret. But how would someone in Scotland have known of it? As to her family, they didn't even go by the same last name as she did. She was Julia Wildthorn, romance author—pen name. Real name—Julia MacPherson. But no one knew that. Not even Maria.

"It's probably just some ticked-off guy who gets off on threats."

Maria cast her a disbelieving look. "You can't deny it sounds personal."

Julia thought about her grandfather and father insisting that she encourage Maria to consider Ian's castle for the film production. What if bad blood existed between her family's ancestors and this person's ancestors? And now Maria was caught in the middle of it.

"Did he say anything about owning a different castle? Maybe he wanted the business instead, and MacNeill is his fiercest competition."

"No."

Julia grimaced as another twinge of pain rippled through her ankle. She compensated by leaning more on her other foot and on Maria's arm. "What did the L.A. police say?"

"Nothing. Without a caller ID name or number, a recording of the phone call, more threats, or anything else to go on, they said they couldn't do anything about it."

Julia pulled Maria to a stop again as she heard distant footfalls. "Whoever's following us is getting closer."

"I know. That's why I'm trying to hurry up and find a town or people or something." Maria started hauling Julia along again.

"You think it's the guy who hit us?"

"Maybe not, but what if it is? What with worrying that the car was going to explode any moment, with the smoke pouring out of the engine and the smell of the leaking gasoline, and you trying to help me out the passenger's side door in a hurry because my door was jammed, we both lost everything in the car, *including* our cell phones. We have no way to call for help."

Julia patted her soaking-wet pants pockets and discovered she had four limp U.S. dollars, a handful of U.S. change, a scrunchie to tie back her hair, and… She touched the pocket of her shell, where the picture of Ian MacNeill was sitting close to her heart and the only thing still warm. She had pulled the photo out of her purse to take one surreptitious look at it, and for some reason, she'd stuck it in her shirt pocket instead of back in her purse.

In her writer's fruitful imagination, she envisioned a bond between them and that through some kind of body heat transference, the laird would know their troubles and come to rescue them. She was hopelessly romantic, which hadn't gotten her anywhere with men, but she wasn't giving up.

She glanced over her shoulder but couldn't see anything except fog and trees. "We could wander for miles and never find anyone. We should sit down and stay quiet. They'll pass us by."

"No. For one thing, it's getting dark. And for another, I have to get to Harold's meeting. And finally," Maria whispered back, "whoever is out there has been tracking us pretty damn well all along. Ever since the Scotsman shouted near the car, calling out to us."

"Was it the same voice as the man who talked to you on the phone?"

"I can't tell. The phone crackled and sputtered when the man called me in L.A., lousy reception. This guy's voice was loud and clear."

And dark and worried and sexy, Julia thought. Not at all like someone who was out to get them. The wolf again came to the forefront of Julia's thoughts. "The wolf has to be one of our kind."

Maria asked quietly, "What if he was with the guy that hit us? What if they worked in collusion?"

Maria and her conspiracy theories.

"Highly unlikely," Julia said, in an attempt at reassuring. But that didn't stop her own small, niggling worry.

She began to look for any signs of a wolf in the area, skulking around in the fog and rain.

The sudden rain shower slowed to a drizzle just as a flicker light in the distance caught Julia's eye. "Over there," she whisper her hopes elevating, and the two changed direction. "A buildi

Distant hearty male singing drifted to them from the direction of the muted light.

"We must look adorable," Maria muttered, glancing down. Their clothes were soaked, but at least Maria was wearing her jacket, and even though she was wet, the fabric didn't cling to her the way Julia's did.

"Road," Julia said. "Dead ahead."

The rambunctious sound of men singing grew louder.

"A pub, maybe," Maria excitedly said, her voice still hushed as she dragged Julia across the deserted road, the music cheering them on. "We'll be safe there and can borrow a phone and call Harold."

Welcoming brass porch lanterns glowed through the fog, illuminating the front of Scott's Pub. The new mixing with the old, ancient stone walls surrounded double glass doors, back-lit from the warm wash of lighting inside. Above the pub, six dark windows overlooked the parking lot, and a sign read: ROOMS FOR LEASE. A corner of the building wrapped around and rose three stories, but it looked ghostly vacant. A sign carved into the stone said, HIGHLAND INN.

Behind the building, trees and hills loomed tall, dwarfing the place. Outside, three cars, a pickup, and a van were parked, and unless tons of people had ridden in the five vehicles, Julia assumed liquor had loosened the singers' tongues to a good-hearted bellow. In her romantic writer's imagination, she envisioned the place filled with braw, kilted Highland warriors who would save them from harm if those following them meant to hurt them.

Maria grabbed the door and opened it, then pulled Julia inside and shut the door. The aroma of juicy burgers grilling made Julia's stomach growl.

She needed food and water. And a towel, a shower, and clean clothes. The place seemed like their salvation.

To keep from tracking in mud, they eased off their muddy heels and left them out of the way on the granite floor against the entry-way wall. Then they padded in stocking feet into a more dimly lit room, complete with paneled bar, several tables, a dartboard on one wall, and the painting of deer on another. The singing had continued, and the men's brogue was so thick that Julia didn't understand a word of it.

A man dressed in a black polo shirt and steel-gray slacks poured drinks from behind the bar, and two others dressed the same way sang along with those sitting at the tables. Julia was disappointed not to see any kilted warriors in Scott's Pub. The six men were wearing trousers and shirts—everyday variety, nothing notewor-thy for her manuscript. But they looked like a hearty lot, smiling and singing and swinging their mugs of ale.

Until a pretty blonde woman—petite and midthirties, wearing jeans and a tank top, and serving another tray of drinks to one of the tables—turned to look at Maria and Julia. The waitress's smil-ing mouth instantly dropped open. She nearly spilled a man's ale in his lap, and he quickly grabbed her hand to steady it.

"Sarah, lass…" But he and the other men quit singing one by one and turned to see what had startled her so.

ACKNOWLEDGMENTS

I wanted to thank Donna Fournier and Darla Taylor for beta reading for me and finding lots of fun mistakes! And Deb Werksman who is always a pleasure to work with, and Susie Benton who tirelessly keeps track of what I should be turning in. And of course the cover artists with their beautiful work who entice everyone to read the book!

ABOUT THE AUTHOR

USA Today bestselling author Terry Spear has written over sixty paranormal and medieval Highland romances. In 2008, *Heart of the Wolf* was named a *Publishers Weekly* Best Book of the Year. She has received a PNR Top Pick, a Best Book of the Month nomination by Long and Short Reviews, numerous Night Owl Romance Top Picks, and two Paranormal Excellence Awards for Romantic Literature (Finalist and Honorable Mention). In 2016, *Billionaire in Wolf's Clothing* was an RT Book Reviews Top Pick. A retired officer of the U.S. Army Reserves, Terry also creates award-winning teddy bears that have found homes all over the world, helps out with her granddaughter, and is raising two Havanese puppies. She lives in Spring, Texas.